_Thank you,
Stena. Your support is
much appreciated._

THE MOTIVE

CYCLE OF VIOLENCE #1

JOSEPH BADAL

SUSPENSE PUBLISHING

THE MOTIVE
CYCLE OF VIOLENCE #1
by
Joseph Badal

PAPERBACK EDITION
* * * * *
PUBLISHED BY:
Suspense Publishing

Joseph Badal
COPYRIGHT
2016 Joseph Badal

PUBLISHING HISTORY:
Suspense Publishing, Paperback and Digital Copy, July 2016

Cover Design: Shannon Raab
Cover Photographer: iStockphoto.com/Roberto A Sanchez

ISBN-13: 978-0692683675 (Suspense Publishing)
ISBN-10: 0692683674

JOSEPH BADAL'S BOOKS & SHORT STORIES

THE DANFORTH SAGA

EVIL DEEDS (#1)
TERROR CELL (#2)
THE NOSTRADAMUS SECRET (#3)
THE LONE WOLF AGENDA (#4)
DEATH SHIP (#5)

CYCLE OF VIOLENCE SERIES

#1: THE MOTIVE
#2: OBSESSED (To Be Released in 2017)

STAND-ALONE THRILLERS

THE PYTHAGOREAN SOLUTION
SHELL GAME
ULTIMATE BETRAYAL

LASSITER/MARTINEZ CASE FILES

#1: BORDERLINE
#2: DARK ANGEL (To Be Released in 2016)

SHORT STORIES

FIRE & ICE (UNCOMMON ASSASSINS ANTHOLOGY)
ULTIMATE BETRAYAL (SOMEONE WICKED ANTHOLOGY)
THE ROCK (INSIDIOUS ASSASSINS ANTHOLOGY)

DEDICATION

Herb, thank you for the inspiration you gave me to write this story. I hope I have done it and your sister, Suzanne, justice. This story is dedicated to her memory.

ACKNOWLEDGEMENTS

This story was inspired by actual events and has been dedicated to a wonderful woman who is greatly missed.

Thank you to the many readers of my novels. I cannot express enough the pleasure I get from your support of my work. You inspire me to write, write, write.

I have been fortunate to have had blurbs for my novels written by many successful and prolific authors, including Tom Avitabile, Parris Afton Bonds, Steve Brewer, Catherine Coulter, Philip Donlay, Steve Havill, Anne Hillerman, Tony Hillerman, Robert Kresge, Jon Land, Mark Leggatt, Michael McGarrity, Michael Palmer, Andrew Peterson, Mark Rubinstein, Meryl Sawyer, and Sheldon Siegel. I know how busy these men and women are and it always humbles me when they graciously take time to read and praise my work.

Frank Zoretich—editor extraordinaire, as usual, made a positive difference in the quality of my writing. Frank's passing earlier this year was both a personal and professional loss.

Thanks to John & Shannon Raab, and your staff, for all you do to publish my novels. From cover art, to editing, to formatting, to publication, and to marketing, you make a huge difference.

PRAISE FOR JOSEPH BADAL

"Badal does what Tony Hillerman told us to do...first, write a good story! A hero in over his head, vicious bad guys, beautiful women... Badal has 'em all in 'The Motive.' "
—Steve Havill, Award-winning Author of "Come Dark," a *Posadas County Mystery*

"Master of Suspense Joseph Badal never disappoints. 'The Motive,' *Cycle of Violence #1*, spins a complicated web of breath-taking intrigue and heart-stopping action. This tightly crafted new thriller introduces a reluctant hero the reader can care about, and adds a well-wrought cast of cohorts and a chilling villain. Well done! Badal knows his way around a good story. I couldn't stop reading."
—Anne Hillerman, *New York Times* Best-Selling Author of "Rock With Wings"

"For novels of international intrigue with gut-wrenching action, twists, and unpredictable developments, no thriller author can beat the high-octane crime writing of Joseph Badal. Suspense is his middle name. Simply put, 'The Motive' is nail-bitingly un-put-downable."
—Mark Rubinstein, Award-winning Author of "The Lovers' Tango"

" 'The Motive' is a nail biter I couldn't put down. Joseph Badal knows how to make his legion of readers sweat to the very last paragraph. He has mastered the art of writing—and suspense. Bravo!"
—Parris Afton Bonds, Award-Winning Author of "Dream Time"

" 'The Motive' is gritty, gripping noir transplanted to a tropical paradise. Joseph Badal's ingenious, postmodern take on a tried and true genre is fresh, vibrant and bursting with colorful characters who practically leap off the page. In a fashion akin to the great James W. Hall, Badal turns the Hawaiian landscape into the perfect backdrop for the dark world that lurks beneath the surface. As close to perfect as a crime thriller can get."
—Jon Land, *USA Today* Bestselling Author

THE MOTIVE

CYCLE OF VIOLENCE #1
JOSEPH BADAL

Inspired by Actual Events

DAY ONE

CHAPTER ONE

A slight tremor snaked through Matt Curtis as though he'd been hit by an errant chill. He looked at his blood-smeared gloved hands and, for a beat, wondered about it. He let the moment pass and announced, "Let's close her up." Matt removed the spreaders that had kept the incision open and used a syringe to inject sterile water into the woman's open hip wound. Then he took the surgical thread from the nurse. About to go to work on the wound, he felt suddenly unsettled. Another tremor hit, but this time it was more severe. It seemed to emanate from within. His hands shook; sweat instantly drenched his body; he gasped for breath. And then, like a shimmering hologram, his sister Susan's image filled his vision. Her body appeared translucent; a brilliant aura radiated from her head.

Matt looked over at John Ransom, the orthopedic surgeon assisting him. Ransom stared back at him, eyebrows raised in question. Matt's gaze shifted to the two surgical nurses. They, like Ransom, seemed frozen in place, concern and wonder etched their faces.

"You okay?" Ransom asked.

Matt grabbed the edge of the stainless steel table and pressed his eyes shut. For a few seconds, his brain seemed foggy. He felt faint, disoriented. Then the feeling stopped and left him only slightly light-headed. He opened his eyes and searched the room for Susan. Matt squeezed his eyes shut again, ordered himself to get a grip, and looked again at Ransom.

"Yeah, I'm fine," he lied. He used an arm to shield his eyes from the intense glare of the overhead lamp. A smoky haze seemed to fill the room and, for a moment, Matt thought the walls undulated. His vision blurred, as though a filter had been placed over his eyes.

Matt forced himself to appear calm. "John, finish up," he said. He wheeled around and left the operating room.

He stripped off his cap, mask, bloodied surgical gown, gloves, and booties and washed his arms up to his biceps at the first sink outside the University of New Mexico's orthopedic surgical suite. He looked up at the wall clock over the sink; had to squint to make out the time. Three-fifteen in the morning. Nothing new in that. Since cancer took his wife, Allison, a decade ago, he'd poured every ounce of energy into his patients with demonic intensity.

He and Allison had tried to have children but, after three miscarriages, she couldn't bear the loss anymore. Allison, Susan, and Matt's mother had been enough for Matt. But not for Allison. So they'd adopted two little boys. Allison was the perfect mother and Matt the perfect provider. But, after Allison died, Matt didn't know how to fill the hole in his sons' hearts. Two years later, they were both off to college. Now they were adults and strangers.

He felt as though he'd just run a marathon. Tired. Weak. Used up. Sure, it was the middle of the night. He'd been on his feet since 7 a.m. the previous day. One operation after another. Too few surgeons, too many patients. But he'd worked that kind of schedule for years. I'm getting old, Matt thought. Fifty-one and I feel seventy.

Matt shuffled to the doctors' locker room, the picture of Susan imprinted on his mind's eye. There was no one, other than his two sons, who meant as much to him as his sister did. Despite the four-year difference in their ages, he and Susan had been like twins their entire lives. They finished one another's sentences; felt the other's pain. But what the hell was that all about back in the operating room?

He stripped off his clothes and dumped them in a laundry basket, then shuffled to a shower stall. He adjusted the water flow to pulse, then placed his two palms against the shower wall, bowed his head, and groaned as the water pounded his skin and cascaded over him. His muscles ached, his backbone felt permanently bent. Matt repeated his daily ritual: He ran a finger down the scar on his lower back, over his spine, and silently thanked God that he could stand at all. The doctors had told him he might never walk again after his car crash in high school.

He reached higher and touched one of the three puckered scars on his upper back—he no longer had the flexibility to reach the other two—and wondered how much luck one person was due in a lifetime. Three bullets in the back, over thirty years ago, compliments of a Serb soldier.

After ten minutes, Matt reluctantly turned off the water. He grabbed a towel from a shelf, rubbed it roughly over his skin, and wrapped it around his waist. Then he snatched another towel and draped it over his shoulders. He walked back to the locker room and eased onto a wooden bench. Bent over, elbows on his thighs, face in his hands, he released a low moan and again wondered what had happened in the operating room. It had been a momentary, eerie sensation. Couldn't have lasted more than a few seconds. Maybe he'd better schedule a physical.

Then another chill hit him, as though an Arctic wind had invaded the locker room. Matt turned to see who had opened the door, but there was no one. Matt's skin prickled, the hair on his arms stood at attention. He felt a presence; certain someone had entered the room. "Damn," he whispered through gritted teeth, as he looked around again. No one.

He stood and shucked the towels, opened his locker, and reached for his street clothes. Even when he finished dressing, the chill he'd felt hadn't completely gone away. Probably just need a good night's sleep, he thought. Then he made a mental note to call Susan.

CHAPTER TWO

"Man, why can't people just swallow a bunch of pills, or walk out into the ocean?" Honolulu Police Sergeant Sal Mokapua said in a thick voice. "No, they gotta take a header off a high-rise. What a fuckin' mess!"

Violent Crimes Lieutenant Dennis Callahan stared at the dozen or so residents of the Sand & Sea Condominiums gathered on the sidewalk near the building, murmuring among themselves. Most wore bathrobes and bedroom slippers. Then he turned to look at Mokapua. "That's why they pay us the big bucks, Sal," he said as he lit up a Marlboro and inhaled the smoke deep into his lungs. "To clean up messes like this. You first on the scene?"

"Yeah. Me and the rookie I'm breaking in."

"Where's the rookie?" Callahan asked and looked around in the glow provided by the pole lights around the parking lot and the nearly full moon.

Mokapua hooked a thumb in the direction of one of the towering palm trees that bordered the parking lot. "Over there fertilizing the flora," he said.

Callahan looked in the direction Mokapua pointed and saw the silhouette of a bent-over man. For a moment, he remembered the first corpse he'd seen when he was a rookie. Back in New York City when he wore NYPD blue. He'd barfed then. Callahan looked down at his brown Santoni loafers and grimaced at the thought of puking on his four hundred dollar shoes, as he'd done on those clunky black lace-ups twenty years ago. Then Callahan turned back to the sergeant and gave him a "go ahead" gesture with his hand.

Mokapua pulled a small notebook from his breast pocket and flipped the pages. "Dispatch got a call from the building's rent-a-cop at . . . 11:20 p.m. We arrived on scene fifteen minutes later."

Callahan tightened his silk Versace tie and pulled on his shirtsleeves so an inch of white cuff showed beyond the arms of his raw silk sport coat. He circled the woman's body, careful not to tread in the blood pools. Her body lay face down, arms and legs unnaturally bent, like a scarecrow. He looked up at the building, a thirty-story pale yellow monolith with balconies that made it look like an enormous chest of drawers. Hell of a long way to fall, he thought. That reminded him of the old joke that homicide detectives tell when they investigate a jumper: It's not the fall that kills them, it's the sudden stop.

He glanced at the moon that shone like a heavenly searchlight, its glow bronzing the windows of one of the Waikiki Beach hotels in the distance. Great way to start the day—with a leaper! But he had no choice. This had to be *his* case.

"You touch anything?"

"No, sir," Mokapua said, indignantly.

A white ambulance turned into the parking lot. The rotating beams of its red and white flashers bounced off the side of the condominium building. Callahan watched it stop, then turned again to Mokapua.

"I want you to write down everything you saw, heard, and smelled. And if some nosy reporter asks you any questions, you say, I-don't-know-nothin'. Got it?"

"Yes, sir." Mokapua started toward his patrol car on the far end of the parking lot, but stopped and turned back. "Don't you want to know the woman's name?" he asked, as he tipped his head in the direction of the corpse.

Callahan hesitated a moment. "Sure, why not?"

"Susan Curtis."

DAY TWO

CHAPTER THREE

The monotonous drone of the airplane engines seemed tortuous. Like high-pitched, buzzing whispers that attacked his sanity. "Susan's dead. Susan's dead. You let her down. You let her down." Then, over and over again, "Susan committed suicide. Susan committed suicide. Susan committed suicide." After hours of the same synchronous hum, Matt thought he would go mad. He balled his hands so tight, the muscles in his forearms cramped.

He thought about the telephone call from his secretary, Linda, that morning. The phone had jarred him from a nightmare-punctuated sleep. Linda's message only accentuated the nightmare. The Honolulu Police had called Matt's office. His sister Susan was dead. He'd dropped the phone, walked to the bedroom window, thrown the drapes aside, and stared unseeing at the Sandia Mountains on Albuquerque's east side.

Susan died just after three o'clock, New Mexico time, Linda had told him. About the time he'd felt disoriented in the operating room. When he thought he'd seen Susan's image. Then he remembered the chill he'd felt moments later in the locker room. The cool presence of someone . . . or something. Tears ran down his cheeks; his throat was suddenly so parched he couldn't swallow. He felt hollow.

"Oh God," Matt muttered as he unclenched, then re-clenched his fists.

Matt knew he wasn't responsible for his sister's death. Not in a legal sense, anyway. He didn't even know for sure if her death had anything to do with what he'd said or done, but he found it difficult to rationalize his innocence, especially with the anvil-heavy burden that weighed on his heart.

Poor Susan. Matt could never tell if she was happy. Most people who knew her would probably say she led a gloomy existence—forty-seven, never married, wedded to her job. That's how he thought of her life. Gloomy.

"Dammit!" Matt muttered, as he turned to the jumbo jet's window to hide his tears.

"Excuse me, did you say something?"

Matt brushed a hand over his eyes and swallowed, then turned and looked at the man seated next to him. "No. It was nothing," he said, and half-waved dismissively at his seatmate.

"You going to Hawaii on business?" the man asked with a smile.

"No."

"Pleasure?"

"To bury my sister."

"Oh, I'm . . . ."

Matt looked back through the window and stared out at a seemingly endless white sea of cotton clouds. He hoped there was a heaven, where all three women he'd loved could be together. Safe. His wife, Allison, dead from cancer ten years ago, his mother felled by a stroke barely a month ago, and now Susan.

He thought about Susan when she was little. She tagged along; wanted to be "one of the boys." Was tougher than most of them. When he pictured her missing-tooth smile and scraped knees, his sadness only escalated. His eyes burned and his throat constricted. God, how he'd loved her!

The Honolulu detective he'd called had said it was suicide. The coroner was expected to make it official in a day or two. After the autopsy. Twenty-four floors from the balcony to the parking lot, the cop had told him.

"Susan would never have killed herself," Matt had protested, through the fog of shock. "Suicide is the ultimate selfish act and Susan wasn't selfish. Just the opposite."

The detective had paused. "I'm sorry for your loss, Doctor

Curtis," he'd said, clearly unconvinced.

Matt could tell the detective's mind was made up. It was suicide—plain and simple. Susan Curtis took a header off a high-rise building. The detective was going through the motions.

Suicide! No way! She wouldn't do that to herself.

She wouldn't do that to *me*.

The last time Matt had talked with Susan was four weeks earlier, in April. He didn't want to recycle the memory, but his guilt wouldn't let him avoid it. She and her boyfriend, Robert Nakamura, had flown into Albuquerque for Mom's funeral.

Since his mother's stroke the previous December, Matt had visited her every evening at the nursing home. He'd watched her groan in her sleep or babble when awake. A stomach tube fed her brown-colored gruel, antibiotics, and sedatives. There were rare moments when she would sing along with the radio, in her contralto voice. "La-la-la." These times raised Matt's hopes that she would recover. But reality had a way of dashing hopes. He'd watched her waste away for five months and held her hand when she died.

Susan arrived like a whirlwind. She took over; allowed Matt to mourn. He'd held Susan when she arrived at the airport; inhaled the peachy smell of her hair. Even the presence of her hovering, ne'er-do-well boyfriend, Robert, couldn't diminish the comfort her presence gave Matt.

"You know you should get away for a while," Susan had said just before the funeral. She'd wrapped him in her arms and pressed her cheek against his chest. "Visit me in Hawaii. We could spend some time on the beach."

She wanted him to come out immediately, but he couldn't get another physician to cover for him until June.

Susan had stood by his side, held his hand during the service and the burial. The reception afterwards turned out to be relatively painless, although Matt hated public displays of emotion and never felt comfortable responding to expressions of condolence.

Susan got him through it.

The last mourner left Matt's house early in the evening. He and Susan helped the catering crew clean up, then joined Robert in the den.

Gangly Robert—one leg bent over a couch arm; the rest of him looked like pickup sticks thrown down at random. His jet-black hair stood up as though intentionally spiked, instead of just the victim of simple neglect. His black eyes zeroed in on the television screen.

Robert grunted acknowledgement of their arrival. Matt took a plush leather chair opposite the couch. Susan sat next to Robert.

"You mind turning that off?" Matt said, his voice even.

Robert huffed a petulant sigh. He lifted the remote from his lap and killed the sound. The NBA basketball playoff game silently scrolled across the screen.

Jesus, Matt thought. What a pain in the ass! How can Susan stand to be around this guy?

Maybe the built-up pain of his mother's physical decline over the past few months had caused it, or the frustration he'd felt grow for eight years over Susan's "going-nowhere" relationship with Robert. Or it could have been simply the three scotches he'd downed during the reception. Whatever the reason, he had a target. He'd confronted Robert before, but this time he was like a bulldog on a bone.

"So, found a job yet, Robert?"

"Matt . . ." Susan interjected, a warning note in her voice.

"Well, it's been kinda difficult, you know," Robert whined while he pulled at his shirt cuffs. "What with my . . . condition . . . and all. It's hard to concentrate. I can't seem to hold down a job."

"Yeah, tell me about it," Matt said. "How much money have you taken from my sister over the years?"

"Matthew," Susan said. "There's no call for—"

"You know, you're not the only person in the world with manic-depression. You could at least get help."

Robert's eyes shifted. The leg he had looped over the couch arm swung down to the floor with a *clump*. He opened his mouth as though he might respond, then dropped his gaze and squirmed in his seat.

For eight years, Robert had taken, taken, taken from Susan, using his psychological problems as an excuse. No marriage, no commitment, no job, no financial contribution. Why had Susan allowed the relationship to continue?

"So why don't you go see a shrink?" Matt said, as he bored in like an auger at soft wood. "There are all sorts of medications that could help you."

Robert's eyes widened and his light-beige complexion went pale. Matt knew Robert was deathly afraid of drugs.

"Dammit, Matt," Susan shouted.

Robert mumbled something unintelligible as he stood and fled like a whipped dog to his bedroom.

"How could you do that, Matthew?" Susan asked in a low, tremulous voice. "You're a doctor. You should know better."

I wish she'd shouted, Matt thought now as he gazed out at the clouds below. But she'd just sat there and stared, her wet, doe-like eyes full of anger.

They sat in silence for several minutes, Matt too ashamed to hold her gaze. He glanced instead at a painting on the far wall. Normally, the violets, blues, and pinks of the Southwestern sky it depicted brought him peace. But at that moment he felt nothing but remorse.

Susan pushed off the couch, sighed, and went after Robert. She was gone for barely a few seconds when her voice carried back to the den.

"You can't leave. Matthew didn't mean anything by it."

Matt heard a door slam. Then muffled voices.

Soon Robert came out, suitcase in hand. He walked straight to the front door while Susan tugged at his arm in a futile effort to stop him. He ignored Matt. Outside, he started the rental car with a roar and drove away.

Susan strode back into the house and again went into the bedroom. Fifteen minutes later, she marched out with her own luggage.

"I need a ride to the airport," she announced. "Will you drive me or should I call a cab?"

Matt stood and spread his hands. "I'm sorry, Suze. I don't know what came over me."

"That was just plain mean, Matthew. I've never seen you like that."

"You're my little sister, and I love you. I don't know why you stay with that guy."

"I'm forty-seven years old. I'm nobody's *little sister*. And who I'm with is none of your business."

Matt drove Susan to the airport. She spoke only once—when she got out of the car at the terminal.

"Matthew, you didn't just hurt Robert, you hurt me, too."

Those were the last words she ever spoke to him.

CHAPTER FOUR

The jet glided to a landing at Honolulu International Airport. The beauty of the sunlit, lush green hills Matt saw through his window seemed wrong, out of place. His mood was dark and icy.

But the soft, tropical breeze that soon caressed his face felt wonderful, and the aroma of flowers was hypnotic. Susan had loved this place. He would try to remember that.

A cab dropped him off at a hotel near Susan's Diamond Head condo. He could have stayed at her place, but decided he couldn't bear it. Dense, jungle-like grounds bordered both sides of the hotel entrance. The lobby was a lanai, open to the air on two sides.

Matt carried his own bag up three marble steps to the open lobby. After he checked in, he took the elevator to his seventh floor room, unpacked, took a quick shower, and dressed in a cotton shirt, tan slacks, and loafers. As he combed his hair at the bathroom mirror, he was struck once again by how similar he and Susan had looked. The same salt-and-pepper hair, ruddy complexion, green eyes, high cheekbones, and aquiline nose. Their differences were minor: His eyebrows were thicker than hers; her mouth was fuller than his. They'd been a matched set all their lives. Even though he was older, they'd often been mistaken for twins. He felt a lump form in his throat. His breath shuddered. He hadn't consciously realized it, but Susan and he had been two parts of one whole. They'd been more than sister and brother. She was his best friend. Now he felt empty, robbed of an irreplaceable part of himself. He was angry she'd taken her own life, but he couldn't get past the feeling that Susan's death could have been his fault.

Matt forced himself to take a deep breath, then reached for a towel and pressed it against his eyes.

The clock radio on the nightstand showed 9:30 a.m. Matt dug into his briefcase for his appointment book and found the entry for Lieutenant Dennis Callahan, the Honolulu violent crimes detective he'd talked to. He went to the phone, punched in the number, and listened to the hollow ring for fifteen seconds. He was about to hang up when a woman answered.

"HPD. How can I help you?" The woman spoke with an easy, rhythmic cadence.

"Lieutenant Callahan, please."

Matt heard a click, then silence. He gazed out the window at azure water beyond a golden beach.

"Violent Crimes. Callahan!"

The sharp bark shocked Matt back to reality. The strong Brooklyn accent out of place.

"Lieutenant, this is Matthew Curtis. You told me to call when I arrived."

"Ah, Mister Curtis, what can I do for you?"

Matt's fuse suddenly smoldered. "Susan Curtis," he said. "You remember Susan, don't you? She's the woman who supposedly jumped off a balcony yesterday. I'm her brother . . . from Albuquerque."

Callahan expelled a stream of air that whistled in Matt's ear. "Of course, Mister Curtis. I remember."

It was worrisome that the man hadn't recalled his name. Matt was afraid the cop had already put Susan's death behind him. Suicide. To Callahan, she was just another jumper.

"I'm here to take care of my sister's affairs. Before I get started, I'd like to come by your office. I need to know more about what happened to my sister."

Callahan cleared his throat. "I'm pretty busy . . ." A pause. "Well, I guess I could spare a few minutes . . . if you come down tomorrow about eleven. I won't have time until then."

CHAPTER FIVE

Lucas Polk leaned against the dirty brown brick building across the street from the Honolulu bus terminal and tried to ignore the acrid smell of urine. Damn street people. He dropped his cigarette to the pavement, crushed it underfoot, and spat out a bit of tobacco. He swept his hands through his thin blond hair and pulled up on the collar of his purple silk shirt. He felt his heart rate accelerate and recognized the quiver in his belly. Hunting nerves. He took a step toward the curb, but stopped when he saw the big Hawaiian patrol cop step out of the Korean grocery store at the end of the block. Lucas leaned on a parking meter as though he was just hanging out.

The cop looked in Lucas's direction, then across the street at the bus station. He stood there for thirty seconds and finally went off in the opposite direction.

Lucas breathed a sigh of relief when the cop disappeared around the next corner. Sonofabitch cop is a problem, he thought. Can't be bought off and treats every little runaway like one of his own kids.

Lucas checked his watch. Almost eleven. Damn bus should have been in ten minutes ago. He pulled his cigarettes from his shirt pocket and shook out the last one. Crumpled the empty pack, tossed it at the gutter, and lit up. He took a deep drag and exhaled as a bus pulled under the terminal canopy.

Lucas crossed the street to get a good look at the passengers. He hoped there would be at least one good prospect. His boss had been all over his ass about building up his stable.

An elderly couple slowly stepped down to the pavement. Then an Asian woman with two little kids in tow. A nun. A couple guys who looked like migrant farm workers. That seemed to be it. Disappointed, Lucas was about to turn away when he saw a final passenger tentatively step down to the sidewalk.

Debbie Stokes looked down the street at the distant skyscrapers and hugged herself. As warm as it was, she felt chilled. This was the big city. She knew the eighty-six dollars in her wallet wouldn't last long here. That's all the cash she could scrounge from the cache in the back of her mother's lingerie drawer. She needed a job but would have to lie about her age. Who would hire a thirteen-year-old?

She waited until the other passengers had retrieved their luggage from the storage area under the bus, then walked up and took her handleless suitcase from the driver. She hooked her fingers under the rope she'd tied around the bag and lifted it under her arm.

"You got a place to go, honey?" the driver asked

"Yeah," she lied. "My mom's gonna pick me up."

"That's good," the man said. "This isn't the best place for a young gal to be alone."

She went inside the terminal and found the ladies room. After she used the toilet and cleaned up a little, she walked back outside. The buildings around the bus station were squat and dilapidated. There weren't many people around. She turned again in the direction of the high-rise buildings. They were blocks away. But there would be businesses and jobs there.

Lucas trailed the girl as she set off toward downtown, clearly unfamiliar with the area. She looked around as though both nervous and fascinated. Her thin cotton dress could have come from a Goodwill store or been handed down by an older sister. It had no shape. Of course, as skinny as the kid was, nothing she wore would have had any shape. Lucas knew this kid would be worth a fortune. There were a lot of clients who liked them real young.

The girl walked eight blocks, then hesitated outside a rundown diner. Lucas guessed she hadn't eaten in hours and probably didn't have much money.

"Come to Papa," he whispered.

Lucas followed the girl into the diner and watched her go to a booth at the back. He took a seat at the counter and listened to her order a hamburger, French fries, and a coke. Later, he stole glimpses of her eating.

When the waitress dropped the check on the girl, he sauntered to the booth and sat down across from her. She jerked back against the booth and pulled her suitcase across the seat to her side.

"Sorry, honey," Lucas said, "I didn't mean to scare you."

"I ain't scared," she said, in a squeaky, brittle voice.

"You lookin' for a job?" he asked.

The girl tilted her head and her eyes went wide. "I . . . I guess I'm gonna need a job."

"I could probably help you out. I know a man who needs workers."

"What kinda work?" she asked.

"Heck, I don't know. I could introduce you to him, if you want."

The girl clutched her suitcase as though it was a life preserver. Her gaze wandered around the little diner as though one of the other customers might give her advice.

"You got a place to stay tonight?" Lucas said. "I could take you to my friend tomorrow."

She looked down at her lap and mumbled, "No, I just got here."

Lucas glanced at the check, then tossed a ten-dollar bill onto the table. "Come on, don't be afraid," he said. "I'll show you where you can rent a room for the night."

She hesitated.

"It's cheap," he said.

Those seemed to be the magic words. She slid out of the booth, dragged her suitcase after her, and followed Lucas out to the street.

"What's your name, honey?"

"Debbie. Debbie Stokes."

"The Tryon Arms will do for one night," Lucas said in a soft, comforting voice. "Tomorrow, I'll find you something nicer." Horseshit! he thought. This fleatrap will be as good as it gets. He patted her shoulder and smiled down at her. "Meet me back at the diner at nine in the morning. Okay?"

Debbie looked around the lobby and cringed. The linoleum floor was stained and gouged. The wood furniture was scrapped and cracked; its cushions threadbare and pocked with cigarette burns. A grizzled old guy with whiskers and worn-out clothes sat on a couch. He sucked the life out of a cigarette stub he held between nicotine-stained fingers. An old whore glared at Debbie as though she was an alien that had invaded her territory. Debbie wanted to cry.

CHAPTER SIX

Matt walked two blocks from his hotel to a rental car office. He drove away in the only vehicle available, a tan Ford mini-van, directions to the funeral home written on a slip of paper he'd placed on the front passenger seat.

Susan had left instructions to have her body cremated. No headstone. No permanent memorial. As little hassle as possible for all concerned. That was Susan. At the mortuary, a receptionist greeted him, took his name, then pushed an intercom button.

"Mister Cleary," she said, "Doctor Curtis is here to see you."

After a few seconds, a middle-aged man with a florid, acne-scarred complexion came out of a room twenty yards down the hall. The Grim Reaper, Matt thought, as the man approached the lobby. He wore a nametag: William Cleary, and looked like a Dickensian character—gaunt and stooped. A crow in his black suit and slicked-down black hair. He skulked, rather than walked.

Cleary folded his hands over his stomach and half-bowed. "How may I assist you?" he asked, in a voice so low it was almost a croak.

"My sister, Susan Curtis. She named your place in her will."

Cleary led Matt to a small conference room, furnished with a mahogany-colored round table and four chairs. Three wooden trays with forms were stacked in the center of the table. Cleary took a form from each tray and filled in information that Matt provided: Present location of Susan's body, when he thought it might be delivered to the funeral home, next of kin, vital statistics, organizations she belonged to.

"Do you have a copy of the death certificate?" Cleary asked.

"Not yet," Matt answered. "The coroner hasn't released her body."

Head bent down over the form in front of him, Cleary asked, "What was the cause of death?"

Matt mentally stumbled. He found it difficult to say *suicide*.

Cleary looked up, his eyebrows arched in a question.

"Put down *accident*," Matt said.

When Cleary learned there would be no casket, no tombstone, no cemetery plot, his eyes narrowed and the solicitous smile slipped away.

Finally, a genuine emotion, Matt thought. Even if it was just disappointed greed.

The obituary notice for the newspaper would not mention the cause of death. Since Susan wasn't a member of any religious congregation, Matt accepted Cleary's offer to arrange for someone to lead a memorial service. Matt knew Susan wouldn't have wanted a service, but he decided it was for him. He was certain there would be dozens of Susan's friends and co-workers who would want to pay tribute to her memory.

Matt and Cleary shook hands after all the papers were signed. Cleary's was moist with perspiration.

Matt wiped his hand on the side of his trousers as he left the conference room.

DAY THREE

CHAPTER SEVEN

Matt looked up at the Honolulu Police Headquarters' stone façade and swallowed the lump in his throat.

A Hawaiian cop who looked like Buddha was hunched over a newspaper at the reception desk. His gut stretched the front of his uniform shirt to the point Matt thought he might have to duck ballistic buttons at any moment. He didn't look up until Matt cleared his throat and said, "Excuse me!"

The cop stared right through him.

"Lieutenant Callahan expects me."

The cop picked up the phone on his desk and tapped in four numbers. "Lieutenant, I got a guy down here askin' for you."

He listened for a moment, covered the mouthpiece. "Your name?"

"Matthew Curtis."

The cop reported this information and listened again. "Take those stairs to the second floor," he said, as he replaced the receiver. "Turn right at the top. Third door on the right." Then he dropped his gaze back to the newspaper, as though Matt had never existed.

Matt stopped in front of an open doorway that led into a large bullpen area crammed with desks. Telephones rang, men's and women's voices bounced off walls and ceiling, and what Matt assumed were detectives sat at desks and typed at computer keyboards. Half-a-dozen men in handcuffs sat with heads hung low beside desks occupied by more detectives. Matt moved to the closest desk and asked, "Inspector Callahan?"

The woman behind the desk snatched the receiver from a ringing telephone as she pointed at an office at the rear of the area.

Matt walked to the office and knocked on the glass of a closed door.

"Come in," a man shouted.

Matt opened the door, entered the office, and closed the door behind him. Callahan: Six feet tall. Barrel-chested. A head of short, black hair, streaked with gray at the temples. Crowsfeet around his eyes and deep furrows on his forehead and around his mouth indicated years of hard-edged experience. A skein of broken blood vessels on his nose hinted at a losing battle with the bottle. The detective paced as he talked on the phone. He waved Matt to a chair.

Callahan wore expensive-looking clothes—a dark-blue blazer, starched white dress shirt with monogrammed cuffs, regimental tie, gray slacks with a knife-edge crease, and spit-shined tasseled loafers. He paced like a caged animal, growled into the phone, alternately looked out the window and glanced at his feet. He stopped once, to place a foot on the edge of a wastebasket, bend down, and flick something—an offensive mote of dust—from one of his shoes. Then he paced anew.

Callahan's desk held an in-box and an out-box—both empty. No piles of paper or files. No clutter. No dust. On one wall, a dozen photographs of uniformed police officers hung like a necklace beneath the mounted head of a fiercely tusked wild pig.

Callahan slammed the receiver into its cradle. "Goddamn bureaucrats!" he spat. He walked around his desk and offered his hand. "Dennis Callahan, Mister Curtis. No, it's Doctor, isn't it?"

"Matt Curtis."

Callahan carefully pulled at the creases in his pants before he settled into his chair.

Matt pointed at the boar's head. "You shoot that?"

Callahan looked at the trophy and snorted. "Nah! My ex-wife found it at a garage sale. Said it reminded her of me. I keep it because it reminds me to send the goddamn alimony check every month."

Matt couldn't think of an appropriate response. "Anything new

35

on my sister's death?" he asked after a moment.

Callahan closed his eyes and leaned his forehead on steepled fingers. Then he looked up again. "Doctor Curtis, I know it's hard to accept. Suicide, I mean. But in your sister's case there's no evidence to the contrary."

So, Susan had killed herself, plain and simple. "Has the coroner's report been released?"

Callahan sighed. "The coroner called a couple minutes ago and left me a message. Said he'd received the serology report—the last thing he needed. He wants me to come down to the morgue. Give me a number where I can reach you. I'll call after I meet with him."

"Any reason I can't go with you?"

Callahan scowled. "I would think the morgue would be the last place you'd want to visit. An autopsy's been performed on your sister, Doctor Curtis. It won't be pretty."

"Lieutenant, I'm an orthopedic surgeon. I think I can handle it. I've seen my share of gruesome injuries."

"None of which was your sister's, right?"

Matt stared at Callahan.

After a few seconds, the detective lifted his hands in surrender. He smirked, then huffed through his nostrils and shrugged. "Okay, let's go."

Matt struggled to keep up with Callahan on the two-block walk to the parking lot where Callahan fast-walked to a white Crown Victoria. Callahan had at least thirty pounds on him, but moved as effortlessly as a powerful cat. Matt perspired in the hot, humid air. His breaths came in gasps. Callahan smiled at him as he slid behind the wheel.

"Better get out and exercise more, Doc," Callahan said.

Matt was breathing too hard to throw a snappy retort at Callahan. Besides, he knew the cop was correct.

Callahan drove to The Medical Examiner Facility, a modern white and glass building on Iwilei Road.

"You're sure you want to go through with this?" Callahan asked as they climbed the steps to the building entrance. "A person who falls twenty-four stories . . . ."

Matt waved a hand and nodded his head. He trailed Callahan

through the entrance, along a corridor, then down a staircase. In the basement, at the end of a long hallway, a door marked: MORGUE.

The reek hit him even before Callahan opened the door. The first time Matt had entered an anatomy lab in medical school, he'd assumed the smell was the odor of death. He now knew that many morgue smells actually came from chemicals and disinfectants. But that knowledge didn't make the stench any easier to take.

The morgue had six stainless steel tables—three to a row. A body lay on each of them. Plastic sheets that hid everything but bare feet covered four of the bodies. Women in surgical scrubs worked on two of the bodies. One wall contained large drawers—six across and three high.

Callahan moved toward a frail Asian man standing in a glass-fronted office in a corner near the morgue entrance. This man wore a white smock over tan slacks, black running shoes, and rubber surgical gloves.

"Hey, Doctor Trang, looks like business is good," Callahan said.

Trang smiled ruefully. "Too much crime. Why don't you get off your butt and hit the streets?"

"We are, we are. We shoot the bad guys as fast as we can. That's why you're so busy."

"Ha, ha, ha. Just what I need. Irish cop make joke."

"You got something more on the Curtis case? This is Doctor Matt Curtis, the deceased's brother."

Trang blinked, as though he couldn't believe Matt would want to be there.

"Please sit," Trang said. "I have your sister's file on my desk."

Trang plopped into his own chair on the other side of the desk. Framed medical degrees and licenses hung on the walls, along with snapshots of a woman and children. Files were stacked precariously high on the edges of the gray metal desk, on the matching file cabinets, even on the cracked and pitted white linoleum floor.

Matt waited—hoped—for Trang to say something that would clear up this nonsense about Susan's suicide. He watched the medical examiner open a file in the center of his desk and look at the top sheet of paper. Hand-written notes were scrawled across one corner.

"I'm embarrassed to admit that, because we found nothing in your sister's blood—no alcohol, no drugs—and there was no sign of a struggle, we assumed she committed suicide."

Trang expelled a semi-audible stream of words that sounded to Matt like Vietnamese expletives.

"But, we found evidence of *flunitrazepan* in her system when we scoped her urine."

"*Flunitrazepan?*" Matt said, bewildered. "Rohypnol?"

"Yes," Trang said, "the date rape drug."

Matt opened his mouth to ask a question, but Callahan laid a hand on his arm.

"The deceased had enough *flunitrazepan* in her to kill five people," Trang said. He gave Matt a sad little smile.

Matt looked from Trang to Callahan, who looked away. Matt turned back to Trang. "Not a common street drug."

Trang shook his head and said facetiously, "Doctor Curtis, it is highly unlikely that an addict's drug of choice would be Rohypnol."

Matt looked again at Callahan, but saw no expression on the policeman's face.

Trang glanced at Callahan, too, then back at Matt. He seemed to measure his thoughts before he voiced them.

"The Rohypnol would have killed her if she hadn't fallen off the balcony. Her respiratory system would have shut down in less than fifteen minutes with that much barbiturate in her. Our tests lead me to believe there may have been—I repeat, *may* have been—foul play involved in your sister's death. But there's not enough evidence to prove it."

"That's a gigantic leap, don't you think, Doc?" Callahan interjected, his voice suddenly strained.

Trang said, "The presence of Rohypnol is very suspicious, but with no other supporting evidence . . . ." He let his regret hang in the room. "I'll release her body to the funeral home this afternoon."

"Wait a minute," Matt said, "I don't . . . ."

Trang raised both hands to silence Matt.

"Doctor Curtis, just because I feel there may have been foul play doesn't mean your sister *did not* perhaps jump. Maybe she accidentally took a lethal dose of this drug—as strange as it may seem—became disoriented, and simply fell from her balcony." He paused a moment, dropped his gaze back to the file on his desk, then looked at Matt. There was sadness in his eyes.

"She could have brought the wrong man home from a bar." Callahan let this statement hang between him and Matt.

"My sister did not pick up men in bars," Matt said.

Trang scowled at Callahan and then said to Matt, "The urinalysis report is not proof someone else drugged her or pushed her off her balcony."

Matt bunched his fists. His stomach muscles cramped. "How many corpses have you autopsied, Doctor, where the deceased had an overdose of drugs in his or her system?" He knew his voice was loud, accusatory, but he couldn't help it. A drug overdose! This is what he'd hoped for. Some sign that Susan hadn't killed herself.

"Take it easy, Doc," Callahan said, but Trang waved off the detective.

"It's okay, Callahan. I understand Doctor Curtis's frustration." He sat back in his chair and rocked slowly. "Hundreds. I've autopsied hundreds of drug overdoses."

"And, in those hundreds of cases, how many autopsies have you performed where the deceased had a lethal dose of Rohypnol?"

Trang compressed his lips into a flat line and gave a half-nod. "None. We've had a couple bodies in here with traces of Rohypnol, but that's not what killed them. Usually, some guy slips his victim a Rohypnol mickey and kills her after she's passed out."

"Last question, Doctor," Matt said. "How does a law abiding citizen in Hawaii buy Rohypnol? Last I heard it was illegal in every state. Harder to get than even heroin or cocaine."

"You're right. It's illegal."

"Why bother to find an illegal drug if you want to kill yourself?" Matt asked. "Why not OD on painkillers or sleeping pills?" He swallowed the lump in his throat. "And if you do intentionally take a lethal overdose, why jump off a high-rise balcony?"

Trang nodded again. He raised a finger. "I'll take what you've said into consideration. I did say she might have fallen rather than jumped."

"Or was pushed," Matt interjected.

Trang's face seemed to sag with sad-eyed sympathy. "My only choices at this point are accident or suicide," he said. "There's no way I can justify a finding of murder with the evidence I have."

Trang pushed up straighter in his chair and rested the palms of his hands on the open file before him. "But I have a question for you, Doctor Curtis. How well did you know your sister?"

A vision of nine-year-old Susan sprang to Matt's mind—pigtails, sunburned nose, freckles, skinned knees. And that smile. When most thirteen-year-old brothers would have done everything possible to ditch a kid sister, Matt dragged Susan along whenever possible.

Sure, Dad had made Matt—only eleven at the time—swear he would take care of Susan and their mother if anything happened to him. He'd taken Matt's hand and stared into his eyes and made him promise. A drunk driver had killed Dad just a month later. Matt accepted responsibility for his sister and his mother as though he had no choice. But Susan was fun to have around, too. She wasn't afraid of a thing and had a mouth on her that scandalized the neighborhood boys.

Matt warmed at the memory of Susan singing lead with a local rock and roll group in high school and winning Athlete of the Year honors in her senior year, after she broke state records in the quarter-mile and the two-hundred-yard dash.

He had always assumed she would become one of the first female Green Berets. He was shocked when she went to UCLA to study accounting.

After she took the job with the law firm in Honolulu, they stayed in close touch, despite the miles that separated them. They talked on the phone three or four times a month, and visited each other—either in Albuquerque or Honolulu—at least once a year.

When Matt's wife had died, Susan flew to Albuquerque and stayed with him for a month. She'd mothered his two sons as though they were her own; showered them with love and attention. Gave Matt time to come to terms with his loss.

Eight years ago, Susan had hooked up with Robert Nakamura. She split her energy and time between Robert and her job at the law firm. She soon seemed to have little left for anything or anyone else.

Matt and his boys had seen Susan only three times since Robert had entered her life—once in Hawaii, twice in Albuquerque. Each time, she'd seemed strangely preoccupied. Focused on Robert. She no longer paid attention to Matt's sons or Mom. Somehow, Matt knew, Susan had changed.

Matt lowered his head and rubbed his forehead. Trang's question was a poignant one. How well *did* he know his sister? Well enough to know it was difficult to get her to even take an aspirin. She referred to pushers and addicts as "scum of the earth."

Matt stood and met Trang's gaze. "I want to see my sister's body."

Trang's face screwed up with a pained expression. His forehead wrinkled and his mouth opened to start an unspoken, "What?" He looked at Callahan, who hunched his shoulders.

"Well, it would be helpful to have a family member ID the body," Callahan said.

Trang sighed, shook his head. "Come with me." He led them to one of the large drawers in the adjoining room and pulled on its metal handle.

Matt steeled himself while Trang unzipped a black vinyl bag.

A cloth covered the head. Matt circled Callahan to the other side of the drawer. Trang lifted the cloth. Matt felt his heart seem to stop. He tried to suck in more air than his lungs could hold. He raised his hands to cover his eyes and spun away. He couldn't identify her. Susan's face had been smashed beyond recognition.

CHAPTER EIGHT

Lucas Polk smiled. A night alone in that flea trap hotel had made little Debbie Stokes anxious to see a familiar face. She'd come back to the diner, as he'd known she would. Her suitcase rested on the floor beside her counter seat.

Lucas said from the stool next to her's, "You're lookin' kinda tired this morning. Gotta get your sleep, you know."

Debbie leaned her elbows on the Formica counter and turned her head toward him. "It was awful," she whispered. "People in the room next door grunted like pigs. It went on for hours. I couldn't sleep. I sure don't want to stay there again."

"What you gonna do? You can't hang around the streets."

"You said you could find me a job," she said, her forehead creased with worry.

"That I can, honey." He squinted. "Don't get me wrong," he said as he dropped his gaze to her clothes. "I don't mean to hurt your feelings, but you can't get a job dressed like that."

She looked down, fingered a button on the front of her dress. Her face reddened. "It was my sister's."

Lucas reached over, tilted her chin up. "Well, I won't let you look for a job wearing hand-me-downs. Finish your breakfast."

"I'm not really hungry."

Lucas dropped a five on the counter. "Come on, little girl, I'm gonna buy you some new clothes."

Lucas saw her hesitate. "You're not the first person I've helped," he said. "What else do I gotta do with my money?"

He gently took her hand and lifted her suitcase off the floor. "You get to pick out whatever you want."

Lucas saw excitement in her eyes. He guessed the kid had never had a brand-new dress.

CHAPTER NINE

Matt followed Callahan out of the morgue and into the humid noon air. He used his hand to shield his eyes against the bright sunlight and walked next to the cop. He was thankful for Callahan's silence.

Matt's mind reeled with questions. How could Susan have had Rohypnol in her? It just didn't add up. And where the hell was Susan's boyfriend, Robert? Matt had called before he flew from Albuquerque and left a message on the answering machine at Robert's apartment. But he hadn't heard a word back. He squinted against the sunlight, brushed a hand through his hair, let his fingers dropped to the back of his neck, and kneaded the tension-stiff muscles there.

He turned to Callahan. "Can we stop somewhere? Get some coffee?"

Callahan looked at his watch. "I guess so." He pointed down the street to a sign over the sidewalk: Mori's Bakery & Deli.

Callahan led the way to Mori's. He opened the door there for Matt. A cowbell fixed to the inside of the door clanged and the heavy odor of grease greeted him. They sat in a back corner, at a table barely big enough for one grown man. The lunch crowd had begun to arrive and the buzz of conversation, the clink of utensils, and the waitresses' shouted food orders reverberated off the tile floor and tin ceiling. It was deafening.

He looked around at the eclectic mix of clientele: Suits, a

longhaired surfer-type, casually dressed but elegant-looking women, and even a couple of bikers with leather vests, bare chests, and beer bellies.

A long-legged, buxom replica of a 1950s-diner-waitress appeared at their table. She had red hair, bright red lipstick, blue eye shadow, a pink uniform. She was about thirty-five, with a deeply lined face and a no-nonsense set to her jaw. Matt noticed that her eyes were violet-blue. She gave Callahan a wink.

"Hello there, Denny," she said. "Who's the *haole?*"

Callahan grinned at Matt. "That's you, white boy," he said. "To the locals, all mainlanders are *haoles*—honkies, gringos, crackers, flatlanders—whatever suits you. But Doris here didn't mean it nasty." He patted her hip. "It's her way of saying *aloha.*"

"Doris, meet Doctor Curtis. He just arrived," Callahan said.

Doris leaned toward Matt and regarded him with closer attention. "You wouldn't happen to know anything about backs, would you, Doc? Mine's killing me."

Matt decided to be polite. "A little," he said.

She straightened up, turned to the side, and placed a hand on her spine just below the small of her back. "It hurts right here. Goes right down my left leg."

"You should see an orthopedic surgeon or a neurosurgeon."

"Aw, Doc. I can't afford that. You think I get medical benefits with this exec-u-tive position I got here?" She laughed, but there wasn't much humor in it.

Matt wasn't about to practice medicine in a cafe. Besides, he wasn't licensed in Hawaii. But he decided to offer her some practical advice.

"At the very least, you should go home and stay in bed for a couple days."

Doris smirked. "Yeah, right!"

Callahan laughed. "You better listen to the doctor."

"You really should go to bed for two, three days," Matt repeated. "No work, no running around, no lifting. Flat on your back, knees bent."

"I can do that," she said, then gave Callahan a leer. "Maybe you ought to drop by, Denny, considering I'll be in such a vulnerable position."

Callahan laughed again. "Now, Doris, you know I'd never take advantage of a damsel in distress."

"Your loss, sweetie," she said.

"What d'ya say your name was, Doc?" Doris asked.

"Matt Curtis," Matt said, hoping she'd go away and let him talk with Callahan.

But she stood there with sudden sorrow in her eyes.

She jerked a hand to her mouth. "My God! The resemblance. I should have made the connection. Was Susan Curtis your sister?"

An electric current ran through Matt. He sat up straighter. "You knew my sister?"

Doris waved her order pad toward the cashier and shouted, "Hey, Mori, I'm on my break."

Mori shouted back, "Doris, it's too busy; you . . . ." He didn't finish what he was about to say because Doris narrowed her eyes at him, raised a finger, and waggled it in warning.

She slid onto the chair next to Callahan and stared across the table at Matt. "I can't believe I didn't notice the resemblance right off. Same gray hair. Same green eyes. Same nose. I'm so sorry about what happened."

Callahan cleared his throat. "Doctor Curtis and I have things to discuss, Doris. You think you could take our order and leave us alone for a minute?"

Doris twisted in her chair. She grimaced. She did the finger-waggling thing again. "I ain't leavin' 'til I tell Doctor Curtis what his sister meant to me." She slowly turned back toward Matt.

"It's no exaggeration when I tell you Susan saved my little girl's life." She placed a hand over her heart. "I thought I'd lost Amy forever, but your sister changed everything."

Matt stared. "You've lost me," he said.

"Save the Kids," she said.

Matt hunched his shoulders.

"You don't know about Save the Kids?"

"Never heard of it," Matt said.

"Save the Kids finds runaways and brings them home. Part of what the group does is patrol Honolulu's rougher areas at night and tries to convince boys and girls to get off the streets. Some of the kids are hooked on drugs. They survive out there any way they can—panhandling, pick pocketing, prostitution."

Doris closed her eyes and shook her head. "My daughter . . . ." She shuddered and wrapped her arms around herself as though suddenly cold. "A pimp got Amy hooked on drugs and then sold her on the street."

"My God," Matt said.

"Amy wanted to go to a rock concert with some friends. I told her she was too young to be out that late. And it was a school night. She snuck out anyway . . . and vanished."

Matt saw Doris's eyes glaze over, as though a cloud had passed through them. They were etched in pain.

Doris reached into a pocket of her uniform, pulled out a tissue, and dabbed at her eyes. "Amy had been gone for three months. One night on patrol, Susan saw a guy shove Amy out of his car. He'd beat her up pretty bad. Susan took her to a hospital. She called me from the emergency room. But that's not all she did. After the hospital released Amy, Susan got her into a drug rehab program and visited my daughter every day for eight weeks. Made sure she stayed in the program. Susan gave my little girl back to me."

Doris's tears now flowed. Her eye makeup ran in blue streaks over her cheeks. She daubed at her eyes, but only succeeded in smudging her makeup even more.

"I've never met anyone like your sister. She didn't seem to give a damn about the danger. Pimps' threats didn't even faze her. At first, I thought she was just naïve." Doris smiled. "Susan wasn't naïve. She was gutsy. When I met her at the hospital where she'd taken Amy, she was shaking she was so damned angry."

"How long had my sister worked with Save the Kids?"

"Quite a while, as far as I know."

"She never mentioned it to me," Matt said.

Doris hunched her shoulders. "Probably didn't want to worry you. It was dangerous. The pimp who had Amy said he'd kill Susan."

"Do you know the pimp's name?" Matt asked.

"I'll never forget the sonofabitch," she hissed. "Name's Chick Hamea. Works for Rubio Gonzales."

47

Doris turned toward Callahan. "Okay, Denny, I'll leave you alone now. You guys can discuss your business in private." She stood, gave Matt a grin, and turned to walk away.

"Whoa, Doris," Callahan said. "Where're you going? You didn't take our orders."

She stopped and looked back over her shoulder. "I know what you want, Denny. You always get the same thing. Black coffee and a fritter." Then to Matt. "For you, Doc, I got something special. On the house."

"You made yourself a friend," Callahan told Matt.

Matt raised his hands in a "what can you do?" gesture. "Lieutenant, I appreciate you taking this extra time to meet with me. I suspect this isn't how you normally deal with a victim's family."

"Doctor, I don't often have family members come all the way from Arizona."

Matt nodded, not bothering to remind Callahan that he was from New Mexico. "It's important you understand that Susan would never have taken her own life," he said. "I don't say that as a distraught relative. I've thought about it a lot. There's no way she could have committed suicide. No way would she have taken any drug, let alone Rohypnol. No way in hell. My sister hated drugs. She rarely even took over-the-counter medication."

Matt kept his voice just loud enough in the noisy café. "I need you to believe me. Please don't write off Susan's death as a suicide or an accidental drug overdose. I knew my sister. Something about this whole thing stinks. You heard what Doris said. What about that pimp she mentioned, or the guy he works for? Couldn't they have murdered my sister?"

Callahan closed his eyes for a couple seconds, opened them, and stared at Matt. "Chick Hamea skipped to the mainland after he stuck a blade in a sailor six months ago. And I can't believe some big-time criminal like Rubio Gonzales would murder your sister because she messed around a little with his prostitution business. Gonzales runs dozens of women. What's a couple teeny-bopper prostitutes to him? Besides, there was no physical evidence at the scene."

"You know this Rubio Gonzales?"

"Know of him. He's into drugs and loan sharking, as well as prostitution and porn."

"How soon will a formal report be released on cause of death?" Matt asked, after a moment's pause

"Depends on Doctor Trang," Callahan said. "It will probably come today, tomorrow at the latest. You heard him say he would release your sister's body soon."

Matt couldn't help himself. He felt his whole body sag.

Callahan relented. "Tell you what I'll do. I'll call Trang and ask him to put your sister's file on the bottom of his pile. That ought to give us another couple of days. But I want you to understand something. I got cases out the wazoo. I'm short on investigators. We're not authorized overtime. So don't expect much."

"I understand, Lieutenant. Thanks. I'll only be here until the funeral. If you find out anything, I'd really appreciate a call."

"You got my word on it," Callahan said. Then he smiled. "Now why don't you call me Dennis? Any friend of Doris's is a friend of mine."

"Only if you call me Matt."

Doris arrived with their meals. She'd repaired her makeup. Callahan scarfed up the fritter and coffee, then reached for his wallet. Matt waved him off. "I'll get it," he said. Callahan thanked him, mumbled something about getting back to his office.

"You go ahead," Matt said. "I'll catch a cab back to my car."

"You sure?"

Matt nodded. "I need some time to think."

Callahan shook Matt's hand and left the restaurant.

Matt stared at his food and suddenly no longer had an appetite. He put a twenty-dollar bill on the table, leaned back in his chair, and stared at the ceiling. He wasn't anxious to go to Susan's condominium.

Callahan stood on the sidewalk outside the restaurant and looked in through the window blinds. His eyes lasered in on the back of Doctor Curtis's head. He squeezed his lips tightly together. Damned civilians, he thought; always meddling. Can't let the pros do their jobs.

CHAPTER TEN

Before he left Mori's in a taxi, Matt used his cell phone to call the Sand & Sea Condominium where Susan had lived. A woman named Michelle in the management office said the complex's maintenance man, Shawn, would let Matt into his sister's unit at 5 p.m.

When Matt stepped from the rental car at the condominium, he saw a tall, hulking man in a khaki uniform, work boots, and a blue baseball cap hose-watering a spectacular bird-of-paradise plant in a white ceramic planter at the building's entrance.

"Excuse me," Matt said. "Are you Shawn?"

The man continued to stare at the planter, but he released the handle on the hose nozzle and cut off the water. Then he turned toward Matt, his eyes downcast. "Yup, that's me," he said, without enthusiasm. "You Mister Curtis?"

"Yes, that's right," Matt said. Shawn had brown-stained teeth and acne pustules on his cheeks and forehead. A pale harelip scar marked the middle of his upper lip.

"I'm suppose'ta let ya into 2408," Shawn said. He slowly coiled up the hose and stowed it behind a nearby bush, then opened the lobby door, and walked inside.

Matt followed him.

"How long have you worked here?" Matt asked.

Shawn just shrugged. He continued toward the elevators, not

once looking back at Matt while they crossed the blue-carpeted lobby.

In the elevator, Matt made another attempt at conversation. "Did you know Miss Curtis?"

Shawn stared at Matt with moist eyes. Then he dropped his head again; looked down at his boots. He pushed the button for the twenty-fourth floor. They rode up in silence.

When the elevator door opened, Shawn loped down the hall to Susan's unit. He unlocked and opened the door.

Matt thanked him and got a grunt in reply.

He watched Shawn quickly return to the elevator, then took a deep breath and entered Susan's unit. He felt odd, as though he had invaded her privacy. The entry hall opened into a spacious living room. The kitchen and dining room were to the right of the living room. The drapes were open, which gave Matt a clear view of the fatal balcony. He shuddered and turned away.

Matt sucked air over his teeth, then turned down the hallway that led to the two bedrooms. Framed photographs covered nearly every inch of wall on both sides of the hallway. Pictures of his sons, of his late wife, of his mother and father, of Susan, of himself. The photos dredged up memories that made his eyes tear. In one, shot by their father, he and Susan stood on a Santa Monica beach. Matt had been about twelve then, Susan about eight. His arm was draped over her shoulders. She had a bright, gap-toothed smile. Such a sweet kid! He swallowed the lump in his throat.

Another picture showed Susan in cap-and-gown at her UCLA graduation. Matt felt conflicted. Maybe it was suicide. But maybe something more sinister had happened. He whispered to the photograph, "Don't let the cops be right about suicide."

Matt searched the condo for an hour. He went through closets and drawers. He even checked the pockets of Susan's clothes. At first he just tried to get a feel for which of Susan's possessions to give away and which to keep or give to his sons. But soon he changed his focus to looking for a clue to what might have caused Susan's death.

There was plenty of evidence of his sister's organized nature. Every drawer was neat. Her bedroom closet had casual clothes on the left, business apparel in the middle, evening clothes on the right. He sat at her desk and went through files. Bills had been paid up-to-date—insurance, utilities, mortgage, medical, health club. She'd kept every birthday card and letter he'd ever sent her. There were other files, each dedicated to correspondence from a friend or relative. He thumbed through them with no particular purpose until he came to one labeled: Robert.

Its contents were an archival record of the tortured relationship she'd had with her boyfriend. There were even letters she'd composed to him but, for whatever reason, decided not to send. They confirmed what Matt already knew, but they also surprised him with their intensity. Robert was emotionally dependent on Susan. But she seemed to have needed Robert every bit as much as he needed her.

He scanned the more recent unmailed letters, all handwritten. One was dated ten days before her death.

Dearest Robert:

I am sitting at the kitchen table, looking out the window at the sunset, wondering where you are. Each time you leave, without a word, without any indication how long you will be gone, I am filled with worry. Why won't you tell me where you go, what you do? I assure you I will understand.

Have I said or done something to offend you? These disappearances are tearing me apart. I never know if you will return.

The letter stopped there, unfinished.

The correspondence was organized in chronological order. The letters and postcards from Robert, also handwritten, began eight years earlier and continued until the previous month. Some had been mailed in Honolulu. Others bore postmarks from places like Guam, the Philippines, Indonesia, Thailand, and several states on the mainland. Many of the letters had been sent from Las Vegas. Robert seemed to have traveled a lot for someone without a job. Probably paid for by Susan, Matt thought as acid burned his stomach.

Generally, in his letters and cards, Robert bemoaned his worthless existence, his mental and emotional problems, his dependence on Susan. The letters she'd drafted and not sent were frequently motherly missives directed at building up his self-esteem. Why hadn't she mailed them? They were all basically the same—installments in a long-running soap opera.

Dearest Robert:

I just received your letter from Los Angeles. Your self-denigrating comments are inappropriate. You are neither untalented nor unintelligent. I have told you so many times that it is your wit and your intellect that first attracted me to you. It hurts me when you put yourself down, and I assure . . . .

Dearest Robert:

Your letter from Bangkok arrived three days ago. I have agonized over your tone. You sound lonely and distressed. You should come home and stay with me. I don't understand why you must take these trips all the time. Please . . . .

Dearest Robert:

I've read the letter you sent me from Las Vegas at least ten times. Your description of the city from the air as you arrived at night was breathtaking. You have a wonderful talent for description. You really should try writing for a living. When you get back to Honolulu, why don't you see if there's a writing course at the university?

Matt dropped the letters on the desk and stood. He examined a three-shelf bookcase against the wall next to the desk and smiled at the titles, neatly alphabetized by author. Susan had always had eclectic taste in reading: Parris Afton Bonds, Catherine Coulter, James Clavell, Anne Hillerman, Elmore Leonard, Michael Lewis, Robert Ludlum, Alvin Toffler.

Matt spied a book with a neon yellow spine placed on its side on top of other books on the middle shelf. It was *Dirty Pool*, a mystery by an Albuquerque author named Steve Brewer. Matt had sent her the autographed copy for her last birthday. It was about the only thing he'd noticed in the condominium that seemed out of place. He lifted the book to place it in the book case, between volumes by Alan Bradley and Stephen J. Cannell, when his finger touched something that stuck out between the pages. An envelope. Sent from Las Vegas, three days before Susan died. Inside, a single sheet of stationery from a casino hotel.

Dear Susan:

I've thought about our relationship more each day, and the more I do, the more convinced I am that Matt's right. I have to stop being a burden to you—the one person I truly love in this world. I've been a depressing weight on you for eight years. I know if I'd gotten my act together you would've married me years ago. And then you would've had the children you always wanted, the life you always wanted.

I know you refused to marry me because of my problem. You've wasted the best years of your life on me, and I've given you nothing in return. This must STOP!

By the time you get this letter, I will no longer be a burden to you.

Thank you for always being there for me. You are truly my one love and I hope and pray you'll finally find someone to make you happy.

Please forgive me.

Love, R.

It read like a suicide note. But Matt found it hard to believe Robert would kill himself. The guy was squeamish about taking an Advil. He couldn't imagine him overdosing, let alone blowing his brains out, hanging himself, or jumping from a balcony. The letter was probably nothing more than a ploy to gain sympathy.

Matt instinctively knew what Susan would have done when she received the letter—call the hotel and ask the operator to connect her to Robert's room. If there had been no answer, she would have asked them to check the room.

So he did exactly what Susan would have done. He called the Las Vegas hotel.

"Carlisle Hotel Casino. Front desk."

"Yes, ma'am," he said. "I'm calling from Honolulu, Hawaii. I'm trying to locate a patient of mine who I believe recently stayed at your hotel, a Robert Nakamura. Would you be able—?"

"Oh, I remember Mister Nakamura quite well. He caused quite

a stir around here. He tried to kill himself in one of our rooms. If it hadn't been for a call to us from a friend of his, he probably would have succeeded."

"Can you remember the friend's name? Was it a woman who called?"

"Yes, it was. If you'll hold a minute, I may have written down the name somewhere."

She put Matt on hold to the accompaniment of soothing music. He sat there, surrounded by all of Susan's worldly possessions. If Susan had called and somehow saved Robert's life, why would she even consider suicide for herself?

"Are you still there?"

"Yes!" Matt said, startled by the sudden return of the hotel receptionist's voice.

"The caller was Susan Curtis. I recall our conversation very well. Her voice had a sense of urgency, but she was very calm. She asked if Mister Nakamura had registered here. I checked the computer and found his name and asked her if she wanted to be connected to his room. She said yes, but insisted I stay on the line and send someone to his room, too. When she told me he might be planning to kill himself, I panicked. But she was so steady. Kept me from losing it. I sent our security man up when there was no answer to my call. Mister Nakamura was unconscious. The police said he had chased a bottle of sleeping pills with a fifth of whiskey."

Matt grimaced at the irony. Robert wouldn't take drugs to correct his manic depression, but he'd overdose to kill himself.

"This place was a circus for hours," the woman continued.

"Do you know when Mister Nakamura swallowed the pills?" Matt asked.

"Oh, one of the policemen said it had just happened. Not very long at all before his friend called here."

Sonofabitch, Matt thought. Robert writes a letter to Susan and threatens to kill himself, then waits three days to pull it off. He wanted Susan to save him. What if the mail had arrived one day later?

"Where did they take Mister Nakamura?" Matt asked.

"To the hospital, that's all I know," the clerk said.

"What hospital?"

"Physicians' Medical Center. They've got the best trauma center in Vegas."

"You wouldn't happen to have their number?"

"Yeah, I do. We keep it handy."

She gave Matt the number and he thanked her.

Matt knew if he called the hospital he'd have little or no chance of getting information about Robert. Patient confidentiality rules prevented information being given to just anybody—even just any physician. So, when he called, he asked for and was connected to the Emergency Room. He got the name of the physician on duty—a Josh Cochran. Then he hung up and redialed.

"Physicians' Medical Center. Can I help you?"

"Records, please."

"Yes, sir. Please hold."

"Records Office. Mark Finch speaking."

"This is Doctor Cochran in Emergency. I need to locate one of our recent patients, a Robert Nakamura. We treated him just a few days ago."

"Give me your extension, Doctor. I'll call you right back."

"That's all right, Mark. I'll hold. No problem." Matt endured a long minute of sappy Vivaldi. "*Spring*," he thought, the middle of the sudden rainstorm.

Then Finch was back on the line. "Got it," he said. "Mister Robert Nakamura was admitted at 1:15 p.m., on the fifteenth. The emergency room physician—that's you, it says—pumped his stomach. He stayed here for observation for an hour, then the police transported him to Silver State Psychiatric Center for observation."

"You have Silver State's number handy?" Matt asked.

"Sure," Finch said.

"Yes, Doctor Curtis, what can I do for you?" Doctor Clarence Sellers, the nightshift administrator of Silver State Psychiatric Center said officiously.

"I'm a physician in New Mexico. I need to locate a patient of mine. The last information—"

"Yes, yes," Sellers said. "The receptionist told me. What's your patient's name?"

Matt took a calming breath. "Nakamura. Robert Nakamura."

"Ah, yes. Mister Nakamura. How could I forget him? What do you want to know?"

"Is he there? How is he?" Matt realized his voice had lost the needed tone of professional dispassion.

"No, Doctor Curtis, Mister Nakamura is not here."

"He was released?"

"No, he just took off."

"Do you have any idea where he went?"

"In fact, I do. One of my nurses saw the taxi that picked him up outside the front gate. Normally, our patients can leave whenever they want. Most of them enter our facility of their own free will. But, in Mister Nakamura's case, he'd been referred here by a court order. So he wasn't supposed to leave until the court approved it. Can you believe it? He called a cab to facilitate his, ah, departure. I contacted the taxi company and they tracked down the driver and called me back. He went to the airport. He told the cab driver he had a flight to Honolulu."

Matt hung up. So Robert could be anywhere in the islands. Matt knew Robert needed Susan as much as he needed oxygen. He could stay away from her for only short periods. Could he have been with her when she died? Could he have been responsible for her death? This wasn't the first time Matt had considered that possibility. He'd almost mentioned it to Lieutenant Callahan. Robert was a bum, as far as Matt was concerned, but he couldn't imagine he was capable of murder.

CHAPTER ELEVEN

"Callahan."

"Lieutenant, it's Matt Curtis."

"It's Dennis, remember? Call me Dennis."

"Right, Dennis," Matt said, as he dropped into the chair behind Susan's desk. "Did you happen to talk to any of my sister's neighbors the night she died?"

"What is this, Matt? You playing detective?"

"No, no. You said you were undermanned. I was just—"

"I'll assume you aren't being sarcastic," Callahan snapped. "Of course we questioned the neighbors."

"No one heard anything? No noise from her condo?"

"Doctor Curtis"—so much for first name camaraderie, Matt thought—"the neighbors we talked to that night, and the next day, all told us they heard nothing. An airline pilot on one side of her unit told us he worked the night she died. We checked. He would have been halfway to San Francisco. According to the building manager, the neighbor on the other side is an old lady who travels a lot. We haven't been able to contact her. No one else on that floor heard a thing."

"Thanks, Dennis," Matt said. "Sorry to bother you."

Matt thought Callahan might hang up then, but the cop asked, "When's the funeral?"

"Services are at one o'clock Saturday, the day after tomorrow, at

O'Connor Funeral Home."

"You flying back home right afterward?"

It sounded more to Matt like a suggestion than a question. "That's the plan," he said.

"Hope your next trip to Hawaii is under better circumstances," Callahan said. "Take care."

Matt replaced the receiver in its cradle and then moved to Susan's computer, perched on a tabletop workspace in the corner of her home office. They'd laughed together once about their passwords. His was "Susan," her's "Matthew." He turned on the machine and, when prompted, typed in "Matthew." A list of options flashed on the screen. He moved the cursor to "File" and a popup window showed the last four files she'd accessed: *savekid, taxretmatt, ltrrn, ltr??*.

He clicked on *ltr??*. Nothing. No file. He tried the other files in turn. Nothing again. This made no sense. But Matt knew he didn't understand computers well enough to figure out the problem. Or even if there was a problem. He had to be doing something wrong.

Matt found a large briefcase in a hall closet and carried it back to the office. He stuffed it with some of Susan's personal papers— things he'd need to clear up her affairs: life insurance policy, bank statements, condominium deed, mortgage papers, legal papers. It was just like Susan to put everything in order so she wouldn't inconvenience anyone after falling off a balcony.

He took the elevator down to the lobby and walked to the entrance when he noticed a door that said *Manager*.

He raised his hand to knock on the door, but changed his mind and opened it. He set the briefcase on the floor inside the door and entered a large room with a beautiful Oriental carpet that covered much of the marble floor. There were three large expensive-looking landscape oil paintings on the walls.

A young, narrow-faced blond woman, with prominent cheekbones, brilliant blue eyes, and a deep tan filed her nails at a secretarial desk.

"Michelle?" he ventured.

"Yes."

He extended his hand. "Matt Curtis. Thanks for arranging to

let me into my sister's unit."

She dropped the nail file in an open drawer, shut it, and reached up to take Matt's hand. "Oh, you're welcome. I'm so sorry about Miss Curtis. She'd been with us since we opened the building. Always paid her fees on time. Never caused a bit of trouble . . . until she jum . . . . Oh, I'm . . . . I was just trying . . . ."

"I understand," Matt said. "I miss her, too. Is the manager in?"

"He's on the phone. I'll slip him a note." Michelle scribbled something on a pad, ripped off the page, and got out of her chair. She reached up with the hand holding the note and brushed back a tendril of hair.

Hip cocked, breasts bulging, she looked, Matt thought, like a *Playboy* cartoon character.

She went through an open door into an inner office and was gone for no more than fifteen seconds before she returned to do nothing more important than move files on her desk from one pile to another. Every once in a while she'd look up and give Matt a hesitant smile.

Matt heard a man's voice drone on in the inner office, but he couldn't make out the words. Eventually, there were the sounds of a handset replaced in its cradle and the squeak of a chair. Then a dark-complected man emerged, medium height, middle aged. He had jet-black, slicked back hair and a pencil-thin mustache. He wore a flowery Hawaiian shirt, open down to the third button. A gold medallion nearly smothered in chest hair hung around his neck on a chain big enough to use as a weapon.

Matt cringed at the sight of the man. The guy looked like a throwback to the seventies, an extra in *Saturday Night Fever*. But when the man winked at the young woman, Matt felt his skin crawl. Smarmy bastard!

"Mister Curtis, my condolences on your sister's death," the man said. His voice was deep and resonant.

"Thank you, Mister . . . ."

"Oh, I'm sorry. Didn't Michelle give you my name?" He turned toward her and shook his finger as though she were an unruly child. "Mustn't forget these things, honey."

Michelle blushed.

"Do you have a moment to visit, Mister . . . ."

"I'm Gabe Muccio," he said and offered his hand. Matt shook his hand, then followed him into the inner office.

"I assume you found everything in order in Miss Curtis's unit," Muccio said.

"Yes, thank you. I appreciate your assistance." Matt glanced around the office. The place was the size of a large living room, with half-a-dozen gold-framed oil paintings—landscapes and still-lifes. The room's centerpiece was a red and blue Persian carpet with an intricate floral design. The only items that seemed incongruous in the elegantly-appointed room were three two-foot-high bowling trophies on top of a corner table—and Muccio himself.

Muccio sat in a plush leather chair some distance from his desk and waved Matt to a couch, on the other side of a glass coffee table. The man slouched in his chair and propped his tasseled alligator loafers on a corner of the coffee table.

"What can I do for you, Mister Curtis?"

Matt felt pissy and thought about correcting him, to insist on being called "Doctor," but decided the man wasn't worth formality. Besides, that wouldn't have been his style. "Did my sister owe anything to the condominium association? I want to make sure all her affairs are settled before I return to the mainland."

Muccio gave Matt a complacent smile. "Your sister was our most reliable resident. She often paid early. She didn't owe us a dime. I assume you'll make the next payment?"

Matt nodded. "But I'll want to sell her unit."

Muccio's smile turned predatory. He dropped his feet to the floor and pushed himself up in the chair. "We've got a waiting list for two-bedroom units. I can make a few calls; probably sell her place in a couple days. Closing in four or five weeks. You'll need a local attorney to help you with the paperwork."

Matt just shrugged, as though to say, Whatever.

"We got all kinds of attorneys right here in this building," Muccio continued. "Any one of them would be okay. But I'd recommend the firm we use. It's the best on the islands." He got out of his chair, walked over to his desk, fished one of his business cards out of a gold cardholder, and wrote something on the reverse side. When he handed over the card, Matt glanced at the front of it, then flipped it over to see what Muccio had written on the back. Then he stuck the card in his shirt pocket.

"We'd be happy to handle the transaction," Muccio said, and here his tongue darted over his lips. "I have a real estate broker's license."

"I'll get back to you," Matt said. Fat chance, he thought. He guessed he'd get screwed doing business with Muccio.

"Anything else, Mister Curtis?"

Matt hesitated. "Just one more thing. I was told that both of Susan's immediate neighbors were away when she died. Have any of the other building residents told you they saw or heard anything suspicious that night?"

Muccio's dark eyebrows bunched together like two wrestling caterpillars. "No, I haven't heard a thing. But, that's not quite correct. About the two occupants next to Miss Curtis's unit being away the night she died. One of them didn't leave until after your sister's unfortunate . . . accident."

Matt felt suddenly rattled. That's not the impression Callahan had left him. "Which neighbor?"

Muccio shifted his gaze away from Matt. "My secretary and I worked late that night," he said.

Matt had the uncomfortable sense that Muccio and Michelle might have been "working" on the couch he now occupied.

"It was about eleven when I walked Michelle out to her car," Muccio said. "She'd just pulled out of the front lot when I heard a scream, then a thud. I ran around the side of the building and found your sister's body. I want to tell you, I was freaked out. Never seen anything like that before. It was the worst damned th . . . ." Muccio stopped, his caterpillar eyebrows grappled once again. "I ran back inside and called the night security guard. He was on his rounds inside the building. Told him to call 9-1-1 and to get his ass downstairs. Then I paged the building owner's attorney. You know you can't be too careful. Everybody sues. The attorney called me back about ten minutes later. I told him there was a woman's body in the parking lot. He asked who the woman was, but I didn't know 'til later that it was Miss Curtis." Muccio paused, then blew out a loud blast of air. "The lawyer was as cool as can be. Like it was no big thing. Told me to stay in my office and wait for the cops. I can tell ya, I was so damned freaked out, I thought I'd jump out of my skin. Then I heard sirens and left my office to go out to the parking lot."

"What about the neighbor?" Matt asked, barely hiding his impatience.

"I was just getting to that," Muccio answered. "On my way back outside, I saw Muriel Goldstein come out of one of the elevators and walk across the lobby with a small suitcase. There was a taxi out front. She went off somewhere in it."

"That's all?"

Muccio frowned as though he resented Matt's question. "Yeah." But then his face lit up and he snickered. "Missus Goldstein really appeared agitated that night. Normally it takes her forever to cross the lobby. She's got bad arthritis. Uses a cane. But she hobbled right past me, like she was on a mission. Now that I think about it, she looked worried. Never even said hello." Muccio seemed to consider what he'd just said. "Never seen her so worked up." His eyes suddenly widened and he leaned forward in his chair. "My God," he said, "do you think she heard something?"

Matt shrugged. "Who knows? Do you think I could talk to her?"

"Don't know how. We haven't seen or heard from her since that night."

Outside, Matt stopped halfway to the parking lot and arched his back. Tropical breezes lightly ruffled his hair. The palm trees around the property swayed with the slight wind. He detected the fragrance of flowers. Welcome to paradise, he thought. Land of my dead sister.

He resumed walking toward the parking lot, but glanced to the right to catch a view of the side lot where Susan had fallen. The corner of the building screened the exact location. Thank God! He turned back to the left to catch a glimpse of the verdant hills in the distance, as though to cleanse his mind's eye of the imagined scene of Susan's death. A sudden movement drew his eyes away from the scenery. Shawn, the maintenance man, spade in hand, stared at him from beneath a palm tree.

Matt wondered if Shawn might know something about where

Muriel Goldstein had gone. He stepped off the walkway and moved across the grass toward him. He'd gone barely ten feet when the man turned and ran off around the corner of the building.

CHAPTER TWELVE

"This has been the best day of my whole life," Debbie Stokes said.

"As sweet as you are, you should have days like this all the time," Lucas said.

Debbie giggled. "You're like Santa Claus. I don't mean, like you're fat, or old . . . ."

Lucas laughed, reached across the table, and put his hand over her's. "I understood you, honey. You don't have to explain yourself."

She looked down at her lap and blushed. "I just meant, like, you're so nice. And now this fancy restaurant. I've never been in a place like this." She reached to set her champagne flute on the table and nearly toppled it over.

Lucas saw the glassed-over look in Debbie's eyes, her flushed cheeks and knew the two champagnes she'd downed had had an effect. He glanced around the room. Lucas didn't have to worry about someone asking the kid for her ID. Rubio Gonzales owned this place . . . and all the cops that worked this beat.

He looked back at Debbie. This restaurant ain't shit, kid, he thought. But, to you, it's a big deal. What a dope! How much would Rubio make off this flat-chested, skinny wretch? She was perfect. She looked no more than ten. The perverts would pay a fortune for her.

Lucas raised his hand and signaled the waitress. It was time to move to the next phase. He'd earned Debbie's trust, fed her, and bought her clothes. Dinner here at one of Rubio's places was just one more step down the staircase from innocence to total degeneration—and absolute surrender.

The waitress carried a tray to the table and, with a flourish, deposited two more bubbly flutes of champagne. "The owner wants to thank you for your business, Mister Polk."

"Tell him thanks," Lucas said, as he slipped the woman a "C" note. Then he raised his glass. "A fitting end to a glorious day," he said. He waited for Debbie to lift her glass, too, but she didn't seem to understand. He leaned forward and whispered, "You're supposed to lift your glass and touch it against mine."

"Oh," she whispered and covered her mouth with her hand. She raised the glass and tapped it against Lucas's, while she stared at him as though he was the most important man in the world.

Lucas downed his champagne in one gulp. "Drink up, honey."

She imitated Lucas; coughed up about half the alcohol. She rubbed her nose and laughed. "It tickles."

The waitress refilled their glasses.

DAY FOUR

CHAPTER THIRTEEN

Matt's sleep was unsettled. It came in installments interrupted by nightmares and night sweats that shocked him awake. One dream scrolled through his mind: Susan pursued by dark, hairy, long-fingered, grasping creatures that carried long iron poles. Matt, in his dream, wanted to save her, but he couldn't move.

The creatures ran Susan down and beat her with the poles. Each blow made a *clang* and sent up a spray of red sparks, as though from a bellows-stoked fire. The noises came in a steady rhythm, louder and somehow more terrifying, until they suddenly transformed into the sound of the telephone ringing two feet from his ear.

He managed to grab the receiver. "Hullo," he said thickly.

"Good morning, this is your 6 a.m. wakeup call."

Matt propped open his eyes long enough to look at the clock radio next to the phone. 6 a.m., right on the button. The tiny LCD light glared at him brightly. He closed his eyes, mumbled thanks to the recorded female voice, and replaced the receiver. He considered all the benefits of going back to sleep, then forced himself to throw off the covers and roll out of bed.

He put on a red T-shirt, gray shorts, and a pair of white socks and running shoes, then set out for the beach. Yesterday's walk with Callahan had convinced him he needed to get back in shape. A one-mile jog would be a good start.

A two-lane road and a patch of forest separated his hotel from the sea. Matt found a hard-packed sand trail that meandered downward through dense bushes and tall, overhanging trees that screened out the dawn-brightening sky. The air felt cool and damp on his skin.

After a few minutes, the path broke out of the trees and merged with the beach sand. After the coolness of the little forest, the beach felt hot, even this early. Sweat poured off his face, neck, and chest as he ran across the deep, dry sand. His lungs burned and his calf muscles felt suddenly tight.

He stopped at the highest reach of the waves, bent over with his hands on his hips, and took rapid, shallow breaths. He raised his head enough to look back up at the top floor of his hotel, visible over the tree tops, and thought how easy it would be to return to his room. A quick shower, then two eggs over easy, homefries, bacon, and toast.

But he suppressed the temptation and continued to jog.

The beach was already busy with other people—joggers, surfers, one old Asian woman going through a graceful *T'ai Chi* routine. He ran on the firm, wet sand until a broad expanse of black, water-eroded lava blocked his path. A thousand tiny pools of water glimmered in depressions in the rocks.

Matt felt exhilarated. He hadn't exercised this hard in a couple years and, despite the length of his run, felt better than he thought he would have. There's nothing like running at sea level, he thought. Especially when you're used to Albuquerque's mile-high atmosphere.

An hour—and four miles—after he'd started, Matt returned to his room, sweat-soaked, sore, and exhilarated.

He showered and shaved, and wondered again, while he dressed, about Susan's neighbor, Muriel Goldstein.

Mori's had to be the most popular eating place on the islands. It was as packed this morning as it had been yesterday. Matt recognized Mori from the day before and asked to be seated at one of Doris's tables.

Mori frowned, then spoke in a rapid-fire mixture of Brooklynese and Yiddish. "The *shiksa* didn't come ta work today. You know what she tells me yesterday when she's leaving? She says, her doctor told her ta go home and lie in bed for at least two days. Her doctor, my *toukas*. So I says, what doctor? When you got time to go see a doctor? She tells me this one did a diagnosis on her right here while she took his order. Now you tell me, what kinda doctor practices medicine in a damn delicatessen? This *meshugeneh* doctor is interfering with my business." The man raised a fist and shook it. "I oughta give this *putz* doctor a piece of my mind. The *momzer*."

Matt tried to look sympathetic. "I guess any table will do," he said.

His waitress's name this morning was Shirley. She was as tall as Doris, with the same statuesque build, and wore an identical pink uniform. But, unlike Doris's red hair, Shirley's was brassy blonde. Her voice was loud and strained.

She filled Matt's coffee cup and squinted at him as she took his order. When she brought his food—a toasted English muffin and a bowl of granola—she asked, "Ain't you the doctor who helped Doris out yesterday?"

Matt wished she'd lower her voice. He glanced over at the register where Mori made change for a customer.

"Yes," he whispered to Shirley.

"Speak up, honey. I can hardly hear ya."

"Yes," Matt said, a little louder. "I'm the doctor."

"Ya think ya could help me like ya did Doris?"

"Well, I'm not in the habit of treating patients outside my office."

"So where's your office?" she asked.

"Albuquerque, New Mexico."

She laughed as though she thought he was teasing her. "That's cute, Doc."

Matt couldn't help himself. He laughed back. "No, I'm serious; my office really is in Albuquerque."

She nodded. "I'd sure appreciate it if ya could help me," she said. Her voice seemed to bounce off the walls and ceiling.

Matt twitched and again looked toward the cash register.

"I can't hear worth a darn," she all but shouted.

"How long have you had the problem?" Matt said.

"What?"

Matt repeated the question, louder.

She scratched her hip with the eraser end of her pencil and looked up at the ceiling for the answer. "Maybe about two months? Yeah, that's right." She returned her gaze to Matt. "My boyfriend decides he's going to teach me how to scuba dive. He takes me out on a boat and loads me up with a ton of equipment and throws me overboard. I could hear fine until then. Now I can't hear worth a darn and my ears hurt all the time. And they itch like crazy."

"Have you tried to clean your ears with anything?" Matt asked.

"Yeah, sure. I swab them out every day. But it don't do no good."

Matt gave her the name of an over-the-counter saline treatment, said her boyfriend should administer it to her. "If it doesn't work the first time, you should go to the nearest emergency room."

"Thanks, Doc," she bellowed.

This time, Mori, seating two men a few tables away from Matt, snapped his head around to look at him.

Matt smiled back, then turned again to Shirley.

"How's your breakfast?" she asked. "Can I get you anything else?"

Matt raised his empty cup in answer, hoping Shirley would find a coffeepot rather than feel compelled to continue the conversation.

"That's it? Just coffee?" she said. "I'm gonna bring you a donut, too."

As she walked away, and as Mori headed back to the cash register, Matt sighed and returned to his granola.

Shirley slapped the check on the table when she brought a donut to Matt. "Maybe I'll see you here again," she said.

Matt raised his eyebrows and shrugged. "Oh, by the way," he said. "You wouldn't happen to know Doris's phone number."

Shirley smiled and winked at Matt. "You know, Doc, there's nothing Doris's got that I don't have."

Matt felt his face get hot. He thought to explain that he just wanted to see if Doris had any more information about Susan's involvement with Save the Kids, but decided it would come across as a lame excuse.

Shirley winked at Matt again and wrote a telephone number and address on her order pad. She ripped off the page and handed it to Matt. "Good luck," she said.

CHAPTER FOURTEEN

Lucas Polk untangled the sheet from around his legs and looked over at Debbie's naked body. You sure as hell weren't no virgin, kid, he thought. Your step-daddy musta done a hell of a job on you.

The girl snored sonorously, surprisingly loud for a kid who looked like a miniature Twiggy. He knew the booze she'd consumed the night before and the speedball he'd given her before dawn would keep her out for a little while. She'd been so drunk when he'd screwed her, he suspected she didn't even know it had happened. She probably wouldn't remember much of anything when she woke up.

Lucas moved from the bed, picked up the cordless phone, and dialed Rubio's number.

"Yeah," Rubio said.

"Lucas, boss. She's all yours."

"You stay there until the guys arrive. Then you can take off. Unless you want another taste?"

"No thanks, boss. I couldn't get it up for a million bucks. I rode that little girl half the night."

Rubio laughed. "What's the matter, Lucas? Can't handle the young stuff, anymore?" Then he hung up.

Lucas quickly showered and dressed. He'd just popped the tab on a beer can when a knock sounded on the apartment door. He opened the door and four of Rubio's crew drifted inside.

"She's still asleep," Lucas told the crew leader. "Better give her a minute. No point in making her miss the action."

"You got anything to drink?" one of the men asked.

"There's beer in the refrigerator under the bar," Lucas said.

"What d'ya give her last night?" the leader said.

Lucas held his hands apart. "Ten inches," he said.

The other men laughed.

"If you screwed her three times, that wouldn't add up to ten inches," one of the others said.

More laughter.

"When I asked you what you gave her last night, I meant the hard stuff," the leader said.

"Booze and a speedball," Lucas answered. "There's smack on the table next to the bed. What I gave her last night should wear off soon."

The leader cocked an ear when a squeaky voice sounded from the bedroom.

"Luuu-cas, where are you? My head hurts awful."

Lucas put his beer can on the kitchen counter and smiled at the group of men. "I guess it's time for Little Debbie to grow up some more," he said.

"Real fast, too," one of the men said. The others laughed.

CHAPTER FIFTEEN

Matt didn't see the red light until he was almost on top of it. The mini-van's tires screeched when he slammed his foot down on the brake pedal at the last second. He ended with the front of the vehicle a foot into the crosswalk. He tried not to make eye contact with any of the half-dozen pedestrians who glowered at him in shocked disapproval. But one old guy squared off with the front of the van and banged the hood with the gnarled handle of a cane that looked like a medieval bludgeon. He shook it at Matt, then continued slowly across the street.

Nice dent, Matt thought.

He took both hands off the wheel and ran them through his hair. He inhaled and blew out a rush of air. Come on, Matt, he thought, pay attention. He looked up and saw the street sign. Dahlia Street. He was at the intersection of Ocean and Dahlia. Dahlia was Doris's street.

When the light changed, Matt turned left, away from the beach, and slowly made his way up the tree-lined street past tiny bungalows. It seemed like a nice neighborhood; well-painted facades, white picket fences, neat lawns and gardens.

Like most of the houses on the street, Doris's was tiny, with red wooden shingles, a white picket fence, and a jungle-like garden of ice plant, bougainvillea, and a bunch of plants Matt didn't recognize. He knocked lightly on the door. No response. It crossed his mind that Doris might be on her back in bed. He knocked harder. This time he heard footsteps thump inside on a wooden floor.

A small, thin girl opened the door. Her hair was highlighted in bright purple and her lips were thickly coated with almost-black lipstick. She wore a tank top and extremely tight cut-off jeans. Her set of headphones was bright yellow. She gave Matt a look as though he'd just interrupted her whole life of fourteen or fifteen years.

Matt assumed the girl couldn't hear him through the music noise that came from the pounding headset. "Does Doris Sutherland live here?" he shouted.

"Yeah," the girl yelled back, around a wad of bubble gum. "Who are you?"

"You mind removing those?" Matt said and pointed at the headset.

"Oh, yeah," the kid said.

Matt gave her his name after she draped the headset around her neck.

She eyed Matt up and down.

"You look okay," she said. "Come on in. Ma, you got a visitor!" she hollered while she led the way inside. She looked back over her shoulder at Matt, grinned, then shouted again, "He's kinda cute . . . for an old guy."

"Who is it?" a voice called back.

The girl looked at Matt. He gave her his name again.

"Matthew Curtis," she yelled.

"Send him back here, honey."

The girl cracked her gum and pointed at a hallway. She moved the headset back on her head, plopped down on the sofa, and picked up a fashion magazine. "Second door on the left," she shouted.

Matt went down the hall and knocked on the closed door.

"Come in."

He entered a world of pink—throw pillows, stuffed animals, bedding, walls and curtains. All pink.

Doris lay on the bed with her legs propped up on two pillows. She laughed when she looked at Matt.

Matt was confused by her reaction. "What's so funny?" he asked.

Doris smiled and said, "The look on your face. I hope you don't think this is my room. I switched with my daughter until my back gets better. The mattress in here is much firmer than mine."

"Good idea," he said. Then he noticed on the wall next to the closet door a poster with four emaciated-looking musicians who wore black masks and waggled their tongues through the masks' mouth openings. It was the only thing in the room that wasn't pink. "I should have guessed this wasn't your room."

Doris pointed at a pink-upholstered bench in front of a pink-painted vanity. "Have a seat."

Matt pulled the bench over to the bed. "How're you feeling?"

"Actually, a lot better. Just being off my feet for one day seems to have made a difference. How'd you know where I live?"

"Shirley at Mori's. I planned to call you, but I noticed your street on the way back to my hotel and took a chance and stopped. I hope you don't mind."

"Don't even think about it," Doris said. "I'm glad to have the company."

"I wanted to talk with you about Save the Kids and this Rubio Gonzales guy."

She gave him a suspicious look. "Save the Kids is one thing. Its office is downtown. Talk to Renee Drummond. She's the founder; runs the organization. But you don't want to have nothin' to do with that asshole Gonzales." She slowly scooted back against the bed's headboard. "What do you want with him?"

CHAPTER SIXTEEN

Matt double-checked the address on the slip of paper in his hand. It was difficult to believe this derelict building was occupied. Paint peelings hung in foot square pieces; serpentine cracks spider-webbed from roof to foundation. Two signs hung over the door. One read: Rape Crisis Center. The second read: Save the Kids, 2nd Floor. Matt opened the door and smelled wet rot. Will these damned stairs hold me? he wondered, as he climbed.

Halfway to the top of the stairs, the temperature seemed to drop. Matt shivered. He felt as though someone was there. He stopped and looked back down the steps. No one. But, this time, instead of his heart pounding with anxiety, as it had in the operating room a couple days ago, he suddenly felt at peace. Susan came to mind. Then he had the feeling he belonged in this wreck of a building. That there was something significant about being here. He shook his head as though to clear it of thoughts that made no sense.

Matt climbed to the top of the staircase to a landing barely large enough to hold a floor mat that announced WELCOME. He tried to turn the handle on the glass-paneled door. Locked. He could just see through the slats of an ancient, yellowed set of venetian blinds hung on the inside of the glass. A woman in jeans and a blue work shirt stood at an open file cabinet at the far end of the office. He knocked and watched her jerk her head around. She went to a desk, took something from a drawer, and held it out of sight behind her hip. She came to the door and peered back at him through the slats.

"Can I help you?" she shouted.

"I'm sorry if I frightened you," Matt yelled. "My name is Matthew Curtis. I wanted—"

"Oh my Lord," the woman exclaimed. She unlocked the door and threw it open. The venetian blinds made a racket as they banged against the glass. Before Matt could take a step inside she stretched her arms toward him as though to hug him. The pistol in her right hand knocked against his chest.

"Jesus!" Matt gasped.

"Oh, I'm so sorry," she said, her face red. She placed the pistol on the top of a file cabinet beside the door and then grasped Matt's arms and looked at him.

"I'm so glad to finally meet you. Susan talked about you all the time. All of us around here were jealous," she said with a smile. "We wished we had a big brother like you."

After his last conversation with his sister, Matt didn't feel much like the Big Brother of the Year.

"I'm Renee. Renee Drummond," she said and stuck out her hand. Matt took it and was surprised at the iron in her grip.

"I understand Susan volunteered here."

"Susan was one of our first volunteers when I started Save the Kids five years ago." Her eyes misted. "Come in," she said. "Have a seat."

Matt stepped through the doorway and watched as she closed and relocked the door. "Security conscious," he said.

"That's the only way to be around here," she said. "It's a war zone down here, and we've made our share of enemies." She walked back toward a desk and sat down.

Matt took a chair across the desk from her.

"I tried to contact you after Susan . . . . I got your answering machine," Renee said.

"Thanks," Matt mumbled. "I flew out here as soon as I heard about . . . ."

Renee sat up straighter and seemed to stiffen her spine. She smiled. "What brings you down to this lovely part of town?" she asked.

"A couple of reasons. I didn't know my sister was involved with your group until a waitress at Mori's Deli told me Susan rescued her daughter."

"That would be Doris Sutherland," Renee said, the smile back on her face. "Yeah, Susan saved little Amy Sutherland as sure as you and I are sitting here. Susan was the most vigilant, hard-working volunteer we've ever had."

"Was what she did dangerous?" Matt asked.

Renee's jaw jutted and her eyes became steely. "Nothing we can't handle."

"What do you think happened to Susan?" Matt asked.

Renee shrugged, but Matt saw the muscles in her cheeks twitch. Her lips compressed into a tight line. She didn't seem to want to answer.

"The police tell me Susan committed suicide," he said.

"Impossible!" Renee replied, her face now scarlet. "There's no way Susan would kill herself."

Exactly what I initially said, Matt thought. "Yeah," he said, "but, without evidence to the contrary, the police can't do much."

"Just like they can't do much to help us get runaways off the streets!" Her voice went up a couple notes. "Just like there's nothing they can do about arresting the bastards who pay to have sex with children!"

She stopped suddenly. "I'm sorry," she said. "I didn't mean to get on my soapbox."

"I understand. It must be frustrating."

Renee nodded.

"She never mentioned you or Save the Kids to me. That surprises me. Susan and I were as close as brother and sister can be. I don't get it."

Renee said, "That's the way she was. Always worried about others. She didn't want you to lose sleep over what she did."

"Do you think it's possible that whatever she did here had something to do with her death?"

Renee gave him a surprised look, her eyes suddenly hard. "You can't—"

"Don't misunderstand me," Matt interjected. "I'm not looking to blame you or Save the Kids." He paused, then leaned forward in his chair. "Look, Miss Drummond, I want to find out what Susan's state of mind was."

She nodded and said, "She'd been quieter than usual since she returned from your mother's funeral. And there was always the continuing saga of her relationship with Robert Nakamura. But she seemed fine. Just a little subdued, maybe."

"Had anyone threatened her?"

"Not her directly. We get anonymous threatening calls here all the time."

Matt sighed. He had hoped that Renee Drummond would be able to provide a name of someone who had threatened his sister. But, even if she had, he couldn't believe, despite the Rohypnol in Susan's system when she died, that someone would want to murder Susan. Murder seemed even more unbelievable than suicide.

"Doris Sutherland told me Susan helped her daughter get away from a pimp who worked for a guy named Rubio Gonzales. What about him?"

Renee puckered her mouth. For a moment it looked as though she might spit on the floor.

"Rubio Gonzales. That SOB is as bad as they come," she said. "He specializes in the kiddie trade. Boys and girls for the chicken hawks and perverts. And the creeps pay big bucks for a couple hours with one of the children in his stable. Doris Sutherland's little girl should have been home playing with dolls and having pajama parties. Instead, he got her addicted to crack cocaine and turned her into a plaything for anyone who could pay the price."

Matt raised his hands to slow her down. "Whoa, whoa. Sounds to me like Gonzales had a strong reason to kill Susan. When Susan took the Sutherland girl away from him, she affected his pocketbook."

Renee said, "Yeah, but Gonzales had no way of knowing that Susan had intervened in the case of the Sutherland girl."

"What's this Gonzales look like? Where can I find him?"

She gave him an incredulous look, her eyes wide as saucers, her mouth open. "Are you nuts? You can't go near that maniac. He finds out you're Susan's brother and you're snooping around, he'll have you killed. He's absolutely psycho about anyone connected with this organization. That's why I keep the door locked, why I go everywhere with a pistol."

"I promise I won't do anything stupid," Matt said. "But from what you've said, it sounds as though Rubio Gonzales could have had Susan killed. That's information I need to give the police."

Renee snorted. "Lotsa luck," she said. "Don't you think I already mentioned Gonzales to the cops?"

"You did?"

"Yeah. I told them it was a whole lot more likely that maniac killed Susan, than her committing suicide."

Matt stared at Renee. He liked the way this woman held nothing back.

She closed her eyes, covered her face with her hands. After a moment, she dropped her hands, opened her eyes, and said, "Let's go eat. We can talk more about Susan."

Matt stood by the door and studied her while she hurriedly retrieved her pistol and put it in her purse, put a few files into a cabinet and locked it, and turned off the window air conditioning unit. She moved with a dancer's fluidity. Tall, slim, but not model-skinny. Long, wavy auburn hair bounced with every step. When she turned and walked toward the door, he admired her full lips and hazel-colored eyes. She was about forty and gorgeous. She wore a wedding ring.

After she locked the office, Renee led Matt down the stairs. At the curb, a half-block from the building's entrance, sat a silver Mercedes sports car. He wondered how it still had its hubcaps.

"Nice car," Matt said as he ran his eyes in a caressing way over the car's lines. "Looks like a 1990."

She nodded. "My husband bought it for me," she said, ". . . just before he died."

His gaze snapped toward her, over the top of the car, but she seemed to pay no attention to him while she opened her door and tapped the door-lock release. Matt slid into the low-slung passenger seat and moved to adjust his seat belt when she put the car in gear and squealed away from the curb, slamming his head against the headrest. He couldn't tell if she was angry about something or just as passionate about her driving as she had seemed to be about Susan, Save the Kids, the cops, and Rubio Gonzales.

Renee drove six blocks to a sidewalk cafe and screeched to the curb next to a fire hydrant. Matt didn't realize he had a death hold on the padded door grip, until she shut off the engine. She got out of the car and he had to scramble to catch up as she walked to the cafe.

He pointed back at the hydrant. "Aren't you concerned you'll get a ticket?"

Renee shrugged. "Now wouldn't that be just great. The cops don't have time to arrest murderers, rapists, pedophiles, and drug dealers, but they have time to bust me on a parking violation. How appropriate."

Matt felt stupid for having said anything.

Inside, Renee approached a Hawaiian man in a short-sleeve Polo shirt, a pair of khakis, and sandals. He had forearms the size of Matt's thighs and a stomach that would have made a Sumo wrestler jealous. He greeted Renee with a toothy smile and a bear hug, then took her arm and escorted her to a table on the open-air veranda. Matt trailed them. Like the other dozen or so tables, theirs had a bright yellow umbrella stuck into its middle. After he gave them menus and kissed Renee on the cheek, the man shot Matt a wary "watch it, fella" look and walked away.

"What's with him?" Matt asked. "He sure gave me the once over."

"Hah!" she exclaimed. "Sam's a little overprotective."

"Why's that?"

She closed her eyes and rubbed her forehead. Matt thought she looked as though she mentally grappled with herself—do I answer, or not? Then she exhaled and looked at Matt. "Two years ago, Susan and I snatched his thirteen-year-old daughter, Kristine, away from a pimp." A faraway look came to Renee's eyes and she wagged her head as though she still couldn't believe what had happened. "Kristine fought us like a mother bear protecting her cubs. She was so deep into the drug scene she wasn't about to be separated from her source—the pimp—without a fight. After we grabbed Kristine, her father put her in a supposedly secure rehab program over on Molokai. But she hadn't been there three days when the pimp somehow found out where she was. The girl was probably so starved for drugs she found a way to call him. Two thugs flew over to Molokai in a helicopter, landed on the rehab center's grounds, picked up Kristine, and started back to Honolulu. A freak storm hit them halfway back. The pilot, the two men, and that poor little kid crashed somewhere in the ocean. Never found the bodies."

Matt realized his mouth hung open and shut it. He glanced at Sam seating a foursome at a table on the far side of the veranda. Matt wanted to say something, but the horror of Renee's story seemed to have sucked the moisture from his throat. He looked back at Renee. Her eyes glistened.

"Sam's just grateful for everything we tried to do for his daughter," Renee said. "Does that answer your question about Sam seeming over protective?"

Matt nodded.

Renee's mouth turned down and her eyes now filled with tears. She spat the words, "If it's the last thing I ever do . . . ."

Matt reached across the table but withdrew his hand before he touched her's.

She smiled at him and dabbed at her eyes with a napkin.

"I admit I'm no expert," Matt said, "but helicopter rescues don't sound like things I'd normally associate with run-of-the-mill pimps."

"Rubio Gonzales isn't run-of-the-mill," Renee said. "He works for a big organization."

"Why can't the cops do something about him? Feeding drugs to juveniles is illegal as hell. So's prostitution. There must be all kinds of political and community pressure to bring the guy down."

"Gonzales has plenty of gofers around to do his dirty work. Men who would rather go to jail than squeal on him. Ratting him out is a quick way to an early and painful death. Witnesses either disappear or refuse to testify against him. We hear that if one of his men gets caught, Gonzales covers his bail. Somehow his men are always granted bail. Once they're out, they leave the islands. And Gonzales keeps these guys on his payroll, whether they're in jail or out of state.

"And we think he must have some cops and judges on his

payroll. Evidence disappears whenever one of Gonzales's men is arrested. And how else does he find out where the cops have witnesses hidden away? Witnesses against Gonzales have a very short life span or they suddenly lose their memories. And why would the judges continually allow Gonzales's men out on bail? They've got to know every one of them is a flight risk."

Matt dropped the fork on the table. "I didn't realize there was enough money in prostitution to buy off cops and judges, pay for lawyers and helicopters. Something doesn't feel right."

"What?" Renee asked.

Matt threw up his hands in frustration. "Hell, I don't know. But I still can't believe Rubio Gonzales would kill my sister just because she snatched one of the kids in his stable. Even if he knew she was involved."

Renee leaned forward. "You know," she said, "some of the boys and girls we've rescued talked about pornography, drug shipments, blackmail, and even murder. Some talked about a Godfather. But most of these kids had been so traumatized, they weren't sure themselves if they'd really seen and heard what they claimed. Not the most credible witnesses in the world."

A silence settled between them. She consulted the menu while Matt processed the information she'd given him. Sam suddenly appeared with an order pad in hand. Renee ordered a fruit salad.

"Make that two," Matt said.

After Sam walked away from the table, Matt whispered, "How the hell does he keep going? How does anyone survive the loss of a child?"

Renee hunched her shoulders. Matt saw the glint in her eyes abruptly change, replaced by a dark, murky stare. The change only lasted a few moments, but the difference startled Matt.

After another silence, Matt told Renee what he knew about Susan's boyfriend, Robert.

"Susan talked a lot about Robert," Renee said. "You know she loved him, despite his problems. But I have to tell you I didn't understand their relationship. I met him once when Susan brought him out to my place. He followed her around like a puppy dog. But she seemed to need him, too. Whenever he left town, which was frequently, Susan seemed lonely." Renee hesitated. "I sure don't have a clue as to where he might be," she said.

"Did Susan ever mention anything about the woman who lived in the unit next to her's?"

Renee smiled. "Muriel Goldstein?"

"Yes."

After a long beat, Renee said, "That old woman was a bit of a busybody, but she watched over Susan like a mother cougar. And Susan looked out for her, as well."

Matt said, "I found out Muriel Goldstein left the Sand & Sea shortly after Susan fell from her balcony. I wonder where she went at that late hour."

Renee shrugged.

After their lunches were served, Matt told Renee stories about Susan as a little girl. He was relieved to hear her laugh and thought how lucky Susan had been to have a friend like her.

Renee placed her fork on her plate and patted her mouth with her napkin. "Susan used to talk about your sons as though they were her own kids. Will they be here for the funeral?"

"We'll have a memorial service in Albuquerque this summer. George is in his last year of law school in Philadelphia. He's in the middle of finals right now. Andrew's up to his butt in alligators. He's in his last year in an ophthalmology residency."

Renee's brow furrowed. "You don't want them here with you?" Then her eyes rounded as though a thought had suddenly come to her. "They don't know about Susan, do they?"

Matt felt a stab of pain hit his throat, as though a wire had been tightened around it. He didn't know how to tell her why he hadn't told George and Andrew about their aunt. His reasoning now seemed lame, and for some reason he didn't want Renee to think ill of him. At the same time, he couldn't admit the reason was he didn't want to break down in front of his sons. He'd never opened up to them before. He was afraid they might think less of him than they already did. He shrugged.

Matt expected Renee to become judgmental, but instead she gave him a half-smile. "Another reason to believe that Susan couldn't have killed herself," she said.

"What do you mean?" Matt said.

"She told me numerous times how much she loved those boys. There's no way she would have done anything that would cause them pain."

They finished their lunch and Matt covered the check.

"You said your husband died," he said, while they walked to the Mercedes. "Was he ill?"

"He killed himself," Renee said flatly.

CHAPTER SEVENTEEN

"How long did you say you've been with Save the Kids?" Matt asked as Renee ignored speed limit signs and raced back to her office.

Her foot hard on the gas; her gaze riveted ahead, she answered, "I started it a little over five years ago."

"What inspired you?"

"Six years ago, one of Rubio Gonzales's clients murdered my fifteen-year-old son."

"Good God!" Matt rasped.

She quick-glanced at him. "I want you to know what you've stuck your nose into here. David was our only child. He'd gone to a school dance, then decided to go downtown with a couple of friends to see if they could get into one of the clubs. They were just a bunch of stupid teenagers pushing the envelope. Apparently, they wandered into the wrong part of town. One of the boys in the group told us later they went to a strip joint."

He noticed her hands clench the steering wheel. Knuckles white.

Renee's voice rose in pitch. "How do fifteen-year-olds get into a strip club?" she asked incredulously. After a beat, she said, "Some guy came over to the boys and offered them a chance to have a private session with one of the dancers. The other boys were suddenly frightened and ignored the man. But not my macho son. He followed the guy. That was the last time his friends saw him. The coroner said the guy in the strip joint must have shot him up with heroin, then sold Davie to a man the police called a chicken hawk. A man who likes young boys. The guy who lured my son away from his friends was a pimp who worked for Rubio Gonzales. That much we learned from the private detective my husband hired. Davie was a target of opportunity. That's what the detective called him."

Renee paused and ground her teeth so hard Matt heard them gnashing.

"Like society is one great big jungle where predators hunt for young boys. They swoop down and prey on the innocent."

Matt wanted to tell her she didn't need to continue. But he didn't, and she did.

"The pimp had a big time client in from the mainland. Somebody willing to pay big bucks for an innocent kid. Virgin goods."

Virgin goods. The way she said it—with despair and venom—made Matt's heart ache.

"A middle-aged state legislator from a mid-western state, here for a conference. He used my son, got carried away, and killed him. The police caught the bastard. But they never found the pimp who delivered my son to his murderer."

She looked at Matt again; her chin trembled. "Witnesses identified the pimp. The cops had to know he worked for Rubio Gonzales, but they said there was no proof Gonzales was involved. The pimp conveniently disappeared. Probably somewhere on the mainland, where he can still supply kids to perverts."

Matt found it difficult to breathe. He knew there was nothing he could do or say to make a difference. He thought she'd finished. He hoped she'd finished.

"My husband was devoted to Davie. Our lives were . . . so . . . perfect. When we weren't hiking, or sailing, or otherwise spending time with Davie, we talked about him. Made plans for his future. My husband killed himself because he couldn't live with the grief and guilt. He felt he'd failed Davie."

Renee had a faraway look—lips slightly parted, head rigid, gaze frozen on the road ahead. They drove the rest of the way to her office in silence.

After she'd parked, Renee scribbled something on the back of a business card.

"Here's my address and home telephone number. If you need to contact me."

Matt got out of the Mercedes, then bent down and looked at her through the open passenger door. "Are you free for dinner tonight?" he blurted. The words just flew out of his mouth.

She stared at him for a second. Matt anticipated rejection. Instead, she said, "Sure."

Carlo Venturi sat in Huey Jackson's black Trans Am and watched a man exit the Drummond bitch's Mercedes and walk to a tan mini-van parked a few spaces away.

Carlo slammed the dashboard with his fist. "Shit. Who is that sonofabitch?"

"What the fuck you think you're doing?" Huey shouted. He leaned over from behind the wheel and inspected the spot on the dashboard Carlo had just struck. "You put a dent in there and I'll fuckin' kill ya."

Carlo looked at Huey, then back at the dash. He knew the big guy could and would kick his ass if he damaged his precious Pontiac. It was the only thing Huey truly loved. Carlo rubbed the padded dash. "See, no dent. Besides, it's just a damn car," he said.

Huey scowled as though Carlo had insulted his mother.

Carlo quickly changed the subject. "Man, the boss will be pissed if we don't take care of that Drummond bitch."

"So, what we waitin' for," Huey asked. "Let's go."

"You don't see that guy behind her?" Carlo answered as he watched the Mercedes pull away from the curb, the van right behind.

"The boss didn't say nothin' about killin' some guy. I think we gotta wait 'til she's alone."

Huey hunched his shoulders and stretched his arms and back. His muscles rippled beneath the fabric of his shortsleeve knit shirt.

Momentarily distracted, Carlo wondered again how Huey found clothes to fit. Then he stared out through the windshield. The Mercedes moved down the street, followed by the mini-van, and vanished around a corner.

"Let's go back and talk to the boss," Carlo said.

CHAPTER EIGHTEEN

"I don't give a shit if she was with goddamn King Kamehameha. I told you I wanted a cap put in her ass."

"But Lonnie, we didn't know who the guy was and we thought . . . ."

Lonnie Jackson sneered up at the two men in front of his desk. "I pay you to do what I say—not to think." Sweat poured from the big black man's forehead. The little Italian had a deer-in-the-headlights look. "Fuckin' idiots!" Lonnie screamed. "Now do you think you can go get the job done?"

Huey brightened "You bet, boss," he said. "Right away."

Lonnie turned to the small one. "Carlo, you and Huey screwed up. This is your last chance."

Carlo's head bobbed as though attached to a spring.

Lonnie pointed his finger at the door.

When the door closed behind them, Lonnie waited a moment, then swiveled in his chair. "They're gone," he said loudly. "Come on in."

The door to the adjoining office opened and John Dunning entered, drink in hand. Dapper as ever: Armani suit, Versace tie, and Santoni loafers. He sat in one of two overstuffed leather chairs that bracketed a glass coffee table, propped his feet up on the table, and ran a hand through his thick, straight, black hair.

"You look too damned comfortable, Johnny-boy," Lonnie said.

John smiled and took a sip from his drink. "It's just business, Bro. Doesn't bother me a bit, as long as those muscleheads don't see my face." He took another sip from the glass. "This is great scotch."

"Hell, it's some thirty-year-old single-malt shit. Can't tell one from another. Give me a can of ice-cold Bud any day. Nothing like good old American beer. Breakfast of champions."

John snorted.

"How's things at the firm?" Lonnie asked.

"Humming right along. More business than we can handle. Best thing we ever did was get into maritime law."

"Maritime law, my ass," Lonnie said and laughed. "Call it what it really is. You stuffed-shirt lawyers are pushers—just like me. Trunk of a car or hold of a ship, the shit's the same."

John smiled again. "As far as the firm is concerned, we handle import-export business for certain clients." He raised his glass in a salute.

"Yeah, right," Lonnie said. He intertwined his fingers, put his hands behind his head, closed his eyes, and yawned. Then he slid his chair forward and leaned his elbows on his desk and glared at John. "You know I don't lose no sleep whackin' anyone who gets in my way. And the cops don't mind lookin' the other way when it comes to drugs. But they take it personal when corpses start to pile up. They could be watchin' me. You take a big risk comin' here."

"I know, I know," John said. "But it couldn't be helped. Mister C called, and I didn't want to talk about it over the phone." He paused, then set his glass on the table, and looked purposefully at Lonnie. "You know, as far as that Drummond woman is concerned, I agree she's got to go."

Lonnie stabbed a finger at John. "You forget you heard anything about Renee Drummond!" he growled. "I don't want you tied to what will happen to her."

John set his drink on the table and raised his hands in a sign of surrender.

Lonnie clucked his tongue and wondered at the curve balls life threw. He and Johnny were half-brothers. But Lonnie didn't even have a high school diploma—and he was half-black, the ultimate minority in the islands. Johnny had graduated from an Ivy League law school—and he was all white. But Lonnie and Johnny were both crooks by choice. Made Lonnie want to laugh sometimes. Him and his kid brother, partners in crime. And getting richer every day.

John downed the remainder of his scotch and stood up. "Thanks for the drink, Bro. Catch you later. I'll let you know when Mister C gives me the exact time the shipment is due."

Lonnie stood, too, and walked around his desk. They embraced and patted each other on the back.

After John left through the same side-office door he'd entered from, Lonnie pressed his intercom button.

"Yeah, boss."

"Tell Rubio I want to see him."

CHAPTER NINETEEN

Lonnie watched Rubio Gonzales, one of his three lieutenants, strut into his office like a bantam rooster. Short and wiry, the man still weighed the same as he did years ago when he was Hawaiian Golden Gloves Flyweight Champ.

Lonnie pointed at one of two leather chairs in front of his desk. "Take a seat," he said. "I got a couple things I want to talk to you about." Lonnie always *told* Rubio what to do, never asked. Rubio would perceive asking as weakness. With men like Rubio, you never showed even a hint of that. Lonnie knew Rubio's loyalty to him was based on two things: Fear and money.

"Carlo and Huey just left here," Lonnie said.

"Yeah, I saw them."

"They've got a job to do. Already fucked it up once."

Rubio huffed. "Those two idiots could screw up a wet dream," he said.

Lonnie nodded. "That's why I need someone with a brain to go with them. That's you."

Rubio shifted in his chair. "Must be important," he said.

Lonnie saw a momentary gleam in Rubio's eyes. He knew the cocky little bastard was already trying to figure out an angle he could use.

"You could say that," Lonnie said. "I want them to get rid of that Save the Kids woman, Renee Drummond." Lonnie saw Rubio's eyes light up again. Rubio's tongue darted serpent-like and slid across his lips.

"I've wanted to take out that woman for years," Rubio said. "She and that damned do-gooder group of her's been messin' with my business for too long. You've always told me to back off. Why now? Why the sudden change?"

"Let's just say I got tired of your complaints."

Rubio smiled.

Lonnie could tell he hadn't bought his explanation.

"I'll see to it," Rubio said.

"Good."

Rubio turned to leave. "Whoa, hold on a minute. I got something else," Lonnie said.

"This must be my day," Rubio said.

"I hear you got a new girl."

"Just started breakin' her in. The boys been workin' her over day and night. Probably won't have her cashflowing until a week, maybe two."

"How much you figure?"

Rubio's tongue slithered out again and slid back and forth over his lips, as though testing the air for the scent of prey. "Maybe a hundred grand, if she doesn't OD, get AIDS, or get killed by a john. I give her two, three years, max. I'll work her like a machine. She'll be very popular. Got a lot of clients that like the young stuff."

"Take fifty grand for her right now?"

Rubio's eyebrows shot up in two perfect upside-down Vs. "Why would I give her up for fifty when I can make a hundred?"

"Time value of money, Rubio," Lonnie said, as though lecturing a business school student. "Fifty grand today is a whole lot better than a hundred grand over three years. Besides, who's to say she'll last even a month, what with some of the tough trade you deal with?"

Rubio's eyes narrowed. "Seventy-five grand."

"Sixty-five. And you get to keep her for a week. You ought to be able to clear ten grand in that time if you work her hard."

Rubio growled. "Dammit, Lonnie. You won't let a guy make a buck."

Lonnie laughed, reached into the humidor on the corner of his desk, and took out two cigars. "Have a Cuban," he said and tossed one to Rubio. He watched the man bite off one end, drop the plug into an ashtray, and use the lighter on the desk. While smoke swirled around Rubio's head, Lonnie calculated the profit he'd just made. His Thai contact had already agreed to pay him a hundred grand for a very young white girl to star in a snuff film.

CHAPTER TWENTY

Huey looked at Carlo over the top of his beer, then glanced down at the glass sweating in his enormous hand. He pressed the cold glass against his forehead and exhaled an "aah." Then he lowered the glass, slurped the head off the beer, and replaced it on the little cardboard coaster. "So whattaya think, Carlo?" he said in his booming voice. "Shoot her ass now or later? Got me a date tonight."

"Shit, Huey," Carlo rasped, his New York accent evident even in those two words, "keep your voice down." Carlo leaned to the side and looked down the bar's row of booths, then craned his neck to look over the back of the booth he shared with Huey. Except for the bartender across the way, the place was still empty. "We can't go prowlin' around a high-falutin' neighborhood in the middle of the day in that pimpmobile of yours. Those tight-assed snobs on the hill will sic the cops on us so fast. *Capisce*?"

"Yeah, I guess we'll have to wait until it's dark. But I'd sure hate to miss seeing Selina tonight."

Carlo had seen Huey's girlfriend only once, but he'd wondered many times how that tiny woman—couldn't weigh more than one hundred and ten pounds—handled Huey. Half his height and weight, she'd have to be the damned eighth wonder of the world.

Carlo watched Huey tip his head up at the ceiling. He knew that was how Huey did his thinking—turned his head up, closed his eyes, and screwed up his mouth. Quite a sight, this muscle-bound, black Hercules making like he was contemplating the creation of the universe.

Finally, Huey opened his eyes and dropped his head. "Why's Lonnie want the woman killed?"

Carlo lowered his head to his hands; covered his face. He sighed, raised his head, and sat back against the booth. "What do you care, Huey? What difference does it make?"

"It don't make no difference to me," Huey said. "I just find it more interesting if I know why I'm offin' someone."

"Didn't you hear Lonnie say he didn't want us thinking? We got a job to do. That's all there is to it. You try to figure out what's goin' through Lonnie's head and you'll get us in trouble."

"Can't stop a man from thinkin'," Huey said.

Carlo shot forward and poked a finger at Huey's chest. "Listen to me, you big dummy. We fuck this up and we're finished. It's bad that Rubio called and said he would go with us tonight. Don't you understand what that means? Lonnie don't trust us to get the job done on our own." He fell back against the booth and blew out a giant sigh. He hoped his explanation would be the end of it.

"How?" Huey asked.

"How, what?"

"How's she messin' with the boss's business?"

Carlo scratched the tip of his nose. "I guess it's the way she's pulled some of the young whores off the street. Her and that Save the Punks group. Getting' them into rehab programs. I hear Rubio and some of the other pimps been wanting him to do something about her."

"Which whores?"

"The teenyboppers. You know, the kids."

"Oh-h-h," Huey said. Then he adopted his thinking pose again.

"Take your time," Carlo said. His words dripped with sarcasm that was lost on Huey.

CHAPTER TWENTY-ONE

John C. Dunning, III, walked into the nineteenth-floor offices of Rawson, Wong & Ballard. His perfectly tailored suit showed off his tall, lithe figure and aristocratic good looks. His fifty-dollar haircut and four-hundred-dollar shoes complemented his image. John felt a glow inside while he moved down the hall to his office. These tight-assed lawyers—his colleagues—had no idea how much money he'd raked in already this year. Even Nathan Ballard didn't have a clue. He and Lonnie had it made.

Rawson, Wong & Ballard, the top law firm on the islands, occupied three floors of the high-rise tower and housed nearly a hundred attorneys, plus legal secretaries, clerks, and paralegals.

John was aware that a few of the senior partners were concerned about the reputations of the clients he brought to the firm, despite his protestations that those clients were legitimate businessmen. That they paid so well—and so often—helped the few concerned partners stifle their objections.

He caught the look one of the secretaries gave him when he strode past her desk. She was a sweet young thing with an ass that made his heart rate leap every time she strutted past his office. He never failed to get a kick out of the reactions he got from the women in the firm, but he knew enough not to mess around on the job.

He stopped at his secretary's desk to pick up messages.

"Anything urgent, Claire?"

"Just Mister Chongsawartha. He called a minute ago. I just tried to patch him through to your cell phone."

"I left it in the car. Get him on the line for me."

He walked into his office, closed the door, lowered himself into his desk chair, and waited for Claire to place the overseas call to Mister C. After a minute had passed, John pulled his wallet from his suit jacket pocket and opened it to the photograph he always carried. He left his chair to stand in front of his office window and let the light play on the faded picture. The photo had been taken thirty-five years ago—before Lonnie's father shipped out to Lebanon. Lonnie had given it to John the year he went off to college. The three Jerrells, one happy family—Roland, Nora, and little Lawrence—stood in front of fake scenery in a portrait studio. John focused on Nora—his and Lonnie's mother. A beautiful woman. Blond, blue-eyed, with aristocratic features. A young Grace Kelly. What a scandal, he thought. Society dame marries black man. The fact that Jerrell had been an officer and had a Masters Degree didn't make a bit of difference then. Probably wouldn't be any different today.

John grimaced and reflected bitterly on what Lonnie had told him their mother went through after Roland Jerrell died in Lebanon. Things she'd never been prepared for: Waitress jobs; taking in laundry. She did okay, though, John thought. But she wasn't going anywhere saddled with a half-black kid—a reminder of her "shame."

Mom returned to Hawaii when Lonnie was ten. John chuckled. That's when Lonnie first got into trouble. Lonnie had told him he'd first run away from home at thirteen. Best thing he could have done for mom, John thought, despite the fact he guessed Lonnie'd broken her heart. And it must have been damned tough for Lonnie. Alone on the streets.

Mom finally took a job as a receptionist in the office of an investment banker who wasn't afraid of her father. That's where she met Clarence Dunning.

John smiled at the memory of his mother's tale. He suspected she wasn't really in love with Clarence. But John knew his father had treated mom like a queen. Clarence and Nora married a year later and John was born eleven months after that.

John thought about the secret meetings with Lonnie in downtown Honolulu hotels. Those clandestine get-togethers occurred half-a-dozen times a year over a ten-year period. Until Lonnie refused to meet them after his picture was in newspapers. Arrested for assault and battery, Lonnie was miraculously acquitted. But, at that point, it made no difference. He'd become a big-time hoodlum. He didn't want his mother and brother seen with him.

Lonnie had infrequent contact with his family over the next fourteen years. Then John, newly graduated from law school, showed up two years ago with a proposition too good for Lonnie to pass up.

His secretary's voice interrupted his daydream. "Mister Chongsawartha is on line one."

John sighed, turned, and dropped the wallet on his desk. He picked up the receiver and swiveled so he could see Pearl Harbor and the Pacific Ocean beyond.

"John Dunning," he said firmly into the mouthpiece.

"Ah, Mister Dunning. It's Chongsawartha here. How are you today?" the forty-year-old Asian said in a singsong British accent.

"Very well, Mister Chongsawartha. And you?"

"Oh, I am doing spectacularly well, my good man. Life is excellent. Don't you think?"

"Yes sir," John said.

"May I assume all arrangements have been made for delivery of my fabrics?"

John smiled. "Everything has been taken care of. The bolts of cloth will be in the consignee's hands as soon as they clear Customs. All I need to know is the name of the ship and its estimated time of arrival."

"Tomorrow morning, around eleven o'clock. The ship's name is the *Sea Sprite*. It will immensely benefit my well-being if I can be sure the shipment will experience no delays."

"You have my assurances, Mister Chongsawartha," John said.

"You sound very confident, Mister Dunning. Good, good. You are a splendid young man. I look forward to a long and profitable relationship."

"Thank you. I'm sure of it."

After Chongsawartha hung up, John continued to stare out the window. He ticked off in his mind the details he'd already taken care of: Longshoremen on the payroll, bribes to select people in Customs, trucks to move the cloth, the crew at the garment manufacturing plant alerted, Lonnie in the loop. Nothing would go wrong.

CHAPTER TWENTY-TWO

Matt checked the dashboard clock: 5 p.m. He decided to stop at Susan's condominium building again; maybe someone would still be in the office.

Michelle looked up when he walked in. She held a lipstick suspended a few inches from her lips. She frowned, looked at the wall clock, and then went back to work on her mouth.

He waited for her to finish. She screwed the lipstick down in its tube, capped it, and dumped it in her purse. She gave Matt a pouty look, her mouth making a red circle, like a miniature inner tube. Then she stood and picked up her purse. "Mister Muccio's not here," she said. She glanced up at the wallclock again.

"It's about my sister," he said. "This won't even take a minute. I promise."

"Oh, okay," she said. "What do you need?"

"Is Muriel Goldstein back?"

"No. At least I don't think so."

"Would you mind calling her apartment to check?" Matt asked.

She pouted again, dropped her purse on her desk, sighed, and turned to her computer. She booted it up, opened a Contact file, and then dialed a number on her desk telephone. "No answer," she announced, after a few seconds. She raised her eyebrows at Matt.

"Could you check her file and tell me if there's a name and a number of a family member to call in case of an emergency?"

"Has something happened to Missus Goldstein?" Michelle asked in a suddenly worried voice.

"No, no," Matt said, "nothing like that. I want to check with someone who might have heard from her."

"I guess it's all right," she said. She went to a file cabinet and knelt to open the bottom drawer. Matt was amazed she didn't split the seam of her form-fitting dress. She took a file from the drawer, stood, and looked inside.

"Beth Nadler," she said. "Muriel Goldstein's daughter lives on Kauai."

Matt got back into his car before he noticed a piece of paper stuck under the windshield wiper. He got out from behind the steering wheel, pulled the paper from under the wiper, and unfolded it. It was a note scrawled in crude block letters: *I loved Miss Curtis. She was always nice to me.*

CHAPTER TWENTY-THREE

Matt hadn't thought about what type of house Renee would have. But he began to get an inkling of its grandeur when he drove up the steep road to The Palisades. There were no homes here that could be described as modest. Large manors on what appeared to be five-acre or larger plots stood majestically-high above the road. Most were hidden behind high wrought-iron fences or stone walls. But, occasionally, Matt caught sight of tiled roofs that soared above statuesque trees. The Pacific Ocean lay off to his right, at least two hundred feet below the road, and then curved around the top of The Palisades. The farther the road climbed, the more it curved, following the cliff edge and the shoreline below.

Matt found her address—foot-high numerals built into the design of an ornate wrought-iron gate set between twelve-foot-high stone pillars. He checked the dashboard clock and saw he was a few minutes early. He drove past the entrance gate for two miles to where the road ended in a cul-de-sac. A sandy parking area big enough to hold four cars bordered the road, and a two-foot high metal safety fence separated the parking area from a gazebo that housed a couple wooden benches and a viewfinder.

What the hell, Matt thought. I've got a couple minutes. He stepped around the safety fence and up into the gazebo, which rested on a promontory that overlooked the water and offered breathtaking views of Oahu's verdant hills on the far side of the bay, highlighted in red by the setting sun. Matt turned left and noticed that the bay formed an inlet, cut between the edge of the cliff where he stood and a similar, but slightly lower promontory a half-mile or so away. When he turned back toward the van, he spied the backs of mansions.

"I could get use to this," he said. He glanced at his wristwatch and saw it was time to go.

Matt drove back down to Renee's gate, pulled up to it, and could see in the distance, through the gate's metal curlicues, the peaked roof of a large house—no, a mansion—above towering palms. A meandering, brick-paved driveway disappeared into the trees. He lowered his window and pressed a button on a speaker box beside the gate.

Her voice answered, "Hello."

"Renee, it's me, Matt."

"I'll open the gate," she said. "Just follow the drive."

Matt noticed the gate close behind him as he followed the rising driveway upward between ever-dense foliage. But soon, the driveway opened into a bricked circular area twice the size of a tennis court, with a fountain at its center, like an exclamation point. The three-story house that stood regally on the far side of the circle could have been transplanted from Provence—smooth-cut stone façade; scrolled shutters that framed leaded glass windows.

Renee waited for him in the recessed arch of the main entry. The lights at the top of the arch illuminated her as though she were on stage. She was beautiful. Her hair was up in an elegant twist. She wore high heels and a black dress with a high oval neckline and a hem just below her knees. Renee waved when he stopped the car. Her wedding ring flashed in the light.

"I hope the mini-van won't scandalize the neighbors," Matt said, though no other house was visible. She'd come forward to greet him when he exited the van.

"Oh, don't give it a thought," she said with a mischievous smile. "The pool boy has one just like it. The neighbors will think he's entertaining the lonely widow."

"Not the sort of scandal I had in mind," he said.

She laughed. "If you really were the pool boy," she said, "I'd be at least the fourth woman in the neighborhood I know he's *entertained.*"

"Randy group of women around here," he said.

"You ought to see the pool boy."

"You look nice," he said, but wished he'd said, "Gorgeous."

She smiled, then turned and led him into the house.

Inside the foyer, Matt stopped a few feet from the bottom of a curved, marble staircase to admire a rose-crystal chandelier that dangled from the ceiling. Its sparkling light softly illuminated a five-foot-high flower arrangement that graced a round table in the middle of the area. Delicate furniture and a marble sculpture tastefully added to the room's elegance.

Beyond the staircase, the house was open all the way to open French doors that revealed a patio and an expanse of lawn. Two hallways radiated off the foyer on the left side.

"This is quite a surprise."

"My husband's ancestors did very well for themselves," she said.

"They owned the Hawaiian Islands?"

"Something like that. Let's go outside. I have a bottle of wine chilling."

Matt followed Renee down one of the hallways. It separated a sitting room and conservatory from closed-off rooms on the other side of the corridor. The hallway ended in a semi-circular space that led to another set of French doors that led onto the patio. The lawn, punctuated here and there by shade trees, sloped gently downward for fifty yards to an abrupt edge. And beyond that, the Pacific. Matt heard waves break, but couldn't see the shoreline.

"Must be a heck of a drop down to the water," Matt said.

"Several hundred feet," Renee said. "Come on, I'll give you a quick tour of the grounds."

He followed her past a kidney-shaped swimming pool, a large cabana, and a greenhouse, all located along the left side of the vast lawn. From there, she took a flagstone path that meandered through trees and bushes and ultimately skirted the edge of the precipice.

"This is quite an improvement over your office," Matt said as he looked over the edge of the cliff. In the air beneath his feet, dozens of sea birds lazily soared above the water. Waves crashed on truck-sized boulders that studded the shoreline like sleeping whales. He looked up at the highest point of land and saw the silhouette of the gazebo, where he'd stood minutes earlier. "Some view," he said.

Renee nodded, then suggested, "Why don't we open that bottle of wine now?"

"Sounds good to me," Matt said, although he would have been quite content just to stand there and stare out at the now-darkened Pacific.

They walked back up the slope to an array of wrought-iron patio furniture and sat on cushioned chairs.

"Would you open the wine?" she said.

"My pleasure." While he worked to remove the wine cork, he continued to gaze out at the yard. "This is what I imagine heaven looks like," he said.

When he looked at Renee again, she seemed sad. She'd slumped suddenly in her chair, and looked at her hands in her lap. A solitary tear glided down her cheek.

"Did I say something wrong?" Matt asked.

"Oh no. Please forgive me," she said. "It's just . . . your sister said almost the same thing the first time she came here." Then Renee smiled. "I used to call her Fitz."

"For her middle name, Fitzgerald," Matt said

Renee nodded.

"Was she here often?" he asked.

"Many times. She was my best friend."

Matt's throat constricted. He swallowed. "Mine, too," he said.

They sat quietly. Renee's chin trembled for a moment.

"Thanks," Matt said.

She glanced up at him. "For what?"

"For being Susan's friend."

Renee's smile returned.

He removed the cork from the wine bottle with a "pop" and poured half-a-glass for each of them.

Renee lifted hers. "To Susan."

"To Susan," Matt repeated.

"So," he said, "tell me about your husband's ancestors."

"Ha!" Renee laughed. "The Drummonds were nineteenth

century merchant princes, New England traders, and ship owners who sent one of their missionary sons to Hawaii—to win the hearts and minds of the natives. Other members of the family followed him here and appropriated as much of the natives' land as they could get their greedy hands on. Stole their hearts, minds, and everything they owned. Today, some of the Drummond land has skyscrapers on it, some has pineapple plantations. The estate is one of the largest real estate owners in the islands. Plus banks, insurance companies." She hunched her shoulders as though to indicate that the list was too long to mention. "The Drummonds became world class land and business barons.

"My son David would have inherited all of it. When David, and then my husband, Palmer . . . died . . . everything went into the family trust. A board of trustees runs the whole kit and caboodle. This place"—she gestured to include the house and grounds— "will revert to the trust upon my death, or in the event I remarry. But I have an income from the trust. That's how I can afford to operate Save the Kids without any help—or interference—from any government agency."

She looked at her watch. "My Lord, it's getting late. I made dinner reservations for eight-thirty. We'd better go."

Matt stood up, inserted the cork in the bottle, and reached for the wine bucket.

"Just leave it there," she said. "Maybe we can finish it later."

"I hope they'll let me into the restaurant without a tie."

"Very few restaurants in the islands require a jacket, let alone a tie. You'll be fine."

"You look so elegant. I just thought . . . ."

She curtsied. "Why, thank you, kind sir."

Renee led Matt back through the house and out the front door. Matt stepped ahead of her and opened the passenger door of the van, but she hung back. "I've got an idea. Let's take the Mercedes. We can put the top down. It's a perfect night for it."

He gave her a playful, sour look. "Afraid the neighbors will think I'm the pool boy?"

She winked. "The thought never crossed my mind. But now that you've mentioned it, let's take the van. My reputation could use the scandal."

"Oh no! I'm not passing up the chance to ride in your Mercedes. But only if I can drive."

"Deal," she said.

Renee led the way around the side of the house to a four-car garage. She flipped a wall switch.

"My God!" Matt said, in the sudden glare of lights, "automobile paradise."

Renee laughed. "My husband's hobby, classic cars. You should see the warehouse downtown. There's another fifty cars there. The trustees turned it into a museum."

Matt prowled around the garage. "I haven't seen a '41 Lincoln Continental Cabriolet since I was a kid in California," he said. He walked around the Continental to the next car in line. "It's a Cord!" His voice cracked and he heard Renee laugh. He looked over its hood and then turned to her. "I don't recognize the white one in the far bay."

Renee gave him a doleful look. "It's a '32 LaSalle. My husband was nuts about these cars. But the Cord was his favorite." She cleared her throat, put a cheerless smile on her face, and reached for a set of keys on a wall hook. She tossed them to Matt. "Let's get out of here," she said, while she hit a button on the wall to open the garage door.

Matt pulled the car from the bay. Renee got in and closed the garage door with a remote hooked to the passenger side sun visor.

"Madame, your chariot is set to go," Matt said. "Top down, engine revved."

She rewarded him with a glowing smile. "Then, let's go," she said as she tied a scarf over her head.

As Matt headed down the driveway; a sensor automatically opened the gate. When he pulled onto the street, he noticed a 1990s vintage black Trans Am, with a shiny customized rearing horse for a hood ornament, heavily tinted windows, and a telephone aerial affixed to the roof, parked nearby under a large tree. It hadn't been there when he arrived earlier.

"Pool boy get a new car?" he asked as he pointed with his chin at the Pontiac.

She laughed. "Probably just a couple kids necking. When you

look at the view, can you blame them?"

"Kids must be different today," he said.

"How so?"

"When *I* parked with a date, I had absolutely no interest in the view."

CHAPTER TWENTY-FOUR

"It's the same guy we saw with her this afternoon," Carlo said from the Pontiac's rear seat.

"You sure?" Huey said. "It's kinda dark."

"Yeah, I'm sure. I ain't blind."

"It don't make any difference," Rubio said from the right front bucket seat. "That's Renee Drummond's car. You heard what Lonnie said. If somebody gets in the way, tough shit. Follow 'em."

"Come on, Huey," Carlo shouted. "Get this hog moving. Lonnie's pissed off at us enough as it is. I don't want him on my ass anymore."

Huey turned the key and the car roared to life. He approached the Mercedes at the bottom of The Palisades.

"Hang back," Rubio ordered. "There's too much traffic around to take them out here."

Huey hit the power switch on the car's stereo system with his cigar-sized index finger. The heavy beat of James Brown's *Sex Machine* thundered from the speakers.

Carlo covered his ears with his hands. "Damn, do you have to play that thing again, Huey?"

"What's wrong, Carlo?" Huey shouted back. "You don't like ma man James?"

"Not fifty times a day, I don't. And not so damn loud. Why don't you get yourself another CD? And turn that damn thing down."

Huey pouted. "I like it this way. Louder the better."

111

Rubio intervened. "Do what Carlo said, Huey. Turn it down. My fuckin' chest is vibrating."

Huey muttered something about honkies, but he reduced the volume.

"How come you never played football, Huey?" Rubio asked. "You coulda made a fortune in the pros."

Carlo laughed. He poked Huey in the shoulder. "Go ahead, Huey. Tell Rubio about your big try-out with the Chargers."

Huey slapped at Carlo's hand. "I don't feel like it," he said.

"Rubio, you're not gonna believe what Huey did." Carlo blurted a laugh, but then devolved into hysterically laughing, tears rolling down his cheeks. It didn't take but a few seconds before he had Rubio laughing, too.

"Jeez," Rubio coughed, "you got me crackin' up and I ain't even heard nothin' funny yet."

"You better shut up, Carlo," Huey growled.

"Come on, man, don't be that way," Carlo said. "I ain't badmouthing ya. I think it's great what you did." Then Carlo shifted back to Rubio. "The Chargers hear about Huey from his high school coach in Los Angeles," Carlo said. "Huey flunked outta school and is providing muscle for a loan shark in East L.A. That's where Huey and I first met up. Anyway, the Chargers send this scout out to see Huey. Guy finds him hanging out at some playground in Watts."

"You're an asshole, Carlo," Huey said.

"Yeah, yeah," Carlo said.

"Shut up, Huey," Rubio ordered. "I want to hear the story."

"Okay," Carlo said, "so here's my boy Huey lounging around this basketball court. The scout goes up to him and says, 'How'd you like to play football with the Rams?'

"Huey says, 'How'd you like it if I shove my foot up your ass?'

"You can imagine the scout's bein' a little intimidated. Guy's white. Maybe the size of Barney Fife. You know, the guy on that Opie show?"

"Yeah, yeah. Huckleberry, USA, or some shit like that," Rubio said. "Get on with it."

"So, this little scout is in the middle of the ghetto and tryin' to make nice with a guy the size of the Empire State Building, with an attitude."

"Don't tell me Huey kicked the guy's ass?" Rubio said, barely able to get the words out, he was laughing so hard.

"No, no," Carlo said. "The guy convinces Huey he's on the up and up. Gives him his business card. Schedules a tryout for the next afternoon down in San Diego. I find out about the tryout that night from Huey and make sure he does something he's never done in his life before—show up early. A couple other players are already there, all decked out in their pads and uniforms. Rookie camp. The veterans don't show up for another week or so. Huey goes over to ask one of them where he should report.

"Guy looks at him and says, 'This ain't amateur hour.' Tells Huey to get lost.

"Huey walks away and sits down next to me in the bleachers. He's stewin' about the way this clown talked to him. He's sittin' there for maybe fifteen minutes, when he decides he's gonna give the guy one more chance to answer his question.

"He crosses the field and taps the guy on the back. 'Who do I gotta report to?' "

"So, what happened?" Rubio asked.

"The guy turns and pokes Huey in the chest. Tells him to get lost. Huey grabs the guy's hand and breaks his fuckin' wrist, hits him a few times in the gut, coldcocks him. It's amazing Huey didn't kill the guy."

"That's it?" Rubio asked. "What about Huey's tryout?"

"What tryout?" Carlo said. "You think the Chargers are gonna give a break to the guy who busts the wrist and ruptures the spleen of their number one draft choice. Huey ruined the guy's career."

Rubio punched Huey on the arm. "Way to go, Huey."

"See, Huey, Rubio loved the story."

"Fuck you, Carlo," Huey said.

"You guys pay attention," Rubio said, all humor now gone from his voice.

"Look, they've pulled into Monte's," Carlo shouted. "Shit! We got ourselves a long wait."

"Should I pull in after them?" Huey asked.

"Hell no!" Rubio said. "See them golden arches down the street?

We'll grab a couple Big Macs and wait there."

CHAPTER TWENTY-FIVE

"Nice place," Matt said, while the maitre d' guided them to a table.

"I'm glad you like it," Renee said. "The food's great and they have a wonderful wine list." She pointed at the gleaming wood floor in the center of the room, two tiers of tables below. She grinned at Matt and raised her eyebrows. "And they even have dancing after ten."

Matt thought he saw a challenge in her look. He felt lightheaded having Renee so close to him. "It's been a long time since I've been on a dance floor," he said. "Not since my wife died. She loved to dance."

After they were seated, he ordered cocktails and made small talk about his sons, his practice, and the mundane aspects of New Mexico life. Renee looked directly at him, appearing to listen intently. Talking to her seemed so easy.

"I haven't talked this much in a long time," Matt said. "Your turn. I want to know about you. Where you . . . ."

The waiter intruded. After he explained additions to the menu, he took their orders. They both picked the Ahi. Matt ordered a bottle of Chardonnay.

As soon as the waiter left, Renee leaned forward and touched Matt's hand. "I'm sorry I mentioned the band here. We don't have to dance."

Matt frowned. "Why do you say that?"

Her brow knitted and she looked down at her folded hands. "It's just that you looked so sad when you said your wife loved to dance."

Matt smiled. "I loved Allison. She was my first love. But she's been gone a long time. Cancer. The reason I looked sad was because it's been that long since I've been out dancing. Susan told me for years that I needed to get a life."

She smiled radiantly. She seemed relieved. "Maybe we can do something about that tonight. It's been more than six years since I've been out dancing. Maybe you'd better pour me some more wine. A little liquid fortitude might be in order."

Matt reached for the bottle in the standup ice bucket. He poured more wine into both their glasses.

The waiter returned with their entrees. They spent an hour eating and talking about everything and nothing. The band started its first set shortly after the busboy cleared the table and the waiter served coffee.

The strains of Hoagie Carmichael's *Stardust* filled the room and Matt closed his eyes and moved his head to the rhythm. Then he looked across the table at Renee. She wore an expectant, wide-eyed expression.

"Are you ready to take your chances with me on the dance floor?" he asked.

"I thought you'd never ask."

Matt rose and took her hand, which felt soft and warm and fit perfectly in his. They walked down the steps to the dance floor and came together in a way that seemed just right. She yielded to the pressure of his hand on her back and closed the distance between them. Her body felt trim and firm.

The scent of her perfume filled him with an almost overpowering sensation. Like the heady aroma of a fine wine—with sexual overtones added. A bit of vanilla, a hint of sandalwood. Matt hadn't experienced this sort of sexual tension with a woman in years. Since Allison. For a moment, he felt guilty about how much he was enjoying himself, considering the reason he was in Hawaii. But the moment passed. There was something right about being here with Susan's best friend.

Renee pressed against him without any encouragement. They moved together slowly, comfortably over the wood floor. When the tune ended, he continued to hold her for a few extra moments. She didn't resist. When he finally released her, she opened her eyes and looked up at him.

"You were sandbagging, Matthew. You dance divinely."

"A total klutz would look like Fred Astaire with you as a dance partner."

Renee put both hands on the back of his neck and rose up on her toes to kiss his cheek. An electric shock shot through him.

The band began another tune, an old Skyliners' song, *Since I Don't Have You*, which took Matt back years. By the end of the music set, Matt felt wired with energy. Butterflies erupted in his stomach. He led her back to their table and pulled out her chair.

She reached for her bag on the table. "Why don't we go back to my place," she said. "The coffee's better there and we still have that bottle of wine to finish."

Matt left cash on the table to settle the tab. He took Renee's arm when they left the restaurant. The parking valet retrieved the Mercedes and Matt helped Renee into the passenger seat, then walked around the car and tipped the attendant before he slid behind the wheel. He pulled out onto the street.

Afraid he might say the wrong thing and spoil the mood, Matt drove in silence. They left the garish lights of the commercial district behind and headed up the coast road toward The Palisades. Widely spaced streetlights cast isolated cones of brightness on the pavement. Each time Matt drove through one of the light beams, he glanced at Renee. Each glimpse of her face carried him through the darkness until the next streetlight.

"What was that wine again? I haven't felt this good in a long time," Renee said.

Matt laughed. "Neither have I. But, in my case, I don't think the wine is responsible for it."

She made a little laughing sound. "You're really pumping up my ego," she said and leaned back against the headrest.

Feeling better than he thought possible, Matt checked the speedometer. He'd had a lot to drink, and he didn't want to attract a cop by going too fast, even though what he *really* wanted to do was to slam the accelerator to the floor to get to Renee's as quickly as possible. He checked in the rearview mirror. A pair of headlights kept pace. He looked at the speedometer again.

Then Matt did a doubletake. He'd been looking for a cop, so the dark-colored car hadn't registered at first. He kept his eyes fastened to the mirror and watched until the trailing car passed under one of the streetlights. It appeared to be the same metallic black as the one he'd seen earlier outside Renee's gate. He remembered the car had a garish chrome hood ornament. He stared at the mirror when the Pontiac passed under another streetlight. Yes, there it was.

Matt glanced at Renee to make sure she had on her seatbelt. He wanted to think that the car behind them was merely a coincidence. But something told him they wouldn't be that lucky. He took the turn onto the road up to The Palisades. He held his breath and tightly gripped the steering wheel as he watched to see if the black car followed.

Shortly after he turned onto The Palisades road, Matt heard the deep-throated roar of a high-powered engine and saw the Trans Am pull around on the left of the Mercedes.

Matt shifted in his seat. He looked at Renee again, her head against the headrest, her eyes closed. Matt cleared his throat. "I think we've got trouble," he said.

Renee jerked upright as the Pontiac closed the distance. Matt slowed down to let it pass. It swung out and pulled nearer on the left, but it didn't pass. It just stayed there off the left rear fender and seemed to fill the convertible with the vibrating roar of its engine.

Matt glared at the Trans Am's passenger window, but couldn't see a thing through the tinted glass.

"What's happening?" Renee shouted to Matt.

"No clue," Matt yelled. "But I think you'd better tighten your seat belt."

Matt stood on the accelerator and the Mercedes lunged forward, leaving the Trans Am and its roar behind. Matt slapped at himself, touching the pockets of his pants and jacket.

"What are you looking for?" Renee shouted.

"My cell phone. To call 9-1-1. But I must have left the damn thing in the van."

Renee opened her handbag and extracted a cell phone. She

flipped it open and punched in numbers. "Damn!" she shouted, after a few seconds. "I got a recording. Can you believe it, I got a recording?"

The two-lane road twisted and turned in a series of S-curves between stretches of straight-aways. To Matt's right: A sheer drop to the ocean. On the left: Luxury mansions behind gates and walls. He concentrated on the pavement ahead, tromped on the accelerator again, and futilely tried to shake the Trans Am.

"Rubio Gonzales," Renee suddenly yelled, sounding more angry than afraid.

"What?" Matt shouted, not taking his eyes off the road.

"Rubio Gonzales," she pointed at the Trans Am. "It's him. It's got to be. We've got to get out of here, Matt."

Then Renee screamed.

The Trans Am came closer again on the left. Its passenger windows slid down. A man in the front seat pointed a pistol at Matt. And so did another in the back seat.

"Bastard!" Renee shouted. "You bastard!"

Matt hit the brakes as hard as he could. The Mercedes skidded on the mist-dampened road. Its rear end fishtailed and for a moment Matt thought he might lose control. The Pontiac shot past them, also in a braking skid. Matt stepped on the gas and veered to the left, rocketing the Mercedes at the bigger car's passenger door. The Mercedes' front bumper slammed into the side of the Pontiac. After a long moment filled with the screech of metal, the cars disengaged. Matt kept his foot down on the gas and the Mercedes pushed the Pontiac aside, then shot up the hill, past the gate to Renee's house.

"We don't have much road left," Matt called out over the noise of the car's engine and the wind sweeping over the windshield.

"Another two miles uphill. Then it ends in a cul-de-sac," Renee shouted, while she pushed numbers on her cell phone. "There's a hairpin turn just below the cul-de-sac. Even this car won't take it at over thirty miles an hour. I—"

"Yes, I've got an emergency," Matt heard Renee yell into the cell phone. "Several men in a black Pontiac Trans Am are trying to kill us."

Matt goosed the Mercedes to greater speed. He checked the

rearview mirror. The Pontiac was there again, and coming up fast. A shot rang out over the noise of the two straining motors. The Mercedes' windshield spiderwebbed into a maze of tiny fractures, obscuring Matt's view of the road.

"That sound," Renee screamed at the 9-1-1 opeartor, "was a gun being fired. We need help up here on The Palisades Road."

Matt had ducked his head into his shoulders like a turtle. Three more shots sounded. It took him a second to realize they'd come from inside the Mercedes. The glove box hung open. Renee held the cell phone in one hand and a revolver in the other.

"I can't see a damn thing," Matt shouted as he rose in his seat and looked over the top of the windshield. He glanced at his sideview mirror. The Trans Am crept up on them.

"Keep your eyes on the road," Renee yelled. "The hairpin turn is just ahead." Then, she turned around, knelt on her seat, and fired three more thunderous shots at their pursuers.

Matt felt as though someone had banged a bass drum inside his head.

"Shit!" Rubio screamed as he jerked his arm back inside the Pontiac. But he banged his elbow on the door and lost his grip on his pistol, which fell to the pavement. He ducked below the door panel. "The bitch has a gun! Huey, ram those assholes over the cliff."

Huey roared as though he'd been gored. "My goddamn car!" he shouted. "I'll kill those bastards. They've ruined my car."

The woman fired another bullet at them and sparks flew as the round ricocheted off the hood ornament. Rubio slid down in his seat. "Sonofabitch!" he yelled.

"You ain't gonna give a shit about your damn car if you're dead," Rubio screamed, "you dumb fuck. Ram them! Now!"

Huey pulled alongside the Mercedes and yanked the steering wheel hard to the right. The Pontiac shuddered when it hit the other car.

Carlo leaned over the front seat, stuck his arm out Rubio's window, and fired off two rounds.

The shock of the collision sent Renee's pistol flying. Then the percussion sound of a pistol firing caused her to duck low on her seat.

Matt peered ahead through a tiny gap in the windshield. He knew the road must end soon. The hairpin turn would be his one chance. He pictured what he wanted to do while he raced uphill, his head now barely above the bottom of the dashboard. He twisted the wheel to the left and rammed the Trans Am. But the other driver maintained control and rammed the Mercedes back.

Matt leaned his head out the driver side window and saw the hairpin turn ahead. He knew he had to act now. He crashed once more into the Trans Am, then slammed on the brakes.

"Now, Huey, do it now!" Carlo shrieked, after the Mercedes rammed the Pontiac, then bounced off. "Push those bastards over the cliff."

Huey floored the gas pedal and twisted the wheel to the right. But by then the Mercedes was no longer there.

The screech and smell of burning rubber filled the night. Matt hung on as the Mercedes careened into a curb just feet short of the abyss. It scraped along the curb and tires burst with a sound like muffled gunshots—*pop! pop!* The car started to tip toward the ocean.

"Oh God! Oh God!" Renee cried.

There was nothing Matt could do. It seemed surreal to be so calm, knowing he was so close to death. The Mercedes teetered on the flattened right-side wheels and hung there like a stunt car. Time seemed suspended.

Matt gripped the steering wheel with all his might, afraid that if he slid down the seat, the extra weight on the right side of the car would push them over the cliff. Out of the corner of his eye, he saw bright red lights, like demon eyes, seemingly hanging in mid-air past the edge of the cliff. The sound of a racing engine bellowed.

Then the Mercedes listed away from the cliff and crashed down onto the street. Matt's head smashed into the steering wheel.

CHAPTER TWENTY-SIX

Dennis Callahan rubbed his sleep-deprived eyes, then pressed the palms of his hands against his temples. The headache persisted. The inside of his mouth tasted sour and his stomach felt as though he'd ingested battery acid. But the physical sensations weren't nearly as bad as the feeling that he'd fallen into an emotional black hole.

If only the girl had left. What the hell was her name? Started with a D. Oh yeah, he remembered, Debbie. Rubio's man had said she was new. "Next best thing to virgin goods," he'd said.

Callahan looked to his left. No such luck. Debbie was still beside him in bed, her frail form just a foot away, curled in a fetal position, her thumb in her mouth.

He swallowed back his self-disgust and watched the girl's mouth reflexively tug on her thumb. He carefully reached over her, took the glass of champagne off the nightstand, tipped the glass, and shuddered as the flat, warm liquid hit his throat and slid down to his queasy stomach.

He set the glass down on the nightstand on his side of the bed just as the cell phone chirped. He snatched it up and recognized the telephone number: Violent Crimes.

"Callahan," he answered hoarsely, as he got out of bed, grabbed his undershorts, staggered into them on his way to the kitchen, and sat at the kitchen table. "Damn!" he gasped at the cold of the vinyl chairback against his skin.

"What was that, Lieutenant?"

"Is that you Saleamuu?"

"Yeah, Lieutenant. Some car took a swan dive off the top of The Palisades. Three men inside."

"Don't tell me," Callahan said. "Right at the hairpin turn."

"You got it."

"So why page me? Since when do I get accident calls?"

"There's more. Two officers who responded to 9-1-1 calls about gunshots found a banged-up Mercedes at the scene. There was a guy behind the wheel with a nasty bump on his forehead. He was disoriented, but the woman with him was madder than hell. She kept screaming something about Rubio Gonzales and how us cops let criminals run free."

A bubble of bile erupted from the base of Callahan's stomach and burned his throat. He tasted stale champagne mixed with stomach acid.

"What the hell does Rubio Gonzales have to do with this?"

"I don't know if he does, Lieutenant. But that's what the woman claims."

"I still don't get it, Matty. Why'd you—?"

"The woman said the three guys that went over the cliff tried to kill them. We found a pistol in the middle of the road. There was another pistol in the Mercedes. The woman said it was her's. Both had been fired."

"Who were the three men?"

"Don't know yet. She swears one of them was Gonzales. The water's pretty deep there. We've got a boat and divers on scene."

Callahan sighed. "Who was in the Mercedes? Please don't tell me it's one of our politicians. That's all I need."

Saleamuu laughed. "No, we got a break there, Lieutenant. Just some guy from the mainland named Matthew Curtis and—"

"Oh shit!"

"What's wrong, Lieutenant? You know him?"

"Who's the woman?" Callahan demanded.

"Your old friend, Renee Drummond."

Callahan hung up the phone. His nausea got worse. He took a deep breath and tried to muster the will to stand and go back to the bedroom. To shower, to get dressed. Movement caught his eye and he turned to look at the kitchen doorway. The girl stood there—naked, one foot on the other, supporting herself with arms braced against both sides of the doorjamb.

"Whatsamatter, Mister? You don't look so good."

He looked at her thin, hairless, adolescent body and shook his head.

"Can I have the present you promised me? I was real nice to you, wasn't I? I tried my best," she said in her little tremulous voice. "I did. I really tried to make you happy."

Hearing her plead made Callahan feel lower than pond scum. Sex with a little girl in return for a vial of crack—the present—he'd pocketed from a drug bust.

"Please, can I have the present now?" she begged again.

She fidgeted; shifted her weight from leg to leg. He could tell she was coming down from her last fix.

"I'll do you again," she said. "Whatever you want." She abandoned the doorway and got down on her knees in front of him.

He seemed paralyzed as she put her hand under the waistband of his shorts and took him in her hand. A tidal wave of nausea rose up in him. He pushed her away and rushed to the bathroom.

CHAPTER TWENTY-SEVEN

Renee stood rigidly in a corner of the hospital emergency treatment room, her arms folded defensively. The steely look in her eyes seemed to say, Don't even think about messing with me. She peered at the young Pakistani physician putting a dressing over the sutures he'd sewed into Matt's forehead. Matt looked up at the doctor.

The young doctor shined a light into Matt's eyes. "How do you feel, Doctor Curtis?" he asked. "Any dizziness, nausea?"

Matt said, "Just a killer headache. How'd the CT scan look?"

"No sign of either epidural or subdural hemorrhaging. You appear alert and attentive, so I don't believe any serious damage occurred. But that doesn't mean you don't have a concussion. The symptoms can come on twenty-four to forty-eight hours after an injury."

Matt nodded.

The physician turned to Renee. "If his headache gets worse, or if you notice his pupils change—one bigger than the other—get him back here immediately."

"What about medication. Can he have anything?" Renee asked.

"Nothing. No aspirin, no alcohol. Absolutely nothing." He jabbed a finger at her to emphasize the point.

Matt touched the patch now on his forehead.

"The stitches will dissolve in about a week," the doctor told him. "I did my best to minimize scarring."

Matt smiled. "I appreciate your skill. But I've always wanted a dueling scar."

"Humpf. Better be careful," the doctor said, as he turned to leave. "Dueling can be lethal."

Matt looked at Renee. "Hell of a way to end a romantic evening."

She came over, put her arms around his neck, and kissed his cheek. "I'm so sorry," she said.

Matt gave her a quizzical look. "For what?"

"Because of me, you got hurt." Tears rolled down her cheeks. "Susan probably died because of me, too. Because of me and Save the Kids."

Matt held her tightly. "You don't know that." Her body trembled. "Everything will be fine," he said.

Then Matt's voice turned angry. "I think it's time I cashed in an IOU. Come on, Renee," he said as he slid off the exam table and slowly walked out of the treatment room, his arm around her shoulders. He drew her closer to him and they entered the waiting room.

"What do you mean?" Renee asked. "An IOU?"

Matt started to explain, just when Lieutenant Dennis Callahan walked in.

Callahan moved toward them, looked at Matt's forehead, and nodded at Renee. "Hello, Missus Drummond," he said.

"What brings you here?" Renee asked. Before he could respond, she blurted, "It couldn't possibly be because we were almost killed tonight."

"I got a call that you claim someone tried to kill you. Want to tell me about it?" Callahan said.

"What do you mean *claim*?" Renee practically snarled. "Three guys in a car shot at us, tried to run us off the cliff."

Callahan's jaw tightened.

Matt looked from Renee to Callahan, and back to Renee. "You two know each other?"

"Oh, Lieutenant Callahan investigated my son's murder. He still hasn't found the pimp who doped up David and handed him over to the pervert who killed him. Have you, Lieutenant? And, of course, you could never tie Rubio Gonzales to it."

Callahan's voice vibrated with barely-controlled anger. "Look, Missus Drummond," Callahan said, "I'm trying to find out what happened tonight. We haven't pulled any bodies out of the ocean yet, but we found two pistols near the scene of the accident—one registered to you. Both had been fired. So talk to me here or you'll talk to me down at the station."

Matt suddenly felt dizzy and nauseous. He looked at Renee. She glared at Callahan as though she wanted to scratch his eyes out. Then she looked at Matt and her angry, narrow-eyed expression changed to one of surprise, then concern.

"Matt, you look terrible." She gently patted his back. "Let's sit down." She took Matt's arm and helped him past rows of occupied chairs to a grouping of chairs in a corner.

When they'd all settled into chairs, Matt asked in a weak voice for some water.

Renee glared at Callahan and the cop seemed to get the message. He got up and walked across the room to a water cooler.

Matt laid a hand on Renee's thigh. "Let's get this over with."

Renee grimaced. "You know nothing will come of what we tell Callahan. The cops are more interested in protecting the criminals than innocent people. I've put up with police incompetence and indifference for years. Rubio Gonzales and his men have preyed on little kids for a long time, and the police have done nothing to put an end to it." Renee leaned her head against Matt's shoulder. "I'm sorry about my temper. It's just that those men tonight pushed me over the edge."

"Not quite," Matt said.

She drew back, her mouth open, eyes wide. "How can you joke about it?"

Callahan returned with a paper cup of water. The cop looked at Renee. "Do you think you could tell me what happened tonight . . . without biting my head off?"

Renee nodded. She related the story of the attack. Callahan took an occasional note.

"What about the possibility they were carjackers?" he asked.

Matt saw Renee's face redden; she squinted.

"Okay," Callahan said as he raised his hands in surrender.

"Stupid question."

Renee just glared at him.

"You're sure it was Rubio Gonzales?"

"Yes. But don't take my word for it. You'll see when you pull his body out of the water. He was in that car."

"You're absolutely sure of that?"

"Yeah, I'm sure. He was no more than ten feet away. He had a gun pointed right at me."

The cop turned to Matt. "Do you have anything to add, Doctor Curtis?"

Matt's eyes had been half-closed, but they popped fully open at hearing his name. He merely slowly and deliberately shook his head.

Callahan closed his notebook and put it back inside his jacket pocket. "I'll look into it," he said and walked out.

"Jesus," Renee exclaimed. "He'll look into it. Thank God for small favors."

The cab stopped at the front gate to Renee's place. She got out of the back seat and punched in the code on the security system keypad. At the house, she let Matt lean on her when they got out of the cab. By the time they reached the front door, he perspired as though he'd just run a marathon.

She shut the door behind them. "You look awful," she said.

Matt pressed his hands against the sides of his head. "Headache's worse; and I feel nauseous and dizzy," he said in a syrupy voice. "My vision's blurred. How are my eyes?"

She turned him so the light from the chandelier shone on his face. The glare made him squint. "They look normal."

"I could use some water," he said weakly, and sank into a chair. "And a place to lie down. I'm exhausted. But you need to wake me every couple hours or so, to check my pupils."

"Yes, Doctor," she said.

DAY FIVE

CHAPTER TWENTY-EIGHT

Matt squinted and turned away from the sunlight that peeked through one side of the thick bedroom curtains. The rest of the room was dark. He felt a sharp pain in his brow and reached up and gingerly touched the patch just below his hairline.

How'd I get here? he thought. He couldn't recall coming to bed. But he did remember other events of the night: The car chase, the shots, the wreck, the hospital. He slowly eased into a sitting position. The nausea seemed to be gone. But when he lowered his feet to the floor and slowly stood up, the dizziness came back with a rush. He grabbed the edge of the headboard; the spinning feeling subsided as quickly as it had come.

As his eyes adjusted to the room's darkness, he noticed Renee asleep in a chair at the foot of the bed.

Matt turned on the bedside lamp and stared across the room at her. Even without makeup, even with her hair ajumble, she was beautiful. She breathed in a rapid, shallow rhythm. Her head rested on one of the chair wings. He walked over to her and, when he touched her hand, she flinched and her eyelids blinked open. She smiled, and he felt his breath catch in his chest.

He helped her out of the chair. "Come on, nurse," he said, "it's your turn to go to bed."

She yawned. "No, no, I'm fine," she said in a scratchy voice.

Matt ignored her protests, led her to the bed, and gently pushed her down. She curled up with a groan. He covered her with the sheet and, after only a moment, she was asleep again.

Matt left the bedroom and went downstairs to the kitchen. There he discovered a dumpling of a woman in a black dress, clunky black shoes, and a white apron. Her back was to the doorway. Her gray-streaked black hair was pulled back in a bun. She hummed a tune. Matt knocked lightly on the wood doorframe.

She looked over her shoulder. "How be ya feelin' this bright, sunny morn?" she said, her voice floating with a musical Irish brogue.

"Not bad, considering," he said. "I'm Matt Curtis."

"I figured as much. Me name is Lily O'Brien, Doctor Curtis. Miss Drummond told me ye had an accident. She called and asked me to be acomin' in early this morn. Would ye care for somethin' to eat?"

"A cup of coffee and some toast would be great."

"I think I can handle that. Sit yeself down at the table while I fix yer breakfast."

Matt spotted a telephone on the wall. "Mind if I use the phone?"

"Of course not," she said.

There was a phone book sandwiched between cookbooks on a nearby shelf. He opened it and searched the M's for Maldonado. There was an Esteban, as Matt had hoped. He hadn't seen Esteban Maldonado for more than thirty years. He dialed the number. A woman finally answered.

"Esteban Maldonado, please," Matt said.

"Esteban's out back," she said. "Can I take a message?"

"It's important," Matt said. "I need to talk to him as soon as possible." He gave his name and Renee's phone number.

While he'd been on the phone, Lily had placed a cup of steaming coffee, a plate of buttered toast, and a plate of pastries on the table. Matt lifted the coffee cup to his lips with shaky hands. The telephone rang.

"Drummond residence," Lily said. "Yes, he's here. A moment please." She covered the mouthpiece. "It's a Mister Maldonado."

Matt set down his cup, slopped coffee onto the saucer, and rose quickly. He held onto the back of his chair in case of another dizzy spell. When nothing happened after a few seconds, he stepped over to Lily and took the receiver. He sucked in a deep breath. He and Esteban had frequently talked by telephone over the five years after Matt left the Army. They'd had little contact since—maybe a call every other year, or so. Matt released the air in his lungs.

"This is Matt Curtis," he said.

"*Chapulin*. Is it really you?" The man's voice rumbled like thunder, and Matt knew he'd found his old friend from the Fifth Special Forces.

"You can forget about that *Chapulin* nonsense. I'm no grasshopper anymore," Matt said. "No skinny kid."

"God, you were built like a rail back then."

"Yeah, but a steel rail." Matt said. "A hundred fifty pounds of twisted blue steel and sex appeal."

Esteban laughed. "In your dreams, a*migo*. What are you doing here on the islands?"

"Long story, pal. Any chance we can get together this evening. Say about seven?"

"Try to keep me away."

Matt gave directions to Renee's home.

"Man, you must be moving up. That's the high rent district. I'll see you at seven."

Matt put the phone in the cradle and returned to the table. Lily replaced his coffee cup with a fresh one.

"Should I plan on dinner guests?" she asked.

"Just one. A very old, very dear friend."

CHAPTER TWENTY-NINE

Lonnie Jackson snatched the phone from his desk and yelled, "What!" He immediately regretted the shout. His head already ached from too damned much booze and too little sleep. The mid-morning sun glare that came through his office window only made him feel worse.

"It's me," Callahan said. "Having a bad day?"

"You could say that."

"You want to share your problems?" Callahan said.

"Screw you, asshole!" Lonnie spat. "What d'ya want?"

Callahan snickered. "No point in getting angry. Just trying to help. You missing a few of your men?"

Lonnie paused. "Yeah, how d'ya know?"

"Turn on the news," Callahan said.

"What d'ya mean?"

"Your boys were fished out of the Pacific this morning. They tried to kill Renee Drummond and a doctor named Matthew Curtis up in The Palisades last night."

" '*Tried* to kill?' "

"Correct. Assignment botched. Apparently, they weren't tough enough to handle the woman and her doctor friend," Callahan chuckled.

Lonnie let the comment pass. He knew Callahan was a smart-ass. But if Rubio, Huey, and Carlo were in the morgue and the

Drummond bitch was alive, Callahan wasn't wrong, either. They hadn't been tough enough.

"Who's this Curtis guy?"

"Remember the gal who took a header off the Sand & Sea?"

"Sure. How could I forget her?"

"Curtis is her brother."

Lonnie remained silent for a full fifteen seconds. "I want a meeting," he said. "Usual place. Midnight." He hung up without waiting for a response.

Lonnie grabbed a cigar from the middle desk drawer and bit off the end of the almost black, seven-inch cylinder. He spat the tobacco plug into his free hand and threw it at the wastebasket in the corner. The plug bounced off the wall, two feet above the basket, and hit the floor.

"Shit," Lonnie growled. "Nothing's workin'." He attacked the end of the cigar with a gold lighter and stoked the flame until smoke plumed to the ceiling. He then punched the intercom on his desk. "Koney, get your ass in here."

Koney Moto rushed into Lonnie's office. A fireplug-of-a-man, Moto had a bowling ball-round head and a bull neck. He made up for his lack of height with unparalleled courage and an insatiable desire to please Lonnie.

"What ya need, boss?"

"You made a disk run lately?" Lonnie asked.

"S'been 'bout two weeks," Moto said.

"Well, it's time for another run," Lonnie said. "And don't forget that asshole Callahan's place. He tasted Little Debbie last night."

CHAPTER THIRTY

John Dunning checked his tie in the hall mirror and pulled the knot a little tighter. He looked again at his Rolex—for at least the tenth time in the last fifteen minutes. Still an hour before he really needed to be at the docks. He brushed his hands through his thick black hair, then stuck them in his pants pockets and crossed the room. The papers were in his briefcase. But despite being confident he'd taken care of everything, he noticed his fingers tremble. His stomach felt as though it would erupt at any moment. John smiled. It was the adrenaline, he thought. He loved the feeling.

"Oh, what the hell," John muttered. So I get there a few minutes early. He took the elevator to the condo parking garage, walked to his BMW, and tossed his briefcase on the passenger seat. He revved the engine, put the car in gear, peeled out of his slot, and fishtailed on the greasy surface. The echo of his squealing tires bounced off the concrete walls as he headed up three levels to the street. He gunned the BMW into traffic. Horns blared, brakes screeched, drivers cursed. John laughed as he sped down the street.

The *Sea Sprite* had arrived at one of Honolulu's massive berths. Men and equipment scurried to unload cargo. A towering crane lifted semi-truck-sized containers from the ship's hold and lowered them to the dock. Workers opened the containers and removed boxes which forklifts carried inside a cavernous warehouse.

John parked his car on the street, a block from the pier, away from the dockworkers. He walked along the concrete pier where uniformed inspectors already hovered over unloaded goods. They checked the containers against manifests and opened some of them to examine the contents. John spotted Chief Inspector Macaluso standing in the shadow of the ship. He waited until Macaluso noticed him, then nodded his head, turned away, and walked to the Customs shed at a corner of the warehouse. Macaluso followed.

"Little early, aren't you?" Macaluso said. "Thought we said noon."

"Yeah, That a problem?" John asked.

"Nah, Let's get it over with."

John handed Macaluso a file with the usually required documents: Bill of lading, Customs forms. The file also contained an unsealed envelope stuffed with hundred-dollar bills.

The money ensured that none of Macaluso's agents would search John's shipment, that it would be released immediately upon being offloaded.

Business completed with Macaluso, John drifted away from the activity on the pier. He dialed his cell phone. "The ship's in," he reported. "Send the trucks."

"Right, Bro," Lonnie said.

John hung around the dock during the two hours it took longshoremen to remove the containers that held Chongsawartha's fabric bolts from the ship's cargo hold. For another hour, he watched them move the thirty plastic-wrapped, twenty-foot-long, four-foot-high bolts from the containers and load them onto Lonnie's trucks. Three hours of his time. It was the middle of the afternoon by the time he returned to his car and used his cell phone to first call Chongsawartha about the safe arrival of the goods. Then he cranked up the stereo, raced away from the port, while hammering his hands against the steering wheel to the beat of *Journey*.

"Piece of cake," he exclaimed. He thought about how much money Rawson, Wong & Ballard would make from his work. The firm would bill T.I.S. Trading Company, Island Garment Wear's parent company—another of Lonnie's corporations—seventy-seven thousand dollars in legal fees. That was the agreement between the law firm and Lonnie. Seventy-seven thousand dollars for two hundred twenty hours of John's time—a month of work. A like bill would be sent to Worldwide Fabric Mills, a textile-manufacturing firm owned by Chongsawartha. All billed hours would be scrupulously documented on law firm time sheets fabricated by its rising star, John C. Dunning, III. Not bad for half an afternoon of work.

John beat the trucks from the docks to the Island Garmentwear factory and watched from his car. The trucks arrived twenty minutes later and drove into the building through giant bay doors. As soon as all four trucks had vanished inside, he roared off to Lonnie's office.

Lonnie lifted a can of Michelob in salute. "Not bad, little brother. Thirty bolts of the finest linen and silk. Twice the size of the last three shipments combined." He put the beer down, picked up a large athletic bag from the floor next to his desk chair, and tossed the bag at John.

John had to jerk his drink out of the way. Half the scotch in the glass splashed on his suit pants. "Shit, Lonnie. Look what you did. You just fucked up a brand-new two-thousand-dollar suit."

Lonnie laughed as though he'd never heard anything funnier. He got up, came around his desk, and playfully tousled his little brother's perfectly coifed hair. That made John spill the rest of his drink.

"Get a grip, boy," Lonnie said. "There's two hundred grand in that bag. Your personal cut. Go buy yourself a hundred suits." Lonnie laughed again. "Or go to Sears and get a thousand suits."

Lonnie looked at his watch. "I'd better get over to the factory. Make sure everything's all right. You ought to get out of here. Don't want anyone to see you hanging around."

John hefted the gym bag. "Not as heavy as I thought it'd be."

"You want to count it?"

"Nope. If I can't trust you, who can I trust?"

Lonnie smiled. "What you doin' tonight. Got a hot date?"

"Thursday night. I'm having dinner with Mom."

Lonnie slapped him on the back. "You're a good son, Johnny-boy." He watched John leave the office and close the door behind him. A cold shiver went through him. He knew his brother couldn't care less about the money. Johnny's daddy, Clarence Dunning, left him all the bucks in the world. He was in this for the thrills. That's what worried Lonnie.

CHAPTER THIRTY-ONE

Matt felt rage bubble up when the funeral service began. Like water in a pot over a flame, his anger surged while the service progressed. He fought to control his temper, but the unresolved questions about Susan's death picked at his brain. Instead of mourning, he focused on revenge.

Rubio Gonzales' name cycled through his head. The man—or one of his minions—surely had a motive, Matt thought. But, he couldn't reconcile Gonzales killing Susan just because she had worked with Save the Kids. Sure she'd harassed him, been a pain in the neck. But so had a dozen other volunteers, according to Renee. There had never been an assault on any of the Save the Kids' people before. There was something bigger involved and Matt thought a hoodlum like Rubio Gonzales had been too low on the totem pole to be the brains behind whatever it was. No crime *capo* would have been in that Trans Am, so close to the action.

Until last night, he'd vacillated between the anger that went with believing someone had murdered Susan and the depression over the lingering possibility she had committed suicide. The attempt to kill him and Renee had resolved the issue; had obliterated the possibility of suicide in his mind. There's a connection between yesterday's attack and Susan's death, he told himself. But what connection? The attack had only raised more questions.

Matt looked around at the small group gathered in the funeral home's chapel. Only a couple dozen mourners. Not much of a tribute to a woman like Susan, he thought. Mostly Save the Kids volunteers and members of families Susan had helped, according to Renee. No Robert. No law firm employees.

Renee stood at his side and dabbed at her eyes with a Kleenex. Matt put an arm around her as he stared at Doris Sutherland, the waitress from Mori's, and her daughter, Amy, standing in a corner. Besides the undertaker, William Cleary, and another man from the funeral home, he didn't recognize any of the other people.

When Cleary handed him the urn with Susan's ashes, a lump closed Matt's throat and his heart felt as though it were drained of blood. But the feeling passed quickly. There wasn't enough room inside him for anger, revenge, *and* mourning.

People murmured regrets as they filed past Matt. Several told him how his sister had saved their children's lives. No one mentioned the word "suicide." Amy Sutherland came over to Matt with another young girl in tow. She introduced the girl as 'my friend, Sissy.'

Amy's hair was now more blue than purple. But her face lacked the garish makeup she'd worn the last time Matt saw her at the Sutherland home. A long, prim dress had replaced the tight short-shorts and tank top she'd worn then.

Amy looked down at the floor and shifted her feet. "We loved Susan," she said. Sissy stood next to Amy and held her hand. Then Amy looked up. "You know Susan saved Sissy, too." Sissy nodded.

Matt shuddered at the thought of these adolescents servicing grown men in seedy hotel rooms, alleys, and the backseats of cars. The images of such perversions scrolled through his mind and stoked the anger already there, which now threatened to blow like a volcanic eruption. He saw the sudden fear in Amy's eyes and realized his emotions must show on his face. He smiled down at her and put his hands on her shoulders. "Thanks, honey," he said.

Amy let go of Sissy's hand, put her arms around Matt's waist, and buried her face in his chest. Then Sissy hugged him, too. The two girls cried. Matt couldn't hold back his own tears.

Then the girls released him and walked out into the brilliant sunshine that showed through the open chapel doors.

Matt watched them walk away, then turned to Renee, who

walked to him. She took Matt's face in her hands, and surprised him with a kiss on his lips. He wrapped an arm around her shoulders and they walked toward the open doors together.

The sky was cloudless, except for a few wisps of white over the mountains. A middle-aged woman outside stepped toward Matt, then stopped, seeming to hold back. She met his gaze, then glanced away as he and Renee walked down a path to the street.

Then the woman seemed to overcome her hesitation. "Do you have a minute?" she whispered as they passed by.

Matt stopped. The woman twisted a handkerchief in her hands. Her voice had sounded strained. She wore a plain black silk suit, appeared to be about fifty, and fell somewhere between stylish and matronly. Her strawberry blond hair was cut in a bob and framed her face like two parentheses.

"Sure," Matt said.

The woman stepped forward and extended her hand. "I'm Jean Nelson, the head of human resources at Susan's law firm."

Matt took her hand.

"Thank you for coming, Ms. Nelson," Matt said. "I hope it didn't put the firm out sending you as its one and only representative." Renee's hand tightened on his arm, but he didn't let that slow him down. "It would have been nice if you'd bothered to come inside during the service."

The woman's face reddened and her eyes performed a little dance, avoiding his face. "I'm sorry, but we were told—"

"You were told what, Ms. Nelson?" Matt demanded.

She waved off Matt's question. "Oh, nothing." She handed him a business card and said in a shaky voice, "You can reach me at that number. Susan had a 401-K account and a life insurance policy through the firm. I'll be happy to work with you to settle everything."

Matt watched her flee down the path to the car she'd left parked at the curb.

"Little hard on her, weren't you?" Renee said.

"I guess so," Matt said as he watched the Nelson woman drive away. "But think about it. One person from the law firm shows up at the funeral of a twenty-year employee."

At Matt's rental van, they found Callahan leaning against the front passenger-side door.

Matt, surprised to find the cop there, gave Callahan a questioning look.

Callahan pushed off the van. "Head all right?" he asked and pointed at Matt's forehead.

Matt's hand seemed to move on its own to touch the bandage. "Fine. Thanks for asking. And thanks for coming. Anything more about those men who tried to kill us last night?"

Callahan looked out through hooded lids and pulled on an ear. He seemed to think twice before answering. "Hell, the media's already got the information. The three men in the car all had criminal records going back years. We've got several unsolved murder cases in which one or more of them figured as suspects. But we could never prove anything."

Renee scowled. "That's it?"

"You were right," Callahan said. "One of them was Rubio Gonzales."

"What a revelation!" Renee said.

Callahan shrugged. "Do either of you have any thoughts about why they would have tried to kill you?"

Matt didn't even try to keep sarcasm out of his voice. "Do you think maybe it had something to do with my sister's death?"

Callahan's face turned red. He looked away from Matt, dug in his jacket pocket for a notebook. "Can you give me all your numbers in Arizona in case I need to talk to you?"

"Jeez, Callahan. It's New Mexico, not Arizona. And I'm not returning to New Mexico just yet."

"Oh."

Matt wondered at the sudden chagrin—eyes closed, lips pressed together—that suddenly showed on Callahan's face.

"After last night," Callahan said, "I would think you'd want to leave the islands as quickly as possible."

"You don't know me very well," Matt said. He gave Callahan his office phone number and email address; watched him write them down.

Callahan nodded and narrowed his eyes. Then he walked away.

After Callahan drive off, Matt turned to Renee. The muscles in her face were rigid.

"Let's get out of here," Matt said. When he reached to take her hand he realized he still held Jean Nelson's business card. He looked at it: Jean Nelson, Director of Human Resources, Rawson, Wong & Ballard, Attorneys at Law.

CHAPTER THIRTY-TWO

"I invited an old friend of mine to meet me at your home tonight," Matt said on the drive back to Renee's. "I hope you don't mind."

"Of course not," she said. "Who is he?"

"An old Army buddy. Haven't seen him in years."

"I was surprised when you told Callahan you weren't leaving right away," Renee said after a moment of silence. "What changed your mind?"

Matt looked at her for a couple seconds. "A couple reasons. You were right when you got on my butt about not leaving," he said. "About not letting the cops write off Susan's death as a suicide. But as long as there was nothing to really convince me Susan had been murdered, I couldn't justify staying. Even with everything I'd heard about Rubio Gonzales and his possible connection to my sister's death. But after last night . . . ."

"You said a couple reasons," she said.

He felt his face warm. "I decided I wouldn't leave until we went dancing again."

Renee blushed. "Dancing, huh."

Matt glanced at her and thought he saw suspicion in her expression.

"Tell me about this friend who you invited over tonight," Renee asked.

"Just an old Army buddy I haven't seen in decades. Guy named

Esteban Maldonado."

Matt looked straight ahead and was grateful she didn't ask anything else. He didn't know how to tell her what he had in mind without worrying her. As he headed the van up the drive toward her house, he felt a twinge of conscience about not having been wholly candid. But he rationalized his motive was honorable. He wanted to protect her, without frightening her. Those men in the Pontiac last night might have been after him, but Matt didn't think so. Something told him that Renee was their target. He had just been in the wrong place at the wrong time.

He parked at her house and she reached for the car's door handle. He touched her arm. "Hold up a second."

Renee twisted in the seat to look at him.

"Something strange is going on," he said.

She huffed a loud sigh. "That's the understatement of the century."

"Yeah, I know. But whatever it is, I can't figure it out. There's no question your life's in danger. Whoever sent those men after you last night might try again."

"It's not *whoever*," she said. "It was Rubio Gonzales. He's dead now. It's over."

Matt knew he was acting paranoid, but he'd learned over the years not to ignore his instincts. He somehow knew that Susan's death and last night's attack had to be more than mere revenge against Save the Kids.

"I don't buy it," he said. "Why murder a woman who pulls kids off the street. There are new runaways every day. Why not just rough up a few people at Save the Kids? Scare them off. And why Susan? Why you? What about all the other volunteers? There's got to be something else involved."

"Like what?"

"Like big money."

"And what's that got to do with Susan and me?"

"Hell, I don't know," Matt said, exasperation etching his words. "But I don't think you should be alone."

Her hands clutched the skirt of her dress and her face went pale. Then she seemed to make a valiant effort to smile. "That's the most underhanded way I've ever heard any man try to get into a woman's house."

Matt decided to play along, although he wasn't feeling playful. "I had to give it the old college try," he said.

Renee laughed and touched his hand. "I was just about to ask you to stay here anyway. This house is enormous. No point in you paying for a hotel room."

"I should confess something else," Matt said. "The old friend coming here this evening is part of my plan to protect you."

Renee looked sidelong at him. "You're really worried, aren't you?"

"Yeah. I've got a feeling I haven't had in decades. The circumstance of Susan's death smells to high heaven. If we hadn't gotten lucky last night, it would have been our bodies in the ocean, not Gonzales and his men. I've got so many questions, my head's spinning."

"Like what?" she asked.

"Give me time to think about them. When Esteban gets here, we can all sit down and hash it out."

She got out of the car and walked to the front entrance. Lily opened the front door before Renee could use her key.

"Thanks, Lily," Renee said. Her voice now sounded very tired. "Doctor Curtis will be our guest for several days." Renee turned to Matt. "Why don't you give Lily the key to your hotel room? She'll arrange to have your things brought to the house."

Matt watched Renee pat Lily on the shoulder and walk past her into the foyer. As he followed, he noticed the sudden change in Renee's posture. He quickly walked over and put an arm around her slumped shoulders. "You okay?" he asked.

Renee turned her head and smiled. She touched his face with her fingertips. "No. But I will be." She kissed him on the cheek. "Thanks for noticing. I just need some time to catch my breath."

Then Matt saw her jaw jut out and the muscles in her cheeks twitch. She clenched her fists.

"I'll tell you one thing, Matt. Whoever was responsible for my son and Susan's deaths, he won't be as lucky with me." She made an obvious effort to stand erect and walked up the staircase to the second floor.

Matt heard the sound of the front door close behind him and looked around at Lily.

"Poor woman," Lily said. "Too much pain for one person to handle alone. And now Miss Susan. They were such good friends."

CHAPTER THIRTY-THREE

Although the direct route from Lonnie's office to the Island Garmentwear factory took twenty minutes at the posted speed limit, the circuitous route Lonnie followed took almost an hour. His driver/bodyguard switched cars once inside a high-rise parking structure. Twice, the driver doubled back to make sure they weren't followed. Lonnie knew he'd lived as long as he had because he always exercised extreme caution.

The final ploy, to shake off any tail, was to go into a small Chinese restaurant that shared a wall with the factory. After he and his bodyguard entered the restaurant, he went to the kitchen, input a code into a keypad, disabled the alarm, and unlocked a metal-clad door. His bodyguard remained inside the restaurant while Lonnie slipped through into the adjacent factory.

The factory's large warehouse wing buzzed with activity. Men moved a bolt of cloth from one of the trucks and placed it on a wheeled metal table as long as a tanker truck. Lonnie watched one of them use a hammer and wedge to knock hubcap-sized metal covers off both ends of the bolt. The man used grippers—an oversized pliers-like tool—to reach deep inside one end of the bolt and yank out two wood struts inside the core. He did the same from the other side of the core.

Another man took a long pole with a leather pad shaped like a large tin can attached to one end and carefully inserted it into the core. He looked like an artilleryman ramming a charge into a cannon barrel. Four men stood at the opposite end of the cloth bolt. One held a flashlight and stared intently into the cylinder. The other three waited in single file behind him.

Lonnie stood on a bench behind the line of men and looked over the tops of their heads. The first man set the flashlight aside. Lonnie's heart hammered in his chest when a tape-wrapped bundle fell into the man's hands. The package would be worth one hundred thousand dollars on Honolulu's streets. Lonnie rubbed his hands together and watched the worker carry the bundle over to a stainless steel counter. The second man in line took his place at the end of the cylinder. He, too, caught a similar-sized package. By the time the last man carried off his bundle, the first man had returned to start the process all over again. Twenty packages were ultimately extracted from the bolt of cloth's core.

After all the cores were emptied, six hundred packages of uncut heroin lay piled three feet deep on the stainless steel counter. A street value of sixty million dollars. His chemist had tested the first thirteen packages and reported them pure. Lonnie ordered the chemist to finish all the packages as quickly as possible.

Lonnie walked around the warehouse and surveyed the operation. He returned to the cloth bolt the men then worked on and watched them wedge the wood support pieces back into the cylinder core and recap the ends. They wheeled the bolt of cloth out of the warehouse and into the Island Garmentwear factory next door, where ninety seamstresses—many of whom were illegals from mainland China and the Philippines—would turn the cloth into dresses.

Confident that things were under control at the warehouse, Lonnie went out the back door through the Chinese restaurant. While his driver checked the sidewalk to make sure there was no threat, Lonnie decided he had to do something, once and for all, about the Drummond woman. She remained a loose end he couldn't afford. A threat to him and Johnny.

CHAPTER THIRTY-FOUR

Matt buzzed Esteban through the gate at sunset. He waited at the front door as a beat-up, old Chevy pickup skidded to a stop beside the fountain. The end of a surfboard stuck out over the closed tailgate. Matt walked down the two steps to the drive. He immediately recognized Esteban, despite the years that had passed, when his old friend stepped from the truck's cab. Though he was heavier and now sported a beard, there was no question it was Esteban. He'd put on thirty or forty pounds since Matt had last seen him, but the extra weight looked solid on his six-foot, five-inch frame. Esteban used to be lean and strong, Matt thought. Now he looked forbidding—World Wrestling Federation material. His hair, now gray, was pulled back in a long ponytail. His mustache and beard were gray, too.

Esteban looked up at the Drummond house and shook his head, as though in amazement, then walked toward Matt. He stopped and stared with coal black eyes. Then he stepped forward, let out a joyous bellow, and wrapped Matt in a bear hug that lifted him off his feet.

Matt roared at his friend's exuberant hello, despite thinking his ribs might break at any moment, and gasped for air.

Esteban put Matt back down. "I can't believe it. After all these years. *Compadre! Mi compa!*"

"*Tantos anos*, Esteban," Matt said and punched his friend's arm.

"Too long," Esteban agreed. He gripped Matt's shoulder as they entered the house.

Renee stood in the foyer.

"And who is this little lady?" Esteban asked. His voice reverberated off the walls like an unmufflered engine.

"This little lady, as you put it, is the mistress of this grand house—our hostess. Esteban Maldonado, meet Renee Drummond."

Esteban stepped forward and engulfed Renee's hand in one of his. He bowed and touched his lips to the back of her hand. "*Encantado, Bella.*"

"Oh my," Renee said. "There are refreshments out on the patio. Why don't you two go there and catch up on old times?"

"Only if you join us," Esteban said as he took Renee's hand and hooked it over his arm. He looked back over his shoulder and winked at Matt.

It took Matt and Esteban an hour to catch up. Esteban laughed at Matt's surprise that he now owned six surf shops on the islands. Renee shuttled drinks and snacks for them.

"What's the matter, Matt? Don't I look like an entrepreneur?"

Matt chuckled. "No, it's not that. I just wondered what it must be like to work for you. What do you do to an employee who screws up? Threaten to shoot him?"

Esteban pushed out his lower lip. "Now that's cold. I've mellowed. I am an enlightened employer. When one of my people makes a mistake, I merely explain to him the error of his ways."

"Yeah, and what if he fouls up again?" Matt asked.

"*Then* I shoot him."

Renee came out of the house with a tray with two more beers and another platter of snacks on it. "Whose shooting who?" she asked as she placed the tray on the table.

Matt laughed and waved a hand at Esteban. "It was just a joke."

"Oh," she said. "When would you like me to put on the steaks?"

Matt stood and took her hand. "Why don't you sit with us? Relax for a minute."

"No, no. You boys want to talk about old times."

"Please, Renee, join us," Esteban said.

She sat down, then popped up again. "I forgot the wine."

"Oh no you don't," Matt said. He stood. "I'll get it. You sit. Stay here and listen to Esteban's lies. Lily can show me where to find the wine."

"She's not here. Her son picked her up. I called the hotel. They drove over to get your things."

"Well, I'll just have to find the wine all by myself."

"Having a good time catching up?" Renee asked.

"You bet," Esteban answered. "I can't tell you how happy I am to see Matt again. I've thought of him every day for the past thirty years."

Esteban saw the skeptical, wide-eyed look on Renee's face. "When a man saves your life, you think about him every day. I wouldn't be here today if it weren't for Matt."

"My God," Renee said. "What happened?"

Esteban hesitated. He heaved a giant sigh, suddenly uncomfortable. Combat conversations with someone who'd never been there made him uncomfortable. But, he'd seen the way this woman looked at Matt. It was obvious she cared for his friend. He sighed again.

"It was 1986. The United States sent Special Operations units into Bolivia to assist the government there to combat drug cartels. We were at a Bolivian Army base camp on a training mission." He made air quotes with his fingers. "Suddenly, everything was chaos. We got hit with rockets and automatic weapons one night by what must have been a coupla' hundred men. A drug cartel army. Against fifty of us—forty-three Bolivian soldiers and seven Green Berets."

"You and Matt were Green Berets?" Renee said.

Esteban nodded. "We lost half our men in the first thirty minutes. Then they sent in men who blew up our perimeter gun emplacements and came through the fence."

Esteban took in a slow, deep breath. He then loudly exhaled and stared out toward the ocean. He swigged his beer, finishing off half the bottle, and finally turned back toward Renee.

"Some of us were able to fall back into a bunker complex on the far side of the camp and set up a defense. Couldn't get air support because of the weather. I ended up alone at one end of the bunker, about twenty yards away from the others. The cartel's soldiers looked like ghosts as they slipped in and out of the light from our flares. They bayoneted our wounded out on the perimeter. They yelped like hyenas every time they finished one off."

Tears sprang to Renee's eyes, but she did nothing about them, just let them glide down her cheeks.

"When another one of our flares went off, I saw one of the Bolivian soldiers on the ground, fifty feet from my position. He was covered with blood and tried to crawl toward us. Then a bad guy went after him. I sprayed the bastard with a burst from my rifle, but there were more behind him. I ran out to get the wounded guy. Hoisted him to my shoulder. That's when I took a round in the back and another in my left leg. I fell to the ground with the soldier mostly on top of me, rolled over, and turned toward the enemy. I had about half a clip in my rifle and a spare on my belt. I took out as many of the enemy as I could—slowed them down for a while. But I knew I'd bought the farm. I couldn't kill all of them and, with my leg broken, knew I couldn't crawl out of there fast enough.

"Then Matt was there. How the hell he got to us without being shot, only God knows. He gave me his rifle, grabbed the Bolivian soldier, and dragged him to the bunker. Then he came back for me."

Renee's eyes widened.

"He was just a skinny kid then," Esteban continued. "Couldn't have weighed more than a hundred fifty pounds with full pack and soaking wet." He laughed, but it caught in his throat. Esteban coughed; got control of his voice. "Matt hefted me onto his shoulder and carried me out of there. I weighed at least two hundred then. To this day I can't believe Matt could have done it. By the time he dumped me in the bunker, he'd taken three rounds in the back."

Renee's hand shot to her mouth.

Esteban stood and walked to the edge of the patio. He stared at the starlit black nothingness of the Pacific sky. "The weather had suddenly cleared," he said. "If the jet jockeys hadn't showed up at that moment and dumped ordnance all over the cartel soldiers, neither of us would be here now."

Renee looked at Esteban through tear-glistened eyes. "Thanks," she whispered.

"*De nada,*" he said.

Just then Matt came back outside, wineglass and bottle in hand.

"Lily and her son just brought my stuff," he said. "She was madder than hell when I told her to take a couple days off. You need to go in and smooth her feathers. She said she only takes orders from you. I don't think it's a good idea for her to be here, at least until we straighten out this . . . business."

Renee rose and kissed him on the lips, then left the two men.

Matt frowned at Esteban. "What?" he said.

Esteban shrugged. "Women! Go figure."

CHAPTER THIRTY-FIVE

Esteban patted his stomach. "Whew!" he said. "I shoulda stopped after the steak. That blueberry pie did me in."

"The first piece or the second," Matt said, then laughed.

"I'll let Lily know how much you enjoyed it," Renee said.

Esteban produced two cigars, and soon the cool night air was pungent with the odor of tobacco smoke.

"So, *amigo*, what's the deal?" Esteban asked Matt. "You suddenly show up in Hawaii and wind up in a mansion with a gorgeous woman who is obviously too good for you. What's on your mind?"

Matt looked at Renee. She smiled back, as though to encourage him. Then he turned back to Esteban. "It's complicated," he said. "You want another drink before I get started?"

Esteban shook his head and sat up straighter in his chair. "You sound kinda serious, Matthew. I think I'll hold off on the booze."

"The reason I'm in Hawaii is that my sister died here. The funeral service was this afternoon."

"*Madre de Dios!*"

"The detective in charge of the case thinks it was suicide, but I don't buy it for a second. I think she was murdered." Matt placed his cigar in an ashtray, leaned his elbows on the table, and steepled his fingers. "I'd be lying if I told you I wasn't confused. But I got that old familiar feeling, like there's bad guys on the other side of the fence. I need to spend some time figuring it out, but first I want to make sure Renee is safe."

"Safe from what?" Esteban asked.

"Some guys tried to kill us last night on the road in front of the house. They tried to ram us off the road, over the cliff. One of the men in the car was a pimp named Rubio Gonzales. "

"Rubio Gonzales!" Esteban exclaimed and choked on cigar smoke. His mouth turned down as though he'd tasted something sour. "Why would that bum want to kill you?"

"I run a group called Save the Kids," Renee explained. "We rescue runaways from the streets. We take kids away from the pimps and druggies and return them to their parents. Get them into rehab. Some of those kids hooked for Gonzales's organization. Maybe he wanted me out of his hair."

"That doesn't make any sense," Esteban mused as he waved a hand through the air as though discarding Renee's conclusion. "I don't—"

"How do you know about this Gonzales?" Matt interrupted.

Esteban blinked. "I wasn't always Mister Entrepreneur," he said. "Where I come from, guys like Rubio Gonzales were the role models. I remember Rubio when he was a punk kid. He was a bagman for the local numbers runner. That's the most benign thing he ever did."

Esteban turned to Renee and, in a soft tone, said, "Renee, what you said just doesn't make sense. Gonzales is the worst kind of scum. But he ain't stupid. I don't see him putting out a hit on you because you rescue kids. Even if those kids worked for him. Even a pimp knows better than to retaliate against someone like you. He bumps off solid citizens; it just brings more heat from the cops."

Esteban stuck his cigar in his mouth, drew on it, and blew out a smoke cloud. Then he stubbed the cigar in the ashtray, put his hands behind his head, and stared at the sky. "From what I hear," he said, "Rubio is part of a large crime ring. Prostitution is only a minor part of the operation. I don't see Rubio as Mister Big. There's something missing from this picture."

"My thought exactly," Matt said. "But one clarification. Gonzales doesn't work for anyone anymore. He's dead. He and two of his buddies were the ones who went over the cliff last night."

Esteban looked from Matt to Renee. "You two did that?"

Renee demurely lowered her head. Matt nodded.

"Jeez Louise," Esteban said. "Now I understand why you want Renee protected. Rubio's men won't let this go without payback."

"That's what I figured," Matt said as he reached over and patted Renee's hand. "Esteban," he said, "what else do you know about Gonzales?"

"Like me, he grew up down by the docks. Rubio was just a kid—maybe twelve, thirteen—when I got drafted. But he was already in trouble. A lot of the guys I grew up with still live in the old neighborhood. Those who weren't killed or are in jail. I heard things about Rubio after I came back to Hawaii. He had moved up in the local crime organization."

"You said you didn't think Gonzales was the boss," Matt said. "Do you know who is?"

"I don't think anyone is really sure. You hear names every once in a while, but I think they're just second-level guys. Organized crime in the islands isn't your typical Gambino Family. That may be because we're so far from the mainland; but I think it's more because whoever runs the show here is a different sort of animal."

"How so?" Renee asked.

"I hear things. Like the local crime organization is more like a secret society than a crime family. None of the leaders go out of their way to get public attention. Unlike the New York Dons, the local guys keep a low profile. And I've heard that their influence among the law enforcement community and the judges is huge."

"Anything else?" Matt asked.

"Not really. Just what you read in the papers, which ain't much. Now it's your turn. What makes you think your sister was murdered?"

Matt said, "The cops say my sister killed herself by jumping from her apartment balcony. Then the coroner discovered she had a lethal dose of drugs in her system, enough Rohypnol to kill her ten times over. Susan would never have used drugs. Rohypnol? Give me a break!

"That's odd enough. But Susan's boyfriend of eight years, a guy named Robert Nakamura, lives here in Hawaii. But I haven't heard from him. He didn't even show up at her funeral."

"You think he had something to do with your sister's death?" Esteban asked.

Matt pinched the bridge of his nose and closed his eyes. After a moment, he opened his eyes and shook his head. "Hell, I don't know. I don't know a damn thing. Except, I don't believe Susan would have taken her own life." Matt opened his hands and spread his arms in a helpless gesture. "Do you know that only one employee from the law firm where Susan worked for years showed up at the service? I don't get that either."

"What law firm?" Esteban asked.

"Rawson, Wong & something."

"Rawson, Wong & Ballard," Renee said.

"The big boys," Esteban commented.

Matt pulled several business cards from his wallet. He held them up to the light and shuffled through them. He replaced Callahan's card and then glanced at the condo manager, Gabe Muccio's card, and put it back in his wallet, too. He read Jean Nelson's card and passed it to Esteban. "Jean Nelson is the only one who came to the funeral. And that was only to tell me to call her about closing out Susan's retirement account and insurance policy."

Esteban stroked his beard. "Mighty strange," he said.

Something spiked in Matt's memory. He shuffled through the other cards from his shirt pocket and picked out the one Gabe Muccio had given him. He remembered that Muccio had written an attorney's name and number on the back. He held out his hand to Esteban. "Let me see Jean Nelson's card again."

Esteban passed the card back.

Matt laid Muccio's card upside-down next to Nelson's card. "Well, I'll be damned," he said. "The telephone numbers are the same. The lawyer who Susan's condominium manager referred me to must work for the same law firm." He handed both cards to Renee.

"John Dunning," she read. "Lots of money and top connections. I know his mother. High society. I hear John is rising fast at the law firm."

158

CHAPTER THIRTY-SIX

Nathan Ballard tried to ignore the party noises that came from his backyard. The music, the voices, the occasional high-pitched laugh or raucous shout of one of the hundred or so guests. His headaches now came more frequently and the noise didn't help. He sat behind his home office desk and stared at framed photographs on a nearby bookcase. He knew that no one out there would notice his absence, especially his wife, who had insisted on hosting yet another party for her socialite friends.

He looked at a photo of his daughter and him at her wedding five years ago and thought, God, I've aged. Then he'd had just a touch of gray. Now his hair was completely white. And he'd put on at least twenty pounds. He grabbed a chunk of his belly in two hands and squeezed. He dropped the stomach lard and let it settle back over his belt.

Ballard turned and looked through the large window inset in the wall behind him and inhaled deeply while he stared at the view of his expansive back yard and the ocean beyond. Ballard loved this room, his only sanctuary in the eight thousand square foot house his wife had insisted she couldn't live without. The office had Chinese silk carpets on hardwood floors. Tall bookcases lined three walls.

"Should have divorced the bitch," he said. "Would have been cheaper." He looked at the Rolex on his wrist: 10:30 p.m. Jackson's man should be here any minute.

Ballard covered his ears with his hands to try to shut out the noise of the fifteen-piece orchestra. It was no use. The party roared on full force under the tent out on the back lawn. The noise was like poison gas. It seeped into the house and polluted his peace of mind.

"We've got a fucking mansion here," he said, "and she rents a tent big enough for a circus. Two thousand bucks for a tent—for one night! And the orchestra, too. Another five grand."

He lifted his glass off his desk, drained the twenty-five-year-old single malt scotch, then chewed on the remains of an ice cube. "I can't believe my life. What a mess! How did I let this happen?" He had only his own secret weakness to blame. He'd kept it hidden for almost all his adult life. But it was no longer *his* secret alone. Now Lonnie Jackson was on him like a buzzard on carrion. That gangster had video. Ballard knew his wife's pathological need to spend his money only made things worse. He felt trapped from all sides. And, on top of everything else, he was aware he talked to himself a lot lately.

Ballard shuddered. He felt the frosty hand of fear grip the base of his neck. The fear was always with him now. Why had he let it happen? Just a moment of weakness, really. He'd always had the longing. But he'd disciplined himself his whole life, because he knew the desire, if given in to, could ruin everything. So he'd suppressed it, and he'd been proud of his ability to do so. Made him feel strong. As long as his yearnings went unfulfilled, he took comfort in the illusion he was normal. But one weak moment, that's all it took. One damn drink too many. One mistake. One time with that twelve-year-old boy. And a video camera he never even knew was there.

Ballard rubbed his temples and tried to will his headache away. He once again remembered the meeting with Jackson two years ago and perspired despite the coolness of the room. Jackson had sounded so reasonable, at first; been so soft-spoken.

"I would like you to do me a favor," Jackson had said, after he'd handed over a copy of the video. "There's this young man graduating from Yale Law. He'd make a great addition to your firm."

The Dunning kid had turned out to be a real surprise. Top of his class. Well spoken. Great family connections. Movie star-handsome. Ballard would have hired him without Jackson's "suggestion." There were no objections from any of the partners, either. A couple months later, however, Jackson called again. It was just a small favor. A conversation with a judge who had been one of Ballard's law partners before his appointment to the bench. And, once more, Ballard knew he had no choice.

He did what Jackson asked the second time. And many times after that. The money Jackson fed to the firm—and to Ballard under the table—had become a lifesaver. His wife's spending was like a bucket with a hole in the bottom. Ballard kept filling the bucket with cash but she spent it faster.

Ballard twitched at the polite knock on his study door. "Come in," he called out. The butler stepped into the room.

"Sir, there's a Mister Marcum at the front. He claims to have an appointment with you."

"Thank you, Franklin. Send him in."

"Will you require a beverage for your guest?"

"No, that won't be necessary. He'll only be here for a minute or two."

"Very well, sir."

After the butler left the room, Ballard screwed up his face and mimicked him aloud. "Very well, sir. I am an authentic English butler. Something else my wife can't live without. At a hundred grand a year. Will that be *all*, sir?"

"You talking to someone?"

A man stood in the doorway.

"Just myself," Ballard said.

"Gotta watch that," the man said, his face a humorless mask, as he crossed the room.

He was well-dressed, as though he'd stepped from the pages of GQ. White shirt, dark-red tie, blue-black blazer, gray slacks, tasseled Italian loafers. He seemed unimpressed with the opulence of Ballard's room. Some men's jaws had dropped when they'd entered the room. Not this guy. He could well have entered a car wash.

The man had an animal-like quality. The way he walked, the way he never took his pale blue eyes off Ballard's eyes. He seemed in perfect balance, within himself and with his surroundings. Predator-like.

He stopped in front of the desk and swung a briefcase on top of it. "My employer wishes to once again express his thanks for your assistance. It's extremely important your firm continues to work for him in his many ventures. And he understands the role you play as managing partner to ensure the continuation of that representation. He appreciates your help."

Nice little speech, Ballard thought. What a bunch of bullshit! Even if Jackson didn't pay him a dime, Ballard would still have to perform like a trained seal. What choice did he have? The money was just a courtesy. Extra insurance.

Ballard breathed in through clenched teeth and made a hissing sound. "Please pass on my thanks to . . . your employer," he said, barely able to get the words out.

The man took a step to leave, but turned back. "Oh, I almost forgot. Mister Jackson feels it would be a very nice gesture for the firm to make John Dunning a partner."

Ballard jerked forward and put his hands flat on the desktop. He half rose from his chair and stared at the man. "That's impossible! We have policies about tenure . . . . The other partners . . . ."

The man just smiled back through sparkling clenched teeth.

Ballard dropped back into his chair. At the same time the acid hit his stomach, he thought, Of course it's not impossible. Nothing's impossible. "John Dunning will be made a partner at the next board meeting," he muttered.

The man turned and walked across the length of the room, opened the door, and padded out.

Ballard opened a desk drawer and removed a bottle of liquid, milky-white antacid. He took a pull on the bottle, then wiped his mouth with the back of his hand. He recapped the bottle, replaced it, and shut the drawer, finding the act almost too much for his energy-depleted body. He had become familiar with this feeling, with how his perpetual state of fear affected him. Mind-numbing, gut-wrenching.

He used the desk for support, stood—shoulders slumped, and moved to the other side. He popped open the briefcase and stared down at twelve six-inch high stacks of cash. Then Ballard walked to the bookcase and removed five leather-bound books from a shelf, reached into the space, and dialed the wall safe's combination. He had to make three trips from the briefcase to the safe. After he locked the safe, he replaced the books, put on his party face, and walked outside to join his wife and her friends.

CHAPTER THIRTY-SEVEN

Dennis Callahan paced back and forth along a crushed-shell path that meandered through palm trees. The path ran from a parking lot thirty yards away and dropped steadily to the edge of a sandy beach. He listened to the sound of waves lapping against the shore and the fluttering wings of bats. Through the trees he saw moonlight reflect on dark Pacific waters. He flicked his cigarette butt at a palm tree trunk and watched red embers explode and die. Callahan checked his watch, then lit another Camel and renewed his pacing. He hated standing near this deserted beach, feeling like a lackey—at Lonnie Jackson's beck and call. And he was fearful someone might come along and see him meet with the mobster.

At ten minutes past midnight, Jackson still hadn't arrived. I'll give him another five minutes, then I'm out of here, Callahan thought as he felt more and more irritable and vulnerable by the second.

A sudden stab of light bounced off the trees. The noise of tires crunched over sand that dusted the parking lot and sounded to Callahan like a thousand little explosions. He didn't recognize the shiny white Lincoln Continental, but that wasn't unusual. Jackson seemed to change cars like most men change underwear. He walked up to the edge of the lot as the car eased to a halt in front of him.

A Sumo-sized Hawaiian got out from behind the wheel, stepped around the front of the car through the glare of the headlights, and stopped by the right front tire, ten yards away. Callahan met the man's stare. He wasn't about to let some steroid-popping low-life intimidate him. But the sound of a car window opening diverted his attention. He glanced to his left. Lonnie Jackson stared grimly at him from the dimly lit interior. His face glowed in moonlight.

"How's it going, Denny? You look worried. Whatsamatter, you afraid of muggers?"

Callahan took a deep drag on his cigarette and used the time to control his anger.

Jackson let out a short laugh. "Is that it, Denny, you're afraid of muggers?"

"Muggers, my ass," Callahan growled. "Think about it, Lonnie," he said, after he sent a stream of smoke from his lungs into the damp night air. "I'm on a beach at midnight with public enemy number one. The DEA, FBI, Honolulu Narcotics Division, State Police, and the Hawaiian Organized Crime Task Force could have us under surveillance right now. I'm not afraid; I'm scared shitless."

Jackson pounded his fist on the car door and laughed as though Callahan had told the funniest joke in the world. "You crack me up," he said. "You think I'd let someone follow me? Come on, give me a little credit. Besides, no one's got a thing on me."

"You called this meeting, Lonnie. What's on your mind?"

"Now, now, Denny. Let's not get snippy. Can't I get together with an old friend once in a while?"

Callahan felt sick. He knew Jackson loved to play with him, and there was not a thing he could do about it. He waited for him to get to the point.

"Tell me about this Curtis guy."

Callahan crushed his cigarette underfoot, then looked back at Lonnie. "That's what you wanted to talk to me about? That's why I'm out here on Bumfuck Lane in the middle of the night? The guy's harmless. He's a fuckin' doctor from Arizona, or some such godforsaken place. Came over here to bury his sister. That's all there is to it."

"Yeah, Susan Curtis. The *suicide*."

"Right! He'd like to find out what happened to his sister. He doesn't believe she killed herself. We would have been home free if the damn coroner hadn't found Rohypnol in her system."

"But she *did* kill herself, Callahan. You said you didn't push her off the balcony."

"The hotshot I gave her would have dropped her in less than fifteen minutes. I don't know why she went out to the balcony. Maybe the drugs disoriented her and she just fell."

"I'm concerned," Lonnie said, a cold sharpness in his voice. "Too many loose ends. I don't like it when things get sloppy. I want you to take care of that Drummond woman, and this doctor, too. No more mistakes. No more loose ends."

"Christ, Lonnie. Curtis is a fucking civilian. He'll be out of town in a couple days and we'll never hear from him again. He doesn't have a prayer of finding anything to prove his sister's death was anything but a suicide. He thinks I told the coroner to drag his feet on the autopsy report. I did just the opposite. He'll have his report done tomorrow. It'll be official then. She killed herself, end of story. Curtis will be out of here. I tell you, the guy's harmless."

"Three of my men went after Renee Drummond and your *harmless* doctor and wound up dead."

"You sent idiots. What can you expect?"

"Rubio was no idiot."

Callahan looked down at the ground and rubbed a hand over his face. Then he stared back at Lonnie. "He was no rocket scientist, either."

Jackson stared impassively at the policeman. "You heard me."

"We kill this guy and the Drummond woman and there'll be more heat than you can imagine. I won't be able to cover it up. He's a tourist; she's part of an old-line family. The press will have a field day. You don't want—"

Jackson held up a hand to stop Callahan in mid-sentence. "You don't have a fuckin' clue what I want, Callahan," he said. His voice trembled with rage; his golden eyes eerily highlighted by moonlight. "Except I want them dead." Then his voice became mellow. The words glided over his tongue like melted butter. "You got it? You're a cop. You're handling his sister's case. You have every reason to meet with him. He trusts you. I have no idea what Susan Curtis told that Drummond bitch. But I do know they were best friends.

She must know more than is good for us."

Callahan sighed and hung his head. How much worse can it get, he thought?

Jackson shouted at his driver, "Let's go, Tommy." While the muscle-bound man walked back around the front of the car and opened his door, Jackson leaned his head toward the detective. "Don't fuck up, Denny. You think your life's a mess now? Wait 'til you disappoint me."

CHAPTER THIRTY-EIGHT

Esteban made a dozen phone calls before he located Angelo Caruso, at midnight, at the Twin Coconuts Bar off Waikiki Beach.

"Angelo, you got a phone call," Esteban heard the bartender shout.

Then Angelo's voice: "Take a message. Can't you see I'm busy?"

The bartender again: "I ain't your goddamn secretary, Angelo. It's Esteban."

Esteban heard a noise like a chair being knocked over, then Angelo got on the line.

"You're worse than a damn wife. What the hell you want, *Esse*?" The words were slurred.

"If you're too drunk to drive and I gotta come get you, I'm gonna kick your ass."

Angelo laughed, then burped. "You and what army, you big freak. I ain't met the asshole I can't whup."

"Cut the bullshit, Angelo. I need your help."

"What's wrong, Esteban?" Angelo said, suddenly more alert.

"I'll tell you when you get here. Bring your good-for-nothing brother, too. And don't come empty-handed. You listening, Angelo?"

"Yeah, Esteban."

"Drink some coffee, sober up. Now, put the bartender back on the line."

A sharp noise sounded over the phone, causing Esteban to jerk the receiver away from his ear. When he returned the receiver to his ear, he heard Angelo shout, "Mekeli, he wants to talk to you."

"Yeah, what?" the bartender's voice growled into the phone.

"How drunk is he?"

"I've seen him a lot worse."

"Okay, here's what I want you to do. There's a twenty in it for you. I'll give you the address and directions to a house. After you pour a gallon of coffee into Angelo, pass on my directions to him and tell him to go get Richie. I want their asses up here as soon as possible."

"All right, Esteban. Now what about my twenty?"

"I'll catch you the next time I'm in there. You know I'm good for it."

"Yeah, yeah."

Esteban gave the bartender the directions to Renee's house, repeated them, then hung up the phone. He gave Matt a thumbs-up sign.

Matt frowned. "How drunk is this guy?"

"He's better drunk than most men are sober. He's as good as they come. Angelo and I were in SF together and I did some contract jobs with him and his brother, Richie. Don't worry about the Caruso brothers."

"Contract jobs?"

Esteban waved a hand dismissively. "I'll tell you about that some other time."

Esteban noticed Renee had fallen asleep in a chair. "It'll be a little while before Ange and Richie get here. Why don't you grab some sleep?"

"Thanks, Esteban. But I'm too keyed up to sleep. I'll help Renee upstairs, though. She sat up most of last night keeping an eye on me. She's got to be exhausted."

"Okay. While you're doing that, I'll make the rounds. Check the doors and windows. Get to know the house and grounds."

"Thanks, I really appreciate it. I'm sorry about getting you involved in this. I didn't know where else to turn."

Esteban shook a finger at Matt. "Don't you ever apologize to me for anything, Matt. I would have been pissed beyond belief if I found out you were in trouble and didn't call me."

Matt nodded, then lifted Renee out of her chair. Still asleep, she snuggled against his neck and made a contented sound, like a purring cat.

The Caruso brothers arrived at three-thirty. Matt buzzed them through the gate. Esteban met them at the door and led them into the house.

Richie whistled. "Wow, what is this place?" he said. "It's like a hotel. I seen museums smaller than this."

"You ain't been in a museum in your life," Angelo remarked.

Richie sneered at Angelo. "How the hell would you know?"

"Whoa, guys," Esteban said. "I want you to meet an old friend of mine, Matt Curtis. We served in SF together."

Matt stepped forward and shook hands with both of them. The Carusoes grunted hellos.

"What kind of equipment did you bring," Esteban asked Angelo.

"Probably more than we need." They all walked out to the car. Angelo popped the trunk.

"My God, Ange!" Esteban said. "I expected you to come armed, not prepared for World War Three." Two shotguns, three Armalite rifles, half-a-dozen pistols, camouflage clothing, knives, an unmarked wooden box, and other assorted gear crammed the trunk.

"What's in the box?" Matt asked.

Richie chuckled. "That's a surprise."

Angelo slapped Esteban on the back. "Wanna see our secret weapon?"

Esteban blew out a long sigh. "Yeah, okay Ange," he said.

He followed Angelo to the left rear door. Sitting on its haunches—probably because it was too damned big to stand up on the back seat—was an enormous Rottweiler. It took up most of the rear of the rust-pitted Oldsmobile 98. The dog snarled at Esteban, its lips pulled back to reveal the points of glistening teeth.

"Jeez! Did you have to bring that beast along?" Esteban asked.

"He ain't no beast," Angelo said proudly. "Maximillian is part of the family. You know that. He goes where I go."

Esteban shook his head, too weary to argue. "Leave Max outside.

I don't think the lady of the house would appreciate a dog the size of a Shetland pony roaming around inside."

"You got it, buddy."

"What's up?" Richie asked.

"Let's bring your gear inside," Esteban answered. "I'll brief you there."

"Maybe I'd better make some coffee," Matt said.

"Good idea," Esteban said while he walked back to the trunk.

Esteban helped Richie transfer the gear into the house and pile it against the foyer closet door. They returned to the car to carry in the last of the weaponry when Angelo opened the back door of the Oldsmobile and released the dog.

"Search!" Angelo ordered.

Max vanished into the cover of bushes on the far side of the driveway.

"What's he doing?" Esteban asked.

"Looking for something to kill," Richie said, matter-of-factly.

Esteban arched his eyebrows and gave the Carusoes a questioning look.

Angelo stepped forward and raised his hands, as though to say, It'll be all right.

Esteban shook his head, squinted at Angelo, then led the two brothers inside to the kitchen.

Angelo and Richie each carried a camouflage vest with shotgun shells stuffed in the vests' cartridge loops. Each also had a holstered pistol on his belt. Esteban carried a pistol in a shoulder holster.

"Well, I asked for help," Matt said. "I guess I got what I asked for."

"Sit down, guys," Esteban said. "Matt's got a story to tell you."

Matt repeated for the Carusoes what he'd already told Esteban about Susan's death and the attempt on Renee and his lives.

"So our job's to protect the lady?" Richie said.

"That's it, plain and simple," Matt answered.

"Anybody we should let pass?" Angelo asked.

"Not without a search," Matt answered. "There won't be many visitors. The lady who cleans and cooks won't be around for a few days. Same with the gardener and the pool boy. Renee has no living relatives on the islands."

"Any deliveries expected?" Richie asked.

Matt said, "I don't know. I'll ask Renee when she gets up; let you know."

Richie frowned. "Hope there's a UPS delivery," he said, almost to himself. "I'd love to roust one of them bastards in those ugly brown short-pants uniforms driving those big ugly brown trucks."

Matt stared at Richie, who added nothing.

Matt shrugged, then looked at Angelo. "How much do you get paid?"

Angelo scratched the back of his neck. Then he turned to Esteban. "He's a good friend of yours?" he asked.

Esteban smiled. "The best."

Angelo looked back at Matt. "You get the discounted rate. Thousand bucks a day, for the two of us, room and board, and replacement cost for all expended ammo and any damaged weapons."

Matt nodded.

"Oh," Angelo added with a smile, "we cover our own medical and burial costs."

Matt knew his eyes went wide. "I hope it doesn't come to that."

Angelo shrugged. "You never know."

"Okay, boys," Esteban interjected. "Let's take a stroll around the house and grounds. Get you familiar with everything. I'll take first watch. Angelo second. Richie last. Four hours each." He looked at Matt, waved a hand, and pointed vaguely toward the south end of the house. "I saw a bedroom with two beds at the end of the corridor. If it's okay with Renee, we can take turns sleeping there."

"Should be fine," Matt said.

"What's on your agenda?" Esteban asked Matt.

"I'll fly over to Kauai tomorrow to try to find Muriel Goldstein. According to the records at the Sand & Sea Condominiums, she has a daughter who lives over there. I hope that's where Muriel Goldstein ran to the night Susan died."

"When's your flight?" Esteban asked.

"Noon."

"Did you call to see if this Goldstein woman is there?"

"No. I thought about calling, but decided if she's in hiding, her daughter wouldn't tell me she was there. Of course, I could be wasting my time. But if she *is* there, it would probably spook her if I called. I figure my chances will be better if I just show up." Matt stood up and stretched. The others also stood.

"All right," Esteban said. "Let's do it. I'll show you around."

Matt followed them to the foyer. Angelo and Richie each picked up a shotgun and walked outside. Esteban selected an Armalite AR-15 automatic weapon, ejected the clip, checked the chamber, inspected the clip, and re-inserted it back into the rifle.

"Thanks, *compadre*," Matt said, as Esteban turned toward the front door. "I'll call from Kauai to tell you what I learn."

"Right," Esteban said.

"By the way, what's Richie's thing about UPS?"

Esteban checked to make sure Richie was out of earshot, then looked back at Matt and whispered, "Richie came home one day and found his wife in bed with a UPS deliveryman." Then Esteban walked outside and shut the door behind him.

Matt felt relieved now that reinforcements had arrived. But he also felt bone-tired. He rubbed his eyes. On his way to the staircase he noticed the unmarked wooden carton on the floor, its lid slightly ajar. He peeked inside. Extra ammunition for all the weapons, a dozen grenades, and two Claymore mines.

"God save us!" Matt said under his breath.

DAY SIX

CHAPTER THIRTY-NINE

Shawn Catlett rolled onto his side, switched on the rusted, coil-necked lamp on the orange crate next to his cot, and squinted at the ancient, wind-up alarm clock: 1 a.m. He looked around his room in the basement of the Sand & Sea Condominium building—he had the cot and the wooden crate, a small butcher-block table and two folding chairs discarded by a previous tenant, and a Pullman-sized bathroom with a commode, sink, and shower. The cinderblock walls were sprayed with some sort of insulation that looked like dried-out meringue.

It wasn't much, but he got to stay here for free as long as he worked at the condominium complex. This was the only place he'd ever had of his own. He felt good about it. Proud that he was making it in the world. He shuddered at the thought of losing his job. He knew he had a lot to lose if he was caught in Miss Susan's unit. He shouldn't go up there . . . especially now, he told himself, his mind and his emotions grappling like two snakes in a death struggle. But, in the end, he couldn't stop himself. He just couldn't.

The residents of the Sand & Sea would be tucked into their beds at this late hour. At least, that was his hope. He threw off the blanket and, fully clothed, slipped into the work boots next to his cot. Shawn sucked in deep breaths and tried to ignore his rapidly beating heart. He always felt this way before he snuck up to Miss Susan's apartment, but the compulsion was too strong to ignore.

After he laced his boots, Shawn peeked into the hall outside his room. There were only storage and mechanical rooms along the hall, but he had to be alert for the security guard. That old guy would show up in the most unexpected places at the strangest times. The hall was empty. He tiptoed to the service elevator and pressed the call button. The door popped open almost instantly, startling Shawn.

The elevator car seemed to shake and clatter on the way to the twenty-fourth floor. When it stopped and the door opened, he peeked down the hall, then stepped out. The door eased shut while he tiptoed along the carpeted hallway. He was careful not to make any noise, just like his daddy had taught him years ago when they hunted in Tennessee. Weight on his toes, then the balls of his feet, then to the heels. The closer he came to Miss Susan's door, the more his already thudding heart seemed to hammer at the inside of his chest, as though it wanted to burst free. When he arrived at unit 2408, he rested his palms against the door's smooth surface and felt a warmth invade his hands, travel up his arms, and then through his entire being. He knew he shouldn't linger here in the hall, but this was part of the process, this communing with the places where Miss Susan had been, with the things she had touched. He used his passkey to enter the condominium and shut the door behind him.

Shawn didn't need to turn on any lights. This wasn't the first time he'd been here at night, both before and after Miss Susan had died. Sometimes, while he moved around her home, she'd even been here, asleep in her bed. The memory of those visits made his head ache and his chest heave. In the hall outside her bedroom, he stopped where he knew the photographs hung. He took a penlight from his pocket and shined it on Miss Susan's images. He touched the glass over her face in each of the photos.

Shawn left the pictures and went into the bedroom, where he entered the large walk-in closet, lifted the skirt of a dress hanging there, and pressed it to his face. He inhaled her scent from the garment. The urge to take one of the dresses away with him was powerful, but he knew it would be wrong. Stealing from the dead. Stealing from Miss Susan.

Shawn went into the bathroom next and looked at the perfume

bottles arrayed on the vanity. The delicate glass containers, with their long necks and slender bodies, reminded him of her. He opened one of them and brought it to his nose—lilacs.

His throat felt constricted. He would never again see her leave the building in the morning or return at night. She would never wave to him again. He'd never see her smile. He had scheduled his chores so he would always be near the building's entrance to witness her passage. Every glimpse of her made his life worth living. He stumbled to the queen-sized bed and fell back on it.

The bedroom drapes were open. The just-risen moon cast a pale yellowish glow over the room. Shawn's tears rolled off his face onto the bedspread. "Why'd you have to die?" he sobbed while he pressed his hands against his temples. His chin trembled. "I loved you so much."

CHAPTER FORTY

Gabriel Muccio, manager of the Sand & Sea Condominiums, took his responsibilities seriously, but he was still pissed off about meeting John Dunning on a Sunday, instead of the usual first Monday of the month. He had to ruin his day off just because the silver-spoon-in-mouth, big-shot lawyer needed to go out of town on Monday.

Muccio arrived at his Sand & Sea office at 10 a.m., thirty minutes before the scheduled meeting time. He unlocked his file cabinet and extracted the "DH Ventures, SA" folder. All he knew about DH Ventures was that it was a Netherlands Antilles real estate holding company and that it owned the Sand & Sea Management Company. Dunning was the company's attorney. Muccio tossed the pale blue folder on the center of his desk blotter, dropped into his leather chair, and opened it.

"Lawyers!" he growled. He scratched his crotch and thought about his assistant, Michele, sunbathing without him. That girl twisted his insides into knots; made him scream for mercy. She was the best lay he'd ever had. He couldn't figure how he'd gotten so lucky. Michelle preferred her men middle-aged, dark, and the hairier the better.

Muccio went through the current financial statements and rent schedule, the maintenance log, and the construction progress report and pre-leasing schedule on the second phase of the condominium development. That's what Dunning would want to hear about.

Dunning arrived thirty minutes late, which only aggravated Muccio even more. Especially because there was nothing he could do or say about it. The young lawyer marched into the office as though he owned the place. No hello, or how are you today. Arrogant sonofabitch, Muccio thought. Just a kid; a spoiled mama's boy. Then Muccio wondered how arrogant *he* would be if he had Dunning's money, education, and looks. The guy was a babe magnet.

"You ready to start?" Dunning asked.

Muccio swallowed the bitter lump in his throat. "Yes, sir." He stood up, took the file from his desk, and joined Dunning at the four-seat conference table. He handed the financial statements to the lawyer, and summarized them from his notes. As he always did, Dunning sat without a word and scribbled on a yellow legal pad. Then Muccio passed a copy of the construction progress report to the lawyer. By the time they were finished, two hours had gone by.

"It looks like everything's in order," Dunning said.

"Yes, sir. The existing building is sold out and we're fifty percent pre-sold on the second phase. Place is a cash cow. Except for that poor woman's suicide, everything's great." Muccio paused, waiting for some reaction from Dunning, but the lawyer's face showed zero emotion, as though Susan Curtis's death was no more important than a set of numbers or the weather report. Muccio shrugged. "You can assure the owners that I run a very tight ship."

Dunning smiled. "Yes, it appears you do. I always let them know what a great job you do when I send them my monthly reports." Dunning closed his folio and slid it into his leather briefcase. Then he surprised Muccio. "Any repercussions over the woman's suicide?" he asked as he snapped his briefcase shut.

"Of course, the residents were upset," Muccio said. "Ms. Curtis was one of our most popular owners. But no problems have come up." Gabe hesitated a second. "No problems at all, really."

"You were about to say something else?"

"Oh, it's nothing. I mean, her brother came by a couple days ago and I think I convinced him to list his sister's unit with us for resale." Muccio smiled. "We should make a nice commission."

"That's it?"

"Well, he came back later the same day and asked my assistant for some information about one of Ms. Curtis's neighbors. I figure he just wanted to talk to the neighbor about his sister. You know, maybe he wanted to thank her for being a friend to his sister, or something."

John bit his lower lip. "What are you talking about?"

"Muriel Goldstein. The woman who owns the next door unit. Miss Curtis's brother, Doctor Matthew Curtis from New Mexico, wanted to know the name of Missus Goldstein's next of kin."

"Did your assistant give him the information?" Dunning demanded, his voice slightly strained and his eyes narrowed.

"Sure. Why not?" Muccio said, suddenly uncomfortable.

"Why the hell would he want that information?" Dunning asked, more to himself than to Muccio.

Muccio hunched his shoulders. He wasn't quite sure if Dunning expected an answer to the question. After a moment's hesitation, he offered, "Like I said, maybe he just wanted to thank the old lady."

"Didn't you tell me when you called the night of the accident that some old lady left the building right after Susan Curtis fell from her balcony?"

"Right! That was Muriel Goldstein."

John rose from his chair, shot out a staccato, "Wait here," and left the office.

John walked on the sidewalk in front of the condo building and dialed his cell phone.

"Yeah," Lonnie answered.

"I just learned a man visited the Sand & Sea two days ago and asked about the old lady who lived next door to Susan Curtis. He wanted to know the neighbor's next of kin."

"What man?" Lonnie asked, his voice tense.

"The dead woman's brother. A doctor from the mainland. Matthew Curtis."

"Sonofabitch!" Lonnie groaned.

"You know this guy?" John asked.

"I thought the old lady next door was out of town that night,"

Lonnie said, after five seconds of silence.

"She wasn't out of town. She left right after the Curtis woman swan-dived off her balcony and just before the cops showed up."

"You think she saw or heard something, got spooked?"

"Could be."

"Talk to Muccio or his bimbo and get the neighbor's emergency contact information. Name, telephone, and address. Then call me back. Fast!"

"What's this all about, Lonnie?" John asked. "Is there . . .?"

"Just do it!"

Lonnie threw his cell phone on the couch and paced the floor of the penthouse apartment—one of the half-dozen safe houses he called home in the Honolulu area. What if the Curtis woman's neighbor saw Callahan? What if she heard something that could tie the cop to the woman's death? "Fuckin' loose ends!" he growled.

He crossed to the bar, opened the refrigerator, and reached down for a beer when the phone rang. He jerked upright and lurched for the phone. Receiver to his ear, he moved to the balcony doors, stared out to sea, where seventeen floors below an assortment of sailboats and motorized craft moved across the water and left behind white wake ribbons.

"Go!" he shouted into the phone.

"The old lady has a daughter on Kauai. That's the only relative listed in her file," Johnny said.

Lonnie wrote down the name and address. Then he hung up and dialed a number.

A man answered.

"Get someone to go with you out to the airfield," Lonnie ordered. "Take the helicopter over to Kauai. Here's what I want you to do."

CHAPTER FORTY-ONE

Matt caught the noon flight to Kauai, rented a white, four-door Chevy Malibu at the airport, and drove to the north side of the island. He hoped the trip wouldn't be a waste of time, but there was really nothing else he could think to do. Muriel Goldstein's late night departure from the Sand & Sea, moments after Susan's death, was suspicious.

Forty-five minutes from the Kauai airport, Matt turned into the Crater Hill subdivision, an upscale development with expanses of open space, endless vistas of the Pacific, and a picturesque view of the Princeville lighthouse about a mile up the coast. He found the street Muriel Goldstein's daughter lived on and parked the rental car at the curb outside a rambling, one-story house. He got out of the car, straightened his jacket, and strode to the front door . . . to hopefully speak to Muriel Goldstein. How will I begin? Matt thought? I'm Susan Curtis's brother; you didn't happen to see someone murder her? Matt shook his head and wondered once again why he had come here.

The Nadler home sat on a high point in the development, but well below the spot where Crater Hill peaked, then dropped off precipitously to the sea. Matt turned back toward the home, swallowed his nervousness, and purposefully moved to the front door. He pushed the doorbell; it chimed three times. Through the door, he heard the high-pitched sound of a child's voice. "I'll get it."

A little girl, about six years old, in pink shorts, a white t-shirt, and flip-flops, cracked the chainlocked door and peered out. She had shoulder-length brown hair and bangs, large brown eyes, and a gap-toothed smile.

"Hello there," Matt said. "What's your name?"

"Cheryl, but my mommy says I shouldn't talk to strangers."

"Good for your mommy. Is she home?"

"No," the girl said. "She and Daddy went to the store. My nana's here. Do you want to talk to her?"

Bingo! "Sure, honey. Where's your nana?"

"I'll go get her." The girl slammed the door shut.

Matt chuckled. For someone who'd been told not to talk to strangers, Cheryl was free with information.

Matt heard the chainlock being undone, and then the door opened again—wider this time—and he was looking at a silver-haired woman who appeared to be about eighty years old. Her skin seemed to be parchment thin. Blue veins showed at her temples. She wore a dark-brown dress and brown low-heeled shoes and leaned on a carved, bone-handled cane. An amber choker with beads the size of jawbreakers encircled her thin neck. Ready to go to a tea party, Matt thought.

"Missus Goldstein?"

"How do you know . . . ?" Then her trembling hand shot to her mouth. Her eyes became wide. She tried to close the door, but Matt put his hand against it.

"Please, ma'am. I'm Matthew Curtis. Susan Curtis's brother." He removed his hand from the door as she opened it again. She put a hand over her heart and closed her eyes for a moment.

Matt watched the old woman turn and move away from the door. He followed her inside, closed the door behind him.

Muriel Goldstein walked slowly and stiffly. She sat on a couch in a large family room with a bay window that provided a view of a field of foot-high native grass. The field extended several hundred yards to a promontory overlooking the Pacific. The little girl sat on the floor and watched television.

"Cheryl," the old woman said in a shaky, delicate voice, "would you go to your room and watch your movie there?"

The girl swiveled around on her bottom and frowned at her grandmother. She looked as though she was about to put up an argument, but something in her grandmother's expression must have made her change her mind. She sighed and said, "Oh, o-o-o-kay."

Missus Goldstein waited until Cheryl left the room, then she picked up the remote from the coffee table, and clicked off the television. She rested her cane against the couch arm and pushed back against the couch cushion with a groan. "I loved Susan," she said. "She was very kind to me. We had dinner together about once a week. Oh, Susan made me laugh so." The old woman seemed to retreat into her memories for a moment. Her chest heaved with a deep breath that she slowly let escape. Then she focused again on Matt. She grimaced. "Why have you come here?"

"I apologize for bothering you, ma'am, but I need to talk with you."

"How did you find me?" she asked.

"I found this address through the Sand & Sea management office."

"Of course," she said. "I didn't think about the condominium records." She closed her eyes and pressed a hand at her throat, as though feeling for a pulse.

"I need to find out what happened to Susan."

She looked back at him. A tear dropped from her eye.

"The police think Susan killed herself," Matt said. "I don't buy it. I understand you were in your unit at least some part of the evening she died. Did you see or hear anything?"

A sudden glint of what could be fear showed in Muriel Goldstein's eyes. She sat quietly for several seconds, heaved another giant sigh, and lowered her gaze to her lap. "It disgusted me to read in the papers that Susan supposedly committed suicide. Impossible! She was so happy, so full of life. She would never kill herself. I was so . . . I'm still frightened." Tears welled in her eyes and began to flow freely. "I should have called the police, but I . . . ."

Matt reached over to touch her arm. "I understand, ma'am."

She raised her head and met Matt's gaze again. "Yes, Mister Curtis, I did see *and* hear something. That's why I left Honolulu and came here." She patted her eyes with a hanky she pulled from her dress pocket. Then her eyes rounded and her hands shook. "You know," she said, "your finding me here means anyone else who thinks to ask the condominium manager about my file can find me, too."

Matt sucked in a rush of air. She's right, he thought. "Can you tell me more about what happened that night? Please."

She kneaded her arthritis-deformed fingers in her lap and sat up straighter. "I'd taken a bag out to the trash chute in the hall. It's only a few feet from my door. When I opened the lid to the chute, I saw something out of the corner of my eye. I can't turn my head all the way to the side—arthritis, you know. But I saw a man standing in Susan's doorway. It looked like he was showing her something. I couldn't see what. Maybe a wallet." She shrugged.

"Perhaps some kind of identification," Matt offered.

She shrugged again. "Perhaps. She let him into her place. I dumped the trash and returned to my unit."

"That's what frightened you, Missus Goldstein?"

"Oh, that wasn't it. Although it did seem a little peculiar, being so late for visitors and all. After ten-thirty. I don't sleep very well anymore. I'm lucky to drop off by one o'clock. Susan usually went to bed early, though, because she left for work at 7 a.m. I tried to tell her not to work so hard. She put in very long hours. She was . . . ."

"What was it that did frighten you?"

"Well, about five minutes later I heard her door close again. I looked out in the hall and saw the man hurry toward the elevators. I shut my door and got ready for bed. I was in the bathroom when I thought I heard a knock on Susan's door. I peeked out, very carefully. It was a woman this time. I watched her knock on the door again, then saw her open it and go inside."

"You mean Susan didn't let her in?"

"I couldn't be sure," she said. She waggled her hands and tilted her head. "I didn't see Susan let her in." She blinked her eyes several times and shook her head. "It looked like she just turned the handle and walked right in."

"Did you recognize the woman?" Matt asked.

"Not really. Well, it seems like I've seen her before. I've tried so hard to come up with the woman's name. But my memory's not what it used to be." She closed her eyes again and made a clucking sound, as though criticizing herself for her bad memory. She looked back at Matt. "I know I've seen her somewhere. She was very nicely dressed. I remember thinking how pretty she was."

"How did you see all this, without being seen yourself?" Matt asked. "How do you know the woman went into Susan's apartment?" Please don't let this old lady turn out to be a flake, he thought.

Missus Goldstein reddened and again lowered her head. "I used to keep an eye out for Susan," she said, talking to her lap. "Whenever I heard someone knock on her door, I'd crack my own door a bit and hold a small mirror in the opening. I could see whoever stood down the hall without opening the door too far." She looked up and said, "I have very good eyes, you know."

Thank God for nosey neighbors, Matt thought. "Can you tell me anything else about the woman?"

"She wore a dark-blue silk dress, with heels and gloves. Her hair was curled. She looked older than Susan, but younger than me. Maybe I've seen her before. But I can't recall. I'm sorry."

Matt touched her hand. "It's all right, ma'am. What happened next?"

"A couple minutes later Susan fell off her balcony."

"You saw it happen?"

"Oh, yes. The woman pushed her over the railing."

Matt felt his heart rate accelerate and a shiver race up his spine. This was more information than he could have hoped for.

After the old woman sobbed for a while, she continued with her story.

"When the woman went into Susan's apartment, I closed my door and went to the bathroom. Then I walked out on my balcony. I always sit out there before I go to bed. I love to look at the stars and see the moonlight reflect off the water. Sometimes I can see a man's face in the moon. You know, from the craters. When the moon's full it sometimes reminds me of a beautiful, sparkling pendant. I just love . . ."

"Was the moon full that night?" Matt gently asked her.

"Oh no! We only had a three-quarter moon that night. But it was still beautiful. I stepped toward my balcony, but I heard a strange voice come from Susan's balcony. They're only a few feet apart, you see. I stayed inside. Then I heard a gagging sound, like someone was throwing up. Then grunting. I peeked around the curtains."

"Yes?"

"Susan was sick. She bent over the railing and vomited. The other woman was talking, loudly, about Susan threatening someone. Susan didn't say a thing. She seemed . . . I don't know. She just continued to retch. It sounded like she couldn't breathe. You know, like when someone's been running and is out of breath."

Her eyes widened and her face paled.

"Are you all right?" Matt asked as he moved next to her and took her hand.

She nodded. Tears again streamed down her face. "I saw the woman push Susan over the railing. I was so frightened. I wanted to scream, but I put my hand over my mouth." She looked at Matt. Her face sagged and her mouth drooped. "I was so scared. I didn't know what to do. Susan was . . . she had acted kind of drunk." Missus Goldstein's voice rose, her shoulders shook. "I did nothing to help her. That woman pushed her off the balcony and I did nothing. And then I ran away."

She turned to Matt. He could see it took an effort for her to twist in her seat. More tears. "It surprised me Susan couldn't fight the woman off," she said. "She was younger than the woman. Much stronger, I'm sure."

There was another interval of sobbing, which gradually subsided.

"Can you tell me anything else about the man you saw go into Susan's condominium earlier?"

"I only saw him for a moment, but he . . . ."

"Yes?"

"He had an aura of authority about him."

"How long was it from the time he showed up to when the woman pushed Susan over the balcony?"

"No more than ten minutes, from start to finish."

"Why didn't you go to the police with this information?" Matt asked, trying not to make the question sound like an accusation.

"I . . . I was so scared. I didn't even tell my daughter or her husband. I thought I could hide here. Not get involved."

Muriel Goldstein's granddaughter, Cheryl, burst into the room, her hair flying. Excitement showed in her round eyes. She ran to the window and pressed her nose against the glass. "Did you hear it, Nana?" she cried. "Can you see it? There's a helicopter over by the nature area? Come see it."

Matt rushed to the window and looked out. Two men ran down the grassy slope. One of them carried a rifle. They were about one hundred-fifty yards away from the back of the house. A helicopter sat on a flat spot just beneath the peak of Crater Hill.

Matt tried to keep fear from his voice as he said, "Missus Goldstein, you and Cheryl must come with me. I have a car outside. We need to go right now."

"Oh no," she said. "I can't . . . ."

Matt's instincts roared into hyperdrive. There was no time to debate the issue. She groaned when he lifted her from the couch and moved with her to the front door.

"What are you doing?" she cried.

"Trying to save your life," Matt said. The little girl danced around them and excitedly waved her hands.

"Can you run real fast, Cheryl?" Matt asked.

"Daddy says I run like the wind."

"Good. Let's see how fast you can run out front and open the back door of my car."

Cheryl rushed past Matt and raced for the car. Her heels kicked up behind her and her hair flew. Matt followed and deposited the woman on the backseat. He told Cheryl to get in with her nana. Then he slid behind the steering wheel. "Fasten your seatbelts," he shouted.

CHAPTER FORTY-TWO

From his vantage point in the parked helicopter near the highest part of Crater Hill, Lonnie Jackson's pilot, Jim Brady, used binoculars to watch the Nadler house. He could see down over the residence's roof to the street beyond. A man and a child ran to a white sedan parked on the street. He assumed they'd come from the house. The man appeared to carry someone who he placed in the car's backseat. Then the car sped away.

"They're on the run!" Brady quickly radioed to the two hitmen who had not yet reached the rear of the house. "Get back here."

It took them several minutes to run back through the tall grass to the chopper and climb aboard. After the two had strapped themselves in and put on their earphones, Brady lifted off and raced in the direction the car had gone.

"There it is down there!" Brady shouted into his microphone. He banked the copter and zoomed toward a white car that careened around a curve in the road below. Brady swooped low, a hundred feet above the vehicle, and followed it as it slipped through the curves of the narrow, tree-lined road. Brady angled off to the side of the white car so his passengers could see inside the vehicle.

"You sure it's the same car?" one of the hitmen yelled. "I only see a driver."

"It's the same car," Brady shouted back. "The one I saw leave the house."

"You said you saw three people get into the car. Where the hell are the others?" the second passenger yelled.

"Maybe they're on the floor in the back," Brady said.

"What are we going to do?" the first passenger said.

Brady adjusted his controls to take the helicopter higher. "Let's see if we can find an open stretch of road ahead where I can set down."

Brady left the car well behind as he raced above the road at one hundred twenty miles an hour. He picked out a flat area three miles ahead, where the road went around a hill that would conceal the helicopter until almost the last minute.

Matt stuffed his cell phone and wallet under the Malibu's front seat as he drove around a tight bend at twice the twenty mile per hour speed limit, then he tromped his foot on the accelerator into the straightaway. His heart seemed to dive into his acid-filled stomach. A helicopter sat in the middle of the road, its rotors turning lazily. He stood on the brakes and the car skidded to a stop just feet from the aircraft. A man stood on the pavement and leaned against the pilot's door.

Matt jumped out of the car. "Jesus, you scared the hell out of me," he shouted and wiped his forehead with his handkerchief. "I didn't think I'd be able to stop in time. What happened?"

Two men broke from the bushes by the side of the road. Each of them armed with an automatic rifle. One man aimed his weapon at Matt; the other pointed his at the car.

"Oh my God, oh my God," Matt exclaimed, his hands clasped as though in prayer. "Please don't hurt me." He knew Muriel Goldstein and Cheryl's lives depended on how good a performance he put on.

The man who covered Matt hit him in the stomach with the butt of his weapon. The blow knocked Matt down. He knelt in pain on the road and gasped for breath. The man who'd hit him stood over him and laughed.

The second gunman opened the car's back door. "There's no one here," he shouted. "Where's the old lady?"

"Goddammit, we got the wrong fucking car," the man who guarded Matt said. Then he kicked Matt in the ribs, bent down, and screamed in Matt's ear, "Where's the Goldstein woman?" He pressed the rifle muzzle against Matt's forehead.

"I don't know who you're talking about," Matt cried. "I was going to Princeville to meet my brother. I'm late. Please, you must have me mistaken—"

The man kicked Matt again, driving him off his knees and onto his side.

"Oh shit!" the second gunman said. "Let's get out of here."

"What about this guy," Brady said. "He can identify us. Lonnie ain't gonna like—"

"Shut the hell up!"

"So what? We ain't done nothing yet. Besides, he's a wimp. Fucker's so scared, he ain't gonna remember shit."

This man, the one who'd sunk the rifle butt in Matt's stomach and kicked him, leaned down and said, "Right, Mr.? You gonna forget this happened?"

Matt nodded.

"Good boy," the man said. He raised his rifle and brought it down on the side of Matt's head.

The three men piled into the helicopter. Brady lifted the aircraft off the road and headed for the airport to refuel.

"Did you see that chickenshit beg for his life?" one of the gunmen said. "I coulda bust a gut laughing. Hell, we shoulda taken his wallet just for the hell of it."

The one who had clubbed and kicked Matt said, "I searched him. He didn't have a wallet on him."

"I think you should have shot the sonofabitch," Brady said. "What if he got the registration number off the helicopter? He could ID us. Bring assault charges."

"Give me a break. The guy's some tourist. What the hell harm's he gonna do to us? The last thing he'll remember is your registration number. Besides, he'll have a hell of a story to tell his friends when he gets back home. Probably cut down tourism to the islands by ten percent."

The two passengers laughed.

"Yeah, but—"

"Listen asshole," the first passenger said, "you worry about flying this thing. As soon as we refuel, we've got to come back and find that old broad."

Brady grunted.

A strange voice came from somewhere. Matt's head felt as though it was filled with Jell-O. Someone pressed a cloth his temple. The voice asked something. He heard the words, but they had no meaning. The voice spoke again.

Matt tried to get up, but his legs wouldn't work. He felt an arm around his back, and then he was sitting up. Then hands under his arms helped him to stand. Hard metal supported his butt. He rested his hands by the sides of his legs against the metal to keep from toppling over. The world spun and a wave of nausea overcame him. He bent over and vomited.

The voice again. "What happened? I nearly ran you over. You were in the middle of the road."

Matt's vision cleared a bit, but he still felt as though he had a terrible hangover, that he was in a fog. His head hurt worse now than the last time he'd injured it. When was that? He tried to remember. Just recently? Or was it years ago? He turned his head slowly toward the voice and blinked several times to bring a man's face into focus. He saw a priest's black shirt and white collar.

"Have you been drinking?" the priest asked.

Matt shook his head. Big mistake! "No-o-o," he groaned.

The priest still held a handkerchief against Matt's head. "The bleeding has almost stopped," he said. "But you've got quite a bump. Probably need stitches. You should see a doctor."

The priest moved Matt's rental car to the shoulder, then helped Matt move from the fender to the passenger seat of his own vehicle.

Matt tried to concentrate. Something he had to do. Something important. What the hell was it?

The priest came back to the car. "Were you alone?" he asked. "Anybody else with you?" He spoke slowly and enunciated each word.

The questions jogged Matt's memory. Muriel Goldstein and Cheryl Nadler.

Other recent events flooded back into his mind. The visit to the coroner's office, the conversations with Callahan, meeting Renee, the knock on his head when the Trans Am tried to drive them off the road, the concussion, calling Esteban, all that Muriel Goldstein had told him.

Susan had been murdered. That's what Muriel had told him. Now he had to find out who did it. And why.

"Father, I have friends just up the road in Crater Hill. Could you drive me there?"

"Of course," the man said. "But you really should see a doctor."

"I'll get my friends to take me," Matt lied. Then a thought hit his brain. "My wallet and phone are under the front seat of my car."

The priest retrieved the wallet and phone and handed them to Matt. Then he drove towards Crater Hill. When they were a half-mile from the subdivision entrance, Matt asked him to stop.

"You going to be sick again?" the priest asked urgently while he pulled the car onto the shoulder.

"I'll be back in a couple minutes," Matt said. "Please don't leave."

He opened the car door, slid off the seat, and stumbled into the field, between rows of tall, green plants. His legs felt less rubbery now, but he still felt unsteady. A stand of shade trees bordered the far side of the field. Matt was twenty yards from the trees when he heard a shrill, little girl voice singing.

". . . Bingo was his name-o. B-I-N-G-O, B-I-N-G-O, B-I-N-G-O, and Bingo was his name-o."

He found Muriel Goldstein and Cheryl seated on a large rock, leaning against one another. Cheryl stopped singing when Matt approached.

"This is a little more excitement than I'm used to, Mister Curtis," Muriel said, as she smiled at Cheryl, who bounced up and stared expectantly at Matt. "Do you think we could go back to the house now?" Muriel turned to look at Matt. "Oh my God!" she said, her eyes wide. "Your head! What happened?"

Matt stepped to Muriel and helped her stand up. "I'll explain later," he said. "Our ride's down on the road. Can you walk that far?"

Muriel frowned at Matt. "Try to stop me."

She took his arm for support. Cheryl kicked up little clouds of dust and hummed a tune as she skipped ahead of them through the cane.

It took five minutes to return to the priest's car.

"I don't understand," the priest said when they reached the road.

"Neither do I, Father, but I will," Matt said as he ushered Muriel and Cheryl into the back seat.

CHAPTER FORTY-THREE

A woman wrung her hands as she paced back and forth on the front lawn of the Nadler house. A man stood in the doorway with a cell phone to his ear, his other hand windmilled the air. Then the man ran to the driveway, as the priest pulled up.

Matt shakily slid off the front seat, stepped from the priest's car, and opened the back door. Cheryl scurried from the vehicle and ran to the woman on the lawn. Matt took Muriel Goldstein's hand and helped her out of the car.

"Mommy, Mommy," the little girl yelled, "Nana and I had an adventure!"

The man with the cell phone raced around the car and wedged himself between Matt and Muriel. He shot Matt a narrow-eyed look, then he led Muriel across the lawn. He knelt on the grass and hugged Cheryl. Then he leaped to his feet and charged back toward Matt, who had come around to the driver's side and stood next to the priest.

"Who the hell are you?" he growled.

A queasy feeling came over Matt and his legs suddenly felt like wet spaghetti strands. He felt himself about to fall. The priest grabbed his arm and, in a commanding voice, said to the other man, "Help me. He needs to lie down."

They moved Matt into the house and put him on a couch in the living room. Matt's brain seemed to be on a merry-go-round.

He heard someone offer him a glass of water, but he didn't seem to know how to respond. He had enough synapses sparking that he knew the blow he'd taken on the side of his head, on top of the injury from the car crash, was impacting his thinking and his reasoning. A woman with a kindly voice said something about a lemon-sized lump, then pressed something cold against his head.

Matt closed his eyes and felt as though he might drift off. In the background he heard a man's angry voice. Then nothing. He wasn't sure how long he was out, but the sun was still up when he awoke. He opened his eyes and, at first, wasn't sure where he was. Then he saw Muriel Goldstein at the other end of the couch.

"Did I sleep long?" Matt asked.

Muriel laughed. "Oh, about three minutes," she said.

Matt pushed against the couch cushions and tried to sit up, but he felt as though three gerbils had invaded his head and competed with each other to see which one could run the fastest. Matt shut his eyes again. It took a minute for the spinning feeling to subside. He finally opened his eyes and struggled to sit up.

Muriel introduced Matt to her daughter, Beth, and her son-in-law, Stuart, who sat in an armchair and glared. Beth was in another chair and paid attention to Cheryl's account of the escape from the bad men. The priest was gone.

When Cheryl finished her tale, Matt tried to explain it all, but Stuart cut him short. "So, let me get this straight, Mister Curtis. You came out from Honolulu to question my mother-in-law about your sister's death, but then a helicopter landed here with armed men, and—"

"I believe those men were sent to kill your mother-in-law," Matt said, "because of what she saw the night my sister died. They might have killed all of us, but they got confused when they found me alone in the car."

Stuart Nadler stood and loomed over Matt. "You sonofabitch!" he shouted. "You put us in danger. We could all have been killed. I want you out of here. Now!"

Muriel made a small sound of protest, but Stuart continued to rant at Matt.

Finally, Muriel yelled, "Shut up, Stuart! Enough! This man

saved our lives."

Stuart gaped at her, as though he didn't think she was capable of such an outburst.

Beth gawked at her mother.

"Wow!" Cheryl said.

Muriel shot eye-daggers at her son-in-law and waved at him dismissively. "Now that it's quiet," she said, "I can hear myself think." She turned her gaze on Matt. "Tell me, Mister Curtis, do you think those men in the helicopter followed you?"

Matt considered the question for a moment. "No," he said. "They couldn't have followed the commercial flight I took to Kauai. Their helicopter wouldn't have been able to keep up. And no one knew my destination except two people I trust with my life. Besides, the gunmen didn't know me when they stopped the car. They were after you, Missus Goldstein. They must have guessed you were here the same way I did—by checking your file at the Sand & Sea."

Muriel nodded once, a resigned, grim-lipped scowl on her face. She looked purposefully at Stuart, as though to say, See. She turned to her daughter. "Honey," she said, "if Mister Curtis hadn't come here and taken us in his car to the cane field down the road . . ." Muriel slowly shook her head, then smiled at Matt.

The elements of a thought hit Matt and he had a sudden sinking feeling. But the problem was that the elements were jumbled. It took him a moment to put the pieces together and, when he did, he felt a cold shiver of anger sweep through him. He said to Muriel, "The condo manager told me he saw you leave the complex soon after my sister fell. Wouldn't you think the police would have questioned the condo manager? That they would have asked the manager if he saw anyone enter or leave the building near the time of Susan's death?" Matt already knew the answer.

"Makes sense," Muriel said.

"And wouldn't it be reasonable to assume the manager told the cops the same thing he told me?" Matt asked, again directing the question to Muriel. "That he saw you leave the building after Susan died."

Muriel answered with a nod.

"Then why didn't the police try to contact my mother-in-law

here?" Stuart interjected.

"Because," Matt said, "they didn't think to check the files at the condo office. The manager probably told them what he told me, that Muriel Goldstein traveled a lot and was probably on her way out of town. But here's what's odd. The detective on the case never mentioned to me that the manager saw Missus Goldstein leave right after Susan died. In fact, he told me neither of her closest neighbors was home that night."

"You don't know for sure the manager really gave that information to the police," Beth Nadler said.

"You're right," Matt said. Then another thought came to Matt. "I think we should call the local police. That helicopter might come back."

"Oh dear," Beth said and reached out for Cheryl.

Stuart made the call. After he talked for a few minutes, he passed the receiver to Matt, who gave the officer as many details as he could, including that one of the men who'd attacked him mentioned a name.

"What name, sir?" the officer asked.

Matt's tried to dredge up the name, but it wouldn't come to him.

"A patrol car is on the way to your location," the officer said.

Matt handed the receiver back to Stuart Nadler, who replaced it in its cradle. Matt noticed that Nadler glared at him again. For a moment he couldn't figure out why the guy seemed so angry. Then something stirred a thought.

He took his wallet from his back trouser pocket and fumbled with it. It was as though his fingers were cramped and useless. He reached out his hand to Nadler and said, "There's a card in there . . . Gabriel something."

Nadler took the wallet and sorted through cards there. He found Gabriel Muccio's business card and handed it to Matt.

"Yes, that's the one. Would you call the number?"

Nadler scowled at Matt, but did as he'd asked and handed the receiver to Matt.

"Sand & Sea Condominiums, can I help you?"

"Michelle?"

"Yes?"

"This is Doctor Curtis calling. Is Mister Muccio there?"

"Yes, Doctor. Please hold."

After a few seconds, Muccio came on the line. "How are you Doctor Curtis?"

"Okay," Matt said.

"I have the listing agreement prepared on your sister's unit."

Matt didn't understand what the man was talking about. "Uh-huh."

"We'll get you top dollar, I promise," Muccio said.

"Okay." Matt paused. "By the way, do you remember . . . when you told me you saw . . . Muriel . . ."

"Muriel Goldstein," Muccio said.

"Yes, Muriel Goldstein. You said you saw her leave the building the night my sister died?"

"Sure," Muccio said.

"Did you mention it to the police?"

"Of course," Muccio said. "I'd never hold that back from the cops."

"Do you remember which policeman you told?"

"The detective in charge. Guy named Callahan."

Matt breathed deeply. His insides felt suddenly hot. "Thanks, Mister Muccio. I'll see—"

"What's all this business with Missus Goldstein?" Muccio interrupted. "First, I told the cops about her, then I told you. Then Michelle got you Missus Goldstein's emergency contact number. And just this morning the owner's lawyer asked me for the emergency contact number, too. Is there some connec—?"

"The owner's lawyer?"

"John Dunning. I wrote his name on the back of my card? Rawson, Wong & Ballard?"

CHAPTER FORTY-FOUR

After refueling the helicopter at Kauai Airport, Jim Brady and Lonnie Jackson's two killers headed straight back to the Crater Hill development.

"We'll come in from the north," Brady said. "Use the cliff face as cover. But I gotta tell you guys I got a bad feeling about this. What if that asshole we stopped on the road called the police? I told you to shoot the sonofabitch. Besides, the house is probably empty by now."

"You want to be the one to tell Lonnie we screwed up?" one of them barked. "I ain't going back to Oahu until we figure out where this Goldstein dame went. You under—"

"Shit!" Brady shouted as he veered away from a craggy rock face. A dense cloud of white and gray birds exploded from nesting sites. Thousands of them flew in panicked disarray. Brady leaned heavily on the controls. Once they were clear of the birds and the way was clear between the aircraft and the edge of the cliff, Brady edged back in toward the promontory.

Brady pointed toward the highest point of the cliff face. "There's an old bunker at the top of Crater Hill," he said. "Spotters in that bunker made the first siting of the Japanese attack on Pearl Harbor."

"Who gives a fuck?" one of his passengers said.

The other one laughed. "Why do you think we're here? Sightseeing?"

Brady felt his face warm, but kept his mouth shut. He eased

the chopper upward until its glass bubble compartment rose high enough above the cliff edge for them to look down the sloping field to the house.

"My God!" Brady yelped and jerked again at the control stick.

They'd had a clear view—the police cars with flashing dome lights and cops everywhere, including a pair who stood right at the top of Crater Hill, a stone's throw away, with their automatic weapons tracking the helicopter as it rose in front of them.

"Go, go, go!" one of the men in back shouted at Brady as the pilot banked the chopper away from the cliff and dove toward the sea.

Matt watched the police chopper that had hovered over the Nadler house race toward the cliff edge and move out to sea.

His head ached with the intensity of a world-class hangover, not helped at all by the *whoop-whoop-whoop* of yet another helicopter. He shielded his eyes against the sun's glare and watched what looked like a converted military chopper, a blue Huey, descend toward the road in front of the Nadler home. The letters "HOCTF" were painted on its belly. He tried to decipher their meaning, but couldn't get past "H" for Hawaii.

When it landed, a man in a suit jumped out and ran to Matt.

"Doctor Curtis?" the man shouted against the rotor noise.

Matt nodded.

"I'm George Thefteros with the Hawaii Organized Crime Task Force. Will you please come with me?"

Matt felt as though his heart did a full gainer into the sudden acid buildup in the bottom of his stomach. He hadn't cared much for flying in helicopters in the Army, and nothing had changed in the interim. As far as he was concerned, the only thing different about the chopper that sat thirty yards away and the ones in the Army was its color. Blue, or Army green, the damned things were nothing but flying pinwheels.

"We need you to identify the men who attacked you, Doctor Curtis," Thefteros said.

"You got them already?" Matt asked.

The man smiled. "Not yet, sir. But it won't be long."

What the hell, Matt thought. He'd even risk a ride in a damn helicopter if it meant confronting the bastards who came to murder Muriel Goldstein. He walked to the chopper.

Thefteros sat next to Matt in the seats behind the pilot. Once the aircraft was airborne, he said, "I'm the team leader for the task force office on Kauai. I don't know if you realize how helpful you can be."

Matt cocked his head as though to say, Isn't that a slight exaggeration. "It seems like you brought in an awful lot of men and equipment over a simple assault," he said.

Thefteros smiled. "I suspect there was nothing simple about the attack on you." He leaned closer. "When you called the Kauai Police and said one of your attackers had mentioned the name Lonnie, you caused a great deal of excitement."

"Who's Lonnie?" Matt asked.

"Lonnie Jackson. We've suspected for several years that Jackson is the head of organized crime on the islands. He's one smart fellow, though. Keeps a low profile; let's his underlings do all his dirty work. We hope that if you can identify the men who attacked you, one of them may, to stay out of jail, testify against Jackson."

"What's this task force?" Matt asked.

"The Hawaii Organized Crime Task Force is made up of representatives from the Hawaii State Police, the Honolulu Police Department, the DEA, the FBI, and the Bureau of Alcohol, Tobacco & Firearms. It was created in 1974, shortly after marijuana became Hawaii's biggest cash crop. We've come down hard on the drug runners over the years. Now our focus is on the drug kingpins, the crime bosses."

"Lonnie Jackson?" Matt said.

Thefteros narrowed his eyes. "Yeah, Lonnie Jackson."

Matt noted that Thefteros's jaw tightened when he mentioned Lonnie Jackson's name.

Jim Brady circled the private aircraft terminal at Honolulu International. "It looks clear," he told his two passengers.

"Land this damned thing," one of the men shouted.

Brady lowered the helicopter to the tarmac, shut down the engine, and tied down the skids.

"What the hell will we tell Lonnie?" one of the men said, as they walked toward the terminal with their gear.

"Shit! I don't know. Let's . . . What the . . .?"

Sirens pierced the air. Brady's heart jumped. Police cars roared toward them from around both sides of the building.

One hitman punched Brady in the chest and knocked him down. "I thought you said it was all clear, asshole." Then both of them raised their hands as a dozen police officers, their guns drawn and aimed, approached on foot.

Brady stood and rubbed his ribs. He felt nauseous while he watched more cops pour from police vehicles, automatic weapons, shotguns, and pistols at the ready. A uniformed cop threw Brady roughly back to the tarmac, cuffed his hands behind his back, and searched him. Officers hustled him and the two assassins into separate police vehicles and took them to a hangar on the other side of the airport.

Two officers gripped Brady's arms and led him to a small windowless, green-painted room. The room smelled of stale tobacco, bitter coffee, and sweat. Armed guards dressed in black, wearing bulletproof vests, stood inside the room, on either side of the door. The two officers pushed Brady down onto a metal chair bolted to the concrete floor, then left the room. Another man came in, read Brady his rights, and left.

Brady demanded to call his lawyer. The guards ignored him.

Thirty minutes later, yet another man entered the room. He was big, florid-faced, with light-brown hair being overtaken by gray. He wore an orange-and-blue-plaid sport jackets.

"Nice jacket," Brady said. "Goodwill have a sale?"

The man ignored Brady's jibe. "Hello," he said. "Nice of you to join us, Mister Brady. I'm Frank Murdoch, Agent-in-Charge of the Hawaii Organized Crime Task Force."

"What the fuck is this?" Brady growled. "I know my rights. You can't hold me here. I want my lawyer."

The guards did not ignore him this time. One of them slapped the back of Brady's head.

"Hey, what the . . . ! What's the idea?"

Another slap shut him up.

Murdoch continued. "You think you can fly around my state and assault law-abiding citizens?"

"Bullshit!" Brady shouted. "I don't know a thing about any assault."

Murdoch tipped his head at one of the guards, who nodded back and left the room. Murdoch walked around the table and stopped behind Brady. "You sure you don't want to reconsider your answer?"

Brady jerked around in his chair and sneered up at Murdoch. "I'll sue your ass for harassment, false arrest, assault, and anything else my attorney can come up with."

"How about the automatic weapons we found on your helicopter?" Murdoch asked.

Brady tried to stare Murdoch down, but, after a few seconds, gave up. "Those weren't mine," he said. He realized there wasn't much bravado or conviction in his voice.

The guard who had left a minute earlier, returned with someone new, someone Brady could only gape at.

Murdoch watched the pilot's face pale. He had to suppress a smile. There was no question, from the expression on Brady's face, that the pilot recognized Matthew Curtis.

Curtis gave Brady a long silent look.

"Doctor, have you seen this man before?" Murdoch asked.

"This is one of the three men who attacked me," Curtis said. "He was with the man who hit me in the gut with his rifle—an AK-47, by the way—and then kicked me and clubbed me on the head." Curtis pointed at a spot on the right side of his head where a bandage had been placed. "Another of his friends searched my car. I recall him saying, 'Where's Muriel Goldstein?' "

Brady looked at Murdoch and scowled.

"Sir, would you like to press charges against this man?" Murdoch asked.

Curtis smiled. Brady avoided his gaze. "You bet, Agent Murdoch," he said. "It would be my pleasure."

CHAPTER FORTY-FIVE

One of the HOCTF agents gave Matt a lift to the airport parking lot to retrieve the rental van he'd left there before he flew to Kauai. But Matt turned down the man's offer of an escort to 'wherever you're staying.' Matt had decided there was something rotten about Dennis Callahan. As long as Callahan had access to law enforcement records and information, he guessed he would be able to find out much of what the HOCTF knew, including the address where Matt stayed. He didn't want anyone to know he was at Renee's. Matt knew that Renee thought the men who tried to kill them on The Palisades road a couple nights ago had been after her. He'd thought the same thing at the time. But now Matt wasn't so sure. He had begun to wonder if he had been the target.

He took one of his business cards from his wallet and gave it to the agent. "My cell number's on the card," he said. "That's the best way to reach me."

Matt drove slowly and deliberately. He leaned forward over the steering wheel to better see the road. His vision was fuzzy again and he felt dazed. His ears rang and pain racked his skull, as though spikes had been driven through his temples.

By the time he arrived at Renee's, the spikes felt as though they were being twisted back and forth. And his vision had blurred even more. Two Renees waited for him by the front door.

Renee ran to the car and opened Matt's door. "We were worried," she said. "You were supposed to call from Kauai. Remember?"

Matt stepped out of the car. "Sorry. I've been kinda busy. Guess I forgot."

"Oh my God!" she blurted as she stared at the new bandaged area on the side of his head. "What happened?"

"Just another bump on the head," Matt said as he touched the new bandage, then moved his hand to the other bandage still on his forehead. "I must look a mess." He tried to smile, but a sudden bolt of excruciating pain struck. "I need to lie down . . . catch my breath. I'll tell you the whole story after you get me a beer."

"You know better than that," Renee said. "You can't have a beer. Remember, the emergency room doctor told you no alcohol, no drugs."

Esteban came out at that moment. He stared at the bandage on Matt's forehead and the bandaged lump over his ear. "You've got to stop leading with your head, my friend. You look even uglier than usual."

Matt made a half-hearted attempt to laugh. "I'll try to remember that next time. Where's Angelo and Richie?"

"Angelo's asleep. Richie's on patrol with Max. It's been quiet around here."

"That's good," Matt said, then his legs seemed to give out and he staggered.

"Whoa," Esteban said. He grabbed Matt's arm and put an arm around his waist. "We better get you inside."

Esteban half-carried Matt to a couch and gently lay him there. "What the hell happened, *amigo*?"

Eyes closed, Matt related the day's events, including his call to Gabe Muccio. The he added, "I understand Callahan has no obligation to tell me anything, but that's not the impression he gave me. He seemed to want to help, to tell me what was happening on my sister's case. He even told me he'd call the coroner and ask him to stall the issuance of his final report on Susan's death, to give me time to dig something up. If Callahan were corrupt, would he have agreed to do that? Wouldn't he have wanted me out of Hawaii as quickly as possible?"

"Just the same," Esteban said. "We watch out for Detective

Callahan. We should trust no one but ourselves."

Matt rolled his shoulders and slowly moved his head from side to side. "If you all don't mind, I need to get some sleep. I'm exhausted." He struggled to his feet and moved as though he were an old man.

"Before you go to bed, I think you should try a Jacuzzi," Renee said. "It might relax you. Take away some of the soreness."

Matt wearily crossed the floor. "Sounds good," he said.

"I'll start the tub," she said, almost leaping from her chair.

"Nice lady," Esteban said after Renee'd left the room. "Poor thing's nuts about you."

"What are you talking about?" Matt said.

Esteban stood up and leered at him. "You must be even older than you look. Maybe you're senile. If you can't see how much she cares for you . . . ." He chuckled as he walked toward the front door.

Matt lightly touched the bandage and jerked his hand away when he felt pain. He felt muddled. Not only from the blow he'd taken to the head, but also because, for the first time since he'd become a widower, he thought about what it would be like to have a woman crazy about him. He'd been attracted to Renee the first moment he'd seen her. And, since then, the attraction had grown into . . . something more.

Matt slowly shook his head. He decided to check his cell phone for messages before climbing upstairs.

The Coroner, Doctor Trang, had called. As had Callahan. But it was the last message that surprised him. His office manager had telephoned to tell him Susan's boyfriend, Robert Nakamura, had called. The return number: Susan's condominium.

"Hello," a tired voice said, picking up the receiver after only one ring.

"Robert, is that you?" Matt demanded, suddenly charged with energy.

"Matt? Oh Matt, I'm glad you called back," Robert shouted shrilly, his words spoken in a machinegun cadence. "Your assistant said you're here in Hawaii. Why? Where's Susan? I just got back to Honolulu; I can't find her. Her things are here, but there's nothing in the refrigerator and all the lights were off. I called your office in Albuquerque and got the emergency number. Talked to your assistant. She said I should call you. It's Sunday, so Susan's not at work. I tried her office anyway, but nobody answered. I'm really worried. What's going on?"

"Listen, Robert," Matt said in a deliberately soft tone, "we're all over at Renee Drummond's. Do you know how to find it?"

"Yeah, I was there once. Is Susan with you?" There was hope in each word.

"Robert—"

"Hold on a minute, Matt. Someone's at the door."

Matt heard him put the receiver down. Then he felt his body go hot. Fear raced through him. Who would be at the condominium door this late? "Robert, don't go to the door," he yelled. "Robert!"

Matt held the receiver tight against his ear. Footsteps sounded on the ceramic tile floor. He heard the sound of a door opening. Voices.

Robert's voice. Loud. "What are you doing here? What do you want?"

Silence.

Robert again. Panic in his voice now. "What do you want? I've done everything you asked."

A scream, a grunt, then nothing except footsteps and the click of the phone replaced in its cradle.

Matt redialed. No one answered.

He took out the business cards from his shirt pocket and rifled through them until he found Frank Murdoch's. He punched in the number for the HOCTF.

"I need to talk to Frank Murdoch," Matt yelled.

"Who's calling?" a man asked.

"Doctor Matthew Curtis."

"Agent Murdoch's gone home," the man said. "I'll leave a message for—"

"No!" Matt yelled. "It's an emergency. I need to talk to Agent Murdoch now."

A pause, then the man said, "Okay, hold on, Doctor Curtis."

Matt heard a couple clicks, then Murdoch's voice came on the line.

"Murdoch. What can I do for you, Doctor Curtis?"

"I just talked to my sister's boyfriend, Robert Nakamura. He's in her condominium at the Sand & Sea complex. I think something's wrong. We were talking, then someone came to the door. Robert went to see who it was. I heard shouts, then I think there was a struggle. Robert never got back on the line."

"Why call me, Doctor Curtis? You should telephone the Honolulu Po—"

"I don't trust the police."

Murdoch sighed.

"Look, Agent Murdoch, I know you don't owe me a damn thing, but I have a bad feeling about this."

"Okay, okay, Doctor, I'll send a man over there. What's your sister's unit number?"

After he hung up, Matt felt wired from emotion overload. Anxious, exhausted, angry, he roamed from room to room. On one circuit through the front foyer, he looked up and saw Renee lean over the second-floor railing.

"Are you coming upstairs?"

"Not yet. I'm waiting for a call."

Renee came down the stairs. "What's the matter? What's happened?"

Matt told her about his conversation with Robert, his call to Murdoch.

Renee suddenly slumped as though she carried the weight of the world's problems, then she stood and took Matt's hand. "Come on, let's go upstairs," she pleaded. "The Jacuzzi's full and the water's nice and hot. You can take the call there."

CHAPTER FORTY-SIX

Shawn Catlett hunched down in the dark bedroom closet, between dresses and blouses. His back hurt; knees ached. If only the man doesn't open the closet door, Shawn thought as he shook from fear. Thank God he'd heard the front door lock turn, or he wouldn't have had time to move from the bed. Please don't let it be the night guard. If he catches me here in Miss Susan's apartment . . . . Oh, why did I come back here again? His teeth chattered as though he'd been locked in a freezing meat locker. Usually, the scent of Miss Susan's clothes helped soothe him. But not this time. His heart still beat as though out of control

He'd heard a man's voice after the condo door closed. He couldn't make out the words. But the man sounded worried. Then the voice became louder as the man came into the bedroom.

"Susan, where the hell are you?" the man had shouted.

Maybe it was Robert, Miss Susan's friend. He always hung around her. Sometimes stupid Robert stayed all night. I hate it when that happens, Shawn thought. I can't sleep thinking about him being with her. It makes me mad. I'd like to hurt Robert.

"Susan, where are you?" the man had yelled, his voice a bit fainter.

It had sounded like Robert's voice, Shawn thought. Then, after a minute, he heard the telephone ring. Then the man's voice again.

At last Shawn's knees stopped shaking. For a moment, he

thought about attacking Robert. He'd straightened up, took a tiny step forward toward the closet door. Just a little push on the door, a quick rush at Robert, and it would be over. And Robert would be gone forever. Shawn felt a hot rush of blood heat his face. But just as he placed his hand on the door, he heard knocks come from another part of the condo.

Bang! Bang! Bang!

Shawn yanked his hand back as though he'd received an electric shock. He burrowed deeper into his hiding place among the clothes. Robert's voice again—scared. Shawn shivered uncontrollably.

"What do you want," Robert cried. "I've done everything you asked."

A pause. A scream. A grunt.

Shawn squeezed even farther back into the corner of the closet and huddled down. He pressed his knees together and put his hands between his thighs. He had to pee so badly, but he couldn't move. He didn't dare.

CHAPTER FORTY-SEVEN

The telephone woke Matt. He jerked upright. The Jacuzzi's jets thrummed; his muscles felt as though they'd turned to mush. He splashed water all over the bathroom floor as he lurched for the handset.

"Hello!"

"Doctor Curtis?"

"Yes?"

"Frank Murdoch. I'm sorry to be the one to tell you. One of my men just called from your sister's place. He found Robert Nakamura on the living room floor. Dead. Looks like a massive drug overdose. A needle still in his arm. We've called HPD Violent Crime. They're on the way. I'm sorry."

"They'll probably call this a suicide, too," Matt mused, not realizing he'd spoken his thoughts.

"I can't say much more yet," Murdoch continued, "but I will tell you that we found a guy in your sister's bedroom closet. The maintenance man at the Sand & Sea. Guy named Catlett. I'll get back to you later." The phone went dead.

Just when he thought he knew about all the pieces to the puzzle—even though he didn't know how they all fit together—the puzzle became more complex. Shawn Catlett was an unexpected new puzzle piece. The man who'd opened Susan's condominium for him . . . when was it? Only a couple days ago? Matt struggled to focus through the pain and fog in his head.

The bathroom door opened and Renee leaned in. A hair dryer whirred in her hand.

"Did I hear the phone?" she asked.

"Yeah," Matt said. "There's more bad news."

DAY SEVEN

CHAPTER FORTY-EIGHT

Matt groaned awake when a hand touched his shoulder. Renee stood over him, haloed by the sun streaming through the partially open curtains.

"Time to get up already?" His voice was hoarse.

Renee giggled. "I woke you up every hour to check your pupils. Do you remember?"

"Sort of. What time is it?"

"It's almost ten. That bath really did wonders."

Matt shook his index finger in Renee's face. "You mean I got a whole four or five hours sleep." But he couldn't even pretend to be angry while her eyes were locked on his. Was it just the light or did Renee's eyes seem more green than hazel this morning? He scooted back against the headboard and ran his hands through his hair.

She tugged at his wrist. "Come on, lazybones."

A sudden breeze came through the open window. It furled the sheers and carried the cooing sound of a dove into the room. Renee's perfume mixed with the breeze and drifted over Matt.

Time seemed to stop. Matt wanted to say something, to tell her how much he appreciated her help, how much her friendship with Susan meant to him. How he felt about her. He was dumbstruck. His eyes drifted from Renee's face, to her silver-clasped long hair, to the swell of her breasts against her yellow halter-top. Her long, shapely legs shone bronze in the sunlight. Matt's spine felt as though it vibrated like a violin caressed by a bow.

He wanted to hold her, breathe her in, bury his face in her hair, kiss her lips. But what if that's not what *she* wants? He knew he was in uncharted territory.

Matt saw Renee's breasts heave, then she released a shuddering sigh. "Follow your instincts, Matthew," she said in a throaty whisper.

He felt as though his pulse played a drum riff, and that riff seemed to soar. He gently took her hand and pulled her to him, brushed her hair back from her face, enclosed her with his arms.

She pressed against him; glided her fingers down the side of his face.

"Oh, Matt," she said.

Matt shivered. He felt nervous and giddy. He kissed her. Her mouth opened and she tasted sweet. Matt kissed her deeply. His whole body trembled as though a cold, alien wind had suddenly invaded his being.

Renee removed the clasp from her hair and dropped it to the floor. She fumbled with the buttons on her skirt, almost tearing them off. He pulled her hand away, unbuttoned her skirt, lifted her top over her head, and—while devouring her lips—unclasped her bra.

Matt arched his back and slipped out of his shorts, rolled Renee onto her back, and pulled off her panties. He looked down at her. She was perfect. Every part of her. But it was her face, especially her eyes that mesmerized him. He tried to translate what he saw in their emerald depths, and decided it was trust. This woman who he had known for less than a week looked at him as though he was the most important person in her life. The shuddering cold that had penetrated his body now vanished in a wave of heat that threatened to scald him from the inside out.

He nibbled her neck, her breasts, her stomach, the insides of her thighs. His lips tingled with the touch of her skin as he moved over her, manic with the sight and smell and feel of her.

Matt took her nipple in his mouth and lightly brushed it with his teeth. He felt her tremble. He ran the tip of his tongue over it. She groaned and pushed him to the side. Then she climbed onto him and wildly kissed his chest. He tensed. Small shocks ran through him as she moved down. Matt was on fire. He closed his eyes and heard a whimper escape his lips. Then she kissed her way back up his body until their lips met, their tongues wet and probing.

She raised herself over him and they came together. She moved her hips in what seemed to Matt like a thousand different directions. Her head dropped forward and her hair covered her face.

Matt reached up to push her hair back behind her ears. She opened her eyes, smiled, and took him as deeply as she could. She bent forward and teased his chest with the tips of her breasts. They fell into a natural rhythm—like lovers of many years—until she cried out, "Now, Matt! Now! Please, Matt."

Spent, they lay together as though frozen in time and place, breathing as one. Renee clutched him. Matt moved, to kiss her cheek, and tasted salty tears.

Matt groaned. He felt pain in his ribs and in his head. The curtains were closed and he couldn't tell if it was day or night.

Renee rose up on an elbow. "You okay?" she asked. Worry etched her voice.

Matt chuckled and ran a hand down her back. "How long did I sleep?"

"Maybe an hour."

"That's it?"

"That's it." She kissed his forehead. "Why the frown?"

"I was thinking about Robert. I feel awful about what I said to him the last time we were together. Now he's gone, too."

"Gee, what a revelation, Matthew Curtis is human," she said, hints of sarcasm and reprimand in her voice. "He said things he's sorry for. I wonder if anyone else in the world ever made the same mistake."

Matt snorted. "You have a way of making me feel like a self-absorbed bastard."

Renee kissed his mouth. "But you're a cute, self-absorbed bastard."

Matt suddenly felt part of a team again. There was something about this woman's "take no prisoners" honesty and her tender, but tough personality that gave him confidence that all would be right with the world. Like it had been with Susan when they were kids, similar to feelings he'd had with his wife, Allison. He released an uneven breath. "You're a good woman, Renee Drummond."

Renee blushed. "For that, Matt, you deserve a reward." Then she put her lips to his and moved her hands over his body.

CHAPTER FORTY-NINE

The microwave clock read eleven forty-five. While Renee busied herself at the stove, Matt called his Albuquerque office manager, but had to be satisfied with leaving a message in voicemail. He was about to return the call Doctor Trang had made to his cell the day before, but he put down the phone when Angelo sloshed into the kitchen, drenched and disheveled, with dark half-circles under his eyes.

"Man, you look like you had a rough night," Matt said.

"Damn, it rained for hours," Angelo said. "I gotta check my feet. See if they're webbed." He moved to take a seat at the kitchen table.

Renee held up an oven-mitted hand. "Whoa there, buster. Don't you even think about sitting in my kitchen until you clean up."

Angelo jerked to attention. "Sorry, ma'am," he said, his face red.

"And please leave those boots outside."

"Yes, ma'am," he said as he backed out of the room like a little boy who's been reprimanded.

Matt was barely able to stifle laughter.

Renee smiled at him and winked. "Every army has to have rules," she said.

Matt came to attention in his chair and saluted. "Yes, ma'am, General, ma'am."

"And don't you forget it," Renee said as she shook her spatula at him before she turned back to the oven to check on the biscuits.

After she closed the oven door, Renee switched on a little television on the kitchen counter. "Let's see if there's any news," she said.

Matt swiveled his chair to get a better view of the set, just as a perky blond smiled into the void.

"This is Gail Sturgis of Eyewitness News. We have a breaking story that deepens the mystery behind a tragedy we reported earlier this week. That was the death of a woman named Susan Curtis who fell from her twenty-fourth-floor unit at the Sand & Sea Condominiums near Diamondhead last Monday. Last night, police were called to her condominium unit, where they found the body of Ms. Curtis's long-time boyfriend, Robert Nakamura. The police say he died as a result of a drug overdose. Our . . . ."

The woman looked to her left. Someone passed her a sheet of paper from off-camera. She took a second to glance at it, then stared back at the camera. "This just in. We understand that the Honolulu Coroner is about to release its report on Susan Curtis's death. Our information is that the coroner, Doctor Van Trang, will rule that Ms. Curtis did, in fact, take her own life. We have Jerry Damon, our roving reporter, on scene outside the coroner's office. What can you tell us, Jerry? Is there any connection between Miss Curtis's suicide earlier this week and Mister Nakamura's death last night?"

The male reporter affected a concerned frown. "Gail, we don't know at this point if there is a connection. The police are still investigating Mister Nakamura's death. But, a high-placed police source, who prefers not to be identified, speculated that Mister Nakamura may have been distraught over Ms. Curtis's suicide and killed himself. That's all we know now."

"Thank you, Jerry," the commentator said. "Eyewitness News will bring you more when . . . ."

Matt rose from his chair and switched off the television set. "Sonofa . . ." He paced the kitchen floor; clenched and unclenched his fists. He tried to keep his voice under control, to contain the anger that surged in him. "The Hawaii Organized Crime Task Force knows someone pushed Susan off her balcony. Muriel Goldstein told them that much. Frank Murdoch called me back last night after they found Robert's body. He said they found the condo maintenance man, Shawn Catlett, hiding in Susan's apartment."

"You think the maintenance man killed Robert?" Renee asked.

Matt closed his eyes. "Honestly, probably not. He seemed slow, kinda weird; too simple to stage Robert's death to make it appear to be a suicide. But, hell . . . I don't know. There's enough screwy stuff about Susan's and now Robert's deaths that I can't believe the cops would believe either of their deaths was a suicide."

"The news report's got to be a mistake," Renee said. "Why don't you call Murdoch?"

Matt ran upstairs, found Murdoch's card on the bedroom dresser, and brought it back downstairs to the kitchen phone. He dialed the number and asked to be put through.

"Murdoch."

"Mister Murdoch, this is Matt Curtis. What the hell is going on? Have you seen the news this morning?"

"Actually, I have, Doctor Curtis. Can't always believe what you see or hear."

That surprised Matt. "What do you mean?"

Murdoch expelled a loud breath. "I think we'd better get together. I have some explaining to do. We screwed up not calling you before we leaked that information to the press. Can you come down here in an hour?"

"Yes. One hour," Matt said.

Renee spread her hands out and shrugged her shoulders, the universal gesture for "tell me."

"I don't know, honey," Matt said. "But I think I'm about to find out. Do you think you could save some of those biscuits for me?"

" 'Honey'?"

Matt shot to attention. "Begging your pardon, General. I must have lost my head there for a moment."

Renee walked over and kissed Matt on the lips. Angelo returned just then to the kitchen.

"Whoops, sorry, guys," he said.

Renee laughed. "Sit down, Angelo. Matt was just showing his appreciation to his commanding officer."

"Man, this sure ain't anything like the Army I was in," Angelo said.

CHAPTER FIFTY

Frank Murdoch came out to the reception room at the HOCTF hangar entrance and escorted Matt through the building to his office. Murdoch moved briskly across the concrete floor, and spoke over his shoulder. "Doctor Curtis, I'm sorry about not calling you. I should have given you a warning. It's been a madhouse around here. Let me explain what we're trying to do. Maybe then you'll understand why I told the press that your sister committed suicide."

Murdoch preceded Matt into his corner office, pointed him to a scuffed wooden chair, and closed the door. He dragged a second chair from against the wall, positioned it facing Matt's chair, and sat down. He leaned forward, elbows propped on his knees, and said, "This stays in this room, Doctor Curtis. You understand?"

Matt nodded his head.

Murdoch sat up straight in his chair and slapped his palms against the tops of his thighs. He closed his eyes and his face grew red. "Okay," he said, after a moment. "Again, I apologize for not telling you in advance what we released to the media. It was my responsibility. It must have been a shock to hear that your sister's death had been ruled a suicide. Especially after what Muriel Goldstein told us."

Matt took Murdoch's apology as sincere. There seemed to be nothing pretentious about Murdoch. His wardrobe looked to have been assembled at Goodwill. Green plaid jacket, bright blue shirt, impossible-to-describe tie, black slacks, and brown shoes. The jacket and slacks needed pressing. His close-cropped hair, above a high forehead, fought a losing battle between staying brown and turning gray. Matt saw intelligence in the man's dark brown eyes.

"All we know for sure," Murdoch continued, "is someone pushed your sister off her balcony. Muriel Goldstein verified that. We can't explain the drugs in her system, however. And we sure don't have a motive for murder that I can buy into. We need to let your sister's killer think he dodged a bullet. That's why we released the suicide story. We had the coroner's cooperation, obviously. We do have those three guys we took off the helicopter. We'll keep the pressure on them. Try to get one to crack. We're holding them on assault and weapons charges. We're pretty sure those three are members of Jackson's organization. But, so far, they haven't implicated him. Until they went after Muriel Goldstein, and one of them said 'Lonnie' in front of you, we had no idea Lonnie Jackson might have any connection to your sister's death. I personally talked to the judge. There's no way he'll let them out on bail, which is a nice change from the way that Lonnie Jackson's men are usually treated."

"Assuming you're correct about their connection to Jackson," Matt said.

Murdoch nodded. "But, even if they do work for Jackson, unless one of those hoods spills for us we won't be able to charge their boss."

"Who is this Jackson?" Matt asked.

"He's slime," Murdoch said. "And, like slime, he's hard to get your hands on. We've tried to tie him to prostitution, drugs, even murder. But he seems to be indictment proof. His may be the last criminal organization in the country that still sticks by the code of *Omerta*. His people have never ratted on him. And, I know in my bones he's got judges and cops on his payroll. His people hardly ever draw a prison sentence . . . if they show up for trial." Murdoch put his hands together as though in prayer. "Oh, if I could only prove who Jackson has bribed," he growled.

A man tapped on the glass of Murdoch's office door, opened the door, and stuck his head inside. "Phone call on line two, Chief."

"Excuse me," Murdoch said. He stood, walked behind his

desk, punched a button on the telephone console, and barked, "Murdoch." He listened for a minute. Matt heard him say, "Doctor Trang, I really appreciate"—Matt waved his arms to get Murdoch's attention—"hold a second, Doctor Trang." Murdoch's eyebrows scrunched. "What?" he mouthed.

"I'd like to talk to him when you're finished," Matt said. Murdoch nodded, and continued his conversation.

"As I was saying, Doctor Trang, we appreciate your cooperation. I owe you one." He listened for a moment. "Yeah, I know you stuck your neck out. It'll only be for a day or two. If nothing comes up, you'll be able to release the official autopsy report on Miss Curtis. By the way, Doctor Curtis is here and would like to talk to you."

Matt stood and reached for the receiver, but Murdoch held it against his chest.

"Remember, Doctor, whatever he tells you is confidential."

Matt nodded, then took the receiver from Murdoch.

"I just wanted to thank you for dragging your feet on my sister's autopsy and death certificate," Matt said to Trang.

A long silence on the other end of the line. "Hello," Matt said. "Doctor Trang, are you still there?"

"Excuse me, Doctor Curtis. I don't understand. What are you talking about?"

"Lieutenant Callahan told me you'd agreed to put my sister's file at the bottom of your work? To give me time to—" Matt noticed Murdoch's head snap in his direction.

"No, Doctor Curtis, on the contrary," Trang said. "Lieutenant Callahan called me later on the morning you two visited my office. He was quite adamant about wanting your sister's file processed quickly. He said he wanted the matter cleared up as soon as possible so you could return home."

Matt stood speechless. He almost put down the phone, but remembered his manners in time. "I appreciate . . . uh, thanks."

"I'm sorry, Doctor Curtis," Trang said. "This all must be terrible for you."

Matt replaced the receiver in the console, stared at Murdoch, and moved his head slowly from side to side. "Very peculiar," he commented.

"What about Callahan?" Murdoch demanded.

"Callahan's in charge of the investigation into my sister's death. I—"

Murdoch made a hand gesture that said, Yes, yes, I know.

Matt hesitated a moment, blew out a heavy breath, then said, "I think Detective Dennis Callahan is a liar. He told me he asked the coroner to delay closing my sister's file, to put off finalizing his findings report. But Trang just told me Callahan asked him to close Susan's file as soon as possible."

Matt shook his head. "I know Callahan has no obligation to tell me anything. But why give me the opposite impression? That he wanted to help prove that my sister did not kill herself, that he would be open with me. He kept secret the fact that the manager of the Sand & Sea saw Muriel Goldstein leave the condominium building in the middle of the night, minutes after Susan died. And, according to the manager, the old woman seemed agitated. That seems peculiar and important. And, with what Muriel Goldstein has now told us, we know that bit of information was more than just important. It was critical."

Murdoch shrugged, but he appeared agitated. He rubbed his hands together and paced the small office.

Matt plopped into his chair, then popped up and touched Murdoch's arm as the cop crossed in front of him. "You told me on the phone that Robert Nakamura died of a heroin overdose. I'll bet there was only one needle mark on him."

Murdoch's forehead wrinkled. "Why would you say that?"

Matt held up his hands and signaled Murdoch to give him a moment. "Am I right?" he asked.

"I'll know more when I see the coroner's report," Murdoch said, "but my agent on the scene told me the whole thing appeared suspicious. He specifically noted that there were no apparent needle tracks on the victim's body."

"Robert was scared to death of needles, of taking any drug, for that matter. Legal or not. There is no way he would inject himself."

After Matt Curtis left the HOCTF building, Murdoch called Agent Roy Casper to his office.

"This gets more and more curious," Murdoch said. "You've been checking on Detective Dennis Callahan for a couple years. Right?"

"Yep," Casper said. "Along with a dozen other Honolulu cops. But Callahan's the big Kahuna, as far as I'm concerned. Despite alimony payments, he has a thirty-eight foot catamaran, a BMW, and an expensive condo. Not to mention the fact that at any given time the guy wears a couple thousand dollars worth of designer duds. All on a lieutenant's salary. But, so far, I can't pin anything on him."

"Well, it sounds as though he's involved in the Susan Curtis case—beyond being the officer in charge."

"How's that, Chief?" Casper asked.

"He lied to Susan Curtis's brother about asking the coroner to put a hold on her file. He held back information he could have given Curtis about a potential witness to his sister's murder. Apparently, the manager at the Sand & Sea saw one of the sister's neighbors leave the building very late at night, just minutes after Curtis died. The manager swears he gave the same information to Callahan."

"That's no crime," Casper said. "It's not illegal for a cop to hold back information from a civilian, but—"

"But something stinks?" Murdoch finished the thought.

"To high heaven," Casper said. "And, let me make it smell even worse," he added. "I asked Internal Affairs at HPD to let me look at copies of Callahan's files from the Susan Curtis case. I wanted to try to find something that would implicate him in criminal activity. I don't recall any mention of anyone seeing a neighbor leave the building. In the witness interview section of the file, Callahan specifically mentions talking to a Gabriel Muccio. He wrote that Muccio stated he did not see or hear anything suspicious. Also, that Muccio did not see anyone enter or leave the building immediately before or after Susan Curtis's death."

"What does that tell you?" Murdoch asked.

"Nothing we can take to court. Maybe Callahan's just a sloppy cop. But, I don't think so. I think he intentionally omitted that information from the case file."

Murdoch intertwined his fingers and stretched them. He rolled his shoulders and tried to release the tension that had built there.

"Anything new on the guy found in Susan Curtis's closet? Shawn Catlett."

"That's another matter," Casper said as he scratched his eyebrow with a paperclip. "He's so traumatized, we can't get anything out of him, except he keeps saying how much he loved 'Miss Susan.' Says she was always nice to him. The guy's a little"—he made circles with his finger by the side of his head.

"I'll bet a month's pay Catlett had nothing to do with Susan Curtis or Robert Nakamura's deaths," Murdoch said. "He had a crush on the Curtis woman, maybe even an obsession, and just got caught in the wrong place at the wrong time. We'll continue to question him, but I think we have bigger fish to fry."

CHAPTER FIFTY-ONE

Matt had never been one to be self-indulgent. But he now found himself feeling melancholy. His life as a surgeon was full of more certainties than uncertainties. Sure there were times when he had to conduct exploratory procedures, where he couldn't be certain of what he would find, but they were the exception rather than the rule. Since he'd arrived in Hawaii, the uncertainties around Susan's death had been maddening.

At a school zone, just before driving up to Renee's neighborhood, Matt stopped while a crossing guard escorted several children across the road. He absent-mindedly glanced to his right at the fenced schoolyard, teeming with children, and focused on three little girls on a swing set just inside the fence. Their laughter drifted through the open windows of his car. He caught the eye of one of the little girls and she smiled at him.

In that moment, Matt felt his heart ache. He remembered Susan would kick her legs harder and harder to make the tire-swing their father had hung in the backyard rise higher and higher. Susan's spirit had been like that. Soaring. Never satisfied to be grounded. The lump in his throat threatened to choke him.

The children in the crosswalk had safely reached the far curb and the crossing guard gave Matt a "you can proceed" wave. Matt nodded and continued up the road to Renee's. But as he was about to turn into her driveway, the flash of strobe lights in his rearview mirror startled him. An unmarked police car, and Matt pulled over immediately. He was surprised when Callahan got out of the car.

Callahan bent down to Matt's open window. "Hey, Doc, how ya doin'?"

"Christ, Lieutenant. You gave me a start."

"Sorry. I need to talk with you and thought I'd find you here."

How could Callahan have known to find him at Renee's? Matt wondered if Callahan had followed him, and for how long.

"I want to bring you up-to-date on the investigation into your sister's death," Callahan said."

"What investigation? I just heard they officially ruled Susan's death a suicide. Case closed."

"Uh, well . . . I followed up on a lead—unofficially. I just don't buy the coroner's conclusion."

"Well, that's a surprise," Matt said. "What made you change your mind?"

Callahan pointed at the driveway. "Do you think we could talk up at the house?"

Matt heard a little voice inside caution him. "I guess that would be all right," he said after a few moments.

Callahan slapped the van door. "Good." He stepped away, then stopped and asked, "Is Missus Drummond home?"

"No," Matt lied. "Why?"

"Oh, I . . . wouldn't want to upset her talking about your sister's death."

"She'll be thrilled to learn you're still working Susan's case. Follow me, I'll open the gate."

Matt quickly pulled up to the control panel. He looked in his rearview mirror. Callahan had just turned into the driveway. Matt pretended to tap in the code, but instead hit the intercom button. He faced forward so Callahan couldn't see him talking. Esteban's voice came through the box.

"Yeah, who is it?"

"Amigo, we got company. Callahan. Hide everyone. I want him to think I'm alone. But, Esteban . . . ."

"Yeah, Matt."

"Something's fishy. Stay close."

Matt released the intercom button and punched in the code. When he reached the house, Matt got out of the car and waited for Callahan to join him under the entrance's arched alcove. He had a sudden sinking feeling after he opened the door. The weapons and box of ammunition had been by the foyer closet when he left for Murdoch's office. Callahan couldn't miss them.

He stepped into the foyer and was relieved to find that the stuff had been moved.

"Let's talk in the solarium," Matt suggested. "Want a drink?"

"Bourbon, rocks, if it's no trouble," Callahan said. He settled into a high-backed wicker armchair that faced away from the open patio door and toward the living room they'd just passed through.

Matt noticed the detective examine the room, then crane his neck to inspect the hall to the kitchen. Next, he looked back toward the foyer.

"No trouble at all," Matt said. He went to the wet bar and filled a glass with ice from the under-the-counter freezer. He poured two fingers of Wild Turkey and carried it over to the cop.

"Not joining me?" Callahan asked.

"Maybe a little later. Stomach's been a little queasy lately. And my head still feels like someone's beating on it."

"Yeah, with good reason," Callahan said sympathetically. The cop again seemed to examine the room. "When's Missus Drummond due back?"

"What's on your mind, Dennis?" Matt sat on a couch across from the cop. He noticed the bulge of a shoulder holster under Callahan's blue blazer.

Callahan didn't answer Matt's question.

"What did you think of the coroner's announcement today that Susan committed suicide?" Matt asked.

"Kinda surprised me."

"Especially the timing of it," Matt said. "I assumed the coroner would hold off for a few more days, based on what you told me. You did ask him to drag his feet on issuing his report."

"Oh, right! Of course!" Callahan shrugged. "I tried."

Matt leaned forward and pointed an accusing finger. "Yeah, I found out exactly how much you tried. I talked to Doctor Trang this morning. He said you told him to expedite his report. Why'd you lie about it?"

Callahan opened his mouth. Matt expected him to try to bullshit his way around the answer. But Callahan closed his mouth and set his drink on the table beside his chair. "You know there's no point in prolonging this," he said as he reached down, pulled a small pistol from an ankle holster, and pointed it at Matt. "You should have just buried your sister and gone back home to fuckin' Arizona, Doc. None of this would have been necessary."

"That's New Mexico," Matt said in a calm, but derisive tone. "Not Arizona. Can't you get that straight?" Then he sat back, crossed his legs, and in a voice as calm as he could muster, said, "What do you plan to do, Callahan, kill me? Then wait for Renee and shoot her, too? For what? What have you done that's so bad that you've become a killer?" Matt thought he saw a shadow flit across the cop's flinty eyes.

"Don't fuck with me," Callahan growled. "Where's Renee Drummond?"

"I guess you'll just have to find her yourself."

Callahan's eyes widened and his eyebrows arched. "Ah, I get it. She *is* here. Where is she?"

"Screw you."

Callahan thumbed back the hammer of the pistol. "Fine. It will be fun playing hide and seek with her." He aimed the gun at the middle of Matt's face. "After I shoot you."

Matt uncrossed his legs and folded his arms across his chest. "Tell me one thing before you shoot me," he said. "Who killed my sister?"

Callahan stood and smiled. He lowered his aim to Matt's chest. "I don't have a clue."

That surprised Matt. He had begun to suspect that Callahan was the killer. "Do you know *why* she was killed?"

Callahan laughed and hunched his shoulders. "Strike two, Doc. Don't know the answer to that one either." He paused, then said, "Would you like to know who gave the order to kill her?"

"Sure," Matt said.

"Lonnie Jackson. Who else?"

"Jackson? How do you know that?"

"Because he personally ordered me to kill her. I shot her up with enough Rohypnol to kill an elephant. But she jumped before the drugs could have done the job." He shot a satisfied look at Matt. "Now, if you're finished with twenty questions . . . ." The pistol zeroed in on Matt's face again.

But another movement caught Matt's attention. The jet-black head of Maximillian the Rottweiler appeared in the open patio door; the sheers shifted around the dog in the light tropical breeze. The dog stood as though frozen.

"Callahan, look behind you, very slowly."

Callahan laughed. "You watch too many movies." But he turned his head and saw not just Max in the doorway, but also Angelo now, with a shotgun aimed at his head.

Callahan took a step backward. He bumped his leg against the coffee table and lurched sideways.

Max released a deep-throated growl and launched himself at the cop. Already off balance, Callahan was knocked against a cabinet. His pistol fired as he collapsed to the floor. The bullet impacted the ceiling and a puff of plaster dust drifted down. Max grasped the forearm of Callahan's gunhand in his mouth.

"Jesus," Callahan said breathlessly. "Get him off me."

A low, rumbling snarl came from Max's throat.

Esteban raced into the room from the foyer and jerked the pistol from Callahan's hand. Then he removed the cop's other pistol from his shoulder holster.

Angelo laughed. "He ain't gonna hurt you, unless you resist. Or if I say the magic word." Angelo spelled *m-a-n-g-i-a*. "You understand Italian, Callahan? It means eat."

"Call off the dog," Esteban ordered calmly.

"Release!" Angelo shouted.

Max let go of Callahan's arm, but stood stock-still and panted and drooled.

"Make nice," Angelo said.

Max moved closer to Callahan and slurped his face, then trotted back to Angelo.

Matt couldn't help himself. He snorted a laugh. "Esteban," he said, "do we have any more friends we should introduce to the lieutenant?"

"Oh, *si Senor*," Esteban said in an affected accent. "I got all kinds of *amigos*. Richie, why don't you come out and meet our new *compadre*."

The four men stood around Callahan when Renee walked into the room. She smiled sweetly. "Did you want to talk with me, Lieutenant?" she asked as she showed him a cassette recorder. "Or would you rather listen to the recording I made of your conversation with Doctor Curtis?"

Callahan moved to sit up.

Max growled.

Callahan jerked back down.

The others in the room erupted in laughter. Callahan's face went gray. He seemed to have aged ten years.

CHAPTER FIFTY-TWO

Matt stood at one end of a green felt-covered billiard table and looked at Callahan's spread-eagled body. He walked around the table and checked the ropes tied around the cop's wrists and ankles and secured to the table's bulky carved legs. "Comfortable, Dennis?" Matt asked.

"Go to hell, Curtis," Callahan rasped. He shot Matt a curled-lip, malignant look. "You think you've got me scared? What will you do, have your rich bitch tickle me to death?" Callahan laughed boisterously, until he devolved into a coughing fit.

"Got to stop smoking, Lieutenant. Cancer sticks, you know. They'll be the death of you."

"Fuck you," Callahan gasped, between coughs.

"Callahan," Matt said, "I'd prefer to ask you questions in a civilized manner. But, I was outvoted. One way or the other, though, we'll get our answers. If you won't cooperate, I'll have no other choice but to turn you over to my friends."

Callahan just stared.

"That recording is the end of your career. You'll spend time in jail. What's the point in not cooperating?"

"You hard of hearing? Fuck off! You got nothing on me. That disk will never make it into evidence. You don't know what you're up against."

Matt knew that wasn't quite true. Then he remembered what

Renee had told him about witnesses and evidence disappearing in past cases. He suspected that had a lot to do with Callahan's cockiness. Matt walked to the door and nodded at Angelo who stood just outside the room. When Angelo took a step forward, Matt grabbed his arm and whispered, "You sure Max won't hurt him? He'll just scare him."

Angelo smiled. "As long as I don't give him the "*m-a-n-g-i-a*" command, he'll be as sweet as can be."

Matt raised his eyebrows.

Angelo smiled. "Okay, okay. Maybe he won't be sweet, but he won't do any damage. Unless the cop gets belligerent . . . or he's got a bad ticker."

"Oh, Jesus," Matt exhaled as Angelo unsnapped Max's leash, but held onto the dog's collar. "Guard!" Angelo said and released the dog. Then he followed Max into the game room.

Matt watched from the doorway. The dog sniffed around the room, raised his big square head, and circled the billiard table. He pranced away from the table, turned around, took a running leap, and landed atop it. He moved forward and pressed his front paws on Callahan's chest, back paws planted between the cop's legs. The dog's back cleared the lamp that hung over the center of the table by only a few inches.

Angelo backed away and joined Matt inside the doorway.

The Rottweiler lowered its head to within inches of Callahan's throat and drooled through bared fangs. A low, steady snarl and Callahan's shouts reverberated off the wood-paneled walls.

"Get him off me," Callahan shouted over and over again. "I'll talk."

Matt stepped into the room. "Man, that was fast," he said.

Angelo gripped Matt's shoulder. "Let's wait for another minute," he said.

Matt screwed up his face in a "What gives?" look.

Angelo walked out of the room, Matt right behind him.

"The way that cop's dressed," Angelo whispered, "I'd guess he's pretty fussy about his appearance. He'll really be ready to talk after he pisses his pants."

"And when do you think that'll be?"

"Oh, it's probably already happened. But, I think we ought to let him suffer a bit longer. Just for the hell of it." Angelo chuckled and slapped Matt on the shoulder.

Two minutes later, Matt and Angelo re-entered the billiard room, with Esteban, who'd just come inside after patrolling the grounds. The only sound in the room came from Max. Callahan's normally ruddy skin color had turned gray. Matt rushed to the pool table. Callahan lay still, eyes closed. Max hadn't moved. Deep snarls resonated. Callahan's face was wet with dog drool.

"Shit!" Angelo exclaimed. "He looks dead."

A faint gurgle came from Callahan's throat. His eyes popped open and his chin trembled. "Please," he whimpered. "Get him off me. I'll talk. Please."

Callahan looked as though he'd been ridden hard and put away wet. His hands shook and his eyes darted from Matt, to Angelo, to Esteban, to Matt, avoiding the Rottweiler's face. His face and hair were wet with what appeared to be a mixture of sweat and drool. His shirt was plastered to his chest. The acrid odor of urine hung in the air.

"Angelo, why don't you get Max off the table," Matt said.

In a calm, conversational voice, Angelo ordered, "Max, make nice."

As though Angelo had turned a switch, the dog stopped growling and enthusiastically licked Callahan's face. Then he stepped back and snuffled and nuzzled Callahan's crotch.

"*Aeeyi*," Callahan cried out.

"Max, come," Angelo commanded.

The dog bounded off the table, circled Angelo, and sat next to his owner's left leg.

Angelo leaned down and stroked the dog's head. "Good boy," he said.

Max gazed adoringly up at Angelo.

Matt went to the far side of the billiard table and worked on the ropes on Callahan's wrist and ankle. Esteban took care of the ropes on the near side.

"I hope Renee isn't too angry about the stain in the middle of her table," Angelo said. He reached down again and scratched the dog's ears.

Callahan reached a hand toward Esteban, who took the sickly-looking cop's arm and helped him off the table. Matt watched Callahan lean into Esteban for support. Then, in a surprisingly fast movement, Callahan reached an arm across Esteban's chest and yanked the 9mm pistol from Esteban's shoulder holster. He jammed the gun into Esteban's side.

"You assholes think you're cute," Callahan yelled. "Well, you fucked up. Now toss your weapons on the pool table." He pushed Esteban away.

Matt and Angelo did as Callahan instructed.

Esteban, his back to Callahan, met Matt's gaze. Matt thought he'd never seen anyone with such a hangdog expression.

Matt said, "Everyone relax."

"Shut up," Callahan screamed. He took one step forward and slugged Esteban on the back of the head with the butt of the pistol. A sound like someone breaking a broomstick over his knee bounced off the walls.

Esteban groaned, sagged to the floor, and lay still.

Callahan then glared at Angelo. "You've got a great sense of humor, don't you? Well, let's see how funny you think this is." He aimed the pistol at Max.

Angelo's roar sounded like a lion on the attack. He threw himself at Callahan just as the cop pulled the trigger. The roar of the 9mm in the confined space sounded like a cannon. The shot's percussion ricocheted off the room's surfaces and sent whining shockwaves of pain into Matt's ears. But despite its noise, the shot didn't cover Angelo's painful cry. He fell in front of Max.

The dog growled like a primordial beast. From a standing position, it leaped at Callahan, like a rocket off a launcher. A one hundred and fifty pound missile made of sinew, muscle, and bone, with terrifying fangs bared.

Callahan squeezed off another round, but the bullet missed its mark as Max hit the cop with incredible force. The charge knocked the detective backward and sent him ten feet across the room. His arms windmilled. He discharged the pistol again, sending a bullet that whizzed past Matt's left ear as Callahan slammed backwards into a protruding edge of a game table. A loud *crack* sounded in the room. The pistol slipped from Callahan's hand as he slumped to the floor.

Matt watched the dog rush at Callahan, fully expecting it to continue its attack. But, instead, Max reversed direction and trotted over to Angelo. It nuzzled its owner and licked his face. No sound came from Angelo. Max whimpered and lay down next to Angelo.

Angelo lay in a heap next to where Esteban had fallen. Blood poured from a wound in his chest.

Richie, assigned to guard the outside of the house, stormed into the room, cried, "Oh no, Angelo," and knelt beside his brother.

Renee entered a moment after Richie. Her hand shot to her mouth.

Matt picked up the pistol Callahan had taken from Esteban, took a quick look at the cop's twisted, still form, and rushed to Angelo. He heard a sucking sound with each breath Angelo took. "Richie, get something to put under Angelo's head," he said.

"Please, Ange, say something," Richie cried.

Matt grabbed Richie's shoulder. "Richie, go get a pillow and blanket. Now!"

Richie gave Matt a demented, wide-eyed look, then seemed to get control of himself and rushed from the room.

"Renee, call 9-1-1," Matt said. "Tell them we need ambulances. Explain we have a gunshot wound and two other serious injuries."

Renee ran to a wall phone on the bar at the far side of the room.

Richie returned and dropped next to Angelo's right side, next to where Matt knelt. He slipped a pillow under his brother's head and handed Matt the blanket.

"You think you can help me?" Matt asked.

Richie nodded and swallowed. His Adam's apple bobbed.

Matt ripped off his shirt and passed it to Richie. He pointed at Angelo's chest wound. "I want you to apply pressure right here," he said. "We've got to stop the bleeding. Understand?"

"Ye . . . yeah."

"Good," Matt said while he scrambled on hands and knees over to Esteban, who had turned on his side. Esteban shook his head as though to clear cobwebs there and moaned.

"Are you all right, amigo?" Matt asked.

Esteban squeezed his eyelids shut and displayed a toothy grimace. "I've had worse headaches from hangovers." But he groaned in contradiction.

Matt took a handkerchief from his pants pocket and placed it over the split, already swollen lump on the back of Esteban's head. "Hold this," he said. "You need to keep pressure on the cut. Scalp wounds bleed like a lot."

"You ought to know," Esteban said.

"Very funny. You okay to take Max out of here. I got a feeling that dog won't take kindly to paramedics hauling Angelo out of here."

"How 'bout I take care of Angelo and let Richie handle Max?"

"Whatever works."

Matt stood and offered his hand to Esteban.

Esteban swayed while he moved to a sitting position, gripped Matt's outstretched hand, and unsteadily got to his feet. He walked a crooked path to where Richie knelt next to Angelo.

"I'll spot you, bro. You need to get Max out of here."

Max whimpered.

Matt heard Renee hang up the phone. He looked over at her while she crossed toward him. "How soon will they be here?"

"Fifteen minutes. I'll open the gate and wait out front."

Matt nodded, then walked over to Angelo and Esteban. He squatted and took Angelo's hand. "Ange, can you hear me?"

A low moan came from Angelo.

Matt tried again. "Angelo, can you hear me?"

Angelo peeked out through hooded lids. "I need a drink," he said. The words were moaned versus spoken.

Matt could see pain in Angelo's eyes. "Hang in there, Ange." He looked at Esteban. "Just keep the pressure on that spot."

Matt crawled over to Callahan. The cop's eyelids fluttered. He looked up, opened his mouth as though to say something, but seemed to change his mind. His eyes now darted back and forth.

"I can't feel my legs," Callahan moaned. "What's wrong? Touch my legs."

Matt complied.

"Are you touching my legs?" Callahan asked.

"Yes."

"Oh, God. No-o-o."

"It's over, Callahan. It's time to make it right."

"I don't want to be a cripple. I can't live like that."

"Callahan." Matt shouted. "The paramedics are on the way. You'll be in the hospital soon."

"Give me a gun," the cop demanded. "Give me a gun and I'll tell you what you want to know."

Matt had no intention of helping Callahan, or anyone, take his own life. But he had no compunction about lying to this dirty cop. "Okay, Callahan, I'll give you a pistol if you answer my questions."

The cop looked at Matt with wide, moist eyes.

"Do you still claim you don't know the reason my sister died?"

"Yes!" He closed his eyes and grimaced.

"But Lonnie Jackson gave the order?"

"That's right."

"He sent you to kill her?"

A burp of a laugh escaped the cop's lips. He coughed. He said nothing for a long beat. Then, "That's right."

Matt stared at Callahan.

"He sent me to do the job. At least I tried to kill her. Just like I killed her good-for-nothing boyfriend. Same place. Gave them both a shitload of drugs." The cop laughed feebly. He coughed again.

Matt's astonishment competed with his rage. Callahan had confessed to two murders as though admitting to shoplifting. But this didn't make sense. Muriel Goldstein said a woman pushed Susan off her balcony.

"You pushed my sister off her balcony?"

Callahan winced and squinted at Matt. "Pay attention, Curtis. I didn't push anyone off any balcony. I took care of your sister the same way I offed her boyfriend—with a drug overdose. I told her I was investigating a robbery in the building. She was more than happy to help." Callahan smiled at Matt. "Women are so fuckin' gullible. She asked me in. I saw a full coffee cup on a table in the living room. I asked her if she wouldn't mind getting me a cup. While she went to the kitchen, I loaded her coffee with Rohypnol."

Callahan sniggered. "I figured she'd stop breathing in ten or fifteen minutes, max."

Matt wanted to strangle Callahan. He clenched his fists until they ached, but forced himself to stay under control.

"How'd Susan fall?"

"That wasn't my doing. Maybe she just lost her balance." He laughed. "You can imagine my surprise when I was called to the scene a few minutes later and found her down there."

"Could someone have pushed her?" Matt asked.

"How the fuck do I know?" Callahan said in a raspy voice. "I'd already left the apartment."

"Why kill Robert?"

Callahan smirked. "Your saintly sister lived with one of Lonnie Jackson's mules. He carried drugs for Jackson—from the mainland to the islands. Sometimes from the Orient to Hawaii. He worked for him for years."

Now Matt understood all the travel Robert had done. Robert had a job—of sorts— after all.

"Jackson changed his operations less than a year ago," Callahan continued. "He moved drugs in bulk shipments aboard cargo ships, instead of in small amounts on human mules. He didn't need the mules anymore, and didn't want to take the risk of any of them rolling over on him. I assume that's why he wanted me to kill Nakamura. Could be he thought Nakamura had said something to your sister. Maybe that's why he wanted her out of the way, too."

Matt had never had any regard for Robert, but now the possibility existed that the sonofabitch got Susan murdered. It hadn't been her involvement with Save the Kids. But then Matt wondered, Why the attack on Renee and him?

A thought slammed against the inside of Matt's head, like a racquetball against a wall: Who did Muriel Goldstein see push Susan over her balcony railing?

Matt took a calming breath. "Okay, Callahan, have you heard of the Rawson, Wong & Ballard Law Firm?"

"Who hasn't? So what?"

"What's its relationship with Lonnie Jackson?"

Callahan closed his eyes for a moment. Then he looked back at

Matt. "None that I know of. I've never known any lawyers from that firm to defend any of Jackson's people in a criminal case." He paused a moment, clenched his jaw and moaned. He worked to catch his breath and then finally continued. "If there's a connection, it's got to mean big bucks. Follow the money, Curtis. When you find the pot of gold, you'll find Lonnie Jackson, and maybe someone from Rawson, Wong & Ballard up to their necks in it."

A wistful look came over Callahan's face. "If someone from there works with Jackson, I'll give odds Jackson's got something on him. Something that would ruin a career, a life, if it ever went public."

Matt noticed Callahan's face darken. "That's Jackson's hold over you, isn't it? Blackmail."

Callahan's eyes found a corner of the room and seemed to fix on a dark place there. "Give me the pistol now, Curtis."

"One more thing. Tell me about Jackson."

Callahan sniggered, but it cracked in his throat. He sneered at Matt. "He's the worst thing that ever happened to me. And he'll be the same with you. He's evil. He'll kill you, Curtis."

"Describe him," Matt ordered.

Callahan coughed. "Six feet, two inches; weighs about two twenty. He's built like a linebacker and has a personality to match. He's handsome, in a way, almost clean-cut looking. But his eyes. Those damn amber eyes. Like a cat's. They make him look . . . satanic." He gulped air and swallowed. He seemed to shudder. "Face of evil. The devil's face," he said so quietly Matt at first wasn't sure he'd heard him.

Callahan seemed to withdraw internally. Then his voice modulated and he spoke again, but more to himself than to Matt. "The first time I saw him was down by Waikiki, ten, eleven years ago. Stopped for a burger. Just sat there in my car. Jackson opens the passenger door and slips in." Callahan paused and looked at the ceiling.

"I'd heard about him for years, but had never seen him before. He was building his organization back then. Nowhere as big as it is now. The guy now keeps a low profile. Let's his men do his dirty work. That's why he's never implicated in anything. Jackson was so cool that day. I couldn't help but be impressed. Dumps a DVD in my lap and tells me it's a copy. He somehow recorded me having sex with . . . ." Callahan paused, swallowed, and then continued. "He said he'd send other copies to the press if I didn't work for him. By the time I figured out a response, he'd disappeared."

"How long has Jackson operated in the islands?"

"Since he was a teenager. I heard he grew up on Honolulu's streets and that every time Social Services picked him up, he'd run away and go back to the streets. I think his parents are dead. No brothers or sisters I know about. Now, give me the gun."

The sounds of sirens drifted up from the road. Matt winced at the rasps of Angelo's labored breaths that came from a few feet away. Max whined. Matt gripped Callahan's jaw in his hand and forced him to look at him. "Do I look like Doctor Kevorkian?" Matt stood and hurried to where Richie gave first aid to Angelo.

"Curtis, you bastard," Callahan shrieked. Then he sobbed.

CHAPTER FIFTY-THREE

Matt paced like a caged tiger in the hospital waiting room. It had been hours since they'd arrived here and he hadn't been able to sit down for more than a couple minutes at a stretch. He now held his cell phone against his ear and listened to the "br-r-r" of its ring. "Come on, Linda, pick up." He alternately stared at Renee and Richie—their faces pale and drawn—seated in plastic chairs against one wall, and at the curtained-off space where Esteban had been taken by hospital orderlies. Angelo had been rushed to surgery two hours ago and they hadn't heard a thing since then.

He needed to keep busy, to take his mind off his injured friends. He knew Esteban would be okay. But Angelo was a different story. He'd lost a great amount of blood, and there was no telling how much internal damage the bullet had done. The idea of Angelo dying tormented him.

"Doctor's office," jolted Matt's attention back to the cell phone.

"Linda, it's Matt."

"Hi, Doctor Curtis. You called at a bad time. It's a madhouse here. I think every kid in town has broken something. Soccer injuries, bicycle crashes, falls from trees. You name it, we got it. I've put off any patients I can until after you get back. Just taking care of the emergencies. How are you?"

"Everything's fine," Matt lied, not wanting to take the time to describe the mess he'd gotten into. "Thanks for handling things. I know extending my trip has put added pressure on you."

"I appreciate you realizing it, but don't worry about a thing."

"I'll probably be back next Monday," Matt told her. "I'll try to call in each day."

"Before you hang up, Doctor," Linda said, "the mailman delivered a package for you today from Hawaii. From your sister. Do you want me to open it?"

Matt felt his stomach lurch. My God, he thought, Susan must have mailed it shortly before her death. "Yes, please. Just take a look inside." He heard Linda put down the receiver. The sounds of paper being torn.

"There's a three-inch stack of tax forms in here, along with a flash drive. Also a handwritten note."

Susan had always done Matt's tax returns. So he didn't think anything about the package. Probably his working papers and a copy of the final tax return she'd done for him. But the note was a different matter. Maybe the last communication between them. He was about to have Linda read the note to him, but hesitated, then decided that the note might be personal and it might make Linda uncomfortable reading it aloud. "Why don't you leave the package in my office, but fax the note to me."

"Sure. What's the fax number?"

Matt covered the cell phone mouthpiece and stopped pacing. He looked at Renee. "You have a fax machine at the house?"

She gave him the number.

Matt repeated the number for Linda, thanked her, and hung up. He turned back to Renee, just when Esteban stepped from behind one of the exam room curtains.

One hour later, a skinny young woman with old eyes, dressed in blood-stained green scrubs, came into the waiting room. Her surgical mask hung limply around her neck. She looked around the room. "Mister Caruso?" she asked in a surprisingly deep voice.

"I'm Richard Caruso," Richie said as he bolted to his feet, his face tight with tension.

The woman walked to Richie. "I'm Doctor Lee. I operated on your brother. He's in the recovery room now. We will know more about his condition in three or four hours."

Richie's voice broke when he asked, "Is he . . . going to make it?"

The doctor had large, wet eyes—fawn-like. Matt saw the sorrowful expression she gave Richie. Most older surgeons would have long since learned to avoid a show of emotion, Matt thought. This gal hasn't lost enough patients, yet.

"The bullet nicked the pericardial sac around your brother's heart and lodged in his left lung," she said. "Significant internal bleeding had occurred. We removed the bullet and stopped the bleeding. I'm still concerned about the risk of infection, and the possibility of pneumonia." She laid a hand on Richie's arm. "He's getting the best of care."

"Can I see him?" Richie asked. Tears welled in his eyes.

The doctor looked at the clock on the waiting room wall. "It's three now. Why don't you come back after seven? We'll know a lot more then, and your brother should have come out of the anesthesia."

Richie thanked the doctor and walked away to a corner of the waiting room, his back to the others, and wiped his eyes on his shirtsleeve.

Esteban gingerly patted the thick gauze bandage taped to the back of his head and smiled at Renee. "Do I look like Matt?"

She smiled back. "Not yet. You have only one bandage."

"You guys break me up," Matt said.

Esteban patted Matt's shoulder. "Why don't we go have some dinner? We can return here afterward."

Matt looked at his watch. "You all go ahead," he said. "I'm not really hungry. I think I'll see if I can get in touch with Jean Nelson at the law firm. I might as well take care of some business. Get it over with."

"And I've got to do something about Max. I can't leave him out there in the van for hours. Angelo will kill me if I don't take good care of his dog."

Renee hooked her arm in Esteban's. "Why don't we drop Max off at my house? He can have the run of the place. We can meet Matt for dinner later." She looked over at Matt and got a nod.

"Sounds good," Richie said.

Esteban said, "Matt, meet us at O'Dool's at 6:30. Get the address off Google. It's close to here."

Matt waved and walked out of the room, his cell phone once again held against his ear, Jean Nelson's business card in his other hand, a rhinoceros-sized weight of guilt on his shoulders.

CHAPTER FIFTY-FOUR

Jean Nelson crossed the lobby, her right hand extended. "Doctor Curtis, thank you for coming down. I have everything ready." She shook Matt's hand, turned, and walked down the hall.

Matt thought her voice sounded strained. Maybe a little defensive.

She led Matt down a bowling alley-of-a-corridor, into a large windowless office furnished with a desk and chair, two visitor chairs and a bank of eight filing cabinets. No art. One photograph of a man, teenaged girl, and Jean Nelson. Another of the same teenager, bandana around her forehead, backpack at her feet, standing on a rocky peak.

She seemed to read Matt's mind. "Some view, huh?" she said. "Here I am in paradise, and I spend at least eight hours a day without seeing the sun." She made a sound that resembled a laugh, but, like her voice, it seemed strained.

Matt offered her an understanding smile, but couldn't think of anything to say.

"Well, I guess we should take care of business." She opened a desk drawer and hefted a large file onto the middle of her desk.

"Quite a file," Matt said.

"Not surprising," she said, "considering the number of years Susan worked here. I've only been with the firm five years myself. After Susan . . . died, I went through her file. I doubt this firm ever had a more conscientious, more respected employee than your sister. Her annual reviews were exemplary."

Matt couldn't let the moment pass. The anger he'd felt at the funeral parlor resurfaced. "Tell me, Ms. Nelson, if Susan was so well thought of, why were you the only person from the firm at her service?" He saw her face redden and the muscle under her left eye twitch.

"I apologize, Doctor Curtis." She paused. Her eyes roamed the room. Then she stood, walked over and closed her door, regained her seat, and looked at Matt. "I guess you deserve an explanation." She hesitated, as though she questioned what she was about to do. "Finally," she sighed and said, "I was told to put out a memorandum to all employees telling them Susan had left instructions in her will that her funeral service would be for family only. The notice we gave our employees also mentioned she didn't want flowers, and instead preferred contributions be sent to Save the Kids."

"That's interesting, Ms. Nelson. I'm the executor of Susan's estate. You're quite correct about the donations to Save the Kids, but the will said nothing about a family-only service."

Jean Nelson's hands trembled. Her eyes widened, then narrowed, while she looked at Matt with what appeared to be an uncomprehending stare. Her gaze again wandered the room. Matt noticed her face had turned an angry-red.

"Who instructed you to distribute the memo, Ms. Nelson?" Matt asked in a softer voice. "I'd just like to know. I've got this resentment in my gut over the way this law firm dealt with my sister's memory. After all those years of service. Had Susan offended someone?"

Jean Nelson's head jerked back in Matt's direction. "Oh no, Doctor Curtis. On the contrary. We all loved Susan. She always did favors for other employees. Such a kindhearted soul. We all would have been at the service if we hadn't been—"

Matt leaned forward. " 'If you hadn't been' *what*?"

She blew out a burst of air and leaned back in her chair. "If Mister Ballard hadn't ordered me to send out the memo." She seemed relieved to have said the words. Her complexion lightened and she breathed a sigh. But she seemed to have trouble getting her breathing back to normal.

"And who is this Ballard?" Matt asked.

"The managing partner. My direct boss."

"I see. And why do think Mister Ballard didn't want any of the employees at Susan's funeral?"

She looked uncomfortable again. "I have no idea." She fidgeted with a pen while she looked down at her blotter.

"If you were ordered to stay away from Susan's service, why were you outside the funeral home?" Matt said, a little more forcefully.

Her face reddened again; eyelids fluttering. "Mister Ballard told me to go," she said. "To talk with you. To get you to come to our office to finalize Susan's business with the firm. As quickly as possible. And—"

"Fine," Matt said stiffly. "Let's finalize our business so I can get out of here."

Her fingers shook even more than before when she handed Matt a document with the name of a mutual fund manager imprinted at the top of the cover sheet. Susan's name was typed across the middle of the sheet. At the bottom of the page the names of the beneficiaries were filled in. Matt saw his sons' names there. It reminded him again of how much Susan loved his boys, and it hurt him that Susan had never had children of her own. He couldn't help himself. He cursed Robert Nakamura under his breath.

Matt turned the cover sheet and looked at the bottom of the next page. The Total Value line of Susan's 401-K account showed $1,231,496.06. He raised his head and looked at Jean Nelson. "Quite a sum."

"Susan had a good salary and the firm matched the first fifty percent of an employee's contributions. Susan had the maximum taken out of her paycheck and invested in her 401-K every month. And the bull market of the nineties made an enormous difference. Even with the recent drop in the market, she has a substantial sum in her account. You can see Susan had everything invested in stock funds. And, of course, there's the life insurance. Three times her current salary. Another $375,000."

She stared at Matt, as though waiting for some reaction. But none came. Finally, she filled the quiet. "Where would you like me to have the proceeds of her 401-K and insurance policy sent?"

"I'd like to talk to my sons, since they're the beneficiaries. I'll call you next week with instructions."

"Sounds fine."

"Anything else I need to deal with, Ms. Nelson?"

"Well, there was one other matter."

Matt noted bitterness in her voice.

"The real reason Mister Ballard wanted me to talk to you. Susan used to do the tax returns for many of the partners and associates. He told me to ask if you found copies of any tax returns in her condo . . . or anywhere else. Like in a safety deposit box. He said he wouldn't want copies lying around."

"Did Susan usually keep copies of these returns?" Matt asked.

"Actually, no. That's what made me think Mister Ballard's request was unnecessary. She did my returns, and she made a point of telling me to maintain good records. After she completed a tax return, she always gave back the original, one copy, and all the employee's working papers and receipts."

"So why would Mister Ballard think she might have copies?"

She hunched her shoulders. "I have no idea."

"I see," Matt said. "You can tell Ballard there were no copies of tax returns in Susan's condo, except her own. And, as far as I know, she didn't have a safe deposit box."

Matt stood and took a step toward the door.

Jean Nelson rose and walked after him.

Matt stopped. Taking his anger out on Jean Nelson didn't feel right. He turned around and put out his hand. "Thank you for your assistance, Ms. Nelson. And thank you for your kind comments about my sister."

"You're welcome, Doctor Curtis." She smiled. "When you get back home, could you do me a favor?"

"If I can."

"Would you send a letter addressed to the employees here and thank them for their contribution to Save the Kids? They raised over fifty-five-hundred dollars. And say something in the letter about your disappointment that they didn't attend Susan's service, that you would have liked to see them there. It would be helpful if you mentioned the misunderstanding about Susan's wishes regarding the service. I'll give a copy of your letter to each of the employees."

Matt smiled in return. "I'll be happy to, Ms. Nelson."

CHAPTER FIFTY-FIVE

Matt glanced in the rearview mirror and watched Esteban bring his pickup to a stop behind the rented mini-van. They'd caravaned back to the hospital from O'Dool's Restaurant. He got out of the van and waited for Richie to leave the pickup.

"We'll wait out here for you," Matt said, when Richie moved toward the hospital entrance.

Richie acknowledged Matt with a hand wave, then walked through the hospital front door.

Esteban left his pickup and joined Matt and Renee in the mini-van. "I hope Ange is okay," he said. That was the extent of conversation during the next twenty-five minutes.

"Here he comes," Renee suddenly said.

They all got out of the van and met Richie on the short path from the hospital.

"He'll be fine, guys," Richie said, a smile across his face.

"Oh, thank God."

"Great!"

"That's wonderful."

The three of them crowded around Richie; showered him with questions.

Richie chuckled. "Whoa, give me a chance." He pumped his hands at them and laughed. "Ange was awake for only a couple minutes; but you should have seen him. He reached out to me, grabbed my hand, and asked, 'Where's Max?' He smiled like a kid at Christmas when I told him that ugly mutt of his was romping, pooping, and pissing all over the Drummond estate. Then the drugs took over and he fell back asleep. The doc said his vital signs are good and there's no sign of infection. His lungs are clear."

Esteban slapped Richie on the back. "Let's go back to the house," he said. "It's been a long day."

Matt drove away from the hospital parking lot. Esteban followed close behind. He drove cautiously, careful not to run any traffic lights or to pull too far ahead of Esteban.

"You okay?" Matt asked Renee.

"Yeah," she said in a low, dry voice.

Matt looked over at her. "What's on your mind?"

"What will happen to that bastard Callahan?" she said.

"He'll probably spend the rest of his life in a state facility. Paraplegic prison. The normal prisons aren't set up to handle criminals with his kind of injuries. The recording and the statements we gave the police at the hospital should ultimately put him away for the rest of his life."

"Good!" she said vehemently.

Matt glanced at Renee. Although the passionate anger in her voice startled him, he understood.

"Did you see Richie's face when he talked about Angelo?" Renee asked softly.

"Yeah," Matt said. "I also saw his face when he said the first words out of Angelo's mouth were, "Where's Max?""

Renee laughed, but the sound seemed to catch in her throat. "It's been one hell of a day."

Matt squeezed her hand. "I liked the way it started," he said, in an attempt to lighten her mood.

"Seems like a long time ago."

He rubbed the back of her neck.

She moaned.

After they arrived at Renee's, Matt completed a quick reconnaissance of the house's interior, while Esteban and Ritchie reunited with Max and checked the grounds. After he'd gone through the house, Matt recalled his conversation with his office manager about the letter and package from Susan. "Could you tell me where your fax machine is?" he asked Renee. "I'm expecting something from my office manager."

Renee winked at Matt. "I'll check the fax machine. Why don't you pick out a nice bottle of wine? I'll meet you upstairs."

"Ah, Miss Drummond, you are a devious, conniving woman," Matt said with a leer.

"I am, aren't I?" Then she smiled and Matt felt his throat tighten and his heart leap.

Matt selected a bottle of pinot noir from the Vinotec, found a corkscrew, and met Renee at the bottom of the stairs to the second floor.

She stuck the fax paper under his arm, took the wine and opener from his hands, and led the way up the stairs.

Matt admired the movement of her hips in her jeans while he took the fax from under his arm.

"You're kind of quiet back there," Renee said.

"Just concentrating on the view."

She looked over her shoulder and saw where his eyes were fixed, laughed, and ran up the remaining steps.

In Renee's bedroom, Matt dropped the fax on the bed and unbuttoned his shirt.

Renee went into the bathroom. The sound of running water came through the closed bathroom door. Matt tossed his shirt over the back of a chair, then picked up the fax sheet. The first sentence made him go cold.

Dear Matt:

Maybe I'm just paranoid, but I think I'm having one of those gut feelings I've heard you talk about. I have a suspicion I'm being followed, but I haven't seen anyone.

I'm afraid I've gotten into a situation I can't back away from. I know something's going on, but I can't figure out exactly what. Someone got into my computer files at work. I think I know who it was. But I can't prove it.

The stuff in this envelope needs to be locked up and I don't want you to do anything with it. I may need to have you send it back to me at some point, but, right now, I'm afraid if I leave it here, someone will find it and take it. Sorry to bother you with this, but there's no one else outside Hawaii I trust. And I don't want to get any of my local friends involved.

I'll call you next week and explain things. You might have an idea about what I should do.

Talk to you soon.

Love, Susan.

P.S. I forgive you for what happened in Albuquerque last month. I know you love me and were only worried.

Renee came out of the bathroom and found Matt seated on the side of the bed. The fax dangled from one hand. "Matt, what's wrong?"

Matt held the fax out to her.

Renee read it. "What's it mean?"

He shook his head, looked up at her, his mouth set in a hard, grim line. "Every time I think I'm about to solve the puzzle of my sister's death, I find more pieces missing. Did Susan ever say anything to you about problems at work? Anything about something she'd discovered that made her nervous?"

"Susan never said anything about the law firm, except to mention she found the work we did with Save the Kids more satisfying than anything she'd ever done. I guess you could interpret that as a backhanded way of saying she didn't get as much satisfaction from her job. But she never complained about anything."

"Did she seem extra nervous or worried lately?"

Renee sucked on her upper lip. "Now that you mention it, I noticed she'd become . . . you know . . . introspective, since she returned from your mom's funeral. She told me about your scene with Robert, so I thought she was just upset about that. Robert took off shortly after that, and then there was the suicide business with him in Las Vegas." Renee shrugged. "I assumed that's why she acted a little different. I tried to get her to talk about it, but she'd just clam up or change the subject."

"She was obviously concerned about something," Matt said. "But not so concerned she thought her life was in danger. She didn't want anyone to find the documents she sent me; otherwise, why send them all the way to Albuquerque. It could be whatever she was worried about got her killed."

Renee handed the fax back to Matt. "Isn't that a stretch?" she asked. "Didn't Callahan say the reason Lonnie Jackson ordered Susan killed was because of her connection to Robert Nakamura? His drug running for Jackson."

Matt rolled his head from shoulder to shoulder as he tried to work the stiffness out of his neck. "But remember, Callahan wasn't sure why Jackson told him to kill Susan. He guessed about the reason. And Susan's comment about someone getting into her files at work," Matt said, as he waved the fax in front of her, "would indicate whatever she was into had to do with the law firm. Not with Lonnie Jackson or Robert's involvement with drugs."

Renee crossed her arms over her chest. "Okay, let's say you're correct. Where does that leave us?"

Matt walked to the bedroom window and parted the curtains. He stared out and thought about Renee's question. "Maybe nowhere," he said. "But based on Callahan's statement, we know Lonnie Jackson ordered Susan's murder. Here are the options, as I see them. One, the documents she refers to in her note and that are in my office right now have nothing to do with Jackson and he had her killed because of her relationship with Robert . . . or, maybe for some other reason. Two, the files *did* have something to do with Lonnie Jackson, and he had her killed because of them. And, three, the files had something to do with the law firm, and that got her killed."

Renee squinted and said, "If the files concern the law firm, why would Lonnie Jackson care?"

Matt shrugged.

"To really mess with your mind," Renee added, "who's the woman Muriel Goldstein says really murdered Susan? Where does she fit into your three options? And why would Nathan Ballard prevent Rawson employees from attending Susan's funeral service?"

"Oh, jeez. I've got a headache," Matt said.

"I can relate."

"I need to get those tax returns and the computer flash drive back here," Matt said. "Maybe they hold the answers to our questions about the motive for Susan's murder."

Matt again went over in his head the options. The more he thought about them, the more he considered the possibility that Lonnie Jackson was somehow tied to the Rawson, Wong & Ballard Law Firm.

But how? What's the tie-in? All the evidence was circumstantial. All smoke and no fire. Like the phone call from a Rawson attorney named John Dunning to Gabe Muccio about Muriel Goldstein's next of kin. Jackson's men flying to Kauai to find Muriel Goldstein right after Dunning's call could have been coincidental. Maybe Dunning passed the information he got from Muccio on to Jackson, but there was no proof that happened. There was Callahan's confession about Jackson's order to kill Susan. But why? Too many unanswered questions.

"It's late," Renee said. "I feel like my mind's on a merry-go-round that won't stop."

"Why don't you open the wine while I check on Esteban and Richie. I'll be right back."

Matt left Renee standing in the middle of the bedroom. "Well, so much for a romantic evening," he heard her say before he left the room.

DAY EIGHT

CHAPTER FIFTY-SIX

Lonnie Jackson glared at Nathan Ballard. Tuesday mornings were usually reserved for his accountant. Lonnie liked hearing his number cruncher tell him how much his businesses had made him in the past week and how much had been put in his offshore accounts. But, he postponed the meeting after Ballard telephoned him. The man sounded rattled. Beyond rattled.

"You haven't found any of the Curtis woman's files? Your tax returns?" Jackson asked.

"Nothing," Ballard said. "We checked her home computer and the one at the office. Nothing but business and personal files in the hard drive. There weren't any flash drives or flash drives with anything loaded on them that could be a problem. Just in case, though, Dunning purged everything."

Lonnie settled back in his chair. "Good," he said. "Hopefully she didn't make any copies and hide them." He bit off the end of a huge black cigar and spit the plug into a wastebasket. Then he lit up and expelled a smoke cloud, which momentarily hung in the air above his head, until the office ventilation system went to work on it. He frowned at Ballard. "You don't think she made copies, do you?"

Ballard leaned forward and churned the air with his arms, his eyes wide with what Lonnie had seen numerous times before in other men: Panic. Ballard's balding head glistened with a sheen of perspiration. "I . . . I don't know. My God! What if she did?"

Lonnie narrowed his eyes. Forearms on the armrests of the leather desk chair, he held the cigar in one hand and raised his other hand to rub his forehead. "We'll deal with that problem when and if it comes up." Then he heaved a sigh. The thought struck him—not for the first time—that Ballard had become a bigger problem than he was worth.

"I understand you told the firm's employees not to attend the Curtis woman's funeral," he said.

Ballard's face screwed up in a "How the hell does he know that?" look.

Lonnie read Ballard's expression and laughed. "Didn't you think that preventing Curtis's friends and co-workers from attending her funeral service would raise questions?"

Ballard hunched his shoulders and became red-faced. "I . . . I guess . . . I thought . . . ."

Lonnie found it difficult to control his emotions. This sonofabitch has a degree from Yale, he thought, and he doesn't have the brains of a fuckin' pineapple. He growled, "Ballard, I'll give you some advice. You can take it or leave it. Take it, and I suspect we'll have a long, profitable association. If you ignore it and cause me any more problems, I will sever our relationship."

Lonnie saw the man gulp. The lawyer's nervousness seemed to grow into full-fledged fright. His eyes bulged. Sweat dripped off his forehead. He crossed, then uncrossed, and crossed his legs again. He wiped his palms on his pants.

"I'm . . . I'm sorry things turned out the way they did," Ballard said.

"Sorry doesn't cut it," Lonnie spat. He pointed a finger at Ballard. "You go through money like it's water. I'd know if you used drugs. I know you don't gamble, and you don't own a yacht." A toothy smile suddenly crossed Lonnie's face. "You know what they say about a boat, Ballard?"

The lawyer just shook his head disconsolately, his eyes downcast.

"It's a hole in the ocean through which you pour money." Lonnie laughed at his own joke. "So, tell me. What rat hole do you pour your money down?"

Ballard looked uncomfortable, embarrassed. His knees were

pressed together. His posture made him look like a question mark.

Lonnie didn't wait for an answer. He already knew about Ballard's problem: his wife. "Close up that hole," he ordered. "You can't spend more than you declare. That's what caused the problem in the first place." He leaned forward and pinned Ballard with a squint-eyed look. "Got it?"

The lawyer rapidly nodded his head. He opened his mouth, as though to speak, but all that came out was a croak.

"You've caused me much inconvenience. I covered your ass with the Curtis woman because of our . . . business association. There will be no more favors like that. Understand?"

Ballard gulped; his Adam's apple bounced up and down. "Ye-e-s," he said.

Lonnie knew Ballard had heard every word he'd spoken. But he had the uncomfortable feeling the lawyer didn't have the balls to correct his problem on the home front. Lonnie knew he'd have to do something about that very soon. Ballard was a liability he couldn't afford.

"What about that little favor I asked of you?"

Ballard's mouth dropped open and his face twisted in a frown. "I don't understand . . . ."

"Johnny Dunning! His partnership!"

Lonnie had noted that Ballard always got a peculiar look on his face—forehead scrunched, brows knitted—when Lonnie referred to John Dunning as "Johnny." He obviously couldn't understand his relationship with Dunning. But that was none of Ballard's business.

"The partners' meeting is next Monday. It will be taken care of then."

"Good," Lonnie said. He rose from his chair. "I think it's time you went back to your office, Ballard."

Ballard blinked like he didn't understand Lonnie's words, then he pushed out of his chair as though it took every ounce of strength he had in him. "Okay," he said. "I guess . . . that's a . . . good idea. I'll talk to you later."

Not if I can help it, Lonnie thought.

After Ballard left, Lonnie called Jimmy Kaneohe's cell phone. He told Jimmy he needed to see him.

"Five minutes," Jimmy said.

Lonnie watched Jimmy walk through the office door and cross toward him. He had the same swagger he'd had since the first time Lonnie met him, when they were teenaged street toughs. Lonnie smiled at the memory. He'd run a gang in Honolulu and learned Jimmy planned to move in on part of his territory, selling drugs and protection. So Lonnie sent three members of his own gang after Jimmy, to rough him up. Jimmy had single-handedly kicked the crap out of Lonnie's three gangbangers. The other members of Lonnie's crew had been incensed and wanted to go after Kaneohe and his people.

But Lonnie disagreed. He offered to meet with Jimmy. One-on-one. Wherever Jimmy wanted. He knew Jimmy had too much testosterone to turn down the offer. That meeting turned out to be the catalyst to elevate Lonnie's organization to a higher level. He convinced Jimmy to join forces with him—Lonnie's first merger with a rival. With their two groups united, Lonnie took the first big step toward becoming the godfather of Hawaii crime. Kaneohe had been Lonnie's right hand man ever since.

"I hear that bigshot lawyer was here," Jimmy said.

Lonnie smiled. "As usual, my friend, nothing eludes you. Yeah, the sonofabitch worries me. He can't get control of his wife's spending and, sooner or later, he'll have to explain how the hell he spends more money than his declared income. The pussywhipped bastard will spill his guts to the first IRS agent who interrogates him."

"You still got the video?" Jimmy asked.

"Locked in the safe. I've always believed as long as we have that video, Ballard is ours," Lonnie said, a sour look on his face. As though he'd tasted something bitter. "What he did to that little boy was . . . ." Lonnie couldn't seem to come up with the right words. "Ruined that kid. Cost me a fortune. But now I'm not so certain. The guy looks like he's at the end of his rope."

"Why pay him so much money?" Jimmy said. "I could make him disappear?"

Lonnie smiled. "Let's go over it one more time," he said, in a patient, paternalistic tone. "Ballard runs the most prestigious law firm in the state. A firm with connections out the gazoo. And I got a man inside who'll be managing partner one day. Our friend Ballard will see to that. What do you think we could do with the most powerful law firm in Hawaii in our pocket? And my man in the firm helps us move more heroin than has ever come into the islands—with Ballard's knowledge and support."

Jimmy held up both hands in a sign of surrender to Lonnie's logic. "Okay, I buy your argument. But I thought you said the guy worries you."

Lonnie said, "I'll let you know if we need to cut our losses and get rid of him."

Jimmy seemed to process what Lonnie'd said, then nodded his head.

"Okay," Lonnie said. "Change of subject. I've got a couple loose ends out there I'd like to cut off. And I need them cut off A-S-A-P."

"Sure, Lonnie. What d'ya need?"

"Guy named Curtis. He's staying with the bitch from the Save the Brats group."

"That Drummond broad? Man, she's hot. She's built like a—"

"Yeah, that's the one," Lonnie interrupted.

"You said, 'a couple loose ends.' You talkin' about this guy Curtis *and* the Drummond woman?"

A broad smile creased Lonnie's face. "You always understand me, Jimmy."

Jimmy smiled. "It's a done deal, Lonnie."

CHAPTER FIFTY-SEVEN

Matt telephoned his office in Albuquerque and asked his office manager, "Linda, how quickly can you send my sister's stuff to me?"

Linda said, "I'll upload the contents of the flash drive that was in your sister's package and email it to you."

Matt pressed the receiver against his chest and asked Renee for her email address, then passed it on to Linda.

"The tax returns, receipts and other stuff are another matter," Linda said. "Must be two hundred pages. Too many to scan. I'll have to send them FedEx tonight."

"You're a genius, Linda," Matt said.

"True," she said. "But you're so technologically challenged you think anyone who uses a fax machine is Mensa material."

"That's an exaggeration," Matt said, knowing Linda was half-right. He thanked her, hung up the phone, and sat at the table across from Renee. "How the hell can she send information on a flash drive in Albuquerque over the Internet to Hawaii?"

Renee got out of her chair, walked around to Matt, and sat in his lap. She nuzzled his neck and laughed. "My poor little boy," she said in a high-pitched, motherly tone. "Still living in the dark ages. I see it will take time to bring you into the new millenium." She moved off his lap and took his hand. "It's time for a quick primer on what every seven-year-old in America already knows."

Matt followed Renee to her office. He watched her boot up her computer and connect to the Internet.

"What's your Internet provider?"

"Yahoo."

She typed for a few seconds and then asked Matt for his email address. Matt gave her his email password. She clicked on the mailbox icon and found the e-mail from Linda already there. After she downloaded the file, with Matt seated in the chair next to her, she pointed at the screen.

Matt read out loud.

To Whom It May Concern:

This flash drive holds summary information about last year's tax returns for Nathan Ballard, managing partner of the Rawson, Wong & Ballard Law Firm, Honolulu, Hawaii. A copy of the returns is included in the envelope with this flash drive.

I prepared tax returns for many of the partners and employees of the firm over the years and never found anything that appeared improper. Until this year. When I approached Ballard about certain discrepancies, he became defensive and angry. Up to that point, I thought he'd merely forgotten to give me all his information on sources of income. But, when he became angry, I became suspicious.

Ballard told me to return all his documents to him. That he would find someone else to do his return. And he was none too nice about it. In fact, he seemed more than just angry, he appeared worried. I gave him back his tax papers, but, for the first time in twenty-one years, I kept copies of what he had given me. I don't know why I did it. I just felt something was terribly wrong.

The reason for my suspicion was that a huge difference existed between what he declared as income and his expenses. I've shown his income and expenses below.

It's clear Ballard lives way beyond his means. Yet he has no loans other than his mortgage. When I questioned him about this, he told me it was none of my business.

Included with this summary is a copy of the tax return I would have filed for Ballard with the IRS and the State of Hawaii, had I not been ordered to give back his original papers.

Matt and Renee stared at the computer screen in silence. Matt turned toward her. "Remember I told you about Jean Nelson at the law firm? About when she asked me if I'd found any copies of Ballard's tax returns at Susan's or in a safety deposit box?"

"Yes."

"This gives me an *Outer Limits* creepy feeling. Something is very suspicious. Maybe we're onto a motive for Susan's murder."

"I don't follow. I thought Lonnie Jackson ordered Callahan to kill Susan. What's Lonnie Jackson got to do with Ballard and the law firm . . . and tax returns?"

"Let's go through the rest of this. Maybe then I'll be able to answer that question."

Renee scrolled down the computer screen to the cash flow statement that Susan had prepared. "Wow," she exclaimed after she'd reviewed it. "Ballard had $450,000 in income from the law firm and total expenses last year of over $1,400,000. I wonder where he came up with nearly $1,000,000."

CHAPTER FIFTY-EIGHT

Jimmy Kaneohe called three members of his crew—Zechariah "Bats" Zarpas, Al "Two Toes" Sullivan, and Terence "Terry" Hill—and told them to meet him at Fanelli's Restaurant at nine that night. These three were his best men, and he needed the best for the job Lonnie had assigned him.

Zechariah had been a member of his crew for ten years. He'd earned the nickname "Bats" because of his preference for beating deadbeat loan shark customers with a Louisville Slugger. And he hated the name Zechariah. No one dared call him anything but Bats. Also known as "The Greek" because of his olive complexion and jet-black hair, he'd adopted the name Zarpas, because it sounded Greek. No member of the crew knew Bats's real name or where he'd come from. Five feet, eight inches tall, weighing two hundred pounds, Bats was as hard as a fireplug and fearless to the point of stupidity. Jimmy knew the man would take a bullet for him.

Al Sullivan, a Chicago transplant, fled the mainland eight years ago, just minutes ahead of his wife's three brothers. The Corey brothers took exception to Al's using their sister as a punching bag. Al heard the Coreys were after him, and this time he knew he was as good as dead. Sullivan had been with Jimmy since he came to the islands. Short and wiry, he wasn't frightened by much—except maybe three irate Irish brothers out to murder his ass. He came by his nickname, "Two Toes," as a result of the second and third toes on his left foot being fused at birth.

Terry Hill joined Jimmy's crew just six months earlier. He'd caught Jimmy's attention one night in a club Jimmy owned, when he'd coldcocked an off-duty cop who'd harassed one of the bar waitresses. Obsessed with physical conditioning, Terry spent most of his spare time in the gym, pumping iron or working out on aerobics machines. And he looked it. At six feet, two inches, two hundred ten pounds, with model-good looks, he was a walking heart throb for women—and one intimidating sonofabitch.

The three crew members were already seated at a booth in Fanelli's when Jimmy arrived. He joined them and listened to their normal bullshit. Who got laid by whom, who'd been whacked, who got sent up to the joint, who had a sure thing at the track.

Jimmy didn't take part in the banter, but enjoyed it just the same. He didn't volunteer information about why he wanted them to meet with him. He didn't like to be rushed and he loved drama and tension. They were into their spumoni before he gave a hint of what he wanted.

"Lonnie has a problem with a coupla people and wants us to get rid of the problem." He could see he had their attention. Even this hardened team took murder seriously. Jimmy met each man's gaze in turn.

"I want you guys to go home right from here; get some rest. You're gonna need to be alert. Wear night gear. I'll bring the weapons. MAC-10s."

Bats's eyes rounded at Jimmy's mention of the MAC-10s. "What's the layout?" he asked.

"I'll brief you at ten tomorrow night at The Bayshore Diner. We'll leave from there. I'll tell you who the targets are on the way there."

Jimmy looked at his watch. "I got eleven here guys. Let's call it a night."

They all stood and drifted toward the door. "I want all of you to stay at Al's place tonight," Jimmy said on the way to the parking lot. "Stay together tomorrow." Jimmy walked to his car and drove off.

Bats made a sound like a leaking tire. "Al, you ever know anyone as paranoid as Jimmy?"

"That ain't paranoid; that's just careful," Al said.

Terry sneered. "Al, you think you can trust me enough to drive to your pad all by myself?" he asked. "I sure as hell ain't gonna to leave my new Vette here all night."

"Don't blame you," Bats said. "We'll meet you at Al's."

"Hundred bucks says I get there before you do," Terry said.

"You're on!" Al said as he ran with Bats to his Cadillac. "You may have more speed, but I know a shortcut," Al jeered back over his shoulder.

The Cadillac's tires squealed when the big blue sedan peeled out of the parking lot ahead of Terry. But Terry had no intention of winning the bet. He tailgated the Cadillac for ten blocks as the two cars roared down Honolulu streets at up to eighty miles an hour, until Al turned off the main drag onto a feeder street. Terry had anticipated he would take that route. He raced another three blocks down the main street, pulled into a convenience store lot, got out of his car, and ran to a pay phone. He tapped his foot nervously and waited for the call to be answered.

"Murdoch."

"Four of us are going out on a hit tomorrow night. At least two people are targeted. I'll try to get back to you in time."

"What car will you be in?" Murdoch asked.

"Don't know."

"Listen. Try to move the locator beacon from the Corvette to whichever car you'll be in. If you can't call, we'll be able to track you."

Terence broke the connection and ran back to his car.

DAY NINE

CHAPTER FIFTY-NINE

Muriel Goldstein knew her son-in-law, Stuart Nadler, wasn't happy about the arrangements made for them by the Hawaii Organized Crime Task Force. He didn't like his family being uprooted and moved to the Kona Coast on the big island of Hawaii. The safehouse they'd been put in was cramped and had few of the conveniences of their own home on Kauai. Stuart was a bright man, so he understood they really didn't have any choice as long as there were killers who might be after Muriel. But he still didn't like it. It was his incessant carping about it that put Muriel on edge. She could see frustration on his face. He had worn a perpetual scowl since they'd been moved.

Muriel walked to the small kitchen table where her family ate breakfast. She spied one of their guards walk past the kitchen window. She shook her head in amazement and sat down next to her daughter. I came to Hawaii to retire, for peace and quiet, and now some *mashugeneh* dope dealer wants to kill me, and I got armed men all around me. She chuckled. At least I'm not bored.

"You want some coffee, Mom?" Beth asked.

"That would be nice, sweetie," Muriel said.

Beth went to the coffeemaker on the kitchen counter and carried the pot to the table. She filled Muriel's cup.

Muriel sipped her coffee. Too hot. She put the cup down and picked up a section of the Wednesday morning newspaper. One of her daily pleasures, Muriel read the *Honolulu Times* from cover to cover. But she always started with the society page. It made her happy to read about the marriages and where the newlyweds planned to honeymoon. And she got a big kick about this or that *shiksa* named Buffy, Muffy, or Fluffy throwing some cockamamie party for a charity.

Muriel turned the page and looked at the photos of the young women in their bridal gowns and read the stories. She felt momentary regret about the way she and Abe had spent their whole life working and never took a trip outside the United States. One summer they'd go to the Catskills, the next summer they'd rent some place on Long Beach Island in New Jersey. Even their honeymoon had been no big deal—two days in a cheap hotel on Atlantic City's boardwalk. She sighed, then turned the page.

The Chadsworth Newells—what kind of name is that? she thought—will vacation in Australia. The Junior League will host a fundraiser . . . . Her heart suddenly seemed to stop.

That face in the center of the page. She would know that face anywhere. Even though she'd only seen it for a moment. After all, how many times would she see someone murdered?

Muriel raised her head and looked at Stuart. Her widened eyes and gaping mouth interrupted another of Stuart's diatribes about their lives being turned inside out and upside down. "Could you go outside and ask one of the policemen to come in here?" Muriel said breathlessly. "I need to talk to him."

"Right this minute?" he asked.

"Yes, now!"

"Sure," Stuart said. "What else do I have to do around here?"

CHAPTER SIXTY

Renee was peeved at Matt for not coming to her bed during the night. She knew she was being childish, but Matt had gotten under her skin and she didn't like him ignoring her. She avoided eye contact with him across the kitchen table. Esteban's presence made it easier for her to nurture her pique, without having to discuss it with Matt. She half-enjoyed the self-indulgence. But when she sneaked a quick glimpse at Matt's face and saw his curved-down mouth and sad, puppy dog eyes, she couldn't continue her performance.

"Can I fix you boys some breakfast?" she said, finally smiling. She held her smile long enough to bring a return smile to Matt's face.

"What's the cook offering this morning?" Esteban asked.

"Watch it, Esteban," Matt said. "Or you'll be lucky to get bread and water. That's no way to talk to the general."

"My apologies, ma'am," Esteban said, a mischievous twinkle in his eyes. "Naturally, anything the general decides to serve would be more than acceptable to this lowly soldier."

Renee laughed. "How about I make something nice?"

Esteban and Matt nodded their heads in agreement, like two chastened little boys.

"I'll be back in a couple minutes," Esteban said, "I want to check on Richie."

After Esteban left the room, Renee turned to Matt. "Sorry about being bitchy. I guess I was disappointed you didn't come to

274

bed last night."

"I can't tell you how much I wanted to be with you," he said. "But with Angelo in the hospital, Esteban and Richie needed me to take a shift on guard duty. They've been at it for too many hours. I slept downstairs so I wouldn't wake you when I got up to take my shift."

She walked behind Matt's chair, put her arms around his neck, and kissed the top of his head. "I feel like an idiot. I wasn't sure you wanted to be with me."

Matt stood up, showed his best smile, and wrapped his arms around her. "Renee, I'm not very experienced at this sort of thing. I've only said, 'I love you' to one woman in my life—my wife. I've known you for less than a week and I already want to say those words to you. Not only did I want to be with you last night, but I want to be with you for the rest of my life."

Renee saw Matt's face turn red. Her own face felt hot. Chills ran up and down her spine. Her eyes leaked tears while she rose up on her tiptoes and kissed him. She took his hands in hers. "I've always been kind of a fatalist. I believe things happen because they're meant to happen. That's the way I feel about our meeting. It was preordained." She smiled and added, "I'd like to pursue this business of you wanting to be with me for the rest of your life."

"I feel like I've been caught in the middle of a maelstrom," Matt said. "I didn't know this sort of thing happened to people over sixteen."

Renee laughed and dabbed away the wetness in her eyes with her fingers. She heard the front door slam shut, turned, and stepped away from Matt. She smiled at him and said, "I guess I'd better start breakfast."

Matt reached out and grabbed Renee's arm, spun her around, and pulled her to him. He hugged her and kissed her passionately.

Renee, her eyes closed, heard Esteban say, "Matt, you're smarter than I thought you were." She heard footsteps leave the room.

CHAPTER SIXTY-ONE

"Mister Dunning, Mister Chongsawartha is on line three."

John Dunning stared at the speakerphone on his desk; noted the time on the digital display. It must be the middle of the night in Thailand, or Indonesia, or wherever the hell the man was now. Doesn't he ever sleep? He picked up the receiver.

"John Dunning!"

"Ah, Mister Dunning. And how is your day?" Chongsawartha said in his singsong cadence.

"Fine, Mister Chongsawartha. How are you?"

"I could not be better. You are making me a very happy man."

It pleased John to know his most important client was satisfied. But he couldn't keep the smile from his face while he listened to the man's accent. He also had the thought, What does Chongsawartha want? He never contacts me just to pat me on the back. The man only calls about one thing—the next drug shipment.

"Thank you, Mister Chongsawartha. That's my job—to provide quality service."

"Good, good," the man said. Pause. Then Chongsawartha cleared his throat. "I must prevail on you for some more... *quality service* quite soon," he said.

"Yes, sir?" John held his breath and waited for the words to come. He hoped Chongsawartha had something entirely different in mind than another narcotics shipment. The last one had been a big one. Lonnie's distributors were still overstocked with heroin.

"I find myself with an unusually large supply of cloth"—their code word for heroin. "This will involve three times as much as the last delivery."

John gasped, but smothered the sound in his throat. "But, Mister Chongsawartha, my client's customers can only absorb just so much . . . fabric. They are barely through a fifth of the last shipment."

Lonnie had intentionally moved only twenty percent of the heroin from the last load. By doling out the dope, the price on the street remained high. Also, if they flooded the streets with heroin, it might raise too many eyebrows at the DEA and at police headquarters. Besides, how much heroin could the junkies in Hawaii consume?

"They'd have to find customers outside the islands to liquidate that much inventory," John said. "I'm sure you can imagine the problems that would cause with my client's . . . competitors."

The line went silent for several seconds, then Chongsawartha chided, "Oh, but Mister Dunning, you assured me your client is a most important, most capable man. If you are telling me he is too small . . . how do you Americans put it? . . . too small potatoes, I shall be forced to find someone who can accommodate my business." The man paused again. "Do you understand me, Mister Dunning?"

John's instincts screamed a warning, but he felt he had no choice. The arrangement with Chongsawartha had made Lonnie more money in a year than he'd made in the previous ten.

"Okay, Mister Chongsawartha. When can I expect the goods to hit the port?"

"I love American slang," Chongsawartha said, laughter in his voice. "Hit the port! How droll!"

John recognized the man's forced laughter. Then Chongsawartha's voice suddenly changed. It sounded steely-cold, and John felt his blood chill.

"Tomorrow, Mister Dunning. I will fax you the name of the ship and the time it is due to arrive in Honolulu."

The phone clicked in John's ear before he could respond. His "Tomorrow?! That's impossible!" bounced off his office walls.

CHAPTER SIXTY-TWO

Frank Murdoch paced the hangar floor. He still hadn't heard from Terry Hill. For about the twentieth time, he looked at his watch. It was still early. Only 10 a.m. But his nerves sparked like a downed electric wire. He had to discover the hit team's target. This was a very dangerous situation for his undercover agent. The only way Terry could protect himself, and stay undercover, would be to actually take part in the hit. And Murdoch hadn't spent his entire adult life in law enforcement to suddenly sanction one of his men committing murder.

"Agent Murdoch, phone call."

Murdoch heard the voice, but didn't respond immediately, too hung up with his thoughts.

"Agent Murdoch . . . ."

Murdoch snapped his head around and glared at the man who'd spoken. "Telephone call," the man said.

Murdoch's heart raced. Please be Terry, he prayed, as he punched the lighted button on his telephone console and lifted the receiver.

"Go," he shouted into the mouthpiece.

"It's Roy Casper. We've got a development over here on Kauai you should know about."

"Yeah, Roy, what is it?" he said impatiently.

"The old lady claims she knows who pushed Susan Curtis off her balcony," Casper said.

Murdoch stiffened. "I'm listening, Roy."

"I don't want to say over this line," Casper said in a whisper. "But it's so incredible, I'm not sure I believe it."

"I understand," Murdoch said. "How do you want to handle this?"

"Sir, we need to fly over there to the hangar. We should be able to keep these people safe there. And I think you should hear firsthand what the old lady has to say. This thing just got stranger."

"Okay," Murdoch said. "I'll send the chopper for you. You'll need two helicopters to move all six of you, so I'll get the one on Maui to fly over, too. Be ready to move in two hours."

CHAPTER SIXTY-THREE

"I don't think it's a good idea you coming here, kid," Lonnie said.

"I know, Lonnie," John said, "but I couldn't do this on the telephone."

"So, what's up? You look like you ate a bad burrito." Lonnie laughed.

"Chongsawartha called. He's got another shipment due in tomorrow."

Lonnie jumped out of his chair and leaned on his hands on his desk. "What the hell," he blurted.

John crisscrossed the office; windmilled his arms. His normally robust color turned wan. Eyebrows knitted; parallel furrowed lines etched his forehead. "And, to make matters worse, it's three times as big as the last one."

Lonnie moved around his desk to his brother, put a hand on John's arm, and led him to a chair. "Sit down, bro. Relax. I'll work it out."

John took a seat, but he drummed his fingers on the chair arms and tapped his feet. "That slant-eyed bastard is playing with us, Lonnie," John said, his voice three notes higher than usual. "How can you move that much smack?"

"Johnny, we won't let him get to us. You hear me?"

John nodded, but he kneaded his hands, his pallid face now scarlet.

"What are you so shook up about?" Lonnie asked. "Losing your cool?"

"Lonnie, that much heroin would take every dime you've got here in the States, and then some. You'd have to move cash from an overseas account to cover the payment. You know damn well Homeland Security monitors large money transfers. The banks are required to disclose such transactions. They track a money wire to you and you're screwed. And if you can't move the dope quickly, how the hell will you keep your organization going with all your cash tied up in inventory? The storage and distribution problems are colossal. Not to mention dealing with Customs."

"Johnny, I can always use a runner to move money from off-shore. Don't sweat the small stuff."

"A runner to move millions of dollars?" John asked incredulously.

Lonnie shrugged. "I'll take care of it. And I'll work something out on the distribution side. I want you to go back to your office. You don't need to worry about this. I got it covered."

John sighed and got to his feet. "Okay, Lonnie."

They hugged, and Lonnie walked John to the door.

After saying goodbye, Lonnie returned to his desk. He ruminated about the drug shipment and his options. A kernel of a plan germinated in his brain. He called Jimmy Kaneohe's cell phone number.

Thirty minutes later, Jimmy entered Lonnie's office and took the same seat on the sofa where Johnny sat earlier. "What's up, boss?" he said.

Lonnie briefed him on the dope shipment due in the next day.

"Shit, I don't feel comfortable with that much *horse* in the warehouse, and it'll take us at least a year to move it. That's a long time to have that much heroin around. Too much exposure."

"No argument," Lonnie said. "But we ain't got a choice."

"Your Asian friend must have a sudden need for a load of cash."

"With all the shit going on in Indonesia right now, I'm not surprised. Chongsawartha owns controlling interest in one of the country's largest banks. I hear their government wants the banks to shore up their capital bases. I bet that's his problem."

"How will we handle this load?"

Lonnie picked up a pack of Marlboros from his desk, shook out a cigarette, and lit up. He rested his head on the back of his chair, blew a smoke ring, and watched it rise toward the ceiling. He looked back at Jimmy and moved forward on the chair; planted his elbows on the edge of the desk. He snapped his fingers. "Just like that, my friend. Just like that. We be scammin' the slant-eyed bastard and be livin' large," Lonnie said in a ghetto accent.

Jimmy's forehead wrinkled and he hunched his shoulders.

Lonnie laughed. "You've seen the crews on the ships Chongsawartha uses. They're nothing but modern day pirates. The crew that comes in tomorrow can't have a clue about the dope on board, or they'd have stolen it by now."

Jimmy shrugged and spread his arms.

"But, if they did know it was aboard and they stole it, what would they do with it? Probably couldn't move that much product. That's our problem, too. And *we're* in the business. If they tried to sell it to the wrong party, they could wind up in jail or dead."

"I don't follow you, Lonnie."

"You still in touch with Furillo in Los Angeles?"

"Sure," Jimmy said.

"What if we were to put someone on the ship before it reaches Honolulu? Our guy has a nice little chat with the captain. Lets him know there's drugs on his ship and that we'll pay him to carry it to another location. We give him a tenth of what we would have to pay Chongsawartha, and"—Lonnie snapped his fingers again—"he's rich beyond his wildest imagination."

"Hell of a deal, Lonnie. But what if the captain won't cooperate? What if he wants to keep the shipment all to himself?"

"We tell him we'll call the Coast Guard about the drugs. How he would wind up spending the rest of his natural life in the joint with a cellmate named Bubba."

"Okay, but if the captain cooperates, we still got the problem of storing the junk somewhere." Then Jimmy smiled and wagged a finger. "That's why you asked about Furillo."

"That's right. We ain't even gonna touch the stuff," Lonnie said. He chuckled, then laughed long and loud. So hard he hacked for a good half minute.

Jimmy frowned. He stood and took a step toward Lonnie, but Lonnie held up his hands.

"I'm okay," he said. Between laughs and coughs, Lonnie explained his plan.

Jimmy was wide-eyed. He slowly shook his head. Then he, too, laughed. And the louder he laughed, the more Lonnie roared.

After a minute, Lonnie staggered to the wetbar, took out two Budweisers, and tossed one to Jimmy. "I propose a toast to that bastard, Chongsawartha. May he have a stroke when he finds out what happens when someone tries to change the rules and threatens me."

Jimmy raised his beer can in salute, pushed off the couch. "I'd better go," he said. "I got work to do."

"Yeah. Let me know if Furillo can handle the shipment."

"I'll call you right away." Jimmy stood up and turned to leave.

"What about that other matter?" Lonnie asked.

"It's all set," Jimmy said.

"When?"

"Tonight. They'll never know what hit 'em."

CHAPTER SIXTY-FOUR

"Got a FedEx package here for a Doctor Matthew Curtis," the man said over the intercom.

"He'll be right down," Renee said. She released the speaker switch and walked outside to the back patio. Matt and Richie were on their knees and intently concentrated on something. "Matt, I think Susan's package from Albuquerque is down at the front gate," Renee announced.

Matt dusted off his hands on the seat of his pants and got to his feet.

"I'd better go with you," Richie said. "You never know."

Matt nodded. He turned toward Renee and pointed at the ground. "Don't go anywhere near this thing," he said.

"What is it?"

"It goes boom. That's why we locked Max in the garage."

Renee waved her understanding and, as soon as the two men entered the house, peered at what she wasn't supposed to go near. A curved contraption rested on a short little tripod-like stand. It sat a couple inches off the ground. She hunched her shoulders and walked away. Boys and their toys, she thought.

The FedEx package contained about two hundred sheets of paper, including the unfiled previous year's federal tax return for Nathan and Julia Ballard, and copies of credit card receipts, invoices, construction documents relating to their new home. Esteban entered the dining room while Matt and Renee spread the papers on the table.

"What you got there?" Esteban asked.

"Evidence, my good man . . . I hope," Matt said.

"Evidence of what?"

"Of a motive for my sister's murder . . . maybe."

"What are you looking for?" Esteban said.

Matt showed Esteban Susan's letter.

"Looks like your sister had reason to be suspicious of this guy," Esteban said. "The cash flow statement she put in her letter says a lot."

"Like what?" Renee asked.

"Like this guy, Nathan Ballard, has a secret source of cash. The fact he didn't disclose the source to your sister, that he got angry when she questioned him about it, says two things to me. He's playing hanky-panky with the IRS and his source of cash may be illegal."

"I guess I'd better go through these tax forms," Matt said without much enthusiasm. "See if I can find something helpful."

"What are you trying to find?" Esteban asked.

Matt felt sheepish. "Well . . . I don't really know. I just thought . . . ."

Esteban took Matt's arm and gently pulled him away from the table. "Why don't you go out and help Richie finish setting up the Claymores? Let me take care of this end."

"What the hell do you know about tax returns?" Matt asked.

"Remember, I have a business," Esteban said. "You either learn to understand these things or you become a target for crooked accountants and employees."

Matt said thanks and, relieved, walked out with Renee.

"What's a Claymore?" Renee asked.

Matt kissed her on the cheek and, on his way outside, said over his shoulder, "Better you don't know."

"How ya comin'?" Matt asked as he stepped out on the patio.

Richie stood and stretched. "They're all unpacked and ready to go. It's been years since I worked with one of these things."

"Let's set them up. I think one down by the gate and the other in the trees between the gate and the house."

"You know we'll have a hell of a time explaining where we got Claymores if the cops find one of them."

Matt scrunched his forehead and stared at Richie. "Second thoughts?"

Richie shrugged. "Aw, what the hell."

After they positioned the two Claymore anti-personnel mines, Matt and Richie patrolled the grounds.

"Where's Esteban?" Richie asked Matt.

"Inside studying tax returns."

Richie gave Matt a questioning look.

"Don't ask. It could be another dead-end." Matt looked at his watch. "Eight o'clock." He pointed at the sky, already bright with the silvery glow of a full moon. The sweet smell of flowers drifted in on a light breeze. "Some evening, huh?"

Richie nodded. "You know you can't go on like this forever, guarding this place. Sooner or later you'll have to get a life."

"I understand," Matt said. "You've been a big help. But you've got a life you have to get back to as well."

"Nah. I just get odd jobs wherever I can find them. I'm in this thing for the duration."

Matt patted Richie on the back. "So am I, Richie."

CHAPTER SIXTY-FIVE

Frank Murdoch watched Muriel Goldstein, the three Nadlers, and their guards leave the helicopters. He waited by the hangar door and greeted them, then led the way into the command center.

They sat in government-issued gray cushioned, metal chairs around a gray metal table. Murdoch sat at the head of the table. "Would anyone like something to drink?"

"Could I have a coke?" Cheryl Nadler asked.

"Shush, honey," Beth Nadler said.

"No, no it's all right, Missus Nadler," Murdoch said. He gave a slight nod. One of the agents left the room and returned a minute later with a glass of ice and a can of Coca-Cola. Murdoch took the glass and the soft drink, opened the can, and poured the soda. He passed the glass down the table to Cheryl, seated between her mother and grandmother.

"What's your favorite subject in school?" he asked the little girl.

Cheryl smiled, then looked at her father. "Recess," she said.

Murdoch saw Stuart Nadler scowl. Murdoch covered his mouth with his hand and coughed in an attempt to hide his smile. The kid already knew how to pull her old man's chain, he thought.

Murdoch was enjoying himself. "Do you play any sports?" he asked.

Cheryl brightened and showed her gap-toothed smile. "Yeah, I'm the goalie on my soccer team. Isn't that great?"

"You bet," Murdoch answered. "How's—?"

"Daddy says I'll get my teeth knocked out playing soccer"—she used both hands to lift her upper lip—"but I don't have enough teeth left to worry about." She giggled, looked sideways at her father, then winked at Murdoch.

I'd better get down to business, Murdoch thought, before I let this little imp antagonize her father any more. Besides, he thought, noticing three of his agents against the wall behind Cheryl, their mouths agape, I'd better not let my men think I've got a soft side. He frowned at them, then turned to Beth Nadler. "Would it be okay if one of my men showed Cheryl around the hangar? She might be interested in the airplanes we have here."

"Ooh, can I, Mommy?" Cheryl asked.

Beth smiled at Murdoch. "Good idea," she said.

After Cheryl and one of the agents left the room, Beth thanked him.

Murdoch waved a hand. "No big deal," he said. He turned to Agent Casper. "Okay, Roy, you called this meeting. Let's have it."

Casper stepped away from the closed door. "Muriel Goldstein saw a newspaper article and a photograph about a charitable fundraiser some society dame is hosting. She thinks the woman in the picture is the same person she saw push Susan Curtis off her balcony."

Murdoch shifted in his chair and looked directly at Muriel. "Is that right, Missus Goldstein?"

Muriel's eyes bored into Murdoch's and her jaw was rigid. "Yes, except for one clarification," she said.

"Yes, ma'am," Murdoch said. "What's that?"

"I don't *think* the woman in the picture is the one I saw on Susan's balcony. I *know* it's the same woman." Muriel lifted her folded hands off the section of newspaper on the table in front of her and handed it to her daughter to pass to Murdoch. "It's her! I knew I'd seen her before. She's in the newspaper every so often. This ball or that fundraiser. Fancy sort of stuff. Real hoidy-toidy."

Murdoch looked down at the newspaper. His heart seemed to compress to the size of a pea. This old dame's nuts, he thought. She wants me to believe some society matron killed Susan Curtis. Next, she'll tell me the woman was part of the Kennedy assassination. Wonderful!

Muriel's face suddenly twisted in a grimace and she shot Murdoch a penetrating look. "From the look on your face, Mister Murdoch," she said, "I can tell you think I'm just some old woman who's touched in the head. Does that about sum it up?"

Murdoch laughed. He felt his face warm. "Yes, that's about it."

"Well, at least you're honest," Muriel said.

Murdoch scooted his chair forward until the edge of the table pressed against his stomach. He looked straight at Muriel. "There's no question in your mind?"

Muriel's eyes were narrowed to slivers. "No question," she said.

Murdoch's chair screeched as he pushed it back. He rose, stuck his hands in his pockets, and drummed his fingers against the sides of his legs. "Thank you, Missus Goldstein, Mister and Missus Nadler. You've been very helpful."

He looked at one of the agents at the other end of the room. "Peter, I want you to arrange to have these people's things brought from the safehouse to Honolulu. Put them up in a first class hotel and post a three-man guard—twenty-four hours a day."

The agent nodded.

"And, Peter, I want you to record Missus Goldstein's statement."

"Folks, if you'll follow me," Peter said, "I'll make all the arrangements."

Stuart Nadler helped his mother-in-law out of her chair. He looked back at Murdoch. "How much longer will this go on?" he asked.

Murdoch rubbed his jaw. "I wish I could give you a definite answer," he said. "I hope not too much longer."

After Muriel Goldstein and the Nadlers left, Murdoch looked at the remaining agent in the conference room. "Sara, I want a complete file on this woman." He stabbed his finger at the newspaper photograph. "Family members, history, finances, whether she sleeps in a nightgown, pajamas, or the nude. Everything there is to know about her. Got it?"

"Yes, sir. I'll get right on it." The agent started for the door.

"Oh, and Sara," Murdoch said, stopping the agent, "go out to this hospice charity mentioned in the newspaper. Get the names of three or four wealthy ladies in their sixties or seventies involved with the organization. Women who've lived in the islands all their lives. Interview them. If there's anything this society dame is hiding, maybe one of her lady friends will be interested in sharing it with us."

CHAPTER SIXTY-SIX

Esteban looked up from the dining room table at Matt and Renee when they entered the room. He extended his arms above his head and grimaced while he rolled his shoulders. "I'm getting old," he said. "Bent over, staring at numbers for hours is hard work. I got kinks where I didn't know I had muscles."

Matt smiled at Esteban. "Remember, you volunteered. Find anything?"

Esteban groaned. "Well, since I'm not getting any sympathy from you, I might as well get to it. Looks like your sister nailed the figures perfectly. Nathan Ballard spends way more than he makes. There's no capital gains income on the tax return or in any of the supporting documentation, including the copy of his check register. No trust, inheritance, or other extraordinary income that I can see. He's in a bunch of partnerships, but they're all tax shelters. The K-1s show they throw off a lot of deductions, but no cash.

"The Ballards built a new home and bought two new cars last year. They also took an expensive trip to Europe. Even without those expenses, they'd already spent more than their declared income. Something fishy is going on. If Ballard's involved in something illegal, and he thought your sister had suspicions, then there's one possible motive for murder."

"What other explanation could there be for Ballard's spending?" Renee asked, while Matt paced around the table.

"Good question," Esteban said. "He could have inherited money, but why not run it through his account? If it went into stocks or bonds, there would have been 1099s showing income from those investments. He might have borrowed the money, but there are no copies of promissory notes or evidence of interest payments. No, I don't think it's anything legitimate. Otherwise, why did he react so angrily when Susan confronted him about the big difference between his income and expenses?" Esteban paused and then said, "I wonder if the whole law firm is up to no good."

Matt completed another circuit of the dining room table. "What confuses me is the connection between Lonnie Jackson and Rawson, Wong & Ballard," he said. "Remember, Callahan said Jackson ordered him to kill Susan. What's Ballard's tax return got to do with it? And, that telephone call from John Dunning to Gabe Muccio, followed by hitmen flying to Kauai has my skin tingling." Matt shook his head and threw up his hands in an exasperated gesture. "Why would Jackson order Callahan to kill Susan because of Nathan Ballard's tax return? That would indicate Jackson and Ballard are involved with one another, that Jackson ordered a murder in order to protect Ballard. I find that difficult to believe. A reputable attorney and the biggest crook in Hawaii."

"What now?" Renee asked.

"Why don't we take this stuff to the Organized Crime Task Force?" Renee suggested.

Matt and Esteban looked at one another and nodded their heads in unison. "Sounds like a hell of an idea," Matt said.

CHAPTER SIXTY-SEVEN

HOCTF Special Agent Sara Olson sat on the raised patio of the Kamehameha Country Club overlooking the eighteenth green. She tilted her head back to let the sun warm her face. Man, I could get used to this life, she thought. Play a round of golf every day, get a massage in the spa afterwards, and have a drink or two here on the patio. The dues probably run about what I make in a month. Oh well, back to work.

Sara watched a foursome of elderly ladies putt out. The women laughed while they walked to their carts, placed putters and balls into golf bags, and drove thirty yards to the clubhouse storage garage. The women disappeared into the building. Fifteen minutes passed and Sara wondered if the information the bartender had provided had been accurate: Round of golf, a quick cleanup in the women's locker room, and then refreshments on the patio. She had just about decided to go into the building to try to track them down when the foursome came out onto the patio and chose a table two removed from her's. A couple of them stared at her as they took their seats.

Sara tried not to appear obvious as she sipped a ginger ale and listened to the women's banter. She paid special attention to the woman the bartender had pointed out earlier: Helen Remington. The woman had the look of affluence: Two hundred dollar coif, large-stoned diamond tennis bracelet, and a lithe and tight figure—

even at her advanced age—that spoke of personal trainers and expensive plastic surgeons. There was only a trace of saggy skin at the knees and elbows. The telltale taut, translucent skin of multiple face-lifts made her appear years younger than Sara's research had told her she was. She knew Remington was sixty-five, but, from a distance, she appeared to be no more than fifty.

Helen Remington wore a short-sleeved white Polo shirt, and pale blue shorts. Sara had to admit the woman must have been a real looker when she was younger. She spoke through perfectly white, clenched teeth in a private school accent.

The more Sara watched and listened, the more assured she became. She knew she'd dressed appropriately: Short, white tennis skirt, a powder blue, sleeveless v-neck knit top, and a cobalt-blue cashmere sweater draped around her shoulders and casually knotted at the throat. As though she'd come to play tennis. She hoped the CZ studs in her ears would pass for the real thing. Her silken blonde hair swept her shoulders.

Sara looked like a woman of leisure who always spent afternoons on the country club balcony having a post-tennis match cocktail.

The ladies had barely taken their seats before they verbally tore apart someone named Lisa Sinclair. Sara had come to elicit dirt—about Nora Dunning. This group of women sounded as though they'd be a first-rate source.

"Did you see what Lisa wore to the Symphony Ball?"

"Oh God, I couldn't tell if it came from a dress maker or a tent maker." Tittering laughter. "She looked as big as a house."

"Maybe we should slip her one of Doctor Krantz's cards. She could use his special talents."

"Good Lord, she'd be on the operating table for weeks. All the fat and cellulite! They couldn't possibly flush it down the drain. It would clog the Honolulu sewer system."

This last sortie sent the four women into paroxysms of glee.

Sara attempted a neutral expression, despite the bile that churned in her stomach. She couldn't abide this sort of cruelty—never could, even as a teen. If these women ran true to form, they'd compliment Lisa Sinclair the next time they saw her, while they surveyed every inch of the poor woman for further gossip material.

Sara watched the four women each polish off three martinis, before one with flaming-red hair broke up the party. "Well, I guess I'd better go home and prepare for the return of my lord and master. You know how Cliff likes things just so when he comes home from the bank."

A long-legged, gaunt woman with bleached blond hair rolled her eyes.

"Put on your smiles, ladies," the Remington woman said. "We have to welcome our conquering warriors home from the battlefields."

They laughed, pushed back their chairs, and stood. The group walked by Sara's table.

Sara stood and asked, "Aren't you Helen Remington?"

The women stopped and turned. Sara felt herself being analyzed by four pairs of predator eyes.

"Why, yes, dear, I am. Sorry, do I know you?"

"Sara Olson. Could I have a minute of your time?"

Helen looked around at her friends and then back at Sara. "Only a moment."

"Of course, Ma'am."

Remington turned to the other three women. "I'll see you all on Friday. Be good."

Sara watched the other women whisper among themselves as they walked away. They all looked back over their shoulders at her. She turned her attention to Remington. "Please sit down," she said, as she sat down in her own chair. "Can I offer you a drink?"

"Oh, I guess *one* more," Remington said.

Sara raised her hand to the waiter, who moved quickly to the table. Her badge had apparently impressed the guy. Of course, it could have been her looks, too. He had been more than accommodating. She ordered a martini for Helen Remington.

"Thank you for giving me a moment," Sara said. "I know you must be very busy."

Remington waved her hand in the air as though to pooh-pooh the idea. "I haven't seen you around here before. Are you a new member?"

"No, Missus Remington, I—"

"Helen, please."

"Sorry, Helen. I'm with the HOCTF, the Hawaii Organized Crime Task Force." She opened her cred pack on the table next to her ginger ale and showed it to the woman, who eyed the photo ID, then inspected Sara's outfit. Sara could almost hear the wheels turn in Remington's head.

Then Sara saw excitement come to Remington's face. Her expression seemed almost salacious. She actually licked her lips—a predator on the scent of licentious prey. She leaned forward in her chair and her eyes bulged.

"We're investigating a woman's death," Sara said. "You might have read about it. She jumped off a balcony in a high-rise building near Diamondhead."

Remington shook her head. "I never read the papers," she said as she raised her nose in the air. "They're full of nothing but bad news about people I couldn't care less about and with whom I have absolutely nothing in common."

How typical! Sara thought. She paused when the waiter returned with Helen's drink, then said, "The dead woman worked for the Rawson, Wong & Ballard law firm. We'd like to get some background to determine if the victim was involved in anything at work that could have gotten her murdered."

"Dear," Remington said, "I thought you said the woman jumped."

Shit! Sara thought. That was careless. "Uh," she said, "the coroner ruled it suicide, but we have new information that could cause him to change his ruling."

"I see." She lifted her drink and sipped delicately at the chilled gin. She seemed to drift off with her internal thoughts for a moment, then set the drink back down. "I don't see how the Rawson firm could be involved in murder. Nate Ballard runs the firm and he's the most respected attorney in the islands. His wife, Julia, is my best friend."

Take your time, be patient, Sara told herself. Don't antagonize her. "Oh, I'm sure the firm has done nothing wrong. You know how these things go. We have to look into every nook and cranny."

"Actually, I do not know how *these things go*," Remington said. She stiffened her spine and looked down her surgically-sculpted nose.

Sara knew she had just about lost any rapport she might have already established with the woman and immediately took another tack. "Are you familiar with a young attorney at the Rawson firm, John Dunning?"

The woman's eyes brightened. Sara sensed she'd given the woman an opening she relished.

"Johnny Dunning, Nora Dunning's son. Of course, I know Johnny Dunning."

"What's he like?"

"Gorgeous creature. Wish I were fort . . . thirty years younger. All the girls swoon over him. He's the number one catch in Hawaii. It's obscene how much money his daddy left him."

"Rich, huh?" Sara said.

"Now, you have to realize I've only heard rumors. But the number is in the eight figures. And, even in *my* crowd, dear, that's real money."

Sara suppressed the anger she felt at what she guessed was an offhanded slap at her by the older woman. "I should be so lucky," Sara said.

Remington gave Sara an appraising look. "Honey, with your looks and body, you could have anything you want. Luck's got nothing to do with it. Two of the women I just played golf with were just little golddiggers, with tight asses and big boobs, who knew how to use their physical attributes to hook rich husbands."

Sara's face now ached from sustaining the fake smile plastered there. This snooty bitch was really getting on her nerves.

Remington squinted and turned her head from side to side. She downed her drink, then placed the empty glass on the table. "Neither one of my golddigger friends could hold a candle to you when they were your age," she slurred. "What are you, twenty-six, twenty-seven?"

"Coming from you that's quite a compliment," Sara replied, deciding that telling the woman she was actually thirty-four might tick her off. "Can you tell me anything else about John Dunning?"

Remington's eyes twinkled. "There's nothing else I can tell you about Johnny. But his mother, Nora, is a completely different story."

She widened her eyes, looked up at the patio roof, and grinned while she used a hand to sweep a few stray strands of blonde hair back from her face.

Sara breathed an imperceptible sigh of relief. At last. The woman did exactly what Sara had hoped she would, segue from John Dunning to his mother, Nora—a woman her own age and of her own social class. "Different how?" Sara asked.

Remington licked the wet rim of her now-empty glass. "Oh, my dear," she said, "you can't imagine the scandal."

Sara took her eyes off Remington for the briefest moment, signaled the waiter with one finger held up, and then looked back. She felt tension build in her stomach as she waited for the woman to continue.

Remington leaned forward in her chair and lowered her voice to a conspiratorial whisper. "Nora Dunning—born Nora Cromwell— was a member of a respectable family here on Oahu. Father a banker; mother came from one of the Seven Sisters."

"Seven Sisters?" Sara asked.

"What the original merchant families were called. There were seven of them and they wound up owning most of the Hawaiian Islands. Nora's mother, a descendant of one of those families, had lots of money in her own right. But Nora screwed it up for herself. Talk about throwing away a fortune."

"How so?" Sara asked.

"She was back home for the summer after her second or third year at Wellesley and took up with an Army officer stationed here. The next thing we knew, she ran off and married the guy. Had a kid."

Remington spread her arms in what Sara thought was a "go figure" gesture. "I mean, really! We all had our little flings with boys from the lower classes. But marry one?"

The waiter moved to the table, deposited another drink in front of Remington, and glided away. Remington didn't seem to notice him. She picked up the fresh drink with an almost reflexive movement, as though the drink was her due. She guzzled half the contents of the glass, exhaled an "aah," and put the glass back on the table. She dabbed her lips with a napkin.

Sara noticed that the woman's eyes were now unfocused and

her head wobbled a bit.

"Nora and her husband moved to some Army base on the mainland," Remington slurred. "Had a kid. True love and all that." She sneered. "Her parents disowned her, you know. Not too many years later, I heard her husband died in some war or something. I didn't hear a thing about her for years. Then, one day, one of the girls said she thought she'd seen Nora in a downtown restaurant." Helen screwed up her face. Her eyes looked suddenly as hard as ball bearings. "Can you imagine?" she asked. "Nora Cromwell waiting on tables. A common waitress. A descendant of one of our best families."

"Did her parents help her out?" Sara asked.

"My goodness, no," she smirked. "If her parents had helped her, do you think she'd have worked like a peasant? Her parents wouldn't have anything to do with her. Nora was on her own. She went from the top of society to the dregs. With no training and only a couple years of college, she couldn't get much of a job." Remington suddenly smiled and Sara thought her eyes looked even harder, flinty and mean. "Besides, I heard her father put the word out among the professional community he would ruin anyone who hired her. He wanted her and her kid out of the islands. She couldn't get a job at any of the banks, law firms, hospitals, accounting offices. Nowhere. She took in laundry and cleaned houses, on top of waitressing." The sneer again.

Sara noticed Remington's words were now beyond slurred. She'd wondered how many martinis it would take. "Her parents disowned her because she married a soldier?" Sara asked. "I don't get it. What's so bad about that?"

Remington gave Sara a supercilious smile and belched loudly. She smiled and said, "'Scuse me." She giggled, then said with a toothy smile, "I thought you'd get around to that question," She seemed to savor the moment. She licked her lips and rolled her eyes. "Nora didn't marry just any Army officer. She ran off with a Ne-gro Army officer." She scrunched up her face in a sour expression and faked an exaggerated shudder. "Or is that black or African-American? I can't seem to keep it straight, anymore." She giggled again. "You see, dear, that sort of thing just isn't done. At least not among our people."

Sara wanted to slap the condescending look off the woman's face. She felt dirty just being with her. "So, how did Nora get back on her feet? How'd she become a society player again?"

Remington showed a lopsided smile. "Marriage. Clarence Dunning, a confirmed bachelor, fell head over heels for Nora." She scowled. "Old Clarence was new money. Self-made man and all that. They got married. Later, when she had Johnny, you'd have thought the old boy had died and gone to heaven. He thought Nora had done the most amazing thing in the world. Giving him a son. Really!"

Sara considered what she'd just heard, while Remington drank the last of her martini. "What happened to Nora's first child?" she asked.

Remington spoke over the lip of her glass, as though she relished the residual scent of the liquor. "No one knows. He, or she—I never heard if the little half-breed was a boy or girl—kind of dropped off the face of the earth. Nora must have smartened up. Old Clarence Dunning was the best thing that ever happened to her. But he might have had a completely different attitude toward a woman with a mulatto kid." She nodded her head and looked at Sara as though she would understand.

Sara breathed in and out as slowly and as quietly as she could. She'd ask one more question. "Do you remember the name of the Army officer Nora married?"

Remington set her glass on the table and made round spots in the dampness as she repetitively turned it in circles. "I thought I'd never forget his name. It was on everyone's lips for months—before and after she ran off with him. Sorry. I can't come up with it." Her eyelids drooped and closed for a moment, and then popped open. "Anything else? I really do need to get home." She winked. "Wouldn't want to make the hubby angry coming home to an empty house."

I think I'll puke, Sara thought.

A woman approached the table when Sara and Helen Remington stood. Sara noticed Remington stagger slightly, then hold onto the back of her chair for support. She still teetered slightly, as though she were on a ship's deck. The other woman stared at Sara, then pecked an air kiss by each of Helen's cheeks. "You look marvelous," she said with as much false sincerity as Sara had ever heard. "How do you do it?"

"Clarice, how nice to see you. Let me introduce you to Sara .... Oh, I'm sorry, dear, I forgot your last name."

"Olson. Sara Olson."

"Of the San Francisco Olsons?" Clarice asked.

"No, the Little Rock Olsons," Sara said.

Clarice blinked.

Remington giggled.

"Clarice, Ms. Olson asked me about Nora Dunning's long, lost love," Remington said. She lowered her voice. "You remember, the black buck she ran off with?"

"Lieu-ten-ant Ro-land C. Jer-rell," Clarice said with obvious distaste, in a comic southern drawl. "Don't you remember how we'd sing that little rhyme Nancy Simpson made up? Nora Cromwell went to hell when she married R. C. Jerrell. Did we laugh about that!"

"I remember now," Remington squealed. "What fun!"

"Have to run. See you later, Helen," Clarice said, not acknowledging Sara. She made her way around the patio tables.

"Clarice is so clever," Remington said. "After all these years, she remembered our little ditty."

Sara leaned forward and put her face just a foot from Remington's. The woman smelled as though she'd been pickled in booze. "This has been quite enlightening, Missus Remington. I've learned a great deal. Thank you." Sara took a step back from the table. "You know something?" she said, "I wonder what evil things your golfing partners say about you behind *your* back."

Sara saw the woman's face tighten. Then Remington fell back against a chair at the next table. She caught herself and straightened. She glared at Sara. Evil radiated from her eyes. Her lips were pressed together so tightly they'd become a white slash. Sara walked away feeling good that she'd made an enemy of Helen Remington.

While Sara walked from the patio to the club lobby, an idea hit her, making her feel warm and fuzzy. She walked briskly to her car, used her radio to call the dispatcher, and report she was back in her vehicle. Then she asked to be patched into the closest radio car to

Kamehameha Country Club. While she waited for the connection, she watched Remington weave one way, then another, as she came down the club's front steps to the walkway to the parking lot. The woman fished around in her purse for nearly a minute, then came up with a key ring. She fiddled with the ring and then Sara heard a loud double "chirp." Another minute passed before the Lexus weaved out of the parking lot and down the long, landscaped drive to the public street.

"This is Officer Natsone," Sara heard over her radio.

"Natsone, this is Detective Sara Olson. Some old gal just left the Kamehameha Country Club parking lot in a silver late-model Lexus." Sara followed close behind Helen Remington's car and saw her run the stop sign at the end of the club driveway and turn left. "She just turned left out of the club's main entrance," she continued. "She looks three sheets to the wind; weaving all over the road. You might want to pick her up before she kills someone."

"Thanks, Detective," Natsone said. "I'll get right on it. I'm only a block away from there. Oh . . . I think I see her."

Sara turned right at the end of the drive and whistled as she drove to HOCTF headquarters.

CHAPTER SIXTY-EIGHT

Sara walked into the HOCTF hangar and spied Frank Murdoch seated at a long table with two other agents. A man she didn't recognize stood nearby. Murdoch talked animatedly as he appeared to look at papers in his hands. Sara walked over and cleared her throat.

Murdoch glanced up and gave her an arched-eyebrow look. "Casual day, Olson?" he said.

"Actually, they're work clothes, Chief," she answered and tried not to laugh.

"Oh, I can't wait to hear you rationalize wearing tennis togs on assignment."

"You know me, Chief. Work, work, work. That's all I ever do."

"Detective Sara Olson, meet Doctor Matthew Curtis. Susan Curtis's brother."

"Hello, Doctor Curtis. I'm sorry about your sister."

"Thank you, Detective Olson," Matt said.

"Sara is one of my agents," Murdoch said.

Sara noticed Matt's look. He gawked at her as most men did—especially when they found out she was a cop. For a brief moment she expected him to say something like, What's a nice girl like you doing in a job like this. But Curtis surprised her.

"Just what we need around here," he said, "a female perspective. We've got lots of information, but the pieces don't seem to fit together. Maybe you can come up with an answer, Ms. Olson."

Sara smiled her thanks at Matt, then turned to Murdoch. "I just got back from a meeting with someone. Got a minute?"

"Unless it's something that implicates Doctor Curtis as a suspect, you can speak freely in front of him," Murdoch said with a smile.

Sara hesitated, got a reinforcing nod from Murdoch, and related her experience at the country club.

"Very interesting," Murdoch said. "But I don't see how it's got anything to do with this. There's no way I can charge Nora Dunning with murder unless I've got more than Muriel Goldstein's statement. We just learned she's about to have cataract surgery. Can you imagine what a defense lawyer would do with that information, if he got her on the stand?"

"Boss, I got a feeling about this Dunning dame. Let me make a few more inquiries."

"It's six. I'll give you 'til noon tomorrow. I need you back here after that."

Sara gave Murdoch a thumbs up and extended her hand to Matt. "Nice to meet you, Doctor Curtis." Then she fast-walked out of the building.

Murdoch turned back to the documents in front of him. "Assuming everything in your sister's note is accurate—about the house, the cars, the vacation—and there's no reasonable and legal reason for the Ballards' excessive spending, we've got the proverbial case of lots of smoke maybe leading to fire."

"What will you do with this information?" Matt asked.

"First, I'll pull a credit report on Ballard."

"Why?"

"Because we may find out Ballard is just up to his neck in debt and there's nothing sinister about any of this."

"If he was in debt, wouldn't there be a record of his paying interest?" Matt asked.

Murdoch shrugged.

"And, if he isn't in debt?" Matt asked.

"Then, I'll try to get phone taps on Ballard's home and office. And I'll have one of my people tail him for a few days." Murdoch paused. "I appreciate you bringing this stuff to us. It gives us another angle on your sister's death. I feel like I've got hold of a three-ring circus, but the rings are disconnected. When I get them all under one Big Top, I'll know the link. Why don't you go home? I'll call you if something comes up."

Matt's voice rose as he said, "Why can't you pick up Lonnie Jackson? You've got Callahan's confession. And, why not question the Dunning woman?"

"The problem with Callahan's confession is he's a dirty cop. And he has no idea about why Jackson told him to kill your sister. So, all we have is the word of a corrupt cop and no motive against the word of Lonnie Jackson, who we have nothing on. The guy's so careful; we haven't been able to pin a damn thing on him. Until we discover motive, we don't have enough.

"And, as far as Nora Dunning is concerned, I ain't touchin' her until I've got all my facts in order. With that gal's money, her lawyers will have me strung up in the public square if I go off half-cocked."

CHAPTER SIXTY-NINE

"Hello," John Dunning said.

"Clear your schedule, Johnny-boy," Lonnie said. "We're going for a ride."

"What's up?"

"Tell you when we meet," Lonnie said. "Helicopter will pick you up in an hour at the landing pad out by the marina."

After he hung up, Lonnie went to the bathroom, pasted on a false mustache and beard, and put in dark-brown contact lenses.

He thought about his pilot and the two men he'd sent to Kauai. He wondered why he hadn't heard from them. If they went into the drink, so be it. If the cops had them . . . . Well, that didn't really matter; they wouldn't talk. He could get to a rat inside prison or out on the streets.

After he adjusted the mustache, Lonnie put on a hand-tailored blue pinstripe suit and red and blue striped tie. Spit-shined cordovan shoes and an alligator briefcase completed the look. He called his driver on his cell phone. "I'll be downstairs in one minute."

Lonnie walked out of the building. His car was running, the right rear passenger door open. "Take me to the Sea Breeze Condos," he said as he slid into the back seat.

At the Sea Breeze, he stepped from the car and briskly moved to the lobby. In the elevator, he inserted a key card in the control panel that locked off the penthouse. The car shot upward to the top floor.

After he placed his briefcase on the dining room table, Lonnie went to the bedroom. He dug a brown leather, soft-sided valise from the closet floor and carried it to the safe behind an oil painting. He took two hundred thousand dollars in crisp bundles of one hundred-dollar bills and stuffed them in the valise. After he zipped it up, he pulled another ten thousand from the safe and carried the money and the valise to the dining room. He neatly laid the ten thousand dollars in the briefcase.

Lonnie grabbed a Budweiser from the refrigerator, went out on the balcony, sat down on a cushioned wrought-iron chair, and stared at the ocean. Chongsawartha's ship was somewhere over the horizon. The biggest payday of Lonnie's life.

Fifteen minutes later he sighted a speck in the sky. Right on time, he thought, as the speck slowly took on the form of a helicopter. He left his chair and went back inside. He climbed an interior staircase to the building's roof, unlocked the latch on a steel maintenance access door, slipped a bolt, strained against the heavy door, and pushed it open on its hinges. The door dropped on the concrete roof pad. Lonnie quickly stepped back down, picked up the briefcase and the valise, and again climbed to the roof. The whine of the aircraft's engines and the thrum of its rotor blades carried to him. Lonnie stepped up through the opening, closed the roof hatch behind him, and stood behind a block wall that shielded him from the helicopter's rotor blast.

As soon as the aircraft set down and its engines slowed, Lonnie calmly walked over and opened the rear door. "Hey, bro," he said.

"Where we goin'?" Johnny asked.

Lonnie smiled. "It's a surprise."

Lonnie reached inside the helicopter and set the two cases on the floor. He closed the rear door, stepped inside the front passenger door, and took the co-pilot's seat.

"Fasten your seatbelt, sir," the pilot said. After he made sure Lonnie had buckled up, the pilot handed him a set of headphones, then revved the engines and lifted the chopper off the roof.

Lonnie sized up the pilot. He was a lanky blond with a shock of hair that drooped over his forehead. Mirrored aviator glasses covered his eyes. "CHET" was stitched on the breast of his jacket.

"Where exactly on the Kona Coast do you want me to set down?" Chet asked.

"Little change of plans, Chet," Lonnie said. He handed the man a slip of paper with the coordinates Chongsawartha's ship captain had given him over the radio that morning. Lonnie jabbed a finger at the slip of paper. "We'll land there." He watched Chet plug them into his navigational controls.

"There must be some mistake," Chet said. "That's over water."

"No mistake, Chet," Lonnie said. "It's a ship."

"Whoa, wait a minute," Chet said as he jerked a look toward Lonnie. "I can't land this thing on a boat."

"It's a beautiful afternoon," Lonnie said, in a deadly calm voice. "Almost no wind. Calm sea. And it's not a boat, it's a ship. A very large ship." He glanced over his shoulder at Johnny and noted his brother's flared nostrils, bright eyes.

"I don't care. I can't land on—"

"And I got a briefcase here with ten thousand dollars in cash," Lonnie added. "You put us on the ship and bring us back, the ten grand is yours, on top of your normal fee."

"Why didn't you say so in the first place?" Chet said as he banked the chopper in a southwesterly direction, toward open water.

Lonnie leaned his head against the top of his seat and closed his eyes. He tried to anticipate everything that could go wrong once they landed on the ship. Over and over, he mentally scrolled through how he would deal with possible problems.

Lonnie snapped alert when Chet asked, "What's the name of the ship? We're about twenty-two miles out. Just about where we need to be."

"*La Concepcion*," Lonnie said. "Look for a Panamanian flag."

"There's a big mother off to the left—about ten o'clock. I'll drop down and check it out."

Chet skirted the side of the ship. "It's her. See? *La Concepcion* on the bow."

Lonnie looked down at the torpedo-shaped vessel. Its hull was painted black, with a red stripe around the top edge. The ship's name was painted on the bow in large white letters.

Lonnie called out a radio frequency from memory. "Radio the ship and ask for permission to land," he ordered. "Tell them your passengers have an appointment with Captain Chin."

"You're the boss," Chet said. He radioed the ship and followed Lonnie's instructions.

"Permission granted to land," a voice responded after a pause.

Chet checked the wind direction and came at the ship with the wind at his nose. Lonnie thought the ship looked too small to land on and held his breath until they landed on deck and the ship's crewmen tied down the helicopter's rails.

A swarthy Asian in wrinkled dress whites and a soiled captain's cap with gold braid on its brim met them. No taller than five feet, four inches, with a belly so pendulous it obscured his belt, the man appeared comical. When he smiled, he displayed blackened, betel nut-stained teeth. He saluted when they stepped forward. "Mister Bingham?" he asked.

"I am Bingham," Lonnie said, acknowledging the false name he'd earlier given the captain. "Captain Chin?"

"Yes, I am Captain Chin," he said in stilted British English. "Welcome aboard my ship. If you will follow me, I have refreshments below."

Lonnie removed the valise from the helicopter and followed Chin, who fired off a rapid stream of words in a language Lonnie didn't recognize. A crewman ran to the helicopter. Lonnie looked over his shoulder and saw the man motion to the helicopter pilot to exit the aircraft.

Chin led them to an interior stairway that descended below decks. Lonnie trailed, Johnny behind him.

They entered a gangway with doors on each side, then turned into a room with "CAPTAIN" painted in gold letters on its door. The room smelled foul—sweaty and mildewed, like a gymnasium locker room.

Chin displayed his black-toothed smile, but glared through piggy eyes that seemed to have seen all nature of deceit and evil. He pointed to two chairs on one side of a rectangular table. "Please sit down." He removed a whiskey bottle from a wood cabinet and carried it to the table, where three murky glasses rested. Lonnie wondered who had used them before and what had been in them. He felt his stomach roil.

The captain poured an inch of booze in each glass, set the bottle down, and hoisted one of the glasses. "To your good health," he said.

Lonnie barely touched his lips to his glass. "And to our mutual profit," he added, before he returned the glass to the table.

The captain's eyes turned even harder and his dark, almost purple lips tightened into a thin line.

"If I recall correctly, Mister Bingham, you mentioned you would pay me a rather large sum of money if I allowed you to board my ship to discuss a business transaction. No obligation. Right?"

"That's right, Captain."

"Then why don't we discuss this matter before we enter United States territorial waters?"

Lonnie looked at the glass of whiskey in front of him and wished it were a beer. "You're in a terrible bind, Captain," he said. He paused and measured Chin's reaction. Nothing. "On board this ship is a fortune in heroin," he continued. "It's quite well hidden. But I know where it is. If you enter U.S waters with the heroin, you'll be arrested and spend the rest of your life in a government penitentiary. Not a happy prospect."

Lonnie noticed a slight movement of Chin's eyes. His only reaction, so far. He admired the man's cool. "I have a way out of this predicament for you."

"I see," Chin said. "And what might that be?"

"Divert your ship toward California. Another ship will rendezvous with you two hundred miles from the California coast, where you will offload the heroin. I'll be advised once the drugs have been moved from the *La Concepcion.*" Lonnie paused and held Chin's gaze for several seconds. "Then I will wire five million dollars to your account at any bank you choose."

Chin's jaw dropped, then banged shut. When fifteen seconds passed and he still hadn't spoken, John interjected, "Do you own this ship, Captain Chin?"

Chin shook his head.

"How long would it take you to earn—or steal—five million dollars?" John asked, boring in.

Chin swallowed. "Five lifetimes," he said.

Lonnie and John sat in silence.

"What's to keep me from throwing you two, your pilot, and your helicopter over the side, then searching for the drugs, and selling them myself?" Chin asked.

Lonnie chuckled. "Good question. First, you wouldn't find the heroin, even if you looked for days. Second, if I don't arrive back on land within one hour, an associate of mine will call the U.S. Coast Guard with your name, the location and name of your ship, and the location of the dope. Third, do you have the contacts to sell a great deal of heroin without getting caught or killed?"

A gargoyle-like smile spread over Chin's face. "Those are very good points, Mister Bingham. Anything else?"

Lonnie smiled, too. "Just one thing." He unclipped a small black box from his belt. "This device is a remote detonator. On board our helicopter is a package of plastic explosive. If I push this button, I'll sink your ship."

"And kill yourself, too, Mister Bingham?" Chin laughed. But the momentary flash of fear Lonnie had seen in the captain's eyes told him he'd won.

"Well, I would only do that if you decided to kill us anyway. That thought has crossed your mind, has it not?"

Chin laughed again, seeming to enjoy the predicament Lonnie had put him in. "You've thought of everything, haven't you, Mister Bingham?" He massaged the back of his neck. "You know, the owner will not be happy. What will I do with the rest of my life? I'll be a dead man if I ever return to the Orient."

You're a dead man, no matter where you go, Lonnie thought. Chongsawartha will hunt your ass down in Hades. "First of all, if you so desire, you can return to Hawaii after you offload the dope," Lonnie said. "All you have to do is claim your navigational instruments were inoperative. You can unload the rest of your cargo then. And, remember, with five million dollars and a little imagination, you should have a wonderful life outside the Orient."

"Quite so, Mister Bingham. Quite so. And what do you propose to give me now to ensure my goodwill."

Lonnie reached down and lifted the valise onto the table. He unlatched the bag, opened and tilted it so Chin could see inside. "There's two hundred thousand dollars in here. Is that enough to earn your good will?"

"Ah!" Chin said. He smiled and stood. Lonnie and John rose, too, and shook hands with him.

Chin escorted them back to the main deck. He shouted at one of his men, who scurried off and came back a minute later with the pilot in tow.

Lonnie shook Chin's hand once again. "Thank you, Captain, for your cooperation."

Chin bowed. "With pleasure, Mister Bingham."

While Chet climbed inside the chopper, Lonnie reached to open the co-pilot's door as the chopper's engine whined. John gripped Lonnie's elbow and moved shoulder-to-shoulder with him.

"Chongsawartha will be pissed. He'll know we scammed him."

Lonnie patted John on the shoulder. "He'll be pissed, all right. Especially when you notify him that his ship never docked in Honolulu." Lonnie winked at John, then slapped him on the shoulder.

John shook his head, as if in wonderment.

Inside the helicopter, while it took off, Lonnie looked back at Johnny. "You really like this shit, don't you?" he yelled over the engine noise.

John looked surprised. "What shit?"

"Landing on a ship in the middle of the ocean. You know. The danger. The adrenaline rush."

"It's what makes life worthwhile," John said.

Lonnie rubbed a hand over his face. "And can get you killed," he said.

"Weren't you excited?" John asked.

"Are you kidding? I was scared shitless," Lonnie said as he reached back behind his seat, took the briefcase off the floor, and placed it on his lap. "That's the difference between you and me. I know when to be scared."

"Would you really have detonated the explosives?" John asked.

Chet's head snapped around.

Lonnie grinned. "Relax, Chet," he said. "Do I look nuts?

Carrying explosives on this flying erector set." Lonnie looked over his shoulder and smiled when he saw the wide-eyed look on John's face.

"What about the detonator you showed Chin?"

"Can't you tell the difference between a detonator and a garage door opener?" Lonnie asked.

"You were bluffing?" Johnny exclaimed. "The guy could have killed us."

"Whatsamatter, bro? Too much of an adrenaline rush for you?" Lonnie could no longer hold his laughter when he saw the shock in his brother's eyes and the sudden paleness of his skin.

CHAPTER SEVENTY

Sara Olson left the task force hangar and drove to her apartment. After a quick meal of yogurt and an apple, she sat at her kitchen table and wrote down questions she wanted to ask. She hoped she'd catch someone in the Army Personnel Office at the Pentagon about 3 a.m., Hawaii time. After she jotted down questions in her notebook, she got her alarm clock, set it for three, and placed it on her living room coffee table. She turned on the television, stretched out on the couch, and, some time during the *Late Show*, drifted off to sleep.

Frank Murdoch hoped he didn't look as tired as he felt. He rubbed his hands over his face and closed his eyes for a moment.

"You all right, Chief?"

Murdoch opened his eyes and scowled at Agent Roy Casper. "Yeah, I'm fine," he snapped. "You got something to do or you just hanging around?"

Casper grinned. "I suppose you want me to go somewhere."

"Go to the hospital and get a signed statement from that bastard, Callahan. Take a stenographer with you."

"That guy's statement ain't gonna carry much weight," Casper said. "He's about as dirty as a cop can get."

"Maybe so," Murdoch said. "But I'd rather have his statement than not have it. It's one more nail in the coffin of the case we'll build against Lonnie Jackson."

"One day, maybe," Casper said.

"Yeah."

Casper drove with a stenographer to Honolulu General. He lugged the steno machine into the lobby and crossed to the elevators. They took one of the cars to the 5th floor, where Casper led the way down the corridor, past the nurses' station, where the hallway turned right.

"God, I hate these places," he growled to himself. "If the smells don't get ya, the germs will."

When he took the turn, he felt his heart lurch. The chair outside Callahan's room was empty! The HOCTF agent had orders to stay at his post unless he arranged for a replacement.

Casper looked at the stenographer and put a finger to his lips. "Anne, I want you to go to the nurses' station," he whispered. "I'll come for you if everything's all right." He lowered the steno machine to the floor and drew his pistol from his shoulder holster. He waited, while Anne turned, and quick-walked down the hall.

Casper knew he could be overreacting. The guard might be in the room. He laid his left hand on the large metal door opener, took a deep breath, pushed the lever, and threw his shoulder into the door. It swung halfway open, then slammed against something. Casper bounced back and momentarily teetered on his heels.

"Shit!" he wheezed. He shoved with added force and struggled to move the door another foot. Two trousered legs splayed on the tile floor between the edge of the door and the baseboard. Casper sucked in his breath and detected the coppery odor of blood. He flipped on the light switch, illuminated the fluorescent fixture over the bed, and entered the room in a semi-crouch. He swept his extended gun hand from left to right and back again. He glanced into the bathroom. Empty! He released the air in his lungs, took a calming breath, and moved to the bed.

Callahan lay facedown, his head turned to the side. A syringe protruded from the side of his neck. Casper moved to him and pressed his fingers against the man's throat. No pulse. His grayish-blue pallor and cold skin told Casper that Callahan had been dead for a while.

He shoved the room door closed and knelt next to the body on the floor. The HOCTF agent assigned to guard Callahan lay on his back, eyes open in a sightless stare, his throat slashed. A stiletto jutted out of his chest—right over his heart. Blood pooled between the body and the baseboard.

"Jackson, you sonofabitch!" Casper hissed.

CHAPTER SEVENTY-ONE

Jimmy Kaneohe spotted Al Sullivan's Cadillac in the diner parking lot. He parked his Suburban and walked across the lot to the all-night joint, one of those places with shiny metal siding that looked like a converted RV. He peered at one of the diner windows and saw Bats, Al, and Terry seated inside. He checked his watch. Good, he thought. It wasn't quite eleven. They're early.

Jimmy entered the diner and looked around to see who else was in the diner. Only one old guy at the opposite end of the place He noticed his guys stopped talking and watched him approach. They suddenly appeared serious.

"Whatsamatter, someone die?" He lowered his voice. "That don't happen for another hour." Then he laughed uproariously.

He let the men burn off tension by talking about women, telling jokes. After twenty minutes, Jimmy waved the counterman over. "Hey, Joey," he shouted. He pointed at the dishes on the table, "How 'bout getting rid of this crap."

Jimmy sat next to Al and looked down his nose at the cigarette butt-stuffed ashtray in the middle of the table. "You guys ready to go to work?" he whispered.

The three men leaned closer to Jimmy.

"You bet, boss. Ready to go."

"Me too, Jimmy."

"Let's do it."

Jimmy scrutinized each man's face, hands, and body language for any sign of nervousness. He especially checked their eyes. Jimmy never went into battle with a man he was unsure of. He saw nothing to worry him.

"Good," Jimmy said. "Terry, settle up the check. We're going up to The Palisades. I'll tell you *who* in the car." He stood. Al and Bats walked with him toward the door.

"Jesus," Terry complained. "I gotta pick up the damn check every time."

Jimmy chuckled. "Newest guy always pays."

"How about finding someone else new so I can save a few bucks."

The others laughed. Bats gave Terry the finger.

"I gotta take a leak first," Terry said.

"Hurry the fuck up," Jimmy said as he pushed the door open and walked outside, Bats and Al close on his heels.

Terry went to the men's room at the far end of the diner and pulled a slip of paper and a pencil from his jacket. Not good, the way this thing was going down, he thought. Unless I can get word to headquarters now, there was little likelihood HOCTF agents would reach The Palisades in time. Even with a helicopter. To make matters worse, this two-bit diner didn't have an inside telephone. The closest phone was in a booth right next to where Jimmy'd parked his truck.

Terry hastily wrote, "Call Frank Murdoch at this number. Tell him it's at The Palisades." He walked out of the bathroom and up to the counter. He laid down two twenty-dollar bills—more than enough to cover the pie and coffee, to get the man's attention—and the slip of paper on the counter. He slid them to the counterman, made eye contact with him. "I need you to call—"

"What the hell's keeping you?"

Terry jerked around. His heart pumped like an overworked piston.

Al stood in the doorway. "Jimmy's having a fit," he said. Then Al walked back outside.

Terry strode out of the diner without another word. By the time he'd descended the three steps to the parking lot, Al had already opened the front passenger door of Jimmy's Suburban.

Terry stuck his right hand in his jacket pocket while he walked over to the vehicle. He pulled out his car keys and the locator beacon and flipped the switch on the beacon. He switched the beacon to his left hand, dropped his keys by the right rear tire of the truck, bent down, and planted the magnetized locator beacon in the rear wheel well while he picked up his keys with his right hand. Then he stepped to the utility vehicle's right rear door and climbed inside. Please God, he thought, let the diner guy call Frank.

Jimmy put the Suburban in reverse and backed out of the parking space. "Somethin' wrong with your bladder?" he said. "You're worse than a goddamn broad."

Chuckles from the other men.

"He's nervous, boss," Bats declared. "Gonna bust his cherry tonight."

"Give me a break, guys," Terry said. "I musta had four, five cups of coffee in there."

Jimmy snorted, but apparently decided to let up on Terry. He moved the gearshift to Drive when the counterman, apron flying, paper cap in one hand, ran across the parking lot toward them.

Terry's stomach ached as though acid had burned a hole in it. He put his left hand on the door handle and his shoulder against the door, ready to bolt. He reached inside his jacket with his right hand and gripped his SIG P210-6. The feel of the weapon, fully loaded with eight rounds, seemed to slow his heartbeat some.

"What the fuck does this asshole want?" Al said.

Jimmy stopped the truck and lowered his window. The diner guy stood beside the driver side door. "What!" Jimmy shouted.

The counterman's eyes did a dance as he seemed to stare everywhere but at Jimmy. "You . . . forgot . . . your change," he stammered and handed the bills to Jimmy. Terry could see the white slip of paper poking out from under the bills. He didn't think it possible, but it felt as though his heart had actually stopped and a giant fist had grabbed his lungs and squeezed the air from them.

"I'll be damned!" Jimmy said. "An honest man. I should give you a tip." He hesitated a second, while the diner guy seemed to relax a bit as a slight smile creased his face. "So here it is," Jimmy continued. "When somebody forgets their change, fuck 'em." Al and Bats roared. "Honesty'll get you nowhere, asshole."

Jimmy drove the truck out of the parking lot as he yelled, "Sucker!" out his window.

"Whatsamatter, Terry, you nervous, leaving your change in there?" Jimmy asked. The bills, with the note sandwiched between them, crumpled in Jimmy's hand. "Whattaya think, guys? Should I keep it for myself? Would serve Terry right." He shoved the money—and note—into his shirt pocket. Jimmy, Al and Bats laughed hysterically.

Terry didn't have enough air in his lungs to laugh, but his heart beat again. He wiped the perspiration from his forehead and took deep breaths. It was only a temporary reprieve, he knew. Jimmy reads that note and I'm dog meat.

"Boss," one of the task force agents yelled across the hangar. "I got a signal from the locator beacon."

Murdoch leaped from his chair and rushed the fifty yards to the other side of the building. "Where is it?"

"Looks like about five miles from here, moving northeast up the coast road. It could go almost anywhere from there."

Murdoch looked over the agent's shoulder at the monitor and followed the beacon's progress. He stood glued to the spot, afraid to take his eyes off the screen for even a second. He picked up the radio transmitter on the table beside the video monitor and keyed the mike twice. "Randy," he shouted.

"This is Randy."

"Murdoch here. Get your team loaded on the chopper. I want that damn bird revved up and ready to go on a moment's notice."

"Right, Chief. Where we . . . ?"

Murdoch keyed off the handset and leaned closer to the tracking screen. Ten minutes passed, then fifteen. Like a primitive video game, a tiny light flashed on the monitor, accompanied by *beep-beep-beep* that marked the beacon's path.

Murdoch glanced at his watch, then back at the screen. He'd stared at the blinking light for almost twenty minutes. The beacon suddenly entered a winding dead-end road along the coast. Murdoch's mouth went dry as ashes. The Palisades. Renee Drummond's neighborhood.

"Oh shit!" Murdoch shouted, startling the agent in the chair in front of him. He yelled at the man, "Scramble every agent. Get them up to the Drummond place in The Palisades. Call up there and warn them. See if the police have any cars in the area. I'll take the chopper."

CHAPTER SEVENTY-TWO

"What time you got?" Richie asked Esteban as they moved toward the east corner of the estate.

Esteban brought his wrist close to his face and turned his arm so the moon's reflection shone on the watch. "Little before midnight. One more hour before Matt spells you."

The ringing telephone woke Matt. It rang again before he could snatch it from its cradle. He brought it halfway to his ear when a thunderous explosion shattered the outside night stillness, rattled the windows, shook the house. Matt dropped the receiver on the bed, moved to the chair where his shoulder holster hung, and pulled out the 9 mm pistol.

"What is it?" Renee cried, her voice hoarse and trembly. She rolled out of bed and came around to where Matt now stared out the window through a narrow space between the curtains. She grasped his arm.

"Sounded like one of the Claymores," Matt said. "I can't see any movement out back. I think it came from the other side of the house." He pulled on a pair of jeans and running shoes, then slipped a tee shirt over his head and shrugged into the shoulder rig. "Stay here," he told Renee. "Don't turn on the lights." He moved toward the door, then remembered the telephone. He ran around the bed to the nightstand. The telephone receiver lay on the bed where he'd dropped it. He picked it up and said, "Hello?"

"Doctor Curtis?"

"Yes."

"Mister Murdoch told me to call. We think there's a hit team on its way to your location. You need—"

"They're already here," Matt shouted. "Renee," he said, "come talk to this guy. I've got to help Esteban and Richie."

Matt dropped the receiver on the bed. Then he pulled Renee's pistol from the nightstand drawer and handed it to her. "Lock the door behind me," he said. "I'll be back as soon as I can."

He raced down the hall that overlooked the foyer and took the stairs two at a time. At the foyer closet, he selected an AR-15 automatic rifle, inserted a clip, and slung a canvas bag with extra clips over his shoulder. He flipped off the switch to the lights that illuminated the large entryway and the front of the house, then cracked open the door. A quick movement just outside startled Matt. He threw open the door and swung the automatic weapon toward a man now crouched behind a bush.

"Whoa, it's me," Esteban rasped. His weapon pointed down the driveway.

Matt closed the door behind him and knelt down. "Wha—?"

The *rat-a-tat-tat* of automatic weapons fire burst from the south side of the house, down by the front gate. The repetitive burp of another automatic weapon answered the first. Then all hell broke loose. It sounded as though three or four weapons fired at the same time.

"MAC-10s and an AR-15," Esteban said. "You hear the difference."

"Yeah," Matt answered. "We've got to find Richie."

Then, as suddenly as the shooting had started, it abruptly ended. The only sounds Matt heard were Max's thunderous barkings coming from the garages.

Then, a man screamed, "I'm hit! Oh God! I'm hit!" Then what sounded like the same voice shrieked unintelligible sounds, then silence.

"Doesn't sound like Richie," Esteban whispered to Matt.

"Where is he?"

"Southeast side. In the trees off the back patio. Someone tripped the Claymore down by the gate." Esteban's toothy smile reflected the moonlight. "Musta cut him in half. Never heard a sound after the explosion, until just now."

"How many got inside the wall?" Matt asked.

"Sounds like Richie hit one of them. From the weapons firing, there's at least two more out there."

Matt pointed at Esteban's headset with the single earpiece. "Is your radio on?"

"Yeah!"

"Good! Tell Richie to cover his eyes in exactly two minutes from"—Matt waited for Esteban to look at his own wristwatch, then he checked his own watch—"now. You too. I'll turn on the floodlight security system. I'll leave it on for five seconds, then cut it off. Ought to screw up the bad guys' night vision. They'll be blind for a few seconds. When the lights go off, you run like hell around the west side to the back of the house. I'll go out back through the kitchen."

Esteban repeated in the radio mouthpiece what Matt had told him. He appeared to listen for a moment. "Richie says he needs some help back there. He's got two men in the trees. He hit a third one who's down somewhere."

"Okay." Matt left Esteban in the alcove and ran back inside the house. He went to the security closet off the kitchen, opened the closet door, and flipped the panic switch on the alarm system. It emitted a low howling noise that began as a sluggish, steady sound and rapidly accelerated into a series of mixed, shrill wails. Then he watched the second hand on his watch sweep toward the two-minute mark.

Matt silently counted down the last five seconds. Then he pushed another switch in the security closet and turned on the floodlights, which illuminated the building and the grounds like a football stadium for a night game. He kept his hand on the switch for five seconds, then shut it off, and ran to the kitchen patio door. A second later, he heard the staccato fire of an automatic weapon from the back of the property. The muzzle blast punctuated the night with light flashes.

The silhouette of a man backlit by the moon appeared in the

middle of the lawn: Richie. He stood over a body. Matt ran to him just as Esteban rounded the corner of the house and moved to them.

"Shit, Matt," Richie said, "when those lights went on it was like a shooting gallery. They were as good as flares. Caught this guy out in the open."

"Speaking of being caught in the open," Matt said, "we'd better move from here. Didn't you tell Esteban there were *two* men back here?"

"Yeah, I thought I saw two of them, but maybe . . . ."

Matt picked up a MAC-10 in the grass next to the wounded man and tossed it to the side. He bent down. The man's clothes were blood-soaked. His breathing was shallow and ragged.

Richie grabbed Matt's arm and pulled him up. "Leave this guy for now. We'd better sweep the grounds."

A shot sounded and Matt felt the air around his head pulse with the supersonic movement of what could only have been a bullet. "Damn!" he shouted as he dropped to the lawn. He heard the sound of glass crash behind him.

"We're sitting ducks out here," Richie shouted.

A burst of bullets erupted in answer.

Matt saw the star bursts of muzzle flashes in the trees. He aimed his rifle at the light flashes and pulled the trigger. The weapon jerked in his hands, spraying lethal missiles at the far corner of the property.

"Going in," Matt heard Esteban shout from ahead of him. Matt sprinted in an arc toward the trees overlooking the ocean.

"Richie, cover the back of the house," Matt said. Then he ran along the back wall. He was still twenty yards from where he'd seen the muzzle flash when he heard Esteban call out.

"You got him good, *amigo.*"

Matt walked forward and found Esteban kneeling next to a man on his back on a bed of ferns. Blood seeped from several wounds where bullets had stitched the man's torso.

They dragged the body out onto the lawn and dumped it next to the man Richie had shot earlier.

"Richie, go inside and check on Renee," Matt ordered. "Make sure she doesn't leave her room. Esteban, I'll turn on the security lights again. Let's make sure there aren't any others still out—"

The *whoop-whoop-whoop* of a helicopter seemed to come from out over the ocean. Matt ran into the trees; Esteban took cover around the corner of the house; Richie disappeared inside the house.

The increasingly loud noise and thrum of the helicopter's rotors rattled Matt's nerves. He momentarily felt as though he was back on a godforsaken battlefield, listening and feeling the pounding of American aircraft beating the air.

A floodlight mounted on the aircraft's belly, just under its nose, moved from side to side and swept the lawn and the roof of the house. Matt watched the helicopter fly high over the house. The pilot appeared to be reconnoitering the grounds. Then it returned to the ocean-side and dropped closer to the ground.

Matt looked up. "HOCTF" was stenciled on the helicopter's undercarriage. He breathed a sigh of relief, dumped his weapon under a bush, and walked out onto the lawn, arms in the air. He looked for Esteban at the rear of the house. He wasn't there.

The chopper's floodlight beam bathed Matt with blinding light. He shielded his eyes with one hand. Sounds of dozens of sirens wailed in the distance. Then the helicopter dropped even lower; its rotors blasted Matt. A loudspeaker blared.

"Doctor Curtis, it's Frank Murdoch. Wave your arms if everything's all right."

Matt waved.

While the chopper moved toward the ocean side of the lawn, Matt ran inside and turned on the security lights. He also switched on lights in some of the first floor rooms, while he raced through the house to the foyer. He punched the remote control button to open the front gate, then raced to the staircase. "Renee," he yelled, as he bounded up the steps.

Matt saw a door open on the second floor. Richie stepped out of Renee's bedroom and smiled as he reached the top step.

"We're fine," Richie said. "Okay to come down?"

"Yeah," Matt said, "but ditch the weapon. The cavalry has arrived."

Then Renee's head peeked out of the room. When she saw Matt, she rushed at him, pistol in hand, nearly toppling him down the stairs.

"Are you okay?" Matt asked.

"Am *I* okay?" she shouted. "What happened down there? Are *you* all right? What about Esteban?"

Matt reached behind his neck where she'd thrown her arms and took the pistol from her hand. Then he crushed her to him and desperately held on.

"I'm fine," Matt whispered in her ear. "We're all fine." He felt his body shake as he came down from the adrenaline high he'd been on. "The police are here. We'd better go downstairs."

Renee and Matt reached the bottom of the stairs just as Esteban burst through the front door, his breathing labored.

"Where'd you go?" Matt asked.

"I had to take care of a few things," Esteban said as he looked behind him, then turned to peer across the foyer. "Wouldn't do for the cops to find the other Claymore we set up in the trees. Not to mention the other weapons and ammunition."

"Where'd you put the stuff?" Matt asked.

A smile creased Esteban's face. "The trunk of your rental van. They'll never look there."

A gang of cops entered the house, their pistols and shotguns pointed at the four of them, just when the roar of the helicopter rotors at the back of the house subsided. Matt slowly bent down and placed Renee's pistol on the floor.

"Hands on your heads," an officer shouted. Other officers searched them, then they were marched outside to the floodlit back patio.

Frank Murdoch appeared from behind a clump of trees. "Enough, Lieutenant," he shouted. "These aren't the people we're after. Have your men search the grounds."

Murdoch turned to Matt and squinted. "There's a wounded man and a corpse over there on the lawn. They both look badly shot up. From the looks of the wounds, they must have been hit with high velocity rounds. Automatic weapons. You wouldn't know anything about that, would you?"

Matt shrugged. *God, there won't be much left of the guy who tripped the Claymore,* he thought. *I wonder how we'll explain that.*

Murdoch gave Matt, then Esteban, Richie, and Renee, in turn, stern, but knowing looks. "Yeah, right. Hear no evil, see no evil, and speak no evil. You have any idea who the dead one is?"

Again, just shrugs.

"It's Jimmy Kaneohe. We've known for a while he's Lonnie Jackson's right-hand man," Murdoch said, then did an about face and took a step toward a couple medics working on the wounded man. He stopped mid-stride and turned back to Matt. "You wouldn't know if there are any more bodies around?" He tried to keep the dread he felt from his face. He knew his voice sounded strained.

"There might be one on the south side of the house and another on the far side of the driveway, about halfway to the street," Esteban said.

Murdoch shouted to two of his men who hovered over the medics. "You two come with me."

"I think I'll make some coffee," Renee said. "I suspect it might be needed." Richie followed her.

Esteban put a hand on Matt's shoulder. "I've had all of this defensive crap I can stand. We both know Lonnie Jackson sent these men up here. I'm going after him. He's a dead man, Matt."

Matt saw hardness in Esteban's eyes. He'd seen that look before. Thirty years ago when one of their A team members was killed by a sniper in Bolivia. Esteban had tracked down the sniper and come back with the man's rifle.

"These guys didn't expect resistance tonight," Esteban said. "They came here to murder you and Renee. The next time, Jackson's men will be a whole lot better prepared. I'm not waiting for a next time."

Matt nodded.

Murdoch felt tension build inside his chest. Neither of the two men on the back lawn was Terry Hill. He raced around the corner of the house; looked for his missing undercover agent.

"Over here," someone yelled.

Murdoch and his men sprinted in the direction of the voice. Two Honolulu police officers stood across the driveway, several yards into the dense shrubbery. One of them was bent over. A pool of vomit glistened in the light from the second cop's flashlight. Murdoch snatched the flashlight from the cop, who stared, as though mesmerized, at the eviscerated corpse a few feet away. His expression seemed frozen—popping eyeballs, sagging jaw.

Murdoch turned the light on the body and saw it had been torn apart. There was nothing left of the front half of the torso. Insides spilled between the corpse's legs, not enough clothing or body to identify gender. The face obliterated.

"My God, Frank," one of the HOCTF agents said. "What did this?"

Murdoch slowly moved the flashlight beam over the corpse's length. He heard someone wretch when the light played over the intestines that had exploded from the mutilated body. A red, white, and gray mush covered the body and the ground nearby. Murdoch circled the remains and inspected the damage more closely. "If I didn't know better," he said, "I'd guess the guy tripped an anti-personnel mine. Claymore, maybe. I haven't seen anything like this in a long time." He handed the flashlight back to the cop. "Thank God it isn't Terry," he murmured. Then he thought, It isn't Terry because the body's too short. Otherwise, I wouldn't have been able to tell.

While Murdoch and his men walked back up the hill, in the direction of the helicopter, he heard a noise. He spread his arms and stopped the agent on either side of him. "Shh, listen," he said.

He stood at the edge of the trees and barely breathed as he tried to filter out the muted sounds of voices from the back of the house, the crash of surf on the rocks far below, and the staccato cadence of night bugs. Suddenly, a different sound came through. Murdoch jerked to his right. There. He heard it again. A low moan.

Murdoch broke through the bushes like a rampaging rhinoceros, flashlight extended. He stopped ten feet into the thicket and stood still. The moan again. He stepped to his left and felt something squish under his shoes.

"Oh my God," Murdoch exclaimed. Terry Hill's dirt-encrusted

face appeared in a beam of light. A large dark puddle soaked the bed of pine needles around him. Murdoch knew with a certainty he would never forget the look in Terry's eyes. The same look he'd seen so many times before. The look of a man in pain, afraid he was about to die.

Murdoch looked over his shoulder at one of his agents. "Spencer, get one of those medics from the back yard. Pick him up and carry him over here if you have to." Then he dropped to his knees, removed his jacket, and pressed it against the gaping wound in Terry's chest. "Hang in there, kid."

CHAPTER SEVENTY-THREE

"Am . . . am I go . . . gonna die?" Al "Two Toes" Sullivan asked.

HOCTF agent Don Ferguson knelt on the lawn next to Sullivan, took in a slow, deep breath, crossed the fingers of his right hand behind his back, and mentally made the sign of the cross. He looked down at Sullivan's bloody, pain-contorted face. "It doesn't look good," Ferguson said.

Sullivan closed his eyes.

"Listen," Ferguson said, "why don't you clear your conscience? There's nothing Lonnie Jackson can do to you now."

Sullivan opened his eyes and half-nodded. "Get me a priest," he moaned.

Ferguson ripped the radio from his belt, pretended to key the transmit button, and demanded that a priest be called. He turned back to Sullivan. "Should be here pretty quick," he said.

Sullivan gripped the front of Ferguson's shirt. "I want to make things right," he said.

You couldn't 'make things right,' you dirtbag, if you confessed a thousand times, Ferguson thought. "Clear your conscience," he said to the wounded hoodlum.

Sullivan began slowly, stuttering, long gaps between his words, as though he found the business of confession physically difficult. But, once he got started, the words seemed to flow like flashflood water in an arroyo. "Lonnie Jackson sent us here to kill Renee

Drummond and some guy named Curtis. Jimmy Kaneohe was in charge."

"Who else was with you?" Ferguson asked.

"Bats Zarpas and Terry Hill."

"Why did Lonnie Jackson order you guys to come up here?"

"I don't know," Sullivan said.

"What else do want to tell me?"

Sullivan confessed to three murders he'd committed for Lonnie Jackson. Then he said, "I ain't saying nothin' more 'til the priest gets here."

Ferguson recorded everything on his cell phone and emailed the file to HOCTF headquarters for transcription. He smiled when he thought about Sullivan's "death bed confession." He suspected Sullivan would survive his wounds, to spend the rest of his life behind bars.

Renee sat on the solarium couch, her head on Matt's shoulder. Despite the evening's events, Matt felt at ease.

Footsteps sounded. Frank Murdoch and one of the HOCTF agents approached. "Sorry to disturb you," Murdoch said.

"It's okay," Matt said.

Murdoch narrowed his eyes and stared at Renee. "How are you doing?"

"Not too bad," she said.

"I've arranged for four policemen to be posted at the entrance gate until further notice. If any of you want to leave here, call me first. I'll arrange for an escort. I'm not taking any chances as long as Jackson's on the loose."

Matt nodded. "I hope you've got enough evidence to put an end to this crap."

Murdoch cleared his throat, flipped back the sides of his suit jacket, and stuck his hands in his pockets. "You can count on it," he said. "Lonnie Jackson's going down hard."

"Thanks," Matt said and smiled at the agent.

"My pleasure," Murdoch said and then wheeled around and walked out of the house.

Murdoch dropped into the front passenger seat of the unmarked car and said to the driver, "I want to get to the hangar as fast as this car will go." As the driver roared down the driveway, Murdoch took his cell phone from his shirt pocket and speed-dialed the home number for the Agent-in-Charge for the Honolulu FBI office.

"Zimmerman."

"Mark, sorry about the late hour, but I figured you'd want to be in on this."

"Frank, you sound like a kid at Christmas," Zimmerman said. "What's up?"

"How'd you like to take down Lonnie Jackson?" Murdoch asked.

"Hah!" Zimmerman exclaimed. "Where do I have to be . . . and when?"

"Meet me at the hangar in an hour."

"You got it."

Murdoch made calls and woke up the local heads of the DEA, the Honolulu Chief of Police and the Hawaii State Police Commander. He then called his dispatcher and ordered her to muster all agents at the hangar.

Murdoch felt a tingling excitement while the car zipped down from The Palisades. The sense of anticipation charged his body as though he'd been struck by lightning. Lonnie Jackson was *his*. Finally. He knew it with a certainty.

CHAPTER SEVENTY-FOUR

Lonnie Jackson's cell phone vibrated on the nightstand. Before he could grab it, it shook itself off and onto the plush, cream-colored carpeting.

"Shit!" Lonnie spat. He looked at the clock on the nightstand. "Fuckin' three in the morning." He reached down from the bed and groped with his fingers until he felt the phone.

"Whatsamatter, Lonnie?" the redhead next to him slurred, her voice heavy from the after-effects of cocaine, booze, sex, and too little sleep.

"None of your business."

The stripper rolled over and pulled the sheet over her head.

He noted the phone number on the cell screen but didn't recognize it. He pressed the TALK button and barked, "What?"

"Hello!" The man sounded out of breath.

"Yeah, who is this?"

"It's Jerry."

It took Jackson a couple seconds to match a name with the voice: Patrolman Jerry Freeman, Honolulu Police Department. He softened his tone and said, "Yeah, what's up?"

"I'm in a phone booth," Freeman said in a voice resonant with tension. "Called you as soon as I could get away."

Jackson knew Freeman appreciated the money he received—two hundred a week, week in and week out. He also knew Freeman was the emotional type. He tended to get excited over little things.

"I was dispatched to an estate in The Palisades tonight," Freeman said. "Bloody massacre . . . dead and wounded all over the place . . . big wigs from the Hawaii Organized Crime Task Force there."

Freeman seemed to measure each word. Usually the cop spoke a mile-a-minute, no pauses. You could hardly shut him up. But Lonnie put aside the change in the man's voice. He felt great. Jimmy must have done the job. 'Bloody massacre,' Freeman had said. I finally got rid of the Drummond bitch, Lonnie thought. One less loose end to worry about.

"Thanks, man. I appreciate the news. There'll be a bonus for you this week."

A pause on the other end of the line.

"Didya have something else?" Lonnie asked.

"You misunderstand, sir. We found two dead, two wounded. Your people."

Jackson's heart sank. Not Jimmy. Not after all these years. Then a thought jolted him. "How do you know they worked for me?"

"One of the wounded men gave a statement. He said you'd ordered the raid."

Jackson cursed under his breath. "Anything else?"

"No, sir."

Jackson slammed down the phone. "Get your ass out of bed," he screamed at the girl.

"Huh?" she said as she uncovered her head.

Jackson grabbed a corner of the bed sheet and ripped it off the bed. "Get up! Get out of here!"

She moved sloth-like, planted her feet on the floor and shook her head, as though to clear it.

He walked around to the other side of the bed and slapped her face. "Snap out of it!" he yelled. "Put on your clothes and get lost."

While she stumbled over to a chair to retrieve her clothes, Lonnie opened a dresser drawer and removed a small plastic bag of coke. He tossed the bag at her. Then he peeled off five one hundred-dollar bills from a stack on the dresser and threw them on the floor in front of her. After she'd put on her underwear and gathered up her clothes, the coke, and the cash, he shoved her out of the condominium into the hall.

Jackson took a quick cold shower and willed himself to think. If the cops and judges on my payroll have the testimony of one of my own men, they won't dare protect me from an attempted murder charge. And they've got Callahan's admission, too. It will be damn easy now for them to connect me to the Curtis woman's death. The heat'll be on me big-time.

He toweled off outside the shower stall. While he dressed, he looked at the clock. Three fifteen. About ten hours until the heroin would be transferred from the *La Concepcion*. Fifty million dollars. One hundred twenty-five million all together in my offshore accounts. He padded over to his wall safe, dialed the combination, and opened the door. Inside were rows of currency—his getaway money—neatly arranged on top of several disks. His blue-jacketed, forged passport sat on top of the currency. In the name of Rocque Bingham.

He turned around, walked to his closet, lifted a suitcase off the floor, and carried it to the safe. He removed the passport and ninety thousand dollars in U.S. currency, and stacked them in the case. He added clothes for three days.

Then Jackson went to work on his disguise. While he applied makeup and the false beard and mustache, he thought, I should call Johnny and Mom. But he couldn't. The less they knew the better off they'd be.

CHAPTER SEVENTY-FIVE

Sara Olson jerked upright at the *buzz-buzz-buzz* of her alarm clock. She blindly slammed her hand down on the clock, cursed it, and then rubbed her eyes. She moaned as she stood, arched her back, and shuffled to the kitchen. After she made coffee and slugged back enough of the hot drink to get her synapses to spark, she returned to the living room, picked up the notes she'd made, and dialed the Pentagon number. It was just after 3:15 a.m., Hawaii time. She held her breath while the phone rang.

A woman with a southern drawl answered, "Department of Defense, how may I direct your call?"

"I'm not sure what the official department is," Sara said, "but I need to talk to someone in Army Records. I'm specifically interested in the file of an Army officer who died in 1982."

"Please hold, ma'am; I'll transfer you."

Sara heard a series of beeps, then a male voice.

"Personnel Office, Sergeant Jensen speaking, sir."

A fellow Swede, Sara thought. "Sergeant Jensen, this is Special Agent Sara Olson of the Hawaii Organized Crime Task Force. I need to track down the records of an officer who died in 1982. Is there any—"

"Ma'am," Jensen said, "I'm afraid you called the wrong number. All officers' records from that period are maintained at the Personnel Records Center in St. Louis."

Sara blew out a sigh. The proverbial runaround, she thought. "Can you give me the telephone number in St. Louis?" she asked.

"Of course, ma'am."

After she jotted down the number, Sara thanked the man and immediately dialed the Missouri location. After being transferred three times, she was finally put through to a woman named Esther Washington.

"This is Sara Olson. I'm a Special Agent with the Hawaii Organized Crime Task Force. We're investigating a murder here on Oahu. You might be able to help me."

"A murder?" the woman said. "How can *I* help?"

"I'm trying to get background on a deceased Army officer."

"That's too bad," Washington said.

"Yes, we've lost a lot of good men," Sara said.

"Oh, of course," Washington said. She sounded embarrassed. "But, what I meant was, most of our files burned in a fire. It destroyed our entire storage facility."

"Damn!" Sara said under her breath. "Is there—"

"Besides, I couldn't give out information from our files over the telephone. No insult intended, but how do I know you are who you say you are?"

"Would it help if I faxed you a copy of my identification?"

"Is this really important?" Washington said after a moment, lowering her voice, sounding conspiratorial.

"Very," Sara said.

"Well, I guess it'll be all right," Esther said.

"But, if the files were burn—"

"Let me check the computer," Esther interjected. "We've reconstructed some files. Give me the officer's name?"

"Roland Jerrell. J-E-R-R-E-L-L."

Sara felt a pulse of hope. She crossed her fingers while she waited for the woman to come back on the line. Please, she thought, let there be a connection between Jerrell . . . and who?

"Ah, here it is. Jerrell, Roland C. Born 13 November 1949. ROTC graduate from Lehigh University in 1970. Infantry officer. Fort Benning, Georgia for Infantry Officer's Basic Course in 1970. Honor Graduate. One tour in Vietnam. Promoted to First Lieutenant.

Bronze Star with "V" device, Silver Star, Purple Heart, Combat Infantry Badge. Real hero. Two years as an instructor at Fort Benning after the basic course. Promoted to Captain. Went to the University of Virginia for two years and received a Masters Degree in Political Science. Then assigned to CINCPAC Headquarters in Hawaii in 1975 as a liaison officer for one year."

Bingo! Sara thought.

"After that, he spent forty-seven weeks in the German Language Course at the Defense Language Institute West Coast in Monterey, California. Then thirty months in Germany. Promoted to Major. In 1980, he was sent to the Special Warfare School at Fort Bragg. Pentagon from 1981 to 1982." Washington paused for a beat. "He was assigned to the Multi-National Force in Lebanon in 1982. They supervised the withdrawal of the Palestine Liberation Organization's forces from Lebanon. He was killed by a sniper that same year."

"Any information about his family?" Sara asked.

"Let's see. Yes. He married a Nora Cromwell in Monterey, California. Son born the same year. Date of birth: 2 December 1976. Missus Jerrell claimed Hawaii as her home state. Not much else."

"What was the son's name?"

"Lawrence Jerrell."

"You wouldn't happen to have a photograph of the wife and son in the file?" Sara asked.

"Major Jerrell's picture was scanned into the computer, but not the rest of the family."

"It's probably not important. I just thought I'd—"

"You know the Passport Office might have a picture of the wife and son," Esther said. "The file shows they accompanied Major Jerrell to Germany. They would have needed a passport to do so. The mother and child would probably have had their passport picture taken together."

Sara glanced at her notes. All her questions had been answered. "Thank you, Ms. Washington. You've been very helpful. If you ever get to Oahu, look me up. I owe you a dinner."

"Why thank you, Ms. Olson. I might just do that."

After she disconnected the call, Sara read her notes again. There wasn't anything to shed new light on Nora Cromwell/Jerrell/

Dunning. Sara sighed. She'd report in at the hangar and try to make herself useful. She felt stupid. She'd struck out on the Pentagon angle. What had she hoped to accomplish, anyway? The more she thought about it, the more she found incredible the whole idea of a socialite like Nora Dunning involved in Susan Curtis's death.

DAY TEN

CHAPTER SEVENTY-SIX

Matt and Renee slept late and came down to the kitchen at 9 a.m. Matt made breakfast—coffee, French toast, and bacon—while Renee sat at the table, her face drawn, chin in her hands.

"What are you thinking?" Matt asked.

Renee raised her head and smiled. "I didn't realize how much tension I've carried around with me for a long time," she said. "Now that the police are finally doing something, I feel relieved. Like a one-hundred pound weight has been lifted off my shoulders."

"Last night's attack finally mobilized law enforcement agencies to come down on Lonnie Jackson," Matt said.

"Man, does that coffee smell good," Richie said as he entered the kitchen, trailed by Max and Esteban.

"How come you guys didn't wake us up?" Esteban asked.

"As far as I'm concerned, you can sleep as long as you want," Renee said.

Matt laughed and poured cups of coffee for Esteban and Richie. "So, what's on the agenda for today?" he asked.

"I hate to desert you," Richie said as he took a seat at the table, "but I really need to go see Angelo."

Renee nodded, reached over, and pressed Richie's hand. "We've got plenty of protection from the police now."

Matt put down a metal spatula and walked to the table. He patted Richie on the back. "Couldn't have done it without you; but

Renee's right. We'll be fine now. You should be with your brother."
He turned back to the stove, transferred the French toast to a
serving platter, and placed it on the table.

Renee stood and walked behind Richie's chair. She bent over,
hugged him from behind, and kissed his cheek. "Thanks for
everything," she said.

Matt hid a smile. Richie's face had turned crimson. "What about
you, Esteban?" Matt asked.

Esteban looked angry. His eyes were slits and his jaw clenched.
"I think I'll hang around a little longer. We've got unfinished
business."

"I can hang around, too," Richie said, now looking confused, his
eyebrows knitted. "What unfinished business?" he asked, sounding
like a kid excluded from something fun.

"You go see Angelo, Richie. I don't want you involved in it,"
Esteban said.

Richie's eyes widened. He pouted for a moment. "What's the
matter? You don't think I can hack it? Whatever *it* is."

"Come on, Richie," Esteban said. "Nothing personal. You don't
need this."

Richie's look hardened. He glared at Esteban, then over at Matt.
"Bullshit. Sorry, ma'am. I ain't leavin'. What are you two up to?"

Renee stared wide-eyed at Matt. "What?"

Esteban sighed loudly.

Matt looked at Esteban and nodded his head.

Esteban turned toward Renee and Richie. "We're going after
Lonnie Jackson."

Renee paced the kitchen, her face flushed.

Matt could tell she was losing the battle of controlling her
temper.

"So," Renee finally shouted, "you'll go into Jackson's playing
field and get killed. Does that about sum things up?"

"Whoa, wait a minute," Matt said. "You need to have a little
confi—"

Renee's voice rose in pitch. "Oh, I've got confidence you both
have too damn much testosterone for your own good. I've got
confidence you'll get yourselves killed. I've got confidence you're

crazy. Why don't you two think with your brains instead of your testicles?"

Matt had trouble making eye contact with Renee. She balled her hands, braced them on her hips, and looked directly at him. "Lonnie Jackson is too smart to come after us with the police here. Let the cops do their job." She paused and Matt saw her eyes mist. She pointed at Matt. "Don't you dare do this to me," she said. Her voice quavered. Tears slid onto her cheeks. "You hear me, Matthew Curtis?"

Matt met her gaze.

Renee held his look for a moment, then rushed from the room.

"Bacon's burning," Richie said.

"Shit." Matt turned to the stove. "Shit." He took the pan from the broiler, walked to the garbage can, and dumped the bacon.

Matt sat down. The room was as silent as a morgue. Then he twisted in his chair and looked at the television. The set was on, but the sound had been muted. A news alert scrolled across the bottom of the screen. The words "BREAKING NEWS" coursed in a repetitive sequence below the image of a reporter who stood across the street from an industrial building. Matt reached over and turned up the sound.

"Just behind me, you can see the Island Garmentwear factory," the reporter said. "Moments ago, the Hawaii Organized Crime Task Force, composed of members from several law enforcement departments, raided that building. The building's owner is alleged to be Lonnie Jackson, rumored to be the head of organized crime in Hawaii. According to informed sources, the Hawaii Organized Crime Task Force has investigated Jackson for years. This morning's raid resulted from that investigation."

At the mention of Jackson's name, Matt let out a noisy stream of air.

"This is only one of six locations the task force raided this morning. Surveillance and intelligence work turned up information on Jackson's involvement in an array of businesses, including manufacturing enterprises, like this business here," the reporter said as he turned slightly and pointed toward the warehouse.

Running footsteps sounded and Renee's voice suddenly

intruded. "Turn on the news," she shouted as she entered the kitchen. "The TV upstairs—" A chorus of "Shhs" greeted her. She plopped into a chair.

"It's our . . . ." The reporter suddenly stopped and looked off camera. "I see the head of the task force. Let me try to get Frank Murdoch to make a statement. Agent Murdoch, Agent Murdoch, could you give us a moment?"

The camera panned to Murdoch, who stood with two other men. Murdoch frowned at the reporter, said a few words to the men with him, then walked to the reporter.

The reporter stuck his microphone in Murdoch's face and said, "This is Frank Murdoch, the head of Hawaii's Organized Crime Task Force. What can you tell us?"

Murdoch turned to the camera and said, "Through the unprecedented cooperation of local, state, and federal law enforcement agencies, our task force has spent years gathering information about Lonnie Jackson's criminal operation. Jackson built an insidious organization that has become a blight on Hawaii and its law abiding citizens. These raids today are the beginning of the end of Lonnie Jackson and his criminal organization."

"What charges have been filed against Mister Jackson?" the reporter asked.

"They include narcotics trafficking, extortion, prostitution, and murder."

"Murder?" the reporter said. "What murder?"

"I'll release a statement in a day or two after formal charges are filed."

While uniformed and plainclothes police in the background marched a group of handcuffed men and women from the warehouse, the reporter asked, "Is Mister Jackson in custody?"

A sour look came to Murdoch's face. He looked away for a moment, then back at the camera. "We have not apprehended Mister Jackson, yet. However, I am confident he will be behind bars soon. We ask citizens to call 9-1-1 if they have information about Jackson's whereabouts."

Murdoch walked away without another word.

Esteban muted the sound on the television. "I guess there's no point going after Jackson."

Renee huffed.

Matt smiled at Renee. "Of course, we had no intention of going after him once you gave us your motherly lecture."

"Bullsh—"

"Ma'am," Richie said. "I think you need to watch your language."

Renee glared at Richie, then laughed uproariously.

CHAPTER SEVENTY-SEVEN

Nora Dunning felt as though sludge had filled her chest. The ache there was much like the ache many years before. When the Army officer came to her door and told her Roland, her first and only real love, had been killed in action in Lebanon.

Her throat felt so tight she could barely swallow. She ignored the tears that dropped onto her burgundy silk blouse. She knew the police had tried for years to frame her son, Lawrence, for crimes he had nothing to do with. But they had never been able to charge him. It was just racial bias, she reminded herself. The police couldn't stand to see a man of color succeed. How could he have been involved in drugs, prostitution . . .? Her own flesh and blood. But they now hunted him like an animal. It couldn't be true. Not her boy.

She shut off the television and picked up the telephone. She tried to control her voice, but her words caught in her throat and vibrated tremulously when they carried over the telephone line. "This is Nora Dunning. May I speak to my son, please?"

"Of course, Missus Dunning," the receptionist at Rawson, Wong & Ballard said. "I'll transfer you."

"John Dunning."

Nora devolved into shuddering sobs at the sound of her Johnny's voice. "Johnny, the police . . . they're after Lawrence. They're saying the most . . . awful things about him on television."

"Mother, what are you talking about?"

"It's terrible."

"Where are you?" John asked.

"At home."

"Stay there. I'll try to find out what's going on. Soon as I do, I'll come out to see you."

After he hung up, John switched on the miniature TV on the credenza behind his chair. He channel-surfed until he found a news bulletin and listened in stunned silence. When the special report ended, he stared out his window, dazed. Perspiration rolled off his forehead while the possible repercussions struck home. The implications of the raids on his brother's businesses were almost too horrid to contemplate. If the police knew about Lonnie's operation, did they also know about the law firm's role? They would, if they didn't know already. Most of Lonnie's businesses were held in the name of nominee owners, interlocking directorates, and dummy corporations. But, every one of them named Rawson, Wong & Ballard as its agent for service. Some of the incorporation documents named John personally. Other documents named Nathan Ballard. John paused and rubbed his face. But wasn't that what lawyers did? Stay calm, he told himself. He took a deep breath and tried to relax. But, he tensed when he thought about what else the reporter had said. Something about Lonnie being under surveillance for years. What if he'd been seen with Lonnie?

Asshole! Johnny thought. You're feeling sorry for yourself. What about Lonnie? Where is he? Was he still in Hawaii, or had he escaped? He mouthed a silent prayer that Lonnie had fled the country.

Besides, what if he had been seen with Lonnie. He was his lawyer, after all. Every American has the right to meet with his lawyer.

John heard his door open and swiveled his chair around. Nathan Ballard stood in his office. Ballard closed the door.

"Did you hear?" Ballard asked in a shaky voice. His face looked pasty-white and glistened with sweat.

John saw a muscle under Ballard's left eye twitch. Ballard rubbed the spot, but the twitch continued.

"Yes, I just saw it on TV."

"Oh my God, what will we do? If the police have investigated Jackson for years . . . they must know the law firm was involved. We're listed on the documents." A low moan escaped Ballard's lips. He sank into a chair.

John stared at the older man and tried to keep contempt from his voice. "As long as we limit what we say to the legal work we did," he said, "we have nothing to worry about. We're attorneys; we have clients. Lonnie Jackson was just one of those clients. He never set foot in our offices. And even if he had, so what?"

John took a breath and let it out slowly. The cops couldn't know about his and Lonnie's personal relationship, could they?

Ballard now perspired profusely and had removed the handkerchief from his jacket. He mopped his forehead and patted his lips, chin, and cheeks. "This is bad, John. You know what the publicity could do to the firm's reputation?"

John now found it more difficult to restrain himself from shouting at Ballard. He breathed in a calming breath, slowly released it, and said, "We never received a check directly from him."

Ballard's eyes were saucers; his skin now lobster-red.

John could tell the man was on the verge of losing control. "Every payment we received," he continued, "was signed by someone other than Lonnie and written on the check of a legally constituted corporation. There is no way the cops can prove we even knew Lonnie had any connection with these companies. And there's no way they'll ever be able to trace the cash he gave us." John seemed to gain more confidence now that the words had been said. Maybe, as it turned out, things weren't so bad.

Ballard nodded as though his neck was made of elastic. "Right! Right!"

John remembered Lonnie telling him about Ballard's conspicuous consumption. If the IRS ever audited the stupid bastard . . . .

"You're right," Ballard said. "They can't prove a thing."

John heard uncertainty in Ballard's voice. A stab of pain tore through his gut as Susan Curtis's face popped into mind. He'd been involved in a great deal more than normal legal work for a client. The question again shocked his brain: Had he been seen with Lonnie?

There was a *tap-tap-tap* on the office door. Then Ballard's secretary poked her head inside. "Sorry to interrupt," she said, "but there are some gentlemen in the lobby who demand to see you, Mister Ballard. They said it was urgent."

"Who are they? What do they want?" Ballard snapped as he stuffed the sweat-soaked handkerchief back into his breast pocket.

She stepped into the office, handed Ballard a business card, and quickly retreated.

Ballard held the card in his hand without looking at it. "I'm glad we had this little talk. Mum's the word." He winked and smiled as though happy to be in collusion with John. Then he glanced down at the card.

Sweat broke out again on his face as though a bucket of water had been thrown on him. His face was pasty-colored again. "God help us," he cried. He again took the handkerchief from his breast pocket and wiped his forehead.

John got up from his chair and walked around his desk. He yanked the card from Ballard's grasp and read it: Roy Casper, Special Agent, Hawaii Organized Crime Task Force. John looked at Ballard and felt disdain for the older lawyer. He slapped the card back into Ballard's hand. "Look at me," he growled, no longer able or inclined to hide his contempt. "You fall apart now and we'll lose everything."

Ballard's already pasty color turned almost gray. John watched him leave his office, moving like a man through wet cement.

John calculated his personal exposure. There was nothing on the record except legal work Ballard assigned me. No one can prove I even know Lonnie—unless the cops have surveillance video that shows me meeting with him—or that I know Lonnie owned any of the companies for which I did legal work. And even if there are surveillance videos, I can claim I met with Lonnie on Ballard's orders. I just need to stay cool. Thank God the partnership in the law firm hasn't materialized yet. I'm just another associate doing work for the bigshot partners. Just another small fry, as far as the cops know.

CHAPTER SEVENTY-EIGHT

"What can I do for you gentlemen?" Nathan Ballard announced in a weak, trembly voice, after he shuffled into the lobby.

One of the three men by the reception desk stepped away from the other two. "Are you Nathan Ballard?" he asked.

"Ye . . . yes, I'm Nathan Ballard."

"We're with the Hawaii Organized Crime Task Force," the man said in a dry, unfriendly voice. "I'm Special Agent Roy Casper." He didn't offer his hand. "These are agents Malkovic and Summers. Could we go to a place where we can talk privately?"

Unsure what to do, Ballard took a step toward the hall to his office, then turned back and stared at the three men. He felt a bubble of spittle leak out of the corner of his mouth. He ignored it and let it hang there. The men watched him without expression.

"Uh, we can go to my office," Ballard said. He turned again, shambled down the hall. He limped and listed from one side to the other.

Ballard entered his office and walked directly to a plush, burgundy-red leather chair behind his desk. He collapsed into it and let the three men pick their own seats. He stared at Casper. Ballard knew his mouth hung open. He tried to close it, but he couldn't seem to muster the energy.

Ballard suddenly felt a need to pee. Should I excuse myself? Wait until these men leave? Or . . .? It was difficult to think with

Agent Casper's eyes augered into his.

Casper passed Ballard a sheaf of papers. "Mister Ballard," the agent said, "That's a court order that gives me authority to take all the files your firm has on fifteen separate corporations owned by Lonnie Jackson. Computer files, billing records, everything. I have twenty agents outside ready to move as soon as I give the word. One way or the other, it will happen in the next few minutes. How I go about it is another matter. I can call the press and have reporters crawl all over here. And, if you don't cooperate, I can take you out in handcuffs so your wife and friends can watch you humiliated on television." The only expression on Casper's face seemed to be flinty anger in his eyes.

Ballard swallowed. He felt desperate, hopeless.

"Or, Mister Ballard," the agent continued, "I can do this quietly. How I do it depends on how you answer my questions. Are you prepared to cooperate with us in providing information about Lonnie Jackson and every person you know associated with him? Or would you like to take a perp walk in front of the cameras?"

Ballard's heart palpitated and his head pounded. A wave of nausea made him glance at his wastebasket to make sure it was within reach. He looked from Casper to the other two agents. He hoped to find refuge, or even the slightest smile. All he saw were contemptuous, implacable stares. He finally nodded his head.

"I take it," Casper said, as he placed a pocket recorder on Ballard's desk, "you just answered my question in the affirmative. You will cooperate?"

Ballard slumped even deeper in his chair. "Yes," he rasped.

"What other employees of this firm knew about Jackson's illegal activities?"

Ballard stared at Casper. He saw the agent's eyes narrow, his jaw tighten, as though Ballard's hesitation might indicate resistance. But he had zero intent to hesitate or resist. His brain felt short-circuited. Something's wrong, he thought. I can't think. My head feels fuzzy. And this headache!

Casper attacked. "Mister Ballard, we know your spending exceeds your reported income."

Ballard felt his heart freeze. The cop just stared at him with implacable, ice-blue eyes. Ballard tried to catch his breath.

Casper leaned forward and rapped his knuckles on Ballard's desk. "We found a safe in one of Jackson's places. Several disks were inside that safe. One showed you in living color." Casper's lips curled back in a snarl. "With a young boy."

Every time the agent said something, Ballard thought he heard a thunderous *Clang*. Like Thor's hammer striking a mighty anvil. *CLANG!* Ballard shuddered and saw a sudden, momentary starburst of light, accompanied by a sharp pain in his temple. His head felt as though it would explode.

"I will use that disk if you don't cooperate," Casper said. "When we search Jackson's other places of business and his homes, I'm sure we'll find even more disks," Casper added.

CLANG! Ballard blinked repeatedly. He felt his vision become cone-shaped. All he could see was Casper's face, his teeth, the squint of his eyes. He felt like a beached fish as he gasped for air. His mouth opened and closed spasmodically.

The cop smiled at him.

"Ja . . . Ja," Ballard stuttered. His voice was barely a whisper. "John . . . ."

Casper leaned forward in his chair, anxious to hear Ballard. The words had been spoken softly, almost under Ballard's breath. Then Casper leaped from his chair and ran around to Ballard's side of the desk. Yellowish drool oozed from the lawyer's mouth. His color had become deathly pale and his eyes had rolled up. Then Ballard pitched forward and slammed his face on his desktop. An overpowering stench told Casper that Ballard had voided his bladder and bowels. He knew the man was dead before he checked for a pulse.

CHAPTER SEVENTY-NINE

Sara Olson leaned against the bedroom wall of Lonnie Jackson's Sea Breeze condo unit. She watched a task force agent pop the wall safe.

"Nice job, Reggie," she said. "Don't suppose you'd like to tell me where you learned your safe-cracking skills?"

Reggie smiled at Sara.

She walked forward and took the safe's contents from him and jotted down a quick inventory of the items: Twenty-one silver disks in sleeves with dates and letters—maybe initials— written on them. Sara carried the disks to a DVD player in the living room, hit the power button, and inserted a disk.

The disk spun and sound crackled when the picture broke up into an explosion of zigzag lines. Sara stepped forward to adjust the picture, when it suddenly focused. The breath caught in her chest when the first frame became clear. She recognized the man immediately: HPD Detective-Lieutenant Dennis Callahan stood naked in the middle of a room, mouth open, chest heaving. Across the room stood a nude girl who appeared to be no more than eleven or twelve years old. From the angle of the picture, the camera must have been mounted on a wall near the ceiling. Callahan seemed unaware of its presence.

Sara scrolled through the video and stopped it each time the characters changed. She recognized a couple other cops. A city counselor. Two judges. A state senator. There were other men and women on the disk she didn't know. Most of the adults on the disk had been filmed having sex with children. Some were filmed having homosexual sex. A couple were into whips and chains.

She ejected the first disk and inserted another. Three of the subjects on the second disk had also been on the first one. What a windfall, if all the disks have more of the same material! she thought. Now she understood how Lonnie Jackson had become the Teflon criminal. He had built, through bribery, blackmail, and extortion, a protective ring of influence around himself and his organization.

Sara returned to task force headquarters and registered the disks into the evidence log. Exhausted and sleep-deprived, she collapsed in a chair and, bleary-eyed, stared at the dozens of other law enforcement personnel who circulated through the building. They carried box after box of items taken under subpoena from Jackson's many businesses, offices, and homes. She suspected Jackson had hangouts and safe houses they'd never find; but the volume of evidence they'd so far uncovered was staggering.

She felt sleep seduce her. She closed her eyes but jerked back when she felt her head sag forward. Her eyes closed again, but a telephone ring startled her awake and rattled her nerves. She forced herself to stand. I need to keep busy, she thought.

Sara walked to a file cabinet outside Frank Murdoch's office, pulled open the top drawer, and finger-walked through the files. She grabbed a three-inch thick file with Lonnie Jackson's name on the label and lifted it from the drawer with both hands. Then she moved across the massive room, found a table that hadn't yet been covered with boxes, sat down, and read about Jackson's criminal history, dating back nearly thirty years to when the mobster was just a kid. Most of his arrests had been for misdemeanors while he was a minor. Sara scanned the mundane entries—dates and places of arrests, statements made by arresting officers, Jackson's height and weight. She concentrated on the nature of the charges and could see a trend develop over the years. Jackson became involved in steadily more frequent, more violent crimes. There was nothing in the file after Jackson turned twenty-five. That must have been when he smartened up, she thought, and got others to do his dirty work. She read until everything seemed to blur.

Then, as if in a dream, something came up from her subconscious and jolted her. She couldn't identify it and felt bitter irritation when she attempted to dredge it up. Something there. But what was it? Sara wanted to scream. So close—just under the surface. She rubbed her hands over her face. If only I weren't so damned tired, she thought. Sara flipped back to the beginning, turned from one arrest report to the next, looked for anomalies. Three times she returned to the first page and went through the entire file. Line by line, page by page.

Suddenly, like the item had been highlighted, it hit her. Lonnie Jackson's birth date. Something about it.

Sara's fatigued mind wouldn't come up with the date's significance. She felt as though her brain was mired in oil. Her nerves seemed to be electrified. Something important picked at the edge of her memory. But why? What? She tried to concentrate, but nothing came to her. She left her chair and mumbled to herself as she wandered around the hangar.

"Come on, Sara, what is it?" she muttered. "December 2, 1976. Twelve, two, seventy-six." She repeated the date; walked in cadence to the numbers. "Twelve"—step, "two"—step, "seventy"—step, "six"—step. She did three circuits of the enclosure.

Then a light seemed to switch on in her head and she was suddenly excited, full of energy. "Sonofabitch!" she shouted. "Sonofabitch!" She ran back to where she'd left the Jackson file, fished her purse from under the table, and pulled out her notebook. She turned the pages until she came to the notes she'd taken during her conversation with Esther Washington of the military records office in St. Louis.

There it was: 2 December '76. Written the same way the woman had said it. The military way of giving dates—day, month, year. Lawrence Jerrell—Roland Jerrell and Nora Cromwell's son—had the same birth date as Lonnie Jackson.

Sara didn't believe in coincidences. Two half-white, half-black males born on the same date. Both with a Hawaii connection. She opened the Jackson rap sheet file and checked the box for Place of Birth on the first arrest form. The initials "CA" stood out. Lonnie

Jackson had given his place of birth as California. Army records showed Lawrence Jerrell was born in Monterey, California, while his father was assigned to the Defense Language Institute.

No longer tired or sleepy, Sara's adrenaline pumped. She collected her thoughts. Lawrence Jerrell and Lonnie Jackson were born on the same date in the same state. They had the same initials. Nora Dunning was married to Roland Jerrell and was Lawrence Jerrell's mother. Nora and Lonnie both live in Hawaii. Lonnie Jackson's rap sheet shows he came to the attention of the police some time shortly after Nora returned to the islands.

Sara hesitated to take the next deductive step. Waiting helped her savor the moment. Her mind skipped ahead and drew the conclusion—slowly and methodically. She said her thoughts out loud. "Muriel Goldstein said she saw Nora Dunning push Susan Curtis off her balcony. Dennis Callahan confessed that Lonnie Jackson ordered him to kill Susan Curtis. Jackson obviously had an interest in Susan Curtis death—whatever that interest was. If Nora Dunning is Lonnie Jackson's mother, could she not, by extension, also have a motive in Susan Curtis death?" But why would she kill Susan? What possible motive could she have had, regardless of Lonnie Jackson's motivation or interest?

Sara flinched and turned at a scraping sound.

Frank Murdoch dragged a chair from an adjacent desk and sat on the opposite side of the table from her. "You look beat, Olson," he said.

"Thanks," she said. "Have *you* looked in a mirror recently?" She tried to laugh, but it came out more like a croak.

"*Touché,*" Murdoch said. "What are you working on? It looked like you were talking to yourself a moment ago."

"I'm shaking like a leaf, Frank. You may think I'm nuts, but I got a feeling about this."

"What the hell are you talkin' about, Sara?"

"Okay, okay, just listen for a minute," she said as she pumped her hands. She methodically went through it all for Murdoch.

He listened, then stood, and paced. He stopped, stared down at her, closed his eyes, and massaged the center of his forehead.

Murdoch met her gaze. "Let me add something to your list of

facts and conjecture. Nora Dunning has a son, John, who works at Rawson, Wong & Ballard. The firm handled most of Jackson's legal work."

Sara opened her eyes wide. "Didn't you send Roy Casper over there to bring in the managing partner?"

"Yep. Except the guy stroked out at his desk, right in front of Roy."

"Will he recover?"

"He's dead," Murdoch said.

"Bad news. The guy might have had a lot to tell."

"There's more bad news. Lonnie Jackson's disappeared. He's probably left the country by now. Somebody must have tipped him off before we raided his businesses." Murdoch's face suddenly turned an angry red. "If I ever catch the sonofabitch traitor . . . ."

"I may have a lead on who the informant is," Sara said. "One of the disks we pulled out of Jackson's safe showed two of Honolulu's finest cavorting with little girls."

Murdoch looked around the hangar and then yelled, "Ferguson!"

"Yeah, Chief?" Ferguson said as he rushed over.

"Go through the box of disks we took out of Jackson's condo. Bring in anybody who's on them. Put them in separate holding rooms. Got it?"

"There's got to be dozens and dozens of people on those disks," Sara said.

Ferguson's jaw dropped.

"I don't give a damn how many there are," Murdoch growled. "I want every one of them in here by the end of the day. Get arrest warrants on every damned one of them."

"Yes, sir. Right away." Ferguson turned to walk away, when Murdoch added, "I want a list of every person you recognize on the disks." Ferguson nodded.

Murdoch turned back to Sara. "I think it's time we put some pressure on the Dunning woman. Get a warrant. Conspiracy to commit murder. Take another agent with you and go pick her up."

CHAPTER EIGHTY

Sara briefed Agent Manny Bartolo in the car on the way to the Dunning residence.

Manny drove and listened to her story. When she finished, he glanced at her and said, "You've gotta be shittin' me. Some white society dame is Lonnie Jackson's mother. She's the one who pushed Susan Curtis to her death?"

"The more I think about it, the more I find the whole thing a little hard to believe myself," Sara said. Then she closed her eyes.

Sara awoke when Manny shook her shoulder. They were parked outside an enormous mansion with thirty-foot white columns, set back from the road behind towering pine trees and fronted by a semi-circular brick-paved driveway.

Sara rubbed her eyes. "We there already?" She looked around. "You know somewhere up here is where Jackson's men tried to kill Susan Curtis's brother and Renee Drummond?"

"Yep," Manny said. "We passed it 'bout a quarter mile back."

She stretched her neck and shoulders. "God! I feel like a bird built a nest in my mouth."

"You look a little like road kill," Manny said.

"Gee, thanks, Manny. How gallant of you."

Manny laughed. "I'd give you a back rub, but I'm afraid you'd kick my ass."

"Keep thinking that way, Manny," Sara said. She opened her door and stepped from the car.

Manny led the way up the walk to the front door. "Jeez, all the boy scouts in Hawaii could camp out on the front lawn," he said. "Can't wait to see the back yard."

"The only difference between people who live up here and the rest of us is money," Sara said as she adjusted her jacket and brushed her hair back with her hands.

Manny gave Sara a "No shit!" look. "That's a big difference, Olson." He rang the doorbell.

A uniformed Polynesian maid opened the door. "How may I help you?" she asked in an imperious voice.

"We want to talk with Nora Dunning," Sara said. She showed her HOCTF identification card and badge.

"I'm afraid she can't be disturbed right now," the maid said. "You may leave a number she can call when it's more convenient for her."

Manny stepped up on the threshold and glared down at the woman. "Where is Nora Dunning?" he growled.

"I told you—"

"Lady, you got two choices," he snapped. "You take us to wherever Nora Dunning is . . . now, or I run you in on an obstruction of justice charge."

The woman's *café au lait* complexion darkened and her eyes went wide. She wheeled around and led Manny and Sara down a mahogany-trimmed, silk-carpeted hall to a rear door, which led out onto a paved patio, bordered by a terraced lawn.

The lawn transitioned to a narrow flower garden that separated the broad expanse of grass from what looked like a precipitous drop to the sea. A woman in a wide-brimmed straw hat and a canvas apron over a summery dress knelt on the edge of the grass, trowel in hand. She wore soil-stained, yellow work gloves. A dozen potted plants lay scattered around her.

"I'm sorry, ma'am," the maid said, when they were five yards from the flower garden. "These people insisted—"

The woman looked up from her kneeling position. "It's all right," she said. "Why don't you go inside and bring out a pitcher of lemonade? It's a bit warm out here."

"Yes, ma'am," the maid said. She scowled at Manny before she turned back toward the house.

Sara looked Nora Dunning over and thought she must have been a world-class beauty at one time. Her piercing blue eyes and patrician features still made her stunning. She showed the woman her badge, gave her name, and introduced Manny. "Nora Dunning, we have a warrant for your arrest on a charge of conspiracy to commit murder."

Dunning stood up. She showed no emotion and didn't say a word.

Sara had expected the usual reaction—that's absurd, you've got the wrong person, or some other cliché. But Dunning continued to hold her gaze and her ground. She dropped the trowel and slowly, calmly removed her dirt-encrusted gloves, which she threw to the ground.

The woman swept an arm in a half-circle that took in the garden. "You know, this is where I come when I need to think. It's so peaceful;"—she looked left, then right—"quite beautiful, don't you think?"

"Missus Dunning, did you hear what I said?" Sara asked.

Dunning waved a dismissive hand. "And who is it I am supposed to have murdered?" she asked as she took a half-step back.

"You'll be charged in the death of Susan Curtis."

"I see," she said. She stepped back again.

Sara noticed the woman didn't ask who Susan Curtis was. Out of the corner of her eye, she saw Manny's hand flex. He was as tense as she was. Dunning had already backed up precariously close to the cliff edge and was now perched on naked lava rock, ten feet from where Sara and Manny stood on the edge of the grass.

Manny reached for the handcuffs on his belt and said, "Missus Dunning, would you please step away from the edge of the cliff?"

The calm demeanor Nora Dunning had shown up to then evaporated. Her fingers twitched as she windmilled her arms. Her face flushed. She narrowed her eyes and lazered a look at Sara.

"She would have hurt my son, you know. I couldn't allow that. You're a woman; you must understand. We can't allow people to hurt our flesh and blood."

Sara lowered her voice. "I understand, ma'am. Why don't you come with us? We'll sit down on the patio and have some lemonade and discuss this."

Dunning's voice became high-pitched. "I went to her apartment, to try to reason with her. But she wouldn't listen. She acted as though she were drunk. Kept babbling something. She had trouble breathing. I thought she needed fresh air, so I helped her out to the balcony."

She looked from Sara to Manny, and back to Sara. "I didn't go there to do her any harm. I just thought I could reason with her, woman to woman. But she just stared at me, as though she were deranged. Then she leaned over the balcony railing and vomited. I was disgusted. I figured the world would be better off without a drunk like her. She could have destroyed my boys."

Boys, plural, Sara thought. Her breath caught in her chest. "Boys?" she asked. Sara took a small step forward.

The woman's eyes blinked furiously; darted about. "Johnny and Lawrence." Her face changed, but only for an instant. A peace seemed to come over her when she mentioned the two names. But then the manic look returned.

Sara inched forward. "John Dunning and Lawrence Jerrell?"

"Of course," Nora Dunning said petulantly. "Do you know my boys?"

"Not personally, Missus Dunning. But I've heard a lot about them." Sara moved to the flowerbed and stood atop a small mound of freshly dug earth. "I believe your son, Lawrence, goes by the name Lonnie Jackson now." She held her breath.

"Lawrence shouldn't have changed his name," Dunning said. She now sounded child-like. "If he'd stayed with me, he would still be my Lawrence." Her eyes seemed unfocused. She stared right through Sara. Then she appeared to remember something, and her eyes became bright. "Johnny's father was a wonderful man. He would have welcomed Lawrence. I . . . don't know . . . why Lawrence . . . ." Her eyes again lost their luster.

Sara now stood five feet away from the woman. Almost within reach. She tried to divert her attention. "What could Susan Curtis have done to harm your sons?"

Dunning laughed. Then she shrugged. "I'm a bit . . . I don't know. It's all very confusing. It had something to do with Nathan Ballard. My Johnny was quite worried about it." She hunched her shoulders again, then lowered her head, and stared at the ground.

Sara was incredulous. Nora Dunning had killed Susan Curtis and didn't know why. She had thought Susan was demented, or drunk, or both. She had had no idea that the woman had been drugged by that bastard Callahan. Manny took a step forward, but. Sara held out her hand to stop him.

"So you killed Susan Curtis, Missus Dunning?" Sara asked.

Nora Dunning's eyes narrowed and her jaw tightened. "You know I could never live anywhere but here."

Sara knew she was losing her. The woman seemed disorientated. She was just beyond Sara's reach. Only one step away. Sara took a tiny step forward, but the woman screamed, "Stay away from me!"

Sara froze.

A voice came from behind Sara. "Mother! Mother!"

Sara saw Manny reach for his pistol as he turned toward the house. She looked over her shoulder and saw a young man dressed in a suit run down the terraced lawn. Her head snapped back to Nora Dunning when she heard a moan come from the woman. Sara's eyes met hers. Sara saw anguish there. Defeat.

Nora Dunning's eyes sparkled in a seeming moment of clarity. "I love my boys," she said. "Tell them for me, would you?" She took two demure steps backward and, without a sound, disappeared over the edge of the cliff.

DAY ELEVEN

CHAPTER EIGHTY-ONE

Renee felt as though every movement, no matter how slight, required extra concentration. Just to turn the pages of the book she held seemed to take Herculean effort. She knew she should feel relieved, but, for whatever reason, she couldn't quite get past a sense of foreboding. As long as Lonnie Jackson was on the run . . . .

She looked at Matt seated on the couch across from her and noticed that he mechanically flipped the pages of the magazine in his lap. He obviously couldn't concentrate any more than she could. She rose from her chair, crossed the room, and sat next to him. She held his hand. They sat there in silence, the only sound the *tick-tick-tick* of the antique grandfather's clock.

Renee sighed. "I badly need a nap."

"Great idea. Let's—" The tone from the control box at the front gate interrupted him.

Renee moaned. "What now?"

Matt put his arm around her and squeezed. "It's okay, honey." He kissed her again. "I'll get it."

Matt stood up and walked to the speaker box in the foyer. "Who is it?" he demanded.

"Frank Murdoch."

Renee heard the exchange and looked at her watch. Ten o'clock. She'd forgotten that Murdoch had called earlier to ask if he could come out. She forced herself to stand and joined Matt by the front door.

Murdoch parked in front of the door and came around the rear of the car. A woman got out of the passenger side.

"Agent Olson," Matt said.

Murdoch introduced Sara Olson to Renee.

Renee and Matt led the two agents through the foyer to the solarium.

"Please sit down," Renee said. "Would anyone care for a drink?"

"No thanks," Sara said.

"I'm okay," Murdoch said.

Matt looked pointedly at Murdoch. "You said you had news about Susan's murder."

Murdoch turned to Sara. "You do the honors."

Sara methodically told her story, from her conversation at the country club, to her call to the St. Louis military records office, to Lonnie Jackson's file, and finally to her visit to Nora Dunning's home yesterday.

"So, Nora Dunning was John Dunning *and* Lonnie Jackson's mother?" Renee said.

"Correct," Murdoch said.

"Was John Dunning involved in Lonnie Jackson's business," Matt asked.

"Yeah, probably, but the problem is I can't prove a thing," Murdoch answered. "His name pops up in the incorporation documents of some of the companies we've tied to Jackson. But it's always in Dunning's role as an attorney. There's no proof Dunning was an accomplice or accessory to any of Jackson's criminal activities, or that he even knew Jackson owned the companies the law firm represented. And, so far, we haven't been able to find any evidence Dunning took money from Jackson. He was just an innocent associate working for the big boys in the law firm."

Matt nodded. "So, I guess that's that."

"Well, indictments will be brought against Lonnie Jackson and all of his people," Murdoch said. "We found enough evidence to put most of them away for several lifetimes. And now that most members of Jackson's gang are singing like little birdies, I'm sure there will be plenty of others who will be implicated."

Murdoch grunted. "The heroin we found in the garment factory was the largest single stash of drugs ever confiscated in Hawaii. Unfortunately, Jackson will be indicted in absentia. But, who knows? Maybe someday . . . ." He let the thought hang while he stood up.

"We appreciate both of you coming out here to brief us," Matt said, while he and Renee escorted them to their car.

"I'm sorry about your sister, Doctor Curtis," Murdoch said. "From everything I've heard about her, she must have been special."

"She was . . . real special," Matt answered.

Murdoch turned to Renee and said, "Lonnie Jackson was directly or indirectly responsible for bringing a lot of tragedy down on you and your family, Missus Drummond. I hope you can take some satisfaction from the collapse of his organization."

"Until that bastard is dead or in prison . . . ."

"I understand," Murdoch said.

Matt shook Sara's, then Murdoch's hand. "Thanks for everything."

Murdoch said, "We couldn't have done it without your assistance."

Matt and Renee walked Murdoch and Olson to their car. Murdoch walked around to the driver side. "By the way," he said. "I'll leave a patrolman on the street down by the gate for a while."

"You think that's really necessary?" Renee asked.

"Probably not," Murdoch said with a smile. "But it makes *me* feel better. Have a good life, you two."

Renee stepped back under the entrance alcove and waved.

Matt stepped down and opened the passenger door for Sara, waited for her to slide into the seat, then closed the door. He looked over the car roof at Murdoch.

"Oh, one other thing," Murdoch said. "From the looks of the damage done to the men who raided this place a couple nights ago, not to mention the destruction to trees and bushes, I would guess someone used Claymores and automatic weapons. I'm sure you know nothing about any of that, but you might want to pass the word that anti-personnel mines and machineguns are illegal in Hawaii."

Matt carefully kept any emotion from his face as he said, "I'll keep it in mind."

CHAPTER EIGHTY-TWO

At dusk, Esteban woke from a long nap and met with Matt and Renee. Matt handed him a cash-stuffed envelope. "Please give this to Richie and Angelo."

Esteban said, "You know they initially got into this for the money, but, at the end, it was something else."

"I know that. But, just the same, do me a favor and give it to them." Matt smiled. "I'm sure it will be expensive to replace the ammunition and the Claymore."

Esteban laughed, then laid a hand on Matt's shoulder. "I'll miss you, a*migo*. I haven't had this much fun in a long time."

"If you don't mind, Esteban, maybe the next time I come to Hawaii we could just lie on the beach and drink beer."

"You got a deal, *cuate*," Esteban said and gave Matt a bear hug. "*Vaya con Dios.*"

Matt watched Esteban drive away. He turned around and looked at Renee. "You know what I'd like to do?"

"What?" she asked, looking as though the half-smile she gave him exhausted her.

Matt wrapped her in his arms and kissed her forehead. "Or, maybe it would be better if we packed some things and got away for a few days." He rubbed her back and kissed her again.

Their eyes met. "You were about to suggest something else."

Matt waved one hand in a dismissive way. "Oh, I was about to suggest reservations at Monte's tonight. A good meal and dancing. Then we'd come back here and make love. No interruptions—no phone calls, no hit squads, no explosions."

She pressed hard against him, her arms wrapped around his neck. "I think I love you, Matthew Curtis."

Matt put a finger under her chin, tipped her head up, and kissed her lips. "I want to talk to you about that."

The sun had fully set by the time Esteban stopped at the bottom of the driveway and shot a thumbs-up to the cop in the patrol car parked by the curb. The cop just sat there with his head against the headrest.

Sonofabitch is asleep, Esteban thought. He turned right onto the road and leaned on the old pickup's custom horn. The noise from the shiny chrome air horn under the hood sounded like a freight train blaring a warning at a crossing. "That'll fix the lazy bastard," Esteban said. He chuckled as he roared past the police cruiser.

Esteban had a sudden pang of conscience. He hadn't seen his wife, Alani, and had only telephoned her twice since he came to help Matt. He figured it would take him at least an hour of sympathetic listening and a dinner at an expensive restaurant before he could get back on her good side.

Renee hummed while she dressed for dinner. It was a simple thing, humming, but she suddenly realized it was something she hadn't done in years. It occurred to her that there were probably lots of simple things she hadn't done in a very long time. She smiled. Humming was a good start. Despite her fatigue, the thought of dinner and dancing with Matt gave her a welcome jolt of energy and enthusiasm.

She laughed at the muted, off-key sounds of singing that drifted from the bathroom shower. The strains of *Santa Lucia* raucously competed with the noise of running water. What an awful voice, she thought with glee. A small price to pay, she decided, to be with a man who put humming back in her life. She turned to the vanity mirror to check her makeup and shuddered as though the icy fingers of an Arctic wind had clutched her insides. Her heart slammed against her rib cage.

A man stood there, not ten feet away, pistol in hand, a finger pressed to his lips. "Shh," he said, as calmly and quietly as a mother might try to silence a restless baby.

Renee whipped around; thought he must be an apparition. Lonnie Jackson couldn't be here. Her mind had to be playing tricks on her. With every cop in the islands looking for him, he would have to be nuts . . . crazy to be here. She tried to scream, but she felt as though a steel band was strapped tightly around her chest and that her throat was frozen.

"You and I will have some fun, Renee," Jackson whispered. "But first I have to take care of your boyfriend."

Jackson's eyes appeared yellow in the muted light in the bedroom. But they also seemed . . . demented.

An electric-like spark sizzled in Esteban's brain and fried his thoughts about Alani. Why the hell would one of Frank Murdoch's men fall asleep on the job? After all that had happened, every cop and every task force agent in town would know that Murdoch would first have his balls, then his badge if he snoozed while on protection detail. The cop in the car he'd just passed hadn't budged when he'd passed him. It would have been difficult to sleep through the reverberating noise of his truck's glass-packed mufflers, let alone the blast from the air horn.

"Dammit!" Esteban shouted. "Dammit!" He stood on the brakes and screeched to a sliding, sideways stop. He turned the truck around and rocketed back up The Palisades road.

Esteban speed-shifted into third gear, then reached over and took his .45 from the glove compartment. He'd only half-noticed the white Lincoln Towncar parked on the side of the road. Now the sight of it stabbed into his consciousness with the efficient sharpness of a scalpel. The police car sat where he'd last seen it, fifty yards farther up the road. He slued the pickup alongside the patrol car at the bottom of Renee's driveway, slammed to a halt, and leaped from the cab. The cop in the car hadn't moved an inch. When Esteban pulled the car door open, the courtesy light showed a gaping wound in the officer's neck; blackened blood soaked the man's uniform blouse and pants.

Jackson gave Renee the finger-to-the-lips sign again and turned toward the bathroom.

There was no doubt in Renee's mind that Jackson was there to kill them. The man had been ultimately responsible for her son's death, her husband's suicide, Susan's murder, and multiple attempts on her's and Matt's lives. The pain, fright, sorrow, and anger those events had birthed suddenly boiled together into one explosive concoction. There was no chance, she told herself, that this vile man would hurt another person whom she loved. She launched herself at Jackson. "A-a-a-ah," she screamed, a war cry filled with hate and fury.

Renee landed on Jackson's back as he reached for the bathroom door handle, her legs wrapped around his waist, her fingers raked his face. She went for his eyes, those damn devil eyes.

She heard the explosion, as though a cannon had gone off inside her head and felt heat blister in her side. She knew she no longer clutched Jackson. She seemed to fly backward. Then, somehow, she lay on the carpet. Freckles of light flashed in her eyes, and slowly dimmed to blackness.

Matt thought he'd heard Renee call him. But it wasn't really a call. Something else. When he called her name and she didn't answer, he walked from the sink to the door.

"*BA-ROOM!*"

Towel around his waist, Matt jerked the door open and saw Renee fall backward, just feet from the open bathroom doorway. Red spray framed her dropping figure like a watery mist around a water fountain sculpture. A tall man in the center of the room whipped around while his gunhand rose. Matt knew it was Lonnie Jackson.

Jackson seemed to move in slow motion. Each micro-movement registered in Matt's consciousness. Propelled by an adrenaline blast, Matt leaped at the man. He saw the expression on Jackson's face change. Surprise showed there, as though the man hadn't anticipated that a doctor would defend himself, would fight for his life.

Matt blocked Jackson's hand; deflected the line of the weapon. The pistol fired; whining shockwaves caromed around the room. Matt threw a left hook at Jackson's face and connected with bone-crushing force that sent agonizing shivers up his arm. Jackson wavered, but he still held the weapon. Matt threw a right cross, missed Jackson's head, but struck his right shoulder. Jackson's gunhand dropped for a moment. As Jackson once again raised the pistol, Matt kicked at his groin.

Jackson crumpled to his knees. He grunted, then roared like a wounded bear. He leveled the pistol at Matt.

Matt snatched a large cut-glass perfume bottle from Renee's dressing table and threw it. Jackson ducked, just when he fired the weapon. Matt felt the bullet burn past his left biceps. His ears hurt from the concussion of the fired pistol. Matt charged Jackson, knocked the pistol loose, and clubbed him with his fists to the carpet. He drove the bottom of his foot into Jackson's chest, which forced a gush of air from his lungs. He delivered a hate-charged fist into Jackson's face and only half-saw a bloody, viscous stream of spit shoot from his mouth. Still on his knees, Jackson listed to the side. Matt shot another blow to the man's head. Jackson fell like a dropped sack of cement. He groaned as he rolled onto his back, his arms stretched to the sides.

Matt leaped for the pistol, scuttled back to Jackson, and straddled his chest. He pressed the pistol muzzle against Jackson's forehead. He could see Renee's limp body spread out in a growing pool of blood beyond Jackson's head. A plate-sized red stain over her side, near her heart, marked her light-blue dress. It was that image imprinted on his brain in a microsecond that broke his heart and flooded him with even more anger than he already felt.

Fire seemed to burn from within him. Rage consumed him and he knew that Lonnie Jackson must die. He squeezed his finger on the trigger as Jackson's eyes popped open. Neither fear nor a plea for mercy showed there. Just amber contempt.

"You don't have the balls, Curtis," Jackson growled.

Matt stared into the nothingness of Jackson's eyes and knew in that instant he'd seen Hell. His finger squeezed tighter on the trigger.

He was an instant away from becoming a murderer. He knew that the man under him was the only person who could make him become something he thought he could never be.

"Oh-h-h. Matt."

Matt's head snapped up. He saw Renee stir, then heard the booming sounds of footsteps, and then a sudden pain manufactured flashes of light behind his eyes.

Esteban had driven through the gate, fractured its hinges, and carried it on the truck grill halfway up the drive, until it fell beneath the pickup's tires. His heart pumped frenetically and seemed to accelerate even higher when he saw the open front door. Then, from its revving pace, his heart seemed to stop when the boom of a gunshot sounded.

He gripped his .45 and rushed into the house. He heard noises on the second level, ran up the stairs, and threw open Renee's bedroom door. Movement dragged his gaze to the right. He extended his gunhand and bent his knees, just as a large man burst through the bank of windows and dropped from sight into the night in a hail of glass.

"Oh Lord," Esteban said when he saw the carnage in the room.

TWO WEEKS LATER

CHAPTER EIGHTY-THREE

John Dunning turned back to his desk, sat down, and picked up the preliminary report the investment advisor had sent him. Between the money his father left him and what he would now inherit from his mother, he was untouchable. He had the old familiar feeling of invincibility. Even the death of his beloved mother and his brother's disappearance couldn't detract from that. The cops had nothing on him. They'd discovered that he and Lonnie were half-brothers, but they hadn't been able to carry it forward from there. He'd miss the excitement of working with Lonnie, but that was a small price to pay for getting off scot-free.

He hadn't heard from Lonnie, but it gave him a warm feeling to know the cops hadn't found him. Lonnie'd find a way to contact him as soon as things cooled off. Then he thought about his mother. Perhaps, things had worked out for the best. She would never have been able to survive even a month in prison. But to die like that. Crushed on the rocks. John shuddered. "Fuckin' cops!" he said.

He dropped the investment report and stared at the legal brief on the desk. He would have to do something about his pissant job at the firm. He had neither the need nor the desire to do mundane legal work. But he would hang around until the firestorm that had built up about Lonnie subsided. He was a partner now. The other partners would expect him to bring in new clients—ones of a more parochial, but still profitable nature. What a joke!

Buzz! John pushed the button on the intercom. "Yes?"

"Mister Chongsawartha is on the phone for you, Mister Dunning."

John's heart momentarily fluttered. He willed himself to calm down and then picked up the receiver. "Hello, Mister Chongsawartha, I expected to hear from you days ago."

"*I* expected to hear from *you* two weeks ago, Mister Dunning. Do I need to remind you of our normal arrangement? The money is transferred to my account when the goods are received."

Chongsawartha's voice had a different timbre to it. An overtone of . . . something.

"But, Mister Chongsawartha, the goods never arrived." John smiled. The dumb shit, he thought. Lonnie really slipped it to him on the last drug shipment. "In fact, the ship didn't dock in Honolulu when you said it would. I called for days. The harbormaster never heard from the *La Concepcion*." John put his Ferragamo-clad feet on the edge of his desk and twirled a rubber band around a finger.

Chongsawartha said nothing for several seconds. Then he snorted. "Of course the ship didn't dock in Hawaii on schedule, Dunning. Do you take me for a fool?"

John dropped his feet to the floor and tossed the rubber band away. Something's wrong. "Excuse me?" he said.

Chongsawartha laughed. "You think you are so clever. You and Lonnie Jackson. Do you really believe I would ship heroin with a street value of two hundred million dollars on a ship captained by a pig like Chin, without certain precautions?" The man laughed again.

John's heart leaped to his throat. Chongsawartha had not only mentioned Lonnie's name on the phone, but he'd also said "heroin."

"I put my dear second cousin on my mother's side on the *La Concepcion* crew," Chongsawartha screamed. "He told me about Captain Chin's little side trip toward the California coast. About the heroin transfer to another ship. Such a simple matter for me to track down that ungrateful pig, Chin. I plucked out his eyeballs with my own two hands. Quite a squishy business."

John felt his bowels rumble. Sweat poured off him.

"Since the drugs have been sold, I want my money. The usual price: twenty-five percent of the going street price. Fifty million dollars. Where is it, Dunning?" Chongsawartha hissed.

John swallowed to get rid of the lump in his throat. "You don't understand, Mister Chongsawartha," he croaked. "I don't know what you're talking about."

"Now, now, Mister Dunning," Chongsawartha said, sounding quite reasonable. "Let's not be disingenuous. I know you landed on the *La Concepcion* in a helicopter the day it was due to arrive in Honolulu. My cousin described you perfectly." He hesitated, then shrieked, "Where's my money?"

Chongsawartha's tone shocked John. The man had never raised his voice to him before. John felt panic sluice through him. He couldn't make his normally facile mind work. He did the only thing he could think to do. He hung up.

Chongsawartha stared at the cell phone in his hand, then calmly slipped it into his jacket pocket. He sucked in air over his teeth and craned his neck to look out his half-open window at the office tower across the street. He stared up at the building and tried to pick out John Dunning's floor. Then he dropped his gaze to the sidewalk, pushed the button by his arm, and fully lowered the tinted window. He stared at the man who stood beside the office building's revolving door. He was dressed in a blue pinstriped suit, red power tie, and shiny cordovan wingtips, and carried a black leather briefcase. Chongsawartha thought the man looked exactly like a banking executive.

The hand signal Chongsawartha gave the man amounted to little more than a half-wave. The man gave him a slight nod in return, turned around, and entered the building.

Chongsawartha then ordered the driver to go to the port where his private yacht was moored. As the limousine pulled away, he tapped his fingers on his thighs and whispered, "Now, how will I find the elusive Lonnie Jackson?"

Across town, two HOCTF agents looked at each other and smiled. The woman agent removed her headphones and raised her arms in victory. "We got him. We got the sonofabitch cold."

The male agent picked up the phone and called Frank Murdoch's office. "We just recorded Dunning talking by telephone with a guy with a heavy accent," the agent said. "Dunning called him Chongsawartha. They discussed a load of heroin that was supposed to have come in on a ship two weeks ago. Sounds like Dunning and Jackson stiffed the guy."

Murdoch had been in law enforcement too long to let much of anything excite him. But this news made him feel as good as he'd felt in a long time.

"Where was this guy, Chongsawartha?" Murdoch asked.

"Don't know. The cell signal was disguised."

"Hang loose," Murdoch said. "I'll get a warrant. We'll meet you in the lobby of Dunning's building. Don't let that asshole get past you." He replaced the receiver in its cradle, pumped his arm up and down, and shouted, "Yes!"

Murdoch and three of his agents stormed into the Rawson, Wong & Ballard offices thirty minutes later. "Where's John Dunning's office?" Murdoch demanded of the receptionist. The look on the agent's face and his badge seemed to stifle whatever the receptionist opened her mouth to say. She pointed down one of the two corridors off the reception area. "Fifth office on the right."

Murdoch hurried down the hall, threw Dunning's door open with more force than necessary, and charged inside. He was really enjoying this. He stopped two steps inside the office. The agents behind him stacked up.

"Goddammit!" Murdoch shouted. The word came out like a complaint, while he stared at John Dunning. "Goddammit!"

The young lawyer sat in his plush leather executive chair. His head lolled to the side. His throat cut. Blood covered his white shirt and pooled in his lap.

CHAPTER EIGHTY-FOUR

"How long could she go like this?" Esteban asked Matt.

Matt released air that had felt trapped in his lungs, as stagnant as the fears that had accumulated in his mind over the past two weeks. There was no way he could answer Esteban's question without preceding the words with "I hope." He looked down at Renee, curled in her hospital bed, and gently took her hand.

"I don't know, buddy," Matt said. "She lost a lot of blood. They've done all they can for her. She's got to come out of the coma." He swallowed. "She's got to."

Esteban squeezed Matt's shoulder. "Hang in there, man. She's tough."

Matt felt his throat constrict. He knew Esteban was correct. She'd survived being shot. The anemia, blood poisoning, and septicemia she'd suffered since hadn't killed her either. Now the coma. But how tough could one person be?

"Your head and arm okay?" Esteban said.

Matt pressed his nose between thumb and forefinger and winced. "Nose is still sore."

Esteban clucked. "You still look like a damn raccoon."

Matt wagged his head. Jackson had cold-cocked him when he'd looked over at Renee. There was no better way to put it. At least the bruises on his face would go away.

Esteban's face sagged sympathetically. "You know, I'll bet you a thousand dollars to a dime that Jackson's long gone."

Matt bunched his fists. Esteban had guessed Matt's thoughts. He couldn't get the idea out of his head that Jackson lurked somewhere close by. "I can't believe that sonofabitch got away," Matt said.

Esteban shook his head. "When the cops found Jackson's car down by the dock, they were convinced he'd escaped on the water. But with that guy, you can never be sure." Esteban hesitated. "I'm glad Murdoch has stationed agents here at the hospital and up at Renee's place."

Matt just nodded.

A silence settled over the room, interrupted by the intermittent tone of the heart monitor machine and the *beep-beep-beep* of the intravenous feeder.

Esteban hugged Matt. "Catch you later," he said, and left the room.

Matt pulled a chair to the side of Renee's bed and held her hand. He talked to her. About everything and nothing. About Susan, and how her death had brought them together. How everything would be all right. How much he loved her and wanted to spend the rest of his life with her. He begged, then ordered her to get well. Minutes turned to hours, and daylight became night, and still Matt talked, until his throat turned dry and hoarse.

Something startled Matt. He eased his head off the side of the hospital bed's mattress and cleared his throat to try to ease the pain there. But it only made it worse. The roof of his mouth was coated, as though he'd eaten a cup of powdered sugar and chased it down with ice-cold milk. He didn't know when he'd fallen asleep, but moonlight beams that shone through the window created a translucent aura in the darkened room. He looked around, but there was no one there but Renee.

He brushed his hands through his hair and stood. Time to go to Renee's place to shower and change. Maybe grab a few hours sleep before he returned to the hospital. Matt turned to the door, when his heart seemed to speed up and his body became hot. He felt suddenly faint; his vision blurred.

His first thought was heart attack. Especially when pain hit his shoulder and his body went awash in sweat. He quickly regained the chair and lowered his head to the bed. The pain disappeared almost immediately and then his body became dry. But his vision remained blurry and he still felt dizzy. Then he thought about the incident in the operating room back in Albuquerque, weeks ago, when the same thing had happened. At the exact time, as it turned out, of Susan's murder. He had the same feeling now that had come over him in the locker room in the doctor's lounge, after he'd left the surgical suite—that there was someone in the room. Someone other than Renee. He jerked to his feet and whipped around when he thought he felt a hand touch his shoulder. Again. No one there.

Then, as though bathing sore muscles in a hot bath, his body suddenly felt loose, relaxed; his mind at peace.

A whimper of a sound drifted up from the bed. Child-like, scratchy, but almost . . . disembodied. So different from Renee's normal voice. "Don't worry, Fitz," the voice said. "I'll take care of him."

Matt raised his head. "Renee, it's Matt." He touched her shoulder.

Renee lay there as though frozen, eyes shut. Her chest rose and fell in a cadence Matt had become accustomed to during the past two weeks.

I must be going nuts, he told himself.

Then Renee's legs twitched. One arm fell from its resting-place on her hip. Her eyelids fluttered. A great exhalation of air burst from her mouth. Then the tiniest smile. "Matt, sing *Santa Lucia* for me."

CHAPTER EIGHTY-FIVE

Lonnie Jackson puckered his lips and breathed a silent whistle. The woman who'd passed his table in the sidewalk cafe had great, no . . . spectacular legs. Just another world-class Brazilian beauty. The woman's spiked heels beat out a rhythmic *clack-clack-clack* against the decoratively-paved sidewalk. Her cadence seemed to match his heartbeat.

After just two weeks, he'd gotten used to the pace of things in Rio de Janeiro. He liked to sit at these outdoor cafes, bask in the late afternoon sun, have a Brazilian beer, and admire women as they promenaded along the mosaic sidewalks. He still missed his Budweisers, but he'd decided being in South America demanded a change in habits. Drinking American beer could bring unwanted attention to himself. He had to be careful about even the smallest detail of his appearance and behavior.

I especially like the way I fit in down here, he thought. Lots of mixed race people in Brazil.

A long-legged redhead with muscular legs and sinewy arms strutted by. Just the way I like my women, Lonnie thought. I'll have to learn Portuguese, he reminded himself. Need to find a tutor. Got more money than I can spend, but need to get into some kind of business . . . don't want to get bored. Maybe the cattle ranch I looked at yesterday.

Lonnie checked his watch and calculated the time difference.

The Honolulu cop should be up by now. He pulled the cell phone from his jacket pocket and dialed a series of numbers, followed by the 808 area code and the telephone number.

"Hello," a grouchy voice said.

"Freeman, do you know who this is?" Lonnie asked.

"Jesus!" Police Officer Jerry Freeman said.

"Let's make this quick. Give me an update."

"Jesus!"

Lonnie snapped, "What the hell's wrong?"

"It's bad, man," Freeman said. "They've arrested dozens of people—cops, judges, lawyers. Bribery, obstruction of justice, sex crimes, racketeering, murder. Everything you can imagine. They found your disks. At least forty of your crew are in jail, and most of them are squealing like stuck pigs. I'm scared shitless."

All acceptable losses, Lonnie thought.

"And that ain't all," the cop continued. "The young lawyer you did business with got his throat slit. Can't remember his name . . . oh, yeah. Dunning. John Dunning. Never caught who did it. His secretary claims some guy in a suit walked into the law office unannounced. Had papers for Dunning. Breezed right past her. Went to Dunning's office. Came out twenty seconds later."

Lonnie felt pain slice through his chest. Acid seemed to pour into his stomach. "Not Johnny," he moaned. "Johnny and Mama."

Lonnie felt the red haze come over him, just as it did every time he thought about what had happened to Mama. What Matt Curtis and Renee Drummond had done to him, to them. It was as though a rosy filter had been inserted in his corneas. He didn't know why people at the other tables now stared at him. Even passersby shot odd looks his way. He didn't remember ending the telephone conversation. He seemed to remember screams. "No! No! Not Johnny!" But he couldn't be sure if they were his words. He wondered why he was on his knees on the sidewalk. Why he sobbed.

Patrolman Jerry Freeman looked at the telephone after he replaced the receiver. He didn't understand Lonnie Jackson's reaction and didn't really care. However, the rapid *click-click-click* sounds he'd heard on the telephone concerned him.

ONE MONTH LATER

CHAPTER EIGHTY-SIX

Matt rested his feet on the edge of his desk in his Albuquerque office and arched his back. "Man, what a day," he said. The rest of his staff had already left. The telephone rang, but he planned to ignore it until he noticed the light on his private line.

"That you, babe?" Matt said.

"Don't you babe me," she said, laughter in her voice. "You promised to call me, remember?"

Matt felt his heart beat accelerate at the sound of Renee's voice. It reminded him of wind chimes. That's the way her voice always sounded, at least now that Lonnie Jackson was no longer around. "Miss me, huh?" he said.

She giggled. "Oh, maybe just a little bit. By the way, I finalized everything with the lawyers today. The house will be deeded to the university and I'll get a nice check every month for the rest of my life. How do you feel about being a kept man?"

Matt chuckled. "That's something I'd have to think about."

"We can discuss it when I get to Albuquerque. My plane gets in Thursday at three in the afternoon."

Matt said, "I'll be there with bells on." The two weeks since he'd last held Renee in his arms had seemed like an eternity.

"As long as that's all you'll wear," she said.

Matt laughed. "I'll see what I can do."

"Matt . . .?"

"Yeah, honey?"

"Did you call your sons?"

Matt sighed. "Yeah," he said.

"How'd it go?"

Matt paused for a heartbeat. "I conferenced them both in. They were surprised to hear from me. When I told them about their Aunt Susan . . . . Boy, were they pissed off at me for not calling them right away. They'll both come home for the memorial service."

"You've got to fix things, Matt," Renee said. "For the boys' sakes, for Susan, and for us."

"I know, honey."

Renee didn't respond for a moment, then said, "Do you think . . . everything will be all right?"

Matt dropped his feet to the floor and sat up straight. "I can't think of anything more right than our being together," he said. "You'll love New Mexico."

"I know that," Renee said. "I mean, do you think everything will be all right . . . about . . . Lonnie Jackson?"

"Honey, he's gone. He wouldn't be crazy enough to come back to the States."

SIX MONTHS LATER

CHAPTER EIGHTY-SEVEN

Matt and Renee sat on the deck of their new home on the east side of New Mexico's Sandia Mountains and stared at the lights of Santa Fe forty miles to the north. Matt reached across the table and rubbed the back of Renee's hand. "Are you sure you don't miss Hawaii?" he asked. "New Mexico's sure different from what you've been used to."

Renee took Matt's hand and brushed her lips across his palm. "How many times will you ask me that question?" She waved an arm toward the sky, as though to emphasize the pinks and reds and purples of the sunset. "This isn't hard to take, you know?"

Matt smiled. "Yeah, but that was some house you left."

"I was just a tenant there. It was never really my home after my husband died. Just a place to stay." She chuckled. "I've got to admit it was a damned nice place to stay, but I like it here a whole lot more. This is my home now, Matt. I've never been happier in my whole life. The Save the Kids chapter I started is doing great, we've got a wonderful house, I've met some new friends, and New Mexico's fantastic. But that's all irrelevant. I'd go to the Gobi Desert . . . or even Bakersfield, if that's where you were."

Matt laughed, stood up, and walked behind Renee's chair. He bent down and kissed the top of her head. "Well, Missus Curtis, I think you deserve another glass of wine." He walked to the kitchen and took a bottle of Chardonnay from the Vinotec. When he lifted the bottle, he happened to glance out the French doors to a tree-shaded patio, and gazed at the pine tree he'd planted in Susan's memory—where he'd buried her ashes. His heart full of emotion, his throat tight, Matt raised his glass and said—as he did every day—"I miss you, Fitz."

CHAPTER EIGHTY-EIGHT

Lonnie sat up in bed. The red haze seemed to cover everything. It happened more frequently—every two or three days. Somehow he knew it was madness. Sweat dripped off his forehead and his heart beat like a rock n' roll riff on a snare drum.

"Johnny! Mama!" he screamed. His voice echoed off the walls and pounded at his ears. "Johnny! Mama!"

Then the faces of Matthew Curtis and Renee Drummond, the people he hated most, flashed like holograms, floated before his eyes, grinned at him.

THE END

ABOUT THE AUTHOR

Prior to a long finance career, including a 16-year stint as a senior executive and board member of a NYSE-listed company, Joseph Badal served for six years as a commissioned officer in the U.S. Army in critical, highly classified positions in the U.S. and overseas, including tours of duty in Greece and Vietnam, and earned numerous military decorations.

He holds undergraduate and graduate degrees in business and graduated from the Defense Language Institute, West Coast and from Stanford University Law School's Director College.

Joe now serves on the boards of several companies.

He is the author of ten published suspense novels, including "The Lone Wolf Agenda," named the top Mystery/Thriller novel in the 2013 New Mexico/Arizona Book Awards competition, "Ultimate Betrayal," named the Tony Hillerman Award Winner for Fiction in the 2014 New Mexico/Arizona Book Awards competition, and "Evil Deeds," the Silver Medalist in the 2015 Military Writers Society of America Awards. "Borderline" was his first mystery. The sequel to "Borderline" will be released in 2017.

He also writes a monthly blog titled *Everyday Heroes*, and has written short stories published in the "Uncommon Assassins," "Someone Wicked," and "Insidious Assassins" anthologies.

"The Motive," is the first in a new series titled *Cycle of Violence*.

Joe has written dozens of articles that have been published in various business and trade journals and is a frequent speaker at business, civic, and writers' events.

"EVIL DEEDS"
DANFORTH SAGA (#1)

"Evil Deeds" is the first book in the *Bob Danforth* series, which includes "Terror Cell" and "The Nostradamus Secret." In this three book series, the reader can follow the lives of Bob & Liz Danforth, and of their son, Michael, from 1971 through 2011. "Evil Deeds" begins on a sunny spring day in 1971 in a quiet Athenian suburb. Bob & Liz Danforth's morning begins just like every other morning: Breakfast together, Bob roughhousing with Michael. Then Bob leaves for his U.S. Army unit and the nightmare begins, two-year-old Michael is kidnapped.

So begins a decades-long journey that takes the Danforth family from Michael's kidnapping and Bob and Liz's efforts to rescue him, to Bob's forced separation from the Army because of his unauthorized entry into Bulgaria, to his recruitment by the CIA, to Michael's commissioning in the Army, to Michael's capture by a Serb SPETSNAZ team in Macedonia, and to Michael's eventual marriage to the daughter of the man who kidnapped him as a child. It is the stops along the journey that weave an intricate series of heart-stopping events built around complex, often diabolical characters. The reader experiences CIA espionage during the Balkans War, attempted assassinations in the United States, and the grisly exploits of a psychopathic killer.

"Evil Deeds" is an adrenaline-boosting story about revenge, love, and the triumph of good over evil.

https://amzn.com/B00LXG9QIC

"TERROR CELL"
DANFORTH SAGA (#2)

"Terror Cell" pits Bob Danforth, a CIA Special Ops Officer, against Greek Spring, a vicious terrorist group that has operated in Athens, Greece for three decades. Danforth's mission in the summer of 2004 is to identify one or more of the members of the terrorists in order to bring them to justice for the assassination of the CIA's Station Chief in Athens. What Danforth does not know is that Greek Spring plans a catastrophic attack against the 2004 Summer Olympic Games.

Danforth and his CIA team are hampered by years of Congressionally mandated rules that have weakened U.S. Intelligence gathering capabilities, and by indifference and obstructionism on the part of Greek authorities. His mission becomes even more difficult when he is targeted for assassination after an informant in the Greek government tells the terrorists of Danforth's presence in Greece.

In "Terror Cell," Badal weaves a tale of international intrigue, involving players from the CIA, the Greek government, and terrorists in Greece, Libya, and Iran—all within a historical context. Anyone who keeps up with current events about terrorist activities and security issues at the Athens Olympic Games will find the premise of this book gripping, terrifying, and, most of all, plausible.

"Joe Badal takes us into a tangled puzzle of intrigue and terrorism, giving readers a tense well-told tale and a page-turning mystery."
—Tony Hillerman, *New York Times* bestselling author

https://amzn.com/B00LXG9QNC

"THE NOSTRADAMUS SECRET"
DANFORTH SAGA (#3)

This latest historical thriller in the *Bob Danforth* series builds on Nostradamus's "lost" 58 quatrains and segues to present day. These lost quatrains have surfaced in the hands of a wealthy Iranian megalomaniac who believes his rise to world power was prophesied by Nostradamus. But he sees the United States as the principal obstacle to the achievement of his goals. So, the first step he takes is to attempt to destabilize the United States through a vicious series of terrorist attacks and assassinations.

Joseph Badal offers up another action-packed story loaded with intrigue, fascinating characters and geopolitical machinations that put the reader on the front line of present-day international conflict. You will be transported from a 16th century French monastery to the CIA, to crime scenes, to the Situation Room at the White House, to Middle Eastern battlefields.

"The Nostradamus Secret" presents non-stop action in a contemporary context that will make you wonder whether the story is fact or fiction, history or prophesy.

" 'The Nostradamus Secret' is a gripping, fast-paced story filled with truly fanatical, frightening villains bent on the destruction of the USA and the modern world. Badal's characters and the situations they find themselves in are hair-raising and believable. I couldn't put the book down. Bring on the sequel!"
—Catherine Coulter, *New York Times* bestselling author of "Double Take"

https://amzn.com/B00R3GTLVI

"THE LONE WOLF AGENDA"
DANFORTH SAGA (#4)

With "The Lone Wolf Agenda," Joseph Badal returns to the world of international espionage and military action thrillers and crafts a story that is as close to the real world of spies and soldiers as a reader can find. This fourth book in the *Danforth Saga* brings Bob Danforth out of retirement to hunt down lone wolf terrorists hell bent on destroying America's oil infrastructure. Badal weaves just enough technology into his story to wow even the most a-technical reader.

"The Lone Wolf Agenda" pairs Danforth with his son Michael, a senior DELTA Force officer, as they combat an OPEC-supported terrorist group allied with a Mexican drug cartel. This story is an epic adventure that will chill readers as they discover that nothing, no matter how diabolical, is impossible.

"A real page-turner in every good sense of the term. 'The Lone Wolf Agenda' came alive for me. It is utterly believable, and as tense as any spy thriller I've read in a long time."
—Michael Palmer, *New York Times* bestselling author of "Political Suicide"

https://amzn.com/B00LXG9QMI

"DEATH SHIP"
DANFORTH SAGA (#5)

"Death Ship" is another suspense-filled thriller in the 45-year-long journey of the Danforth family. This fifth book in the *Danforth Saga*, which includes "Evil Deeds," "Terror Cell," "The Nostradamus Secret," and "The Lone Wolf Agenda," introduces Robbie Danforth, the 15-year-old son of Michael and Miriana Danforth, and the grandson of Bob and Liz Danforth.

A leisurely cruise in the Ionian Sea turns into a nightmare event when terrorists hijack a yacht with Bob, Liz, Miriana, and Robbie aboard. Although the boat's crew, with Bob and Robbie's help, eliminate the hijackers, there is evidence that something more significant may be in the works.

The CIA and the U.S. military must identify what that might be and who is behind the threat, and must operate within a politically-corrupt environment in Washington, D.C. At the same time, they must disrupt the terrorist's financing mechanism, which involves trading in securities that are highly sensitive to terrorist events.

Michael Danforth and a team of DELTA operatives are deployed from Afghanistan to Greece to assist in identifying and thwarting the threat.

"Death Ship" is another roller coaster ride of action and suspense, where good and evil battle for supremacy and everyday heroes combat evil antagonists.

"Terror doesn't take a vacation in 'Death Ship'; instead Joseph Badal masterfully takes us on a cruise to an all too frightening, yet all too real destination. Once you step on board, you are hooked."
—Tom Avitabile, #1 Bestselling Author of "The Eighth Day" and "The Devil's Quota"

https://amzn.com/B016APTJAU

"BORDERLINE"
LASSITER/MARTINEZ CASE FILES #1

In "Borderline," Joseph Badal delivers his first mystery novel with the same punch and non-stop action found in his acclaimed thrillers.

Barbara Lassiter and Susan Martinez, two New Mexico homicide detectives, are assigned to investigate the murder of a wealthy Albuquerque socialite. They soon discover that the victim, a narcissistic borderline personality, played a lifetime game of destroying people's lives. As a result, the list of suspects in her murder is extensive.

The detectives find themselves enmeshed in a helix of possible perpetrators with opportunity, means, and motive—and soon question giving their best efforts to solve the case the more they learn about the victim's hideous past.

Their job gets tougher when the victim's psychiatrist is murdered and DVDs turn up that show the doctor had serial sexual relationships with a large number of his female patients, including the murder victim.

"Borderline" presents a fascinating cast of characters, including two heroic female detective-protagonists and a diabolical villain; a rollercoaster ride of suspense; and an ending that will surprise and shock the reader.

"Think *Cagney and Lacey*. Think *Thelma and Louise*. Think murder and mayhem—and you are in the death grip of a mystery that won't let you go until it has choked the last breath of suspense from you."
—Parris Afton Bonds, author of "Tamed the Wildest Heart" and co-founder of Romance Writers of America and cofounder of Southwest Writers Workshop

https://amzn.com/B00YZSAHI8
Now Available at Audible.com: http://adbl.co/1Y4WC5H

"DARK ANGEL"
LASSITER/MARTINEZ CASE
FILES #2

Award-winning author Joseph Badal brings back Detectives
Barbara Lassiter and Susan Martinez in this sequel to his mystery
"Borderline." "Dark Angel" is a tense, hugely suspenseful story that
will put you on the edge of your seat from the first page to the last.
This tale of revenge is replete with heroic characters, bad guys you
will love to hate, and bureaucrats you will want to strangle. You
will cheer for Barbara and Susan as they attempt to identify a serial
killer who has murdered criminals the justice system has failed
to punish. In the midst of their investigation, they discover a link
between the vigilante killer and a murderous home invasion gang
that has committed crimes from Maine to California. "Dark Angel,"
the second book in Badal's *Lassiter/Martinez Case Files* series, is a
roller coaster ride of action and suspense.

"THE PYTHAGOREAN SOLUTION"
STAND-ALONE THRILLER

The attempt to decipher a map leads to violence and death, and a decades-long sunken treasure.

When American John Hammond arrives on the Aegean island of Samos he is unaware of events that happened six decades earlier that will embroil him in death and violence and will change his life forever.

Late one night Hammond finds Petros Vangelos lying mortally wounded in an alley. Vangelos hands off a coded map, making Hammond the link to a Turkish tramp steamer that carried a fortune in gold and jewels and sank in a storm in 1945.

On board this ship, in a waterproof safe, are documents that implicate a German SS Officer in the theft of valuables from Holocaust victims and the laundering of those valuables by the Nazi's Swiss banker partner.

"Badal is a powerful writer who quickly reels you in and doesn't let go."
—Pat Frovarp & Gary Shulze, Once Upon A Crime Mystery Bookstore

https://amzn.com/B00W4JVIYC

"ULTIMATE BETRAYAL"
STAND-ALONE THRILLER

Inspired by actual events, "Ultimate Betrayal" is a thriller that takes the reader on an action-packed, adrenaline-boosting ride, from the streets of South Philadelphia, through the Afghanistan War, to Mafia drug smuggling, to the halls of power at the CIA and the White House.

David Hood comes from the streets of South Philadelphia, is a decorated Afghanistan War hero, builds a highly successful business, marries the woman of his dreams, and has two children he adores. But there are two ghosts in David's past. One is the guilt he carries over the death of his brother. The other is a specter that will do anything to murder him.

David has long lost the belief that good will triumph over evil. The deaths of his wife and children only reinforce that cynicism. And leave him with nothing but a bone-chilling, all-consuming need for revenge.

" 'Ultimate Betrayal' provides the ultimate in riveting reading entertainment that's as well thought out as it is thought provoking. Both a stand-out thriller and modern day morality tale. Mined from the familial territory of Harlan Coben, with the seasoned action plotting of James Rollins or Steve Berry, this is fiction of the highest order. Poignant and unrelentingly powerful."
—Jon Land, bestselling and award-winning author of "The Tenth Circle"

https://amzn.com/B00LXG9QGY

"SHELL GAME"
STAND-ALONE THRILLER

"Shell Game" is a financial thriller using the economic environment created by the capital markets meltdown that began in 2007 as the backdrop for a timely, dramatic, and hair-raising tale. Badal weaves an intricate and realistic story about how a family and its business are put into jeopardy through heavy-handed, arbitrary rules set down by federal banking regulators, and by the actions of a sociopath in league with a corrupt bank regulator.

Although a work of fiction, "Shell Game," through its protagonist Edward Winter, provides an understandable explanation of one of the main reasons the U.S. economy continues to languish. It is a commentary on what federal regulators are doing to the United States banking community today and, as a result, the damage they are inflicting on perfectly sound businesses and private investors across the country and on the overall U.S. economy.

"Shell Game" is inspired by actual events that have taken place as a result of poor governmental leadership and oversight, greed, corruption, stupidity, and badly conceived regulatory actions. You may be inclined to find it hard to believe what happens in this novel to both banks and bank borrowers. I encourage you to keep an open mind. "Shell Game" is a work of fiction that supports the old adage: You don't need to make this stuff up.

"Take a roller coaster ride through the maze of modern banking regulations with one of modern fiction's most terrifying sociopaths in the driver's seat. Along with its compelling, fast-paced story of a family's struggle against corruption, 'Shell Game' raises important questions about America's financial system based on well-researched facts."
—Anne Hillerman & Jean Schaumberg, WORDHARVEST

https://amzn.com/B00LXG9QFA